Dreamsnake

Books by Vonda N. McIntyre

The Exile Waiting
Dreamsnake

Dreamsnake

Vonda N. McIntyre

Boston

HOUGHTON MIFFLIN COMPANY

Library of Congress Cataloging in Publication Data

McIntyre, Vonda N
Dreamsnake.
I. Title.
PZ4.M1526Dr [PS3563.A3125] 813′.5′4 77-18891
ISBN 0-395-26470-7

Printed in the United States of America

S 10 9 8 7 6 5 4

A portion of this book originally appeared
in ANALOG Science Fiction/Science Fact.

To my parents

Dreamsnake

The little boy was frightened. Gently, Snake touched his hot forehead. Behind her, three adults stood close together, watching, suspicious, afraid to show their concern with more than narrow lines around their eyes. They feared Snake as much as they feared their only child's death. In the dimness of the tent, the strange blue glow of the lantern gave no reassurance.

The child watched with eyes so dark the pupils were not visible, so dull that Snake herself feared for his life. She stroked his hair. It was long, and very pale, dry and irregular for several inches near the scalp, a striking color against his dark skin. Had Snake been with these people months ago, she would have known the child was growing ill.

"Bring my case, please," Snake said.

The child's parents started at her soft voice. Perhaps they had expected the screech of a bright jay, or the hissing of a shining serpent. This was the first time Snake had spoken in their presence. She had only watched, when the three of them had come to observe her from a distance and whisper about her occupation and her youth; she had only listened, and then nodded, when finally they came to ask her help. Perhaps they had thought she was mute.

The fair-haired younger man lifted her leather case. He held the satchel away from his body, leaning to hand it to her, breathing shallowly with nostrils flared against the faint smell of musk in the dry desert air. Snake had almost accustomed herself to the kind of uneasiness he showed; she had already seen it often.

When Snake reached out, the young man jerked back and dropped the case. Snake lunged and barely caught it, gently set it on the felt floor, and glanced at him with reproach. His partners came forward and touched him to ease his fear. "He was bitten once," the dark and handsome woman said. "He almost died." Her tone was not of apology, but of justification.

"I'm sorry," the younger man said. "It's —" He gestured toward her; he was trembling, but trying visibly to control himself. Snake glanced to her shoulder, where she had been unconsciously aware of the slight weight and movement. A tiny serpent, thin as the finger of a baby, slid himself around her neck to show his narrow head below her short black curls. He probed the air with his trident tongue, in a leisurely manner, out, up and down, in, to savor the taste of the smells. "It's only Grass," Snake said. "He can't hurt you." If he were bigger, he might be frightening: his color was pale green, but the scales around his mouth were red, as if he had just feasted as a mammal eats, by tearing. He was, in fact, much neater.

The child whimpered. He cut off the sound of pain; perhaps he had been told that Snake, too, would be offended by crying. She only felt sorry that his people refused themselves such a simple way of easing fear. She turned from the adults, regretting their terror of her but unwilling to spend the time it would take to persuade them to trust her. "It's all right," she said to the little boy. "Grass is smooth, and dry, and soft, and if I left him to guard you, even death could not reach your bedside." Grass poured himself into her narrow, dirty hand, and she extended him toward the child. "Gently." He reached out and touched the sleek scales with one fingertip. Snake could sense the effort of even such a simple motion, yet the boy almost smiled.

"What are you called?"

He looked quickly toward his parents, and finally they nodded.

"Stavin," he whispered. He had no breath or strength for speaking.

"I am Snake, Stavin, and in a little while, in the morning, I must hurt you. You may feel a quick pain, and your body will ache for several days, but you'll be better afterward."

He stared at her solemnly. Snake saw that though he understood and feared what she might do, he was less afraid than if she had lied to him. The pain must have increased greatly as his illness became more apparent, but it seemed that others had only reassured him, and hoped the disease would disappear or kill him quickly.

Snake put Grass on the boy's pillow and pulled her case nearer. The adults still could only fear her; they had had neither time nor reason to discover any trust. The woman of the partnership was old enough that they might never have another child unless they partnered again, and Snake could tell by their eyes, their covert touching, their concern, that they loved this one very much. They must, to come to Snake in this country.

Sluggish, Sand slid out of the case, moving his head, moving his tongue, smelling, tasting, detecting the warmths of bodies.

"Is that — ?" The eldest partner's voice was low and wise, but terrified, and Sand sensed the fear. He drew back into striking position and sounded his rattle softly. Snake stroked her hand along the floor, letting the vibrations distract him, then moved her hand up and extended her arm. The diamondback relaxed and wrapped his body around and around her wrist to form black and tan bracelets.

"No," she said. "Your child is too ill for Sand to help. I know it's hard, but please try to be calm. This is a fearful thing for you, but it is all I can do."

She had to annoy Mist to make her come out. Snake rapped on the bag, and finally poked her twice. Snake felt the vibration of sliding scales, and suddenly the albino cobra flung herself into the tent. She moved quickly, yet there seemed to be no end to her. She reared back and up. Her breath rushed out in a hiss. Her head rose well over a meter above the floor. She flared her wide hood. Behind her, the adults gasped, as if physically assaulted by the gaze of the tan spectacle design on the back of Mist's hood. Snake ignored the people and spoke to the great cobra, focusing her attention by her words.

"Furious creature, lie down. It's time to earn thy dinner. Speak to this child and touch him. He is called Stavin."

Slowly, Mist relaxed her hood and allowed Snake to touch her. Snake grasped her firmly behind the head and held her so she looked at Stavin. The cobra's silver eyes picked up the blue of the lamplight.

"Stavin," Snake said, "Mist will only meet you now. I promise that this time she will touch you gently."

Still, Stavin shivered when Mist touched his thin chest. Snake did not release the serpent's head, but allowed her body to slide against the boy's. The cobra was four times longer than Stavin was tall. She curved herself in stark white loops across his swollen abdomen, extending herself, forcing her head toward the boy's face, straining against Snake's hands. Mist met Stavin's frightened stare with the gaze of lidless eyes. Snake allowed her a little closer.

Mist flicked out her tongue to taste the child.

The younger man made a small, cut-off, frightened sound. Stavin flinched at it, and Mist drew back, opening her mouth, exposing her fangs, audibly thrusting her breath through her throat. Snake sat back on her heels, letting out her own breath. Sometimes, in other places, the kinfolk could stay while she worked.

"You must leave," she said gently. "It's dangerous to frighten Mist."

"I won't — "

"I'm sorry. You must wait outside."

Perhaps the fair-haired youngest partner, perhaps even Stavin's mother, would have made the indefensible objections and asked the answerable questions, but the white-haired man turned them and took their hands and led them away.

"I need a small animal," Snake said as he lifted the tent flap. "It must have fur, and it must be alive."

"One will be found," he said, and the three parents went into the glowing night. Snake could hear their footsteps in the sand outside.

Snake supported Mist in her lap and soothed her. The cobra wrapped herself around Snake's waist, taking in her warmth. Hunger made the cobra even more nervous than usual, and she was hungry, as was Snake. Coming across the black-sand desert, they had found sufficient water, but Snake's traps had been unsuccessful. The season was summer, the weather was hot, and many of the furry tidbits Sand and Mist preferred were estivating. Since she had brought them into the desert, away from home, Snake had begun a fast as well.

She saw with regret that Stavin was more frightened now. "I'm sorry to send your parents away," she said. "They can come back soon."

His eyes glistened, but he held back the tears. "They said to do what you told me."

"I would have you cry, if you are able, " Snake said. "It isn't such a terrible thing." But Stavin seemed not to understand, and Snake did not press him; she thought his people must teach themselves to resist a difficult land by refusing to cry, refusing to mourn, refusing to laugh. They denied themselves grief, and allowed themselves little joy, but they survived.

Mist had calmed to sullenness. Snake unwrapped her from her waist and placed the serpent on the pallet next to Stavin. As the cobra moved, Snake guided her head, feeling the tension of the striking-muscles. "She will touch you with her tongue," she told Stavin. "It might tickle, but it will not hurt. She smells with it, as you do with your nose."

"With her tongue?"

Snake nodded, smiling, and Mist flicked out her tongue to

caress Stavin's cheek. Stavin did not flinch; he watched, his child's delight in knowledge briefly overcoming pain. He lay perfectly still as Mist's long tongue brushed his cheeks, his eyes, his mouth. "She tastes the sickness," Snake said. Mist stopped fighting the restraint of her grasp, and drew back her head. Snake sat on her heels and released the cobra, who spiraled up her arm and laid herself across her shoulders.

"Go to sleep, Stavin," Snake said. "Try to trust me, and try not to fear the morning."

Stavin gazed at her for a few seconds, searching for truth in Snake's pale eyes. "Will Grass watch?"

She was startled by the question, or, rather, by the acceptance behind the question. She brushed his hair from his forehead and smiled a smile that was tears just beneath the surface. "Of course." She picked Grass up. "Watch this child, and guard him." The dreamsnake lay quiet in her hand, and his eyes glittered black. She laid him gently on Stavin's pillow.

"Now sleep."

Stavin closed his eyes, and the life seemed to flow out of him. The alteration was so great that Snake reached out to touch him, then saw that he was breathing, slowly, shallowly. She tucked a blanket around him and stood up. The abrupt change in position dizzied her; she staggered and caught herself. Across her shoulder, Mist tensed.

Snake's eyes stung and her vision was oversharp, fever-clear. The sound she imagined she heard swooped in closer. She steadied herself against hunger and exhaustion, bent slowly, and picked up the leather case. Mist touched her cheek with the tip of her tongue.

She pushed aside the tent flap and felt relief that it was still night. She could stand the daytime heat, but the brightness of the sun curled through her, burning. The moon must be full; though the clouds obscured everything, they diffused the light so the sky appeared gray from horizon to horizon. Beyond the tents, groups of formless shadows projected from the ground. Here, near the edge of the desert, enough water existed so clumps and patches of bush grew, providing shelter and sustenance for all manner of creatures. The black sand, which sparkled and blinded in the sunlight, at night was like a layer of soft soot. Snake stepped out of the tent, and the illusion of softness disappeared; her boots slid crunching into the sharp hard grains.

Stavin's family waited, sitting close together between the dark tents that clustered in a patch of sand from which the bushes had been ripped and burned. They looked at her silently, hoping with their eyes, showing no expression in their faces. A woman somewhat younger than Stavin's mother sat with them. She was dressed, as they were, in long loose desert robes, but she wore the only adornment Snake had seen among these people: a leader's circle, hanging around her neck on a leather thong. She and Stavin's eldest parent were marked close kin by their similarities: sharp-cut planes of face, high cheekbones, his hair white and hers graying early from deep black, their eyes the dark brown best suited for survival in the sun. On the ground by their feet a small black animal jerked sporadically against a net, and infrequently gave a shrill weak cry.

"Stavin is asleep," Snake said. "Do not disturb him, but go to him if he wakes."

Stavin's mother and the youngest partner rose and went inside, but the older man stopped before her. "Can you help him?"

"I hope so. The tumor is advanced, but it seems solid." Her own voice sounded removed, ringing slightly false, as if she were lying. "Mist will be ready in the morning." She still felt the need to give him reassurance, but she could think of none.

"My sister wished to speak with you," he said, and left them alone, without introduction, without elevating himself by saying that the tall woman was the leader of this group. Snake glanced back, but the tent flap fell shut. She was feeling her exhaustion more deeply, and across her shoulders Mist was, for the first time, a weight she thought heavy.

"Are you all right?"

Snake turned. The woman moved toward her with a natural elegance made slightly awkward by advanced pregnancy. Snake had to look up to meet her gaze. She had small, fine lines at the corners of her eyes and beside her mouth, as if she laughed, sometimes, in secret. She smiled, but with concern. "You seem very tired. Shall I have someone make you a bed?"

"Not now," Snake said, "not yet. I won't sleep until afterward."

The leader searched her face, and Snake felt a kinship with her in their shared responsibility.

"I understand, I think. Is there anything we can give you? Do you need aid with your preparations?"

Snake found herself having to deal with the questions as if they were complex problems. She turned them in her tired mind, examined them, dissected them, and finally grasped their meanings. "My pony needs food and water — "

"It is taken care of."

"And I need someone to help with Mist. Someone strong. But it's more important that they aren't afraid."

The leader nodded. "I would help you," she said, and smiled again, a little. "But I am a bit clumsy of late. I will find someone."

"Thank you."

Somber again, the older woman inclined her head and moved slowly toward a small group of tents. Snake watched her go, admiring her grace. She felt small and young and grubby in comparison.

His body tensed to hunt, Sand slid in circles from Snake's wrist. She caught him before he could drop to the ground. Sand lifted the upper half of his body from her hands. He flicked out his tongue, peering toward the little animal, sensing its body heat, tasting its fear. "I know thou art hungry," Snake said. "But that creature is not for thee." She put Sand in the case, took Mist from her shoulders, and let the cobra coil herself in her dark compartment.

The small animal shrieked and struggled again when Snake's diffuse shadow passed over it. She bent and picked the creature up. Its rapid series of terrified cries slowed and diminished and finally stopped as she stroked it. It lay still, breathing hard, exhausted, staring up at her with yellow eyes. It had long hind legs and wide pointed ears, and its nose twitched at the serpent smell. Its soft black fur was marked off in skewed squares by the cords of the net.

"I am sorry to take your life," Snake told it. "But there will be no more fear, and I will not hurt you." She closed her hand gently around the animal and, stroking it, grasped its spine at the base of its skull. She pulled, once, quickly. It seemed to struggle for an instant, but it was already dead. It convulsed; its legs drew up against its body and its toes curled and quivered. It seemed to stare up at her, even now. She freed its body from the net.

Snake chose a small vial from her belt pouch, pried open the animal's clenched jaws, and let a single drop of the vial's cloudy preparation fall into its mouth. Quickly she opened the satchel again and called Mist out. The cobra came slowly, slipping over the edge, hood closed, sliding in the sharp-grained sand. Her milky scales caught the thin light. She smelled the animal, flowed to it, touched it with her tongue. For a moment Snake was afraid she would refuse dead meat, but the body was still warm, still twitching, and she was very hungry. "A tidbit for thee." Snake spoke to the cobra: a habit of solitude. "To whet thy appetite." Mist nosed the beast, reared back, and struck, sinking her short fixed fangs into the tiny body, biting again, pumping out her store of poison. She released it, took a better grip, and began to work her jaws around it. It would hardly distend her throat. When Mist lay quiet, digesting the small meal, Snake sat beside her and held her, waiting.

She heard footsteps in the sand.

"I'm sent to help you."

He was a young man, despite a scatter of white in his black

hair. He was taller than Snake, and not unattractive. His eyes were dark, and the sharp planes of his face were further hardened because his hair was pulled straight back and tied. His expression was neutral.

"Are you afraid?" Snake asked.

"I will do as you tell me."

Though his form was obscured by his robe, his long, fine hands showed strength.

"Then hold her body, and don't let her surprise you." Mist was beginning to twitch, the effect of the drugs Snake had put in the small animal. The cobra's eyes stared, unseeing.

"If it bites — "

"Hold, quickly!"

The young man reached, but he had hesitated too long. Mist writhed, lashing out, striking him in the face with her tail. He staggered back, at least as surprised as hurt. Snake kept a close grip behind Mist's jaws, and struggled to catch the rest of her as well. Mist was no constrictor, but she was smooth and strong and fast. Thrashing, she forced out her breath in a long hiss. She would have bitten anything she could reach. As Snake fought with her, she managed to squeeze the poison glands and force out the last drops of venom. They hung from Mist's fangs for a moment, catching light as jewels would; the force of the serpent's convulsions flung them away into the darkness. Snake struggled with the cobra, aided for once by the sand, on which Mist could get little purchase. Snake felt the young man behind her, grabbing for Mist's body and tail. The seizure stopped abruptly, and Mist lay limp in their hands.

"I am sorry — "

"Hold her," Snake said. "We have the night to go."

During Mist's second convulsion, the young man held her firmly and was of some real help. Afterward, Snake answered his interrupted question. "If she were making poison and she bit you, you would probably die. Even now her bite would make you ill. But unless you do something foolish, if she manages to bite, she'll bite me."

"You would benefit my cousin little if you were dead or dying."

"You misunderstand. Mist can't kill me." Snake held out her hand so he could see the white scars of slashes and punctures. He stared at them, and looked into her eyes for a long moment, then looked away.

The bright spot in the clouds from which the light radiated moved westward in the sky; they held the cobra like a child. Snake nearly dozed, but Mist moved her head, dully attempting to evade restraint, and Snake woke herself abruptly. "I mustn't sleep," she said to the young man. "Talk to me. What are you called?"

As Stavin had, the young man hesitated. He seemed afraid of her, or of something. "My people," he said, "think it unwise to speak our names to strangers."

"If you consider me a witch you should not have asked my aid. I know no magic, and I claim none."

"It's not a superstition," he said. "Not as you might think. We're not afraid of being bewitched."

"I can't learn all the customs of all the people on this earth, so I keep my own. My custom is to address those I work with by name." Watching him, Snake tried to decipher his expression in the dim light.

"Our families know our names, and we exchange names with our partners."

Snake considered that custom, and thought it would fit badly on her. "No one else? Ever?"

"Well . . . a friend might know one's name."

"Ah," Snake said. "I see. I am still a stranger, and perhaps an enemy."

"A *friend* would know my name," the young man said again. "I would not offend you, but now you misunderstand. An acquaintance is not a friend. We value friendship highly."

"In this land one should be able to tell quickly if a person is worth calling friend."

"We take friends seldom. Friendship is a great commitment."

"It sounds like something to be feared."

He considered that possibility. "Perhaps it's the betrayal of friendship we fear. That is a very painful thing."

"Has anyone ever betrayed you?"

He glanced at her sharply, as if she had exceeded the limits of propriety. "No," he said, and his voice was as hard as his face. "No friend. I have no one I call friend."

His reaction startled Snake. "That's very sad," she said, and grew silent, trying to comprehend the deep stresses that could close people off so far, comparing her loneliness of necessity and theirs of choice. "Call me Snake," she said finally, "if you can bring yourself to pronounce it. Saying my name binds you to nothing."

The young man seemed about to speak; perhaps he thought again that he had offended her, perhaps he felt he should further defend his customs. But Mist began to twist in their hands, and they had to hold her to keep her from injuring herself. The cobra was slender for her length, but powerful, and the convulsions she went through were more severe than any she had ever had before. She thrashed in Snake's grasp, and almost pulled away. She tried to spread her hood, but Snake held her too tightly. She opened her mouth and hissed, but no poison dripped from her fangs.

She wrapped her tail around the young man's waist. He began to pull her and turn, to extricate himself from her coils.

"She's not a constrictor," Snake said. "She won't hurt you. Leave her — "

But it was too late; Mist relaxed suddenly and the young man lost his balance. Mist whipped herself away and lashed figures in the sand. Snake wrestled with her alone while the young man tried to hold her, but she curled herself around Snake and used the grip for leverage. She started to pull herself from Snake's hands. Snake threw herself and the serpent backward into the sand; Mist rose above her, open-mouthed, furious, hissing. The young man lunged and grabbed her just beneath her hood. Mist struck at him, but Snake, somehow, held her back. Together they deprived Mist of her hold and regained control of her. Snake struggled up, but Mist suddenly went quite still and lay almost rigid between them. They were both sweating; the young man was pale under his tan, and even Snake was trembling.

"We have a little while to rest," Snake said. She glanced at him and noticed the dark line on his cheek where, earlier, Mist's tail had slashed him. She reached up and touched it. "You'll have a bruise," she said. "But it will not scar."

"If it were true, that serpents sting with their tails, you would be restraining both the fangs and the stinger, and I'd be of little use."

"Tonight I'd need someone to keep me awake, whether or not they helped me with Mist. But just now, I would have had trouble holding her alone." Fighting the cobra produced adrenalin, but now it ebbed, and her exhaustion and hunger were returning, stronger.

"Snake . . ."

"Yes?"

He smiled, quickly, embarrassed. "I was trying the pronunciation."

"Good enough."

"How long did it take you to cross the desert?"

"Not very long. Too long. Six days. I don't think I went the best way."

"How did you live?"

"There's water. We traveled at night and rested during the day, wherever we could find shade."

"You carried all your food?"

She shrugged. "A little." And wished he would not speak of food.

"What's on the other side?"

"Mountains. Streams. Other people. The station I grew up and took my training in. Then another desert, and a mountain with a city inside."

"I'd like to see a city. Someday."

"I'm told the city doesn't let in people from outside, people like you and me. But there are many towns in the mountains, and the desert can be crossed."

He said nothing, but Snake's memories of leaving home were recent enough that she could imagine his thoughts.

The next set of convulsions came, much sooner than Snake had expected. By their severity she gauged something of the stage of Stavin's illness, and wished it were morning. If she was going to lose the child, she would have it done, and grieve, and try to forget. The cobra would have battered herself to death against the sand if Snake and the young man had not been holding her. She suddenly went completely rigid, with her mouth clamped shut and her forked tongue dangling.

She stopped breathing.

"Hold her," Snake said. "Hold her head. Quickly, take her, and if she gets away, run. Take her! She won't strike at you now, she could only slash you by accident."

He hesitated only a moment, then grasped Mist behind the head. Snake ran, slipping in the deep sand, from the edge of the circle of tents to a place where bushes still grew. She broke off dry thorny branches that tore her scarred hands. Peripherally she noticed a mass of horned vipers, so ugly they seemed deformed, nesting beneath the clump of dessicated vegetation. They hissed at her; she ignored them. She found a thin hollow stem and carried it back. Her hands bled from deep scratches.

Kneeling by Mist's head, she forced open the cobra's mouth and pushed the tube deep into her throat, through the air passage at the base of the tongue. She bent close, took the tube in her mouth, and breathed gently into Mist's lungs.

She noticed: the young man's hands, holding the cobra as she had asked; his breathing, first a sharp gasp of surprise, then ragged; the sand scraping her elbows where she leaned; the cloying smell of the fluid seeping from Mist's fangs; her own dizziness, she thought from exhaustion, which she forced away by necessity and will.

Snake breathed, and breathed again, paused, and repeated, until Mist caught the rhythm and continued it unaided.

Snake sat back on her heels. "I think she'll be all right," she said. "I hope she will." She brushed the back of her hand across her forehead. The touch sparked pain: she jerked her hand down and agony slid along her bones, up her arm, across her shoulder, through her chest, enveloping her heart. Her balance turned on its edge. She fell, tried to catch herself but moved too slowly, fought nausea and vertigo and almost succeeded, until the pull of the earth seemed to slip away and she was lost in darkness with nothing to take a bearing by.

She felt sand where it had scraped her cheek and her palms, but it was soft. "Snake, can I let go?" She thought the question must be for someone else, while at the same time she knew there was no one else to answer it, no one else to reply to her name. She felt hands on her, and they were gentle; she wanted to respond to them, but she was too tired. She needed sleep more, so she pushed them away. But they held her head and put dry leather to her lips and poured water into her throat. She coughed and choked and spat it out.

She pushed herself up on one elbow. As her sight cleared, she realized she was shaking. She felt the way she had the first time she was snake-bit, before her immunities had completely developed. The young man knelt over her, his water flask in his hand. Mist, beyond him, crawled toward the darkness. Snake forgot the throbbing pain. "Mist!" She slapped the ground.

The young man flinched and turned, frightened; the serpent reared up, swaying over them, watching, angry, ready to strike, her hood spread. She formed a wavering white line against black. Snake forced herself to rise, feeling as though she were fumbling with the control of some unfamiliar body She almost fell again, but held herself steady, facing the cobra, whose eyes were on a level with her own. "Thou must not go to hunt now," she said. "There is work for thee to do." She held out her right hand to the side, a decoy, to draw Mist if she struck. Her hand was heavy with pain. Snake feared, not being bitten, but the loss of the contents of Mist's poison sacs. "Come here," she said. "Come here, and stay thy anger." She noticed blood flowing down between her fingers, and the fear she felt for Stavin intensified. "Didst thou bite me already, creature?" But the pain was wrong: poison would numb her, and the new serum only sting . . .

"No," the young man whispered from behind her.

Mist struck. The reflexes of long training took over: Snake's right hand jerked away, her left grabbed Mist as the serpent brought her head back. The cobra writhed a moment, and relaxed. "Devious beast," Snake said. "For shame." She turned and let Mist crawl up her arm and over her shoulder, where she lay like the outline of an invisible cape and dragged her tail like the edge of a train.

"She didn't bite me?"

"No," the young man said. His contained voice was touched with awe. "You should be dying. You should be curled around the agony, and your arm swollen purple. When you came back — " He gestured toward her hand. "It must have been a sand viper."

Snake remembered the coil of reptiles beneath the branches, and touched the blood on her hand. She wiped it away, revealing the double puncture of a bite among the scratches of the thorns. The wound was slightly swollen. "It needs cleaning," she said. "I shame myself by falling to it." The pain of it washed in gentle waves up her arm, burning no longer. She stood looking at the young man, looking around her, watching the landscape shift and change as her tired eyes tried to cope with the low light of setting moon and false dawn. "You held Mist well, and bravely," she said to the young man. "I thank you."

He lowered his gaze, almost bowing to her. He rose and approached her. Snake put her hand on Mist's neck so she would not be alarmed.

"I would be honored," the young man said, "if you would call me Arevin."

"I would be pleased to."

Snake knelt down and held the winding white loops as Mist crawled slowly into her compartment. In a little while, when Mist had stabilized, by dawn, they could go to Stavin.

The tip of Mist's white tail slid out of sight. Snake closed the case and would have risen, but she could not stand. She had not quite shaken off the effects of the new venom. The flesh around the wound was red and tender, but the hemorrhaging would not spread. She stayed where she was, slumped, staring at her hand, creeping slowly in her mind toward what she needed to do, this time for herself.

"Let me help you. Please."

He touched her shoulder and helped her stand. "I'm sorry," she said. "I'm so in need of rest . . ."

"Let me wash your hand," Arevin said. "And then you can sleep. Tell me when to awaken you — "

"I can't sleep yet." She collected herself, straightened, tossed the damp curls of her short hair off her forehead. "I'm all right now. Have you any water?"

Arevin loosened his outer robe. Beneath it he wore a loincloth and a leather belt that carried several leather flasks and pouches. His body was lean and well built, his legs long and muscular. The color of his skin was slightly lighter than the sun-darkened brown of his face. He brought out his water flask and reached for Snake's hand.

"No, Arevin. If the poison gets in any small scratch you might have, it could infect."

She sat down and sluiced lukewarm water over her hand. The water dripped pink to the ground and disappeared, leaving not even a damp spot visible. The wound bled a little more, but now it only ached. The poison was almost inactivated.

"I don't understand," Arevin said, "how it is that you're unhurt. My younger sister was bitten by a sand viper." He could not speak as uncaringly as he might have wished. "We could do nothing to save her — nothing we have would even lessen her pain."

Snake gave him his flask and rubbed salve from a vial in her belt pouch across the closing punctures. "It's a part of our preparation," she said. "We work with many kinds of serpents, so we must be immune to as many as possible." She shrugged. "The process is tedious and somewhat painful." She clenched her fist; the film held, and she was steady. She leaned toward Arevin and touched his abraded cheek again. "Yes . . ." She spread a thin layer of the salve across it. "That will help it heal."

"If you cannot sleep," Arevin said, "can you at least rest?"

"Yes," she said. "For a little while."

Snake sat next to Arevin, leaning against him, and they watched the sun turn the clouds to gold and flame and amber. The simple physical contact with another human being gave Snake pleasure, though she found it unsatisfying. Another time, another place, she might do something more, but not here, not now.

When the lower edge of the sun's bright smear rose above the horizon, Snake got up and teased Mist out of the case. She came slowly, weakly, and crawled across Snake's shoulders. Snake picked up the satchel, and she and Arevin walked together back to the small group of tents.

Stavin's parents waited, watching for her, just outside the entrance of their tent. They stood in a tight, defensive, silent group. For a moment Snake thought they had decided to send her away. Then, with regret and fear like hot iron in her mouth, she asked if Stavin had died. They shook their heads, and allowed her to enter.

Stavin lay as she had left him, still asleep. The adults followed her with their stares. Mist flicked out her tongue, growing nervous from the smell of fear.

"I know you would stay," Snake said. "I know you would help, if you could, but there is nothing to be done by any person but me. Please go back outside."

They glanced at each other, and at Arevin, and she thought for a moment that they would refuse. Snake wanted to fall into the silence and sleep. "Come, cousins," Arevin said. "We are in her hands." He opened the tent flap and motioned them out. Snake thanked him with nothing more than a glance, and he might almost have smiled. She turned toward Stavin and knelt beside him. "Stavin — " She touched his forehead; it was very hot. She noticed that her hand was less steady than before. The slight touch awakened the child. "It's time," Snake said.

He blinked, coming out of some child's dream, seeing her, slowly recognizing her. He did not look frightened. For that Snake was glad; for some other reason she could not identify, she was uneasy.

"Will it hurt?"

"Does it hurt now?"

He hesitated, looked away, looked back. "Yes."

"It might hurt a little more. I hope not. Are you ready?"

"Can Grass stay?"

"Of course," she said.

And realized what was wrong.

"I'll come back in a moment." Her voice had changed so much, she had pulled it so tight, that she could not help but frighten him. She left the tent, walking slowly, calmly, restraining herself. Outside, the parents told her by their faces what they feared.

"Where is Grass?" Arevin, his back to her, started at her tone. The fair-haired man made a small grieving sound, and could look at her no longer.

"We were afraid," the eldest partner said. "We thought it would bite the child."

"I thought it would. It was I. It crawled over his face. I could see its fangs — " The wife put her hands on her younger partner's shoulders, and he said no more.

"Where is he?" She wanted to scream; she did not.

They brought her a small open box. Snake took it and looked inside.

Grass lay cut almost in two, his entrails oozing from his body, half-turned over, and as she watched, shaking, he writhed once, flicked his tongue out once, and in. Snake made some sound, too low in her throat to be a cry. She hoped his motions were only reflex, but she picked him up as gently as she could. She leaned down and touched her lips to the smooth green scales behind his head. She bit him quickly, sharply, at the base of his skull. His blood flowed cool and salty in her mouth. If he was not already dead, she had killed him instantly.

She looked at the parents, and at Arevin; they were all pale, but she had no sympathy for their fear, and cared nothing for shared grief. "Such a small creature," she said. "Such a small creature, who could only give pleasure and dreams." She watched them for a moment more, then turned toward the tent again.

"Wait —" She heard the eldest partner move up close behind her. He touched her shoulder; she shrugged away his hand. "We will give you anything you want," he said, "but leave the child alone."

She spun on him in a fury. "Should I kill Stavin for your stupidity?" He seemed about to try to hold her back. She jammed her shoulder hard into his stomach, and flung herself past the tent flap. Inside, she kicked over the satchel. Abruptly awakened, and angry, Sand crawled out and coiled himself. When someone tried to enter, Sand hissed and rattled with a violence Snake had never heard him use before. She did not even bother to look behind her. She ducked her head and wiped her tears on her sleeve before Stavin could see them. She knelt beside him.

"What's the matter?" He could not help but hear the voices outside the tent, and the running.

"Nothing, Stavin," Snake said. "Did you know we came across the desert?"

"No," he said with wonder.

"It was very hot, and none of us had anything to eat. Grass is hunting now. He was very hungry. Will you forgive him and let me begin? I'll be here all the time."

He seemed so tired; he was disappointed, but he had no strength for arguing. "All right." His voice rustled like sand slipping through the fingers.

Snake lifted Mist from her shoulders, and pulled the blanket from Stavin's small body. The tumor pressed up beneath his rib cage, distorting his form, squeezing his vital organs, sucking nourishment from him for its own growth, poisoning him with its wastes. Holding Mist's head, Snake let her flow across him, touching and tasting him. She had to restrain the cobra to keep her from striking; the excitement had agitated her. When Sand used his rattle, the vibrations made her flinch. Snake stroked her, soothing her; trained and bred-in responses began to return, overcoming the natural instincts. Mist paused when her tongue flicked the skin above the tumor, and Snake released her.

The cobra reared and struck, biting as cobras bite, sinking her fangs their short length once, releasing, instantly biting again for a better purchase, holding on, chewing at her prey. Stavin cried out, but he did not move against Snake's restraining hands.

Mist expended the contents of her venom sacs into the child, and released him. She reared up, peered around, folded her hood, and slid across the floor in a perfectly straight line toward her dark, close compartment.

"It's done, Stavin."

"Will I die now?"

"No," Snake said. "Not now. Not for many years, I hope." She took a vial of powder from her belt pouch. "Open your mouth."

He complied, and she sprinkled the powder across his tongue. "That will help the ache." She spread a pad of cloth across the series of shallow puncture wounds without wiping off the blood.

She turned from him.

"Snake? Are you going away?"

"I won't leave without saying good-bye. I promise."

The child lay back, closed his eyes, and let the drug take him.

Sand coiled quietly on the dark felt. Snake patted the floor to call him. He moved toward her, and suffered himself to be replaced in the satchel. Snake closed it, and lifted it, and it still felt empty. She heard noises outside the tent. Stavin's parents and the people who had come to help them pulled open the tent flap and peered inside, thrusting sticks in even before they looked.

Snake set down her leather case. "It's done."

They entered. Arevin was with them too; only he was empty-handed. "Snake — " He spoke through grief, pity, confusion, and Snake could not tell what he believed. He looked back. Stavin's mother was just behind him. He took her by the shoulder. "He would have died without her. Whatever happens now, he would have died."

She shook his hand away. "He might have lived. It might have gone away. We — " She could speak no more for hiding tears.

Snake felt the people moving, surrounding her. Arevin took one step toward her and stopped, and she could see he wanted her to defend herself. "Can any of you cry?" she said. "Can any of you cry for me and my despair, or for them and their guilt, or for small things and their pain?" She felt tears slip down her cheeks.

They did not understand her; they were offended by her crying. They stood back, still afraid of her, but gathering themselves. She no longer needed the pose of calmness she had used to deceive the child. "Ah, you fools." Her voice sounded brittle. "Stavin — "

Light from the entrance struck them. "Let me pass." The people in front of Snake moved aside for their leader. She stopped in front of Snake, ignoring the satchel her foot almost touched. "Will Stavin live?" Her voice was quiet, calm, gentle.

"I cannot be certain," Snake said, "but I feel that he will."

"Leave us." The people understood Snake's words before they did their leader's; they looked around and lowered their weapons, and finally, one by one, they moved out of the tent. Arevin remained with Snake. The strength that came from danger seeped from her, and her knees collapsed. She bent over the satchel with her face in her hands. The older woman knelt in front of her, before Snake could notice or prevent her. "Thank you," the leader said. "Thank you. I am so sorry . . ." She put her arms around Snake, and drew her toward her, and Arevin knelt beside them, and he embraced Snake too. Snake began to tremble again, and they held her while she cried.

Later she slept, exhausted, alone in the tent with Stavin, holding his hand. The people had caught small animals for Sand and Mist. They had given her food and supplies; they had even given her sufficient water to bathe, though that must have strained their resources.

When she awakened, Arevin lay sleeping nearby, his robe open in the heat, a sheen of sweat across his chest and stomach. The sternness in his expression vanished when he slept; he looked exhausted and vulnerable. Snake almost woke him, but stopped, shook her head, and turned to Stavin.

She felt the tumor, and found that it had begun to dissolve and shrivel, dying, as Mist's changed poison affected it. Through her grief Snake felt a little joy. She smoothed Stavin's pale hair back from his face. "I would not lie to you again, little one," she whispered, "but I must leave soon. I cannot stay here." She wanted another three days' sleep, to finish fighting off the effects of the sand viper's poison, but she would sleep somewhere else. "Stavin?"

He half woke, slowly. "It doesn't hurt any more," he said.

"I'm glad."

"Thank you . . ."

"Good-bye, Stavin. Will you remember later on that you woke up, and that I did stay to say good-bye?"

"Good-bye," he said, drifting off again. "Good-bye, Snake. Good-bye, Grass." He closed his eyes.

Snake picked up the satchel and stood gazing down at Arevin. He did not stir. Both grateful and sorry, she left the tent.

Dusk approached with long, indistinct shadows; the camp was hot and quiet. She found her tiger-striped pony, tethered with food and water. New, full waterskins bulged on the ground next to the saddle, and desert robes lay across the pommel, though Snake had refused any payment. The tiger-pony whickered at her. She scratched his striped ears, saddled him, and strapped her gear on his back. Leading him, she started east, the way she had come.

"Snake — "

She took a breath, and turned back to Arevin. His back was to the sun, and it outlined him in scarlet. His streaked hair flowed loose to his shoulders, gentling his face. "You must leave?"

"Yes."

"I hoped you would not leave before . . . I hoped you would stay, for a time . . . There are other clans, and other people you could help — "

"If things were different, I might have stayed. There's work for a healer. But . . ."

"They were frightened — "

"I told them Grass couldn't hurt them, but they saw his fangs and they didn't know he could only give dreams and ease dying."

"But can't you forgive them?"

"I can't face their guilt. What they did was my fault, Arevin. I didn't understand them until too late "

"You said it yourself, you can't know all the customs and all the fears."

"I'm crippled," she said. "Without Grass, if I can't heal a person, I can't help at all. We don't have many dreamsnakes. I have to go home and tell my teachers I've lost one, and hope they can forgive my stupidity. They seldom give the name I bear, but they gave it to me, and they'll be disappointed."

"Let me come with you."

She wanted to; she hesitated, and cursed herself for that weakness. "They may take Mist and Sand and cast me out, and you would be cast out too. Stay here, Arevin."

"It wouldn't matter."

"It would. After a while, we would hate each other. I don't know you, and you don't know me. We need calmness, and quiet, and time to understand each other well."

He came toward her, and put his arms around her, and they stood embracing for a moment. When he raised his head, there were tears on his cheeks. "Please come back," he said. "Whatever happens, please come back."

"I will try," Snake said. "Next spring, when the winds stop, look for me. The spring after that, if I haven't returned, forget me. Wherever I am, if I live, I will forget you."

"I will look for you," Arevin said, and he would promise no more.

Snake picked up her pony's lead, and started across the desert.

2

Mist rose in a white streak against darkness. The cobra hissed, swaying, and Sand echoed her with his warning rattle. Then Snake heard the hoofbeats, muffled by the desert, and felt them through her palms. Slapping the ground, she winced and sucked in her breath. Around the double puncture where the sand viper had bitten her, her hand was black-and-blue from knuckles to wrist. Only the bruise's edges had faded. She cradled her aching right hand in her lap and twice slapped the ground with her left. Sand's rattling lost its frantic sound and the diamondback slid toward her from a warm shelf of black volcanic stone. Snake slapped the ground twice again. Mist, sensing the vibrations, soothed by the familiarity of the signal, lowered her body slowly and relaxed her hood.

The hoofbeats stopped. Snake heard voices from the camp farther along the edge of the oasis, a cluster of black-on-black tents obscured by an outcropping of rock. Sand wrapped himself around her forearm and Mist crawled up and across her shoulders. Grass should be coiled around her wrist or around her throat like an emerald necklace, but Grass was gone. Grass was dead.

The rider urged the horse toward her. Meager light from bioluminescent lanterns and the cloud-covered moon glistened on droplets as the bay horse splashed through the shallows of the oasis. It breathed in heavy snorts through distended nostrils. The reins had worked sweat to foam on its neck. Firelight flickered scarlet against the gold bridle and highlighted the rider's face.

"Healer?"

She rose. "My name is Snake." Perhaps she had no right to call herself that any longer, but she would not go back to her child-name.

"I am Merideth." The rider swung down and approached, but stopped when Mist raised her head.

"She won't strike," Snake said.

Merideth came closer. "One of my partners is injured. Will you come?"

Snake had to put effort into answering without hesitation. "Yes, of course." Her fear of being asked to aid someone who was dying and of being unable to do anything to help at all was very strong. She knelt to put Mist and Sand into the leather case. They slid against her hands, their cool scales forming intricate patterns on her fingertips.

"My pony's lame, I'll have to borrow a horse — " Squirrel, her tiger-pony, was corralled at the camp where Merideth had stopped a moment before. Snake did not need to worry about her pony, for Grum the caravannaire took good care of him; her grandchildren fed and brushed him royally. Grum would see to Squirrel's reshoeing if a blacksmith came while Snake was gone, and Snake thought Grum would lend her a horse.

"There's no time," Merideth said. "Those desert nags are no good for speed. My mare will carry us both."

Merideth's mare was breathing normally, despite the sweat drying on her shoulders. She stood with her head up, ears pricked, neck arched. She was, indeed, an impressive animal, of higher breeding than the caravan ponies, much taller than Squirrel. While the rider's clothes were plain, the horse's equipment was heavily ornamented.

Snake closed the leather case and put on the new robes and headcloth Arevin's people had given her. She was grateful to them for the clothes, at least, for the strong delicate material was excellent protection against the heat and sand and dust.

Merideth mounted, freed the stirrup, reached for Snake's

hand. But when Snake approached, the horse flared her nostrils and shied at the musky smell of serpents. Beneath Merideth's gentle hands she stood still but did not calm. Snake swung up behind the saddle. The horse's muscles bunched and the mare sprang into a gallop, splashing through the water. Spray touched Snake's face and she tightened her legs against the mare's damp flanks. The horse leaped across the shore and passed between delicate summertrees, shadows and delicate fronds flicking past, until suddenly the desert opened out to the horizon.

Snake held the case in her left hand; the right could not yet grasp tightly enough. Away from the fires and the water's reflections, Snake could barely see. The black sand sucked up light and released it as heat. The mare galloped on. The intricate decorations on her bridle jingled faintly above the crunch of hooves in sand. Her sweat soaked into Snake's pants, hot and sticky against her knees and thighs. Beyond the oasis and its protection of trees, Snake felt the sting of windblown sand. She let go of Merideth's waist long enough to pull the end of her headcloth across her nose and mouth.

Soon the sand gave way to a slope of stones. The mare clambered up it, onto solid rock. Merideth held her to a walk. "It's too dangerous to run. We'd be in a crevasse before we saw it." Merideth's voice was tense with urgency.

They moved perpendicular to great cracks and fissures where molten rock had flowed and separated and cooled to basalt. Grains of sand sighed across the barren, undulating surface. The mare's iron shoes rang against it as if it were hollow. When she had to leap a chasm, the stone reverberated.

More than once Snake started to ask what had happened to Merideth's friend, but she remained silent. The plain of stone forbade conversation, forbade concentration on anything but traversing it.

And Snake was afraid to ask, afraid to know.

The case lay heavy against her leg, rocking in rhythm to the mare's long stride. Snake could feel Sand shifting inside his compartment; she hoped he would not rattle and frighten the horse again.

The lava flow did not appear on Snake's map, which ended, to the south, at the oasis. The trade routes avoided the lava flows, for they were hard on people and animals alike. Snake wondered if they would reach their destination before morning. Here on the black rock the heat would build rapidly.

Finally the mare's gait began to slow, despite Merideth's constant urging.

The smoothly rocking pace across the wide stone river had lulled Snake almost to sleep. She jerked awake when the mare slid, pulling her haunches under her, scrabbling with her hooves, throwing the riders back, then forward, as they came down the long slope of lava. Snake clutched her bag and Merideth and clamped the horse between her knees.

The broken stone at the foot of the cliff thinned out, no longer holding them to a walk. Snake felt Merideth's legs tighten against the mare, forcing the exhausted horse into a heavy canter. They were in a deep, narrow canyon, its high walls formed by two separate tongues of lava.

Spots of light hovered against ebony and for a moment Snake thought sleepily of fireflies. Then a horse neighed from a long distance and the lights leaped into perspective: the camp's lanterns. Merideth leaned forward, speaking words of encouragement to the mare. The horse labored, struggling through the deep sand, stumbling once and throwing Snake hard against Merideth's back. Jolted, Sand rattled. The hollow space around him amplified the sound. The mare bolted in terror. Merideth let her run, and when she finally slowed, foam dripping down her neck and blood spattering from her nostrils, Merideth forced her on.

The camp seemed to recede, miragelike. Every breath Snake took hurt her as if she were the mare. The horse floundered through deep sand like an exhausted swimmer, gasping at the height of every plunge.

They reached the tent. The mare staggered and stopped, spraddle-legged, head down. Snake slipped from her back, soaked with sweat, her own knees shaky. Merideth dismounted and led the way into the tent. The flaps were propped open, and the lanterns within suffused it with a pale blue glow.

The light inside seemed very bright. Merideth's injured friend lay near the tent wall, her face flushed and sweat-shiny, her long curly brick-red hair loose and tangled. The thin cloth covering her was stained in dark patches, but with sweat, not blood. Her companion, sitting on the floor beside her, raised his head groggily. His pleasant, ugly face was set in lines of strain, heavy eyebrows drawn together over his small dark eyes. His shaggy brown hair was tousled and matted.

Merideth knelt beside him. "How is she?"

"She finally went to sleep. She's been just the same. At least she doesn't hurt . . ."

Merideth took the young man's hand and bent to kiss the sleeping woman lightly. She did not stir. Snake put down the leather case and moved closer; Merideth and the young man looked at each other with blank expressions as they became aware of the exhaustion overtaking them. The young man suddenly leaned toward Merideth and they embraced, silently, close and long.

Merideth straightened, drawing back with reluctance. "Healer, these are my partners, Alex," a nod toward the young man, "and Jesse."

Snake took the sleeping woman's wrist. Her pulse was light, slightly irregular. She had a deep bruise on her forehead, but neither pupil was dilated, so perhaps she was lucky and had only a mild concussion. Snake pulled aside the sheet. The bruises were those of a bad fall: point of shoulder, palm of hand, hip, knee.

"You said she went to sleep — has she been fully conscious since she fell?"

"She was unconscious when we found her but she came to."

Snake nodded. There was a deep scrape down Jesse's side and a bandage on her thigh. Snake pulled the cloth away as gently as possible, but the dressing stuck with dry blood.

Jesse did not move when Snake touched the long gash in her leg, not even as one shifts in sleep to avoid annoyance. She did not wake from pain. Snake stroked the bottom of her foot, with no result. The reflexes were gone.

"She fell off her horse," Alex said.

"She never falls," Merideth snapped. "The colt fell on her."

Snake sought the courage that had seeped slowly away since Grass was killed. It seem irretrievable. She knew how Jesse was hurt; all that remained was to find out how badly. But she did not say anything. Resting one forearm on her knee, head down, Snake felt Jesse's forehead. The tall woman was sweating coldly, still in shock.

If she has internal injuries, Snake thought, if she is dying . . .

Jesse turned her head away, moaning softly in her sleep.

She needs whatever help you can give her, Snake thought angrily. And the longer you swim in self-pity, the more likely you are to hurt her instead.

She felt as if two completely different people, neither of them herself, were holding a dialogue in her mind. She watched and waited and was vaguely grateful when the duty-bound self won the argument over the part of her that was afraid.

"I need help to turn her over," she said.

Merideth at Jesse's shoulders and Alex at her hips, they eased her up and held her on her side, following Snake's instructions to keep from twisting her spine. A black bruise spread across the small of her back, radiating both ways from the vertebrae. Where the color was darkest, the bone was crushed.

The force of the fall had almost sheared the spine's smooth column. Snake could feel shattered chips of bone that had been pushed out into muscle.

"Let her down," Snake said, with deep, dull regret. They obeyed and waited in silence, watching her. She sat on her heels.

If Jesse dies, she thought, she will not feel much pain. If she dies, or if she lives, Grass could not have helped her.

"Healer . . . ?" Alex — he could hardly be twenty, too young to be burdened with grief, even in this harsh land. Merideth seemed ageless. Deep-tanned, dark-eyed, old, young, understanding, bitter. Snake looked at Merideth, glanced at Alex, spoke more to the older partner. "Her spine is broken."

Merideth sat back, shoulders slumped, stunned.

"But she's alive!" Alex cried. "If she's alive, how — "

"Is there any chance you're wrong?" Merideth asked. "Can you do anything?"

"I wish I could. Merideth, Alex, she's lucky to be alive. There's no chance the nerves aren't cut. The bone isn't just broken, it's crushed and twisted. I wish I could say something else, that maybe the bones would heal, maybe the nerves were whole, but I'd be lying to you."

"She's crippled."

"Yes," Snake said.

"No!" Alex grabbed her arm. "Not Jesse — I won't — "

"Hush, Alex," Merideth whispered.

"I'm sorry," Snake said. "I could have hidden this from you, but not for very long."

Meridith brushed a lock of brick-red hair from Jesse's forehead. "No, it's better to know all this at once . . . to learn to live with it."

"Jesse won't thank us for this kind of life."

"Be quiet, Alex! Would you rather the fall had killed her?"

"No!" Looking down at the tent floor, he said softly, "But she might. And you know it."

Merideth stared at Jesse, saying nothing at first. "You're right." Snake could see Merideth's left hand, clenched in a fist, shaking. "Alex, would you see to my mare? We used her badly."

Alex hesitated, not, Snake thought, from reluctance to do as Merideth asked. "All right, Merry." He left them alone. Snake waited. They heard Alex's boots in the sand, then the horse's slow steps.

Jesse moved in her sleep, sighing. Merideth winced at the sound, sucked in a long breath, tried and failed to hold back the sudden deep sobs. Tears glistened in the lamplight, moving like strung diamonds. Snake slid closer and took Merideth's hand, offering comfort until the clenched fist relaxed.

"I didn't want Alex to see . . ."

"I know," Snake said. And so did Alex, she thought. These people guard each other well. "Merideth, can Jesse bear to hear this? I hate to keep secrets, but — "

"She's strong," Merideth said. "Whatever we hid, she'd know."

"All right. I've got to wake her. She shouldn't sleep more than a few hours at a time with that head wound. And she has to be turned over every two hours or her skin will ulcerate."

"I'll wake her." Merideth leaned over Jesse and kissed her lips, held her hand, whispered her name. She took a long time to awaken, muttering and pushing Merideth's hands away.

"Can't we let her sleep any longer?"

"It's safer to wake her for a while."

Jesse moaned, cursed softly, and opened her eyes. For a moment she stared up at the tent, then turned her head and saw Merideth.

"Merry . . . I'm glad you're back." Her eyes were very dark brown, almost black, strange with her red hair and high complexion. "Poor Alex — "

"I know."

Jesse saw Snake. "Healer?"

"Yes."

Jesse gazed at her calmly, and her voice was steady. "Is my back broken?"

Meridith started. Snake hesitated, but she could not evade

the directness of the question even for a short time. Reluctantly, she nodded.

Jesse relaxed all at once, letting her head fall back, staring upward.

Merideth bent down, embracing her. "Jesse, Jesse, love, it's . . ." But there were no more words, and Merideth leaned silently against Jesse's shoulder, holding her close.

Jesse looked at Snake. "I'm paralyzed. I won't heal."

"I'm sorry," Snake said. "No. I can't see any chance."

Jesse's expression did not change; if she had hoped for reassurance, she did not reveal disappointment. "I knew it was bad when we fell," she said. "I heard bone break." She raised Merideth gently. "The colt?"

"He was dead when we found you. He broke his neck."

Jesse's voice mingled relief, regret, fear. "It was quick," she said. "For him."

The pungent odor of urine spread through the tent. Jesse smelled it and turned scarlet with shame. "I can't live like this!" she cried.

"It's all right, never mind," Merideth said, and went to get a cloth.

While Merideth and Snake cleaned her, Jesse looked away and would not speak.

Alex returned warily. "The mare's all right." But his mind was not on the mare. He looked at Jesse, who still lay with her head turned toward the wall, one arm flung across her eyes.

"Jesse knows how to pick a good horse," Merideth said, attempting cheerfulness. The tension was brittle as glass. Both partners stared at Jesse, but she did not move.

"Let her sleep," Snake said, not knowing whether Jesse was asleep or not. "She'll be hungry when she wakes up. I hope you have something she can eat."

Their frozen attention broke in relieved if slightly frantic activity. Merideth rummaged in sacks and pouches and brought out dried meat, dried fruit, a leather flask. "This is wine — can she have that?"

"She hasn't got a serious concussion," Snake said. "The wine should be all right." It might even help, she thought, unless alcohol makes her morose. "But that jerky — "

"I'll make broth," Alex said. He pulled a metal pot from a jumble of equipment, drew his knife from his belt, and began to cut a chunk of jerky into bits. Merideth poured wine over shriveled sections of fruit. The sharp sweet fragrance rose and Snake realized she was both thirsty and ravenous. The desert people seemed to skip meals without noticing, but Snake had reached the oasis two days ago — or was it three? — and she had not eaten much while sleeping off the venom reaction. It was not good manners to ask for food or water in this region, because it was worse manners not to offer. Manners hardly seemed important right now. She was shaky with hunger.

"Gods, I'm hungry," Merideth said in astonishment, as if reading Snake's feelings. "Aren't you?"

"Well, yes," Alex said reluctantly.

"And as hosts — " Apologetically, Merideth handed Snake the flask and found more bowls, more fruit. Snake drank cool-hot spicy wine, the first gulp too deep. She coughed; it was powerful stuff. She drank again and handed the flask back. Merideth drank; Alex took the leather bottle and poured a generous portion into the cooking pot. Only then did he sip the wine himself, quickly, before taking the broth outside to the tiny paraffin stove. The desert heat was so oppressive that they could not even feel the heat of the flame. It flickered like a transparent mirage against the black sand, and Snake felt fresh perspiration sliding down her temples and between her breasts. She wiped her sleeve across her forehead.

They breakfasted on jerky and fruit, and the wine, which struck quickly and hard. Alex began to yawn almost immediately, but every time he nodded, he staggered to his feet and went outside to stir Jesse's broth.

"Alex, go to sleep," Merideth finally said.

"No, I'm not tired." He stirred, tasted, took the pot off the fire, set it inside to cool.

"Alex — " Merideth took his hand and drew him to the patterned rug. "If she calls us, we'll hear her. If she moves, we'll go to her. We can't help her if we're falling over our own feet from weariness."

"But I . . . I . . . " Alex shook his head, but fatigue and the wine stayed with him. "What about you?"

"Your night was harder than my ride. I need to relax a few more minutes, but then I'll come to bed."

Reluctantly, gratefully, Alex lay down nearby. Merideth stroked his hair until, in a few moments, Alex began to snore. Merideth glanced at Snake and smiled. "When he first came with us, Jesse and I wondered how we could ever sleep with such a noise. Now we can hardly sleep without it."

Alex's snore was loud and low, and every so often he caught his breath and snuffled. Snake smiled. "You can get used to nearly anything, I guess." She took one last sip of wine and returned the flask. Merideth, reaching for it, suddenly hiccupped, then, blushing, stoppered the bottle instead of drinking.

"Wine affects me too easily. I should never use it."

"At least you know. You probably never make a fool of yourself."

"When I was younger — " Merideth laughed at memories. "I was foolish then, and poor as well. A bad combination."

"I can think of better."

"Now we're rich, and I'm perhaps a little less foolish. But what good is it all, healer? Money can't help Jesse. Nor wisdom."

"You're right," Snake said. "They can't help her, and neither can I. Only you and Alex can."

"I know it." Merideth's voice was soft and sad. "But it will take Jesse a long time to get used to that."

"She's *alive*, Merideth. The accident came so close to killing her — isn't it enough to be grateful for, that she's alive?"

"To me, yes, it is." The words had begun to slur. "But you don't know Jesse. Where she's from, why she's here — "

Merideth stared groggily at Snake, hesitating, then plunging ahead. "She's here because she can't stand to be trapped. Before we were together, she was rich and powerful and safe. But her whole life and all her work were planned out for her. She would have been one of the rulers of Center — "

"The city!"

"Yes, it was all hers, if she wanted it. But she didn't want to live under a stone sky. She came outside with nothing. To make her own destiny. To be free. Now — the things she enjoys most will be beyond her. How can I tell her to be glad she's alive, when she knows she'll never walk on the desert again, or find me a diamond for some patron's earring, never gentle another horse, never make love?"

"I don't know," Snake said. "But if you and Alex see her life as a tragedy, that's what it will be."

Just before dawn the heat eased slightly, but as soon as it grew light the temperature rose again. The camp was in deep shade, but even in the protection of the rock walls the heat was like a pressure.

Alex snored and Merideth slept peacefully near him, oblivious to the sound, one strong hand curled over Alex's back. Snake lay on the tent floor, facedown, arms outstretched. The fine fibers in the pile of the rug prickled softly against her cheek, damp with her sweat. Her hand throbbed but she could not sleep, and she did not have the energy to rouse herself.

She drifted into a dream in which Arevin appeared. She could see him more clearly than she could remember him when she was awake. It was a curious dream, childishly chaste. She barely touched Arevin's fingertips, and then he began to fade away. Snake reached for him desperately. She woke up throbbing with sexual tension, her heart racing.

Jesse stirred. For a moment Snake did not move, then, reluctantly, she raised herself. She glanced at the other two partners. Alex slept soundly with the momentary forgetfulness of youth, but sheer weariness lined Merideth's face and sweat plastered down the shiny black curls. Snake left Merideth and Alex alone and knelt by Jesse, who lay face down as they last had turned her, her cheek resting on one hand, her other hand shielding her eyes.

She's feigning sleep, Snake thought, for the line of her arm, the curl of her fingers, showed not relaxation but tension. Or wishing it, like me. Both of us would like to sleep, sleep and ignore reality.

"Jesse," she said softly, and again, "Jesse, please."

Jesse sighed and let her hand fall to the sheet.

"There's broth here when you feel strong enough to drink it. And wine, if you'd like."

A barely perceptible shake of the head, though Jesse's lips were dry. Snake would not allow her to become dehydrated, but she did not want to have to argue her into eating, either.

"It's no good," Jesse said.

"Jesse — "

Jesse reached out and laid her hand over Snake's. "No, it's all right. I've thought about what's happened. I've dreamed about it." Snake noticed that her dark brown eyes were flecked with gold. The pupils were very small. "I can't live like this. Neither can they. They'd try — they'd destroy themselves trying. Healer — "

"Please . . ." Snake whispered, afraid again, more afraid than she had ever been in her life. "Please don't — "

"Can't you help me?"

"Not to die," Snake said. "Don't ask me to help you die!"

She bolted to her feet and outside. The heat slammed against her, but there was nowhere to go to escape it. The canyon walls and tumbled piles of broken rock rose up around her.

Head down, trembling, with sweat stinging her eyes, Snake stopped and collected herself. She had acted foolishly and she was ashamed of her panic. She must have frightened Jesse, but she could not yet make herself return and face her. She walked farther from the tent, not toward the desert where the sun and sand would waver like a fantasy, but toward a pocket in the canyon wall that was fenced off as a corral.

It seemed to Snake hardly necessary to pen the horses at all, for they stood in a motionless group, heads down, dusty, lop-eared. They did not even flick their tails; no insects existed in the black desert. Snake wondered where Merideth's handsome bay mare was. These are a sorry lot of beasts, she thought. Hanging on the fence or lying in careless heaps, their tack shone with precious metal and jewels. Snake put her hands on one of the roped wooden stakes and rested her chin on her fists.

At the sound of falling water she turned, startled. At the other side of the corral, Merideth filled a leather trough held up by a wooden frame. The horses came alive, raising their heads, pricking their ears. They started across the sand, trotting, then cantering, all in a turmoil, squealing and nipping and kicking up their heels at each other. They were transformed. They were beautiful.

Merideth stopped nearby, holding the limp, empty waterskin, looking at the small herd rather than at Snake. "Jesse has a gift with horses. Choosing them, training them . . . What's wrong?"

"I'm sorry. I must have upset her. I had no right — "

"To tell her to live? Maybe you don't, but I'm glad you did."

"It doesn't matter what I tell her," Snake said. "She has to want to live herself."

Merideth waved and yelled. The horses nearest the water shied away, giving the others a chance to drink. They jostled each other, draining the trough dry, then standing near it and waiting expectantly for more. "I'm sorry," Merideth said. "That's all for now."

"You must have to carry a great deal of water for them."

"Yes, but we need all of them. We come in with water and we go out with the ore and the stones Jesse finds." The bay mare put her head over the rope fence and nuzzled Merideth's sleeve, stretching to be scratched behind the ears and under the jaw. "Since Alex came with us we travel with more . . . *things*. Luxuries. Alex said we'd impress people that way, so they'd want to buy from us."

"Does it work?"

"It seems to. We live very well now. I can choose my commissions."

Snake stared at the horses, who wandered one by one to the shady end of the corral. The vague glow of the sun had crept up over the edge of the wall, and Snake could feel the heat on her face.

"What are you thinking?" Merideth asked.

"How to make Jesse want to live."

"She won't live uselessly. Alex and I love her. We'd take care of her no matter what. But that isn't enough for her."

"Does she have to walk to be useful?"

"Healer, she's our prospector." Merideth looked at Snake sadly. "She's tried to teach me how to look and where to look. I understand what she tells me, but when I go out I'm as likely as not to find nothing but fused glass and fool's gold."

"Have you showed her your job?"

"Of course. We can each do a little of the other's work. But we each have a talent. She's better at my job than I am at hers and I'm better at hers than either of us is at Alex's, but people don't understand her designs. They're too strange. They're beautiful." Merideth sighed, holding out a bracelet for Snake to see, the only ornament Merideth wore. It was silver, without stones, geometric and multilayered without being bulky. Merideth was right: it was beautiful, but it was strange. "No one will buy them. She knows that. I'd do anything. I'd lie to her, if it would help. But she'd know. Healer — " Merideth flung the waterskin to the sand. "Isn't there anything you can do?"

"I can deal with infections and diseases and tumors. I can even do surgery that isn't beyond my tools. But I can't force the body to heal itself."

"Can anyone?"

"Not . . . not anyone that I know of, on this earth."

"You're not a mystic," Merideth said. "You don't mean some spirit might cause a miracle. You mean off the earth the people might be able to help."

"They might," Snake said slowly, sorry she had spoken as she had. She had not expected Merideth to sense her resentment, though she should have. The city affected all the people around it; it was like the center of a whirlpool, mysterious and fascinating. And it was the place the offworlders sometimes landed. Because of Jesse, Merideth probably knew more about them and the city than Snake did. Snake had always had to take the stories about Center on faith alone; the idea of offworlders was hard to accept for someone who lived in a land where the stars were seldom visible.

"They might even be able to heal her in the city," Snake said. "How should I know? The people who live there won't talk to us. They keep us cut off out here — and as for offworlders, I've never even met anyone who claims to have seen one."

"Jesse has."

"Would they help her?"

"Her family is powerful. They might be able to make the offworlders take her where she could be healed."

"The Center people and the offworlders are jealous of their knowledge, Merideth," Snake said. "At least they've never offered to share any of it."

Merideth scowled and turned away.

"I'm not saying we shouldn't try. It could give her hope — "

"And if they refuse, her hope is broken again."

"She needs the time."

Merideth thought, and finally replied. "And you'll come, to help us?"

It was Snake who hesitated now. She had already set herself to return to the healers' station and accept the verdict of her teachers when she told them of her errors. She had prepared herself to go to the valley. But she put her mind to a different journey, and realized what a difficult task Merideth proposed. They would badly need someone who knew what care Jesse required.

"Healer?"

"All right. I'll come."

"Then let's ask Jesse."

They returned to the tent. Snake was surprised to find herself feeling optimistic; she was smiling, truly encouraged, for what seemed the first time in a long while.

Inside, Alex sat beside Jesse. He glared at Snake when she entered.

"Jesse," Merideth said, "we have a plan."

They had turned her again, carefully following Snake's orders. Jesse looked up tiredly, aged by deep lines in her forehead and around her mouth.

Merideth explained with excited gestures. Jesse listened impassively. Alex's expression hardened into disbelief.

"You're out of your mind," he said when Merideth had finished.

"I'm not! Why do you say that when it's a chance?"

Snake looked at Jesse. "Are we?"

"I think so," Jesse said, but she spoke very slowly, very thoughtfully.

"If we got you to Center," Snake said, "could your people help you?"

Jesse hesitated. "My cousins have some techniques. They could cure very bad wounds. But the spine? Maybe. I don't know. And there's no reason for them to help me. Not anymore."

"You always told me how important blood ties are among the city's families," Merideth said. "You're their kin — "

"I left them," Jesse said. "*I* broke the ties. Why should they take me back? Do you want me to go and beg them?"

"Yes."

Jesse looked down at her long strong useless legs. Alex glared, first at Merideth, then at Snake.

"Jesse, I can't stand to see you as you've been, I can't bear watching you want to die."

"They're very proud," Jesse said. "I hurt my family's pride by renouncing them."

"Then they'd understand what it took you to ask for their help."

"We'd be crazy to try it," Jesse said.

They planned to break camp that evening and cross the lava flow in darkness. Snake would have preferred to wait a few more days before moving Jesse at all, but there was no choice. Jesse's spirits were too readily changeable to keep her here any longer. She knew the partnership had already overstayed its time in the desert. Alex and Merideth could not hide the fact that the water was running low, that they and the horses were going thirsty so she could be cleaned and bathed. A few more days in the canyon, living in the sour stench that would collect because nothing could be properly washed, would push her down into depression and disgust.

And they had no time to waste.They had a long way to journey: up and across the lava, then east to the central mountains that separated the black desert into its western half, where they were now, and its eastern portion, where the city lay. The road cutting through the west and east ranges of the central mountains was a good one, but after the pass the travelers would enter the desert again, and head southeast, for Center. They had to hurry. Once the storms of winter began, no one could cross the desert; the city would be isolated. Already the summer was fading in stinging dust devils and windblown eddies of sand

They would not take down the tent or load the horses until twilight, but they packed all they could before it became too hot to work, stacking the baggage beside Jesse's sacks of ore. Snake's hand limbered up with the heavy work. The bruise was finally fading and the punctures had healed to bright pink scars. Soon the sand viper bite would match all the other scars on her hands, and she would forget which one it was. She wished now that she had captured one of the ugly serpents to take home with her. It was a species she had never seen before. Even if it had turned out not to be useful to the healers, she could have made an antidote to its venom for Arevin's people. If she ever saw Arevin's people again.

Snake wrestled the last pack into the pile and wiped her hands on her pants and her face on her sleeve. Nearby, Merideth and Alex hoisted the stretcher they had built and adjusted the makeshift harnesses until it rode level between a tandem pair of horses. Snake went over to watch.

It was the most peculiar conveyance she had ever seen, but it looked like it would work. In the desert everything had to be carried or dragged; wheeled carts would bog down in the sand or break in rocky country. As long as the horses did not shy or bolt, the stretcher would give Jesse a more tolerable ride than a travois. The big gray between the front shafts stood calm and steady as a stone; apart from a sidelong glance as it was led between the back shafts, the second horse, a piebald, showed no fear.

Jesse *must* be a marvel, Snake thought, if the horses she trains will put up with such contraptions.

"Jesse says we'll start a fashion among rich merchants wherever we go," Merideth said.

"She's right," Alex said. He unfastened a strap and they let the stretcher fall to the ground. "But they'll be lucky not to get kicked apart, the way most of them break horses." He slapped the placid gray's neck fondly and led both horses back to the corral.

"I wish she'd been riding one of them before," Snake said to Merideth.

"They weren't like that when she got them. She buys crazy horses. She can't bear to see them mistreated. The colt was one of her strays — she had him calmed but he hadn't found his balance yet."

They started back toward the tent to get out of the sun as it crept across the afternoon. The tent sagged on one side where two poles had been removed for the stretcher. Merideth yawned widely. "Best to sleep while we have the chance. We can't afford to still be on the lava when the sun comes up."

But Snake was filled with a restless uncertain energy; she sat in the tent, grateful for the shade but wide-awake, wondering how the whole mad plan could work. She reached for the leather case to check on her serpents, but Jesse woke as she opened Sand's compartment. She closed the catch again and moved closer to the pallet. Jesse looked up at her.

"Jesse . . . about what I said . . ." She wanted to explain but could not think how to start.

"What upset you so? Am I the first you've helped who might have died?"

"No. I've seen people die. I've helped them die."

"Everything was so hopeless just a little while ago," Jesse said. "A pleasant end would have been easy. You must always have to guard against . . . the simplicity of death."

"Death can be a gift," Snake said. "But in one way or another it always means failure. That's the guard against it. It's enough."

A faint breeze whispered through the heat, making Snake feel almost cool.

"What's wrong, healer?"

"I was afraid," Snake said. "I was afraid you might be dying. If you were, you had the right to ask my help. I have the obligation to give it. But I can't."

"I don't understand."

"When my training ended my teachers gave me my own serpents. Two of them can be drugged for medicines. The third was the dream-giver. He was killed."

Jesse reached out instinctively and took Snake's hand, a reaction to her sadness. Snake accepted Jesse's quiet sympathy gratefully, taking comfort in the sturdy touch.

"You're crippled too," Jesse said abruptly. "As crippled in your work as I."

Jesse's generosity in comparing them that way embarrassed Snake. Jesse was in pain, helpless, her only chance of recovery so small that Snake stood in awe of her spirits and her renewed grasp on life. "Thank you for saying that."

"So I'm going back to my family to ask for help — and you were going back to yours?"

"Yes."

"They'll give you another," Jesse said with certainty.

"I hope so."

"Is there any question?"

"Dreamsnakes don't breed well," Snake said. "We don't know enough about them. Every few years a few new ones are born, or one of us manages to clone some, but — " Snake shrugged.

"Catch one!"

The suggestion had never occurred to Snake because she knew it was impossible. She had never considered any possibility other than returning to the healers' station and asking her teachers to pardon her. She smiled sadly. "My reach isn't that long. They don't come from here."

"Where?"

Snake shrugged again. "Some other world . . ." Her voice trailed off as she realized what she was saying.

"Then you'll come with me beyond the city's gates," Jesse said. "When I go to my family, they'll introduce you to the offworlders."

"Jesse, my people have been asking Center's help for decades. They won't even speak to us."

"But now one of the city's families is obligated to you. Whether my people will take me back I don't know. But they'll be in debt to you for helping me, nevertheless."

Snake listened in silence, intrigued by the possibilities lying in Jesse's words.

"Healer, believe me," Jesse said. "We can help each other. If they accept me, they'll accept my friends as well. If not, they'll still have to discharge their debt to you. Either one of us can present both our requests."

Snake was a proud woman, proud of her training, her competence, her name. The prospect of atoning for Grass's death in some other way than begging forgiveness fascinated her. Once every decade an elder healer would make the long trip to the city, seeking to renew the breeding stock of dreamsnakes. They had always been refused. If Snake could succeed . . .

"Can this work?"

"My family will help us," Jesse said. "Whether they can make the offworlders help us too, I don't know."

During the hot afternoon, all Snake and the partners could do was wait. Snake decided to let Mist and Sand out of the satchel for a while before the long trip began. As she left the tent, she stopped beside Jesse. The handsome woman was sleeping peacefully, but her face was flushed. Snake touched her forehead. Perhaps Jesse had a slight fever; perhaps it was just the heat of the day. Snake still thought Jesse had avoided serious internal injuries, but it was possible that she was bleeding, even that she was developing peritonitis. That was something Snake could cure. She decided not to disturb Jesse for the moment, but to wait and see if the fever rose.

Walking out of camp to find a sheltered place where her serpents would frighten no one, Snake passed Alex, staring morosely into space. She hesitated, and he glanced up, his expression troubled. Snake sat down beside him without speaking. He turned toward her, staring at her with his penetrating gaze: the good-naturedness had vanished from his face in his torment, leaving him ugly, and sinister as well.

"We crippled her, didn't we? Merideth and me."

"Crippled her? No, of course not."

"We shouldn't have moved her. I should have thought of that. We should have moved the camp to her. Maybe the nerves weren't broken when we found her."

"They were broken."

"But we didn't know about her back. We thought she'd hit her head. We could have twisted her body — "

Snake put her hand on Alex's forearm. "It was an injury of violence," she said. "Any healer could see it. The damage happened when she fell. Believe me. You and Merideth couldn't have done any of that to her."

The hard muscles in his forearm relaxed. Snake took her hand away, relieved. Alex's stocky body held so much strength, and he had been controlling himself so tightly, that Snake feared he might turn his own force unwittingly back on himself. He was more important to this partnership than he appeared, perhaps even more important than he himself knew. Alex was the practical one, the one who kept the camp running smoothly, who dealt with the buyers of Merideth's work and balanced out the romanticism of Merideth the artist and Jesse the adventurer. Snake hoped the truth she had told him would let him ease his guilt and tension. For now, though, she could do no more for him.

As twilight approached, Snake stroked Sand's smooth patterned scales. She no longer wondered if the diamondback enjoyed being stroked, or even if a creature as small-brained as Sand could feel enjoyment at all. The cool sensation beneath her fingers gave her pleasure, and Sand lay in a quiet coil, now and then flicking out his tongue. His color was bright and clear; he had outgrown his old skin and shed it only recently. "I let thee eat too much," Snake said fondly. "Thou lazy creature."

Snake drew her knees up under her chin. Against the black rocks, the rattlesnake's patterns were almost as conspicuous as Mist's albino scales. Neither serpents nor humans nor anything else left alive on earth had yet adapted to their world as it existed now.

Mist was out of sight, but Snake was not worried. Both serpents were imprinted on her and would stay near and even follow her. Neither had much aptitude for learning beyond the imprinting, which the healers had bred into them, but Mist and Sand would return when they felt the vibration of her hand slapping the ground.

Snake relaxed against a boulder, cushioned by the desert robe Arevin's people had given her. She wondered what Arevin was doing, where he was. His people were nomads, herders of huge musk oxen whose undercoats gave fine, silky wool. To meet the clan again she would have to search for them. She did not know if that would ever be possible, though she very much wanted to see Arevin once more.

Seeing his people would always remind her of Grass's death, if she were ever able to forget it. Her mistakes and misjudgments of them were the reason Grass was gone. She had expected them to accept her word despite their fear, and without meaning to they had shown her how arrogant her assumptions were.

She shook off her depression. Now she had a chance to redeem herself. If she really could go with Jesse, find out where the dreamsnakes came from, and capture new ones — if she could even discover why they would not breed on earth — she could return in triumph instead of in disgrace, succeeding where her teachers and generations of healers had failed.

It was time to return to the camp. She climbed the low rise of jumbled rock that covered the mouth of the canyon, looking for Mist. The cobra was coiled on a large chunk of basalt.

At the top of the slope Snake reached for Mist, picked her up, and stroked her narrow head. She was not so formidable unexcited, hood folded, narrow-headed as any venomless serpent. She did not need a thick-jowled head, heavy with poison. Her venom was powerful enough to kill in delicate doses.

As Snake turned, the brilliant sunset drew her gaze. The sun was an orange blur on the horizon, radiating streaks of purple and vermilion through the gray clouds.

And then Snake saw the craters, stretching away across the desert below her. The earth was covered with great circular basins. Some, lying in the path of the lava flow, had caught and broken its smooth frozen billows. Others were clearer, great holes gouged in the earth, still distinct after so many years of driving sands. The craters were so large, spread over such a distance, that they could have only one source. Nuclear explosions had blasted them. The war itself was long over, almost forgotten, for it had destroyed everyone who knew or cared about the reasons it had happened.

Snake gazed over the ravaged land, glad to be no nearer. In places like this the effects of the war had lingered visibly and invisibly to Snake's time; they would persist for centuries beyond her life. The canyon in which she and the partners were camped was probably not completely safe itself, but they had not been here long enough to be in serious danger.

Something unusual lay out in the rubble, in line with the brilliant setting sun so it was difficult for Snake to see. She squinted at it. She felt uneasy, as if she were spying on something she had no business knowing about.

The body of a horse, decaying in the heat, lay crumpled at the edge of a crater. The dead animal's rigid legs poked grotesquely into the air, forced up by its swollen belly. Clasping the animal's head, a gold bridle gleamed scarlet and orange in the sunset.

Snake released her breath in a sound part sigh, part moan.

She ran back to the serpent case and urged Mist inside, picked Sand up and started back toward the camp, cursing when the rattler in his mindlessly obstinate way tried to twine himself around her arm. She stopped and held him so he could slide into his compartment, and started running again while she was still fastening the catch. The case banged against her leg.

Panting, she reached the tent and ducked inside. Merideth and Alex were asleep. Snake knelt beside Jesse and carefully pulled back the sheet.

Little more than an hour had passed since Snake had examined Jesse last. The bruises down her side had darkened and deepened, and her body was unhealthily flushed. Snake felt her forehead. It was burning hot and paper-dry. Jesse did not respond to her touch. When Snake took her hand away the smooth skin looked darker. Within minutes, while Snake watched, horrified, another bruise began to form as the capillaries ruptured, their walls so damaged by radiation that mild pressure completed their destruction. The bandage on Jesse's thigh suddenly reddened in the center with a stain of blood. Snake clenched her fists. She was shaking, deep inside, as if from penetrating cold.

"Merideth!"

In a moment Merideth was awake, yawning and mumbling sleepily. "What's wrong?"

"How long did it take you to find Jesse? Did she fall in the craters?"

"Yes, she was prospecting. That's why we come here — other artisans can't match our work because of what Jesse finds here. But this time a rim gave way. We found her in the evening."

A whole day, Snake thought. She must have been in one of the primary craters.

"Why didn't you tell me?"

"Tell you what?"

"Those craters are dangerous — "

"Do you believe all those old legends, healer? We've been coming here for a decade and nothing ever happened to us."

Now was not the time for angry retorts. Snake glanced at Jesse again and realized that her own ignorance and the partnership's contempt for the danger of the old world's relics had unwittingly granted Jesse some mercy. Snake had treatments for radiation poisoning, but there was no treatment for anything this severe. Whatever she could have tried would only have prolonged Jesse's death.

"What's the matter?" For the first time Merideth's voice showed fear.

"She has radiation poisoning."

"Poisoning? How? She's eaten and drunk nothing we haven't tasted."

"It's from the crater. The ground is poisoned. The legends are true."

Beneath deep tan, Merideth was pale. "Then do something, help her!"

"There's nothing I can do."

"You couldn't help her injury, you can't help her sickness — "

They stared at each other, both of them hurt and angry. Merideth's gaze dropped first. "I'm sorry. I had no right . . ."

"I wish to the gods I were omnipotent, Merideth, but I'm not."

Their conversation woke Alex, who rose and came toward them, stretching and scratching. "It's time to — " He glanced back and forth from Snake to Merideth, then looked beyond to Jesse. "Oh, gods . . ."

The new mark on her forehead, where Snake had touched her, was slowly oozing blood.

Alex flung himself down beside her, reaching for her, but Snake held him back. He tried to push her away.

"Alex, I barely touched her. You can't help her like that."

He looked at her blankly. "Then how?"

Snake shook her head.

Tears welling up, Alex pulled away from her. "It isn't fair!" He ran out of the tent. Merideth started after him, hesitated at the entrance, and turned back. "He can't understand, he's so young."

"He understands," Snake said. She blotted Jesse's forehead, trying not to rub or put pressure on her skin. "And he's right, it isn't fair. Who ever said anything was fair?" She cut off the words to spare Merideth her own bitterness over Jesse's lost chances, snatched away by fate and ignorance and the remnants of another generation's insanity.

"Merry?" Jesse groped in the air with a trembling hand.

"I'm here." Merideth reached out but stopped, afraid to touch her.

"What's the matter? Why do I . . ." She blinked slowly. Her eyes were bloodshot.

"Gently," Snake whispered. Merideth enfolded Jesse's fingers with hands soft as bird wings.

"Is it time to go?" The eagerness was tinged with terror, with unwillingness to realize something was wrong.

"No, love."

"It's so hot . . ." She started to raise her head, shifting her weight. She froze with a gasp. Information entered Snake's mind without any conscious effort, a cold inhuman analysis she was trained for: bleeding into the joints. Internal bleeding. And in her brain?

"It never hurt like this." She glanced at Snake without moving her head. "It's something else, something worse."

"Jesse, I — " Snake was first made aware of her tears by the taste of salt on her lips, mixed with the grit from the desert's dust. She choked on words. Alex crept back into the tent. Jesse tried to speak again, but could only gasp.

Merideth grabbed Snake's arm. She could feel the fingernails cutting her skin. "She's dying."

Snake nodded.

"Healers know how to help — how to — "

"Merideth, no," Jesse whispered.

" — how to take away the pain."

"She can't . . ."

"One of my serpents was killed," Snake said, more loudly than she had intended, belligerent with grief and anger.

Merideth did not make a second outburst, but Snake could feel the unspoken accusation: You couldn't help her live, and now you can't help her die. This time it was Snake's gaze that fell. She deserved the condemnation. Merideth let her go and turned back to Jesse, looming over her like a tall demon waiting to fight beasts or shadows.

Jesse reached out to touch Merideth but drew her hand sharply back. She stared at the soft center of her palm, between the calluses of her work. A bruise was forming. "*Why*?"

"The last war," Snake said. "In the craters — " Her voice broke.

"So it's true," Jesse said. "My family believes the land outside kills, but I thought they lied." Her eyes went out of focus; she blinked, looked toward Snake but did not seem to see her, blinked again. "They lied about so many other things. Lies for making children obedient . . ."

Silent again, her eyes closed, Jesse slowly went limp, one muscle at a time, as if even relaxation was an agony she could not tolerate all at once. She was still conscious but did not respond, with word or smile or glance, as Merideth stroked her bright hair and moved as close as was possible without touching her. Her skin was ashen around the livid bruises.

Suddenly she screamed. She clamped her hands to her temples, pressing, digging her nails into her scalp. Snake grabbed for her hands to pull them away. "No," Jesse groaned, "oh, no, leave me alone — Merry, it hurts!" Weak a few moments before, Jesse struggled with fever-fired strength. Snake could do nothing but try to restrain her gently, but the inner diagnostic voice returned: aneurism. In Jesse's brain a radiation-weakened vessel was slowly exploding. Snake's next thought was equally unbidden and even more powerful: Pray it bursts soon and hard, and kills her cleanly.

At the same time that Snake realized Alex was no longer beside her, trying to help with Jesse, but had crossed to the other side of the tent, she heard Sand rattle. She turned instinctively, launching herself toward Alex. Her shoulder rammed his stomach and he dropped the satchel as Sand struck from within. Alex crashed to the ground. Snake felt a sharp pain in her leg and drew back her fist to strike him, but checked herself.

She fell to one knee.

Sand coiled on the ground, rattling his tail softly, prepared to strike again. Snake's heart raced. She could feel the pulse throbbing in her thigh. Her femoral artery was less than a handsbreadth from the puncture where Sand had sunk his fangs into muscle.

"You fool! Are you trying to kill yourself?" Her leg throbbed a few more times, then her immunities neutralized the venom. She was glad Sand had missed the artery. Even she could be made briefly ill by a bite like that, and she had no time for illness. The pain became a dull, ebbing ache.

"How can you let her die in such pain?" Alex asked.

"All you'd give her with Sand is more pain." Disguising her anger, she turned calmly to the diamondback, picked him up, and let him slide back into the case. "There's no quick death with rattlers." That was not quite true, but Snake was still angry enough to frighten him. "If anyone dies of it, they die from infection. Gangrene."

Alex paled but held his ground, glowering.

Merideth called him. Alex glanced at his partners, then stared at Snake again for a long challenging moment. "What about the other serpent?" He turned his back on her and went to Jesse's side.

Holding the case, Snake fingered the catch on Mist's compartment. She shook her head, pushing away the image of Jesse dying from Mist's poison. Cobra venom would kill quickly, not pleasantly but quickly. What was the difference between disguising pain with dreams and ending it with death? Snake had never deliberately caused the death of another human being, in anger or in mercy. She did not know if she could now. Or if she should. She could not tell if the reluctance she felt came from her training or from some deeper, more fundamental knowledge that to kill Jesse would be wrong.

She could hear the partners talking softly together, voices, but not words, distinguishable: Merideth clear, musical, midrange; Alex deep and rumbling; Jesse breathless and hesitant.

Every few minutes they all fell silent as Jesse fought another wave of pain. Jesse's next hours or days, the last of her life, would strip away her strength and spirit.

Snake opened the case and let Mist slide out and coil around her arm, up and over her shoulder. She held the cobra gently behind the head so she could not strike, and crossed the tent.

They all looked up at her, startled out of a retreat into their self-sufficient partnership. Merideth, in particular, seemed for a moment not even to recognize her. Alex looked from Snake to the cobra and back again, with a strange expression of resigned, triumphant grief. Mist flicked out her tongue to catch their smells, her unblinking eyes like silver mirrors in the growing darkness. Jesse peered at her, squinting, blinking. She reached up to rub her eyes but stopped, remembering, a tremor in her hand. "Healer? Come closer, I can't see properly."

Snake knelt down between Merideth and Alex. For the third time she did not know what to say to Jesse. It was as if she, not Jesse, were becoming blind, blood seeping across her retinas and squeezing the nerves, sight blurring slowly to scarlet and black. Snake blinked rapidly and her vision cleared.

"Jesse, I can't do anything about the pain." Mist moved smoothly beneath her hand. "All I can offer . . ."

"Tell her!" Alex growled. He stared as if petrified at Mist's eyes.

"Do you think this is easy?" Snake snapped. But Alex did not look up.

"Jesse," Snake said, "Mist's natural venom can kill. If you want me to — "

"What are you saying?" Merideth cried.

Alex broke his fascinated stare. "Merideth, be quiet, how can you stand — "

"Both of you be quiet," Snake said. "The decision's up to neither of you, it's Jesse's alone."

Alex slumped back on his heels; Merideth sat rigid, glaring Jesse said nothing for a long time. Mist tried to crawl from Snake's arm and Snake restrained her.

"The pain won't stop," Jesse said.

"No," Snake said. "I'm sorry."

"When will I die?"

"The pain in your head is from pressure. It could kill you . . . any time." Merideth hunched down, face in hands, but Snake had no way of being gentler. "You have a few days, at the most, from the poisoning." Jesse flinched when she said that.

"I don't wish for days anymore," she said softly.

Tears streamed between Merideth's fingers.

"Dear Merry, Alex knows," Jesse said. "Please try to understand. It's time for me to let you go." Jesse looked toward Snake with sightless eyes. "Let us have a little while alone, and then I'll be grateful for your gift."

Snake stood and walked out of the tent. Her knees shook and her neck and shoulders ached with tension. She sat down on the hard, gritty sand, wishing the night were over.

She looked up at the sky, a thin strip edged by the walls of the canyon. The clouds seemed peculiarly thick and opaque tonight, for though the moon had not yet risen high enough to see, some of its light should have been diffracted into sky-glow. Suddenly she realized the clouds were not unusually thick but very thin and mobile, too thin to spread light. They moved in a wind that blew only high above the ground. As she watched, a bank of dark cloud parted, and Snake quite clearly saw the sky, black and deep and shimmering with multicolored points of light. Snake stared at them, hoping the clouds would not come together again, wishing someone else were near to share the stars with her. Planets circled some of those stars, and people lived on them, people who might have helped Jesse if they had even known she existed. Snake wondered if their plan had had any chance of success at all, or if Jesse had accepted it because on a level deeper than shock and resignation her grip on life had been too strong to let go.

Inside the tent someone uncovered a clear bowl of light-cells. The blue bioluminescence spilling through the entrance washed over the black sand.

"Healer, Jesse wants you." Merideth stood outlined in the glow, voice stripped of music, tall and gaunt and haggard.

Snake carried Mist inside. Merideth did not speak to her again. Even Alex looked at her with a fleeting expression of uncertainty and fear. But Jesse welcomed her with her blinded eyes. Merideth and Alex stood in front of her bed, like a guard. Snake stopped. She did not doubt her decision, but the final choice was still Jesse's.

"Come kiss me," Jesse said. "Then leave us."

Merideth swung around. "You can't ask us to go now!"

"You have enough to forget." Her voice trembled with weakness. Her hair clung in tangles to her forehead and her cheeks, and what was left in her face was endurance near exhaustion. Snake saw it and Alex saw it, but Merideth stood, shoulders hunched, staring at the floor.

Alex knelt and gently raised Jesse's hand to his lips. He kissed her almost reverently, on the fingers, on the cheek, on her lips. She laid her hand on his shoulder and kept him a moment longer. He rose slowly, silent, looked at Snake, and left the tent.

"Merry, please say good-bye before you go."

Defeated, Merideth knelt beside her and brushed her hair back from her bruised face, gathered her up and held her. She returned the embrace. Neither offered consolation.

Merideth left the tent, in a silence that drifted on longer than Snake meant it to. When the footsteps faded to a whisper on sand against leather, Jesse shuddered with a sound between a cry and a groan.

"Healer?"

"I'm here." She put her palm under Jesse's outstretched hand.

"Do you think it would have worked?"

"I don't know," Snake said, remembering when one of her teachers had returned from the city, having met only closed gates and people who would not speak to her. "I want to believe it would have."

Jesse's lips were darkening to purple. Her lower lip had split. Snake dabbed at the blood, but it was thin as water and she could not stop the flow.

"You keep going," Jesse whispered.

"What?"

"To the city. You still have a claim on them."

"Jesse, no — "

"Yes. They live under a stone sky, afraid of everything outside. They can help you, and they need your help. They'll all go mad in a few more generations. Tell them I lived and I was happy. Tell them I might not have died if they had told the truth. They said everything outside killed, so I thought nothing did."

"I'll carry your message."

"Don't forget your own. Other people need . . ." She ran out of breath, and Snake waited in silence for the command that would come next. Sweat slid down her sides. Sensing her distress, Mist coiled tighter on her arm.

"Healer?"

Snake patted her hand.

"Merry took the pain away. Please let me go before it comes back."

"All right, Jesse." She freed Mist from her arm. "I'll try to make it as quick as I can."

The handsome ruined face turned toward her. "Thank you."

Snake was glad Jesse could not see what was about to happen. Mist would strike one of the carotid arteries, just beneath the jaw, so the poison would flow to Jesse's brain and kill her instantly. Snake had planned that out very carefully, dispassionately, at the same time wondering how she could think about it so clearly.

Snake began to speak soothingly, hypnotically. "Relax, let your head fall back, close your eyes, pretend it's time to sleep . . ." She held Mist over Jesse's breast, waiting as the tension flowed away and the slight tremor ceased. Tears ran down her face, but her sight was brilliantly clear. She could see the pulse-beat in Jesse's throat. Mist's tongue flicked out, in. Her hood flared. She would strike straight forward when Snake released her. "A deep sleep, and joyful dreams . . ." Jesse's head lolled, exposing her throat. Mist slid in Snake's hands. Snake felt her fingers opening as she thought, Must I do this? and suddenly Jesse convulsed, her upper spine arched, flinging her head back. Her arms went rigid and her fingers spread and tensed into claws. Frightened, Mist struck. Jesse convulsed again, hands clenching, and relaxed completely, all at once. Blood pulsed in two thin drops from the marks of Mist's fangs. Jesse shuddered, but she was already dead.

Nothing was left but the smell of death and a spirit-empty corpse, Mist cold and hissing atop it. Snake wondered if Jesse somehow had felt the pressure grow to breaking point, and had stood it as long as she could to save her partners this memory.

Shaking, Snake put Mist in the case and cleaned the body as gently as if it were still Jesse. But there was nothing left of her now; her beauty had gone with her life, leaving bruised and battered flesh. Snake closed the eyes and drew the stained sheet up over the face.

She left the tent, carrying the leather case. Merideth and Alex watched her approach. The moon had risen; she could see them in shades of gray.

"It's over," she said. Somehow, her voice was the same as ever.

Merideth did not move or speak. Alex took Snake's hand, as he had taken Jesse's, and kissed it. Snake drew back, wanting no thanks for this night's work.

"I should have stayed with her," Merideth said.

"Merry, she didn't want us to."

Snake saw that Merideth would always imagine what had happened, a thousand ways, each more horrible than the last, unless she stopped the fantasy.

"I hope you can believe this, Merideth," she said. "Jesse said,

'Merry took the pain away,' and a moment later, just before my cobra struck, she died. Instantly. A blood vessel broke in her brain. She never felt it. She never felt Mist. Gods witness it, I believe that to be the truth."

"It would have been the same, no matter what we did?"

"Yes."

That seemed to change things for Merideth, enough to accept. It did not change anything for Snake. She still knew she would have been the cause of Jesse's death. Seeing the self-hatred vanish from Merideth's face, Snake started toward the crumbled part of the canyon wall where the slope led up to the lava plain.

"Where are you going?" Alex caught up to her.

"Back to my camp," she said dully.

"Please wait. Jesse wanted to give you something."

If he had said Jesse had asked them to give her a gift, she would have refused, but, somehow, that Jesse left it herself made a difference. Unwillingly, she stopped. "I can't," she said. "Alex, let me go."

He turned her gently and guided her back to the camp. Merideth was gone, in the tent with Jesse's body or grieving alone.

Jesse had left her a horse, a dark-gray mare, almost black, a fine-boned animal with the look of speed and spirit. Despite herself, despite knowing it was not a healer's horse, Snake's hands and heart went out to her. The mare seemed to Snake the only thing she had seen in — she could not think how long — that was beauty and strength alone, unmarked by tragedy. Alex gave her the reins and she closed her hands around the soft leather. The bridle was inlaid with gold in Merideth's delicate filigree style.

"Her name is Swift," Alex said.

Snake was alone, on the long trek to cross the lava before morning. The mare's hooves rang on the hollow-sounding stone, and the leather case rubbed against Snake's leg from behind.

She knew she could not return to the healers' station. Not yet. Tonight had proved that she could not stop being a healer, no matter how inadequate her tools. If her teachers took Mist and Sand and cast her out, she knew she could not bear it. She would go mad with the knowledge that in this town, or that camp, sickness or death occurred that she could have cured or prevented or made more tolerable. She would always try to do something.

She had been raised to be proud and self-reliant, qualities she would have to set aside if she returned to the station now. She had promised Jesse to take her last message to the city, and she would keep the promise. She would go to the city for Jesse, and for herself.

Arevin sat on a huge boulder, his cousin's baby gurgling in a sling against his chest. The warmth and activity of the new being were a comfort to him as he stared across the desert, in the direction Snake had gone. Stavin was well and the new child healthy; Arevin knew he should feel grateful and glad of the clan's good fortune, so he felt vaguely guilty about his lingering sorrow. He touched the place on his cheek where the white serpent's tail had struck him. As Snake had promised, there was no scar. It seemed impossible that she had been gone long enough for the cut to scab over and heal, because he remembered everything about her as clearly as if she were still here. About Snake was none of the blurriness that distance and time impart to most acquaintances. At the same time it felt to Arevin as if she had been gone forever.

One of the huge musk oxen the clan herded ambled up and rubbed herself against the boulder, giving her side a good scratch. She whuffled at Arevin, nuzzling his foot and licking at his boot with her great pink tongue. Nearby, her half-grown calf chewed at the dry, leafless branches of a desert bush. All the beasts in the herd grew thin during each harsh summer; now their coats were dull and rough. They survived the heat well enough if their insulating undercoats were thoroughly combed out when they began shedding in the spring; since the clan kept the oxen for their fine, soft winter wool, the combing was never neglected. But the oxen, like the people, had had enough of summer and heat and foraging for dry and tasteless food. The animals were anxious, in their mild-mannered way, to return to the fresh grass of winter pastures. Ordinarily Arevin too would be glad to return to the plateaus.

The baby waved tiny hands in the air, clutched Arevin's finger, and drew it down. Arevin smiled. "That's one thing I can't do for you, little one," he said. The baby sucked at his fingertip and gummed it contentedly, without crying when no milk came. The baby's eyes were blue, like Snake's. Many babies' eyes are blue, Arevin thought. But a child's blue eyes were enough to make him drift off into dreams.

He dreamed about Snake almost every night, or at least every night he was able to sleep. He had never felt this way about anyone before. He clung to memories of the few times they had touched: leaning against each other in the desert; the touch of her strong fingers on his bruised cheek; in Stavin's tent, where he had comforted her. It was absurd that the happiest time in his life seemed to him the moment just before he knew she must leave, when he embraced her and hoped she might decide to stay. And she would have stayed, he thought. Because we do need a healer, and maybe partly because of me. She would have stayed longer if she could.

That was the only time he had cried in as long as he could remember. Yet he understood her not being willing to stay with her abilities crippled, for right now he felt crippled too. He was no good for anything. He knew it but could do nothing about it. Every day he hoped Snake might return, though he knew she would not. He had no idea how far beyond the desert her destination lay. She might have traveled from the healers' station for a week or a month or half a year before reaching the desert and deciding to cross it in search of new people and new places.

He should have gone with her. He was certain of that now. In her grief she could not accept him, but he should have seen immediately that she would never be able to explain to her teachers what had happened here. Even Snake's insight would not help her comprehend the terror Arevin's people felt toward vipers. Arevin understood it from experience, from the nightmare he still had about his little sister's death, from the cold sweat sliding down his body when Snake had asked him to help hold Mist. And he knew it from his own deathly fear when the sand viper bit Snake's hand, for already he loved her, and he knew she would die.

Snake was associated with the only two miracles in Arevin's experience. She had not died, that was the first, and the second was that she had saved Stavin's life.

The baby blinked and sucked harder on Arevin's finger. Arevin slid down from the boulder and held out one hand. The tremendous musk ox laid her chin on his palm and he scratched her beneath the jaw.

"Will you give some dinner to this child?" Arevin said. He patted her back and her side and her stomach and knelt down beside her. She did not have a great deal of milk this late in the year, but the calf was nearly weaned. With his sleeve Arevin briefly rubbed her teat, then held his cousin's baby in reach of it. No more afraid of the immense beast than Arevin was, the child suckled hungrily.

When the baby's hunger was satisfied, Arevin scratched the musk ox under the jaw again and climbed back up on the boulder. After a while the child fell asleep, tiny fingers wrapped around Arevin's hand.

"Cousin!"

He glanced around. The leader of the clan climbed the side of the boulder and sat beside him, her long hair unbound and moving in the faint wind. She leaned over and smiled at the baby.

"How has this child been behaving?"

"Perfectly."

She shook her hair back from her face. "They're so much easier to carry when you can put them on your back. And even put them down once in a while. " She grinned. She was not always as reserved and dignified as when she received the clan's guests.

Arevin managed a smile.

She put her hand over his, the one the baby was holding. "My dear, do I have to ask what's the matter?"

Arevin shrugged, embarrassed. "I'll try to do better," he said. "I've been of little use lately."

"Do you think I'm here to criticize?"

"Criticism would be proper." Arevin did not look at the leader of his clan, his cousin, but instead stared at her peaceful child. His cousin let go of his hand and put her arm around his shoulders.

"Arevin," she said, speaking to him directly by name for the third time in his life, "Arevin, you are valuable to me. In time you could be elected the clan's leader, if you wish it. But you must settle your mind. If she did not want you . . ."

"We wanted each other," Arevin said. "But she couldn't continue her work here and she said I must not go with her. I can't follow her now." He glanced down at his cousin's child. Since his own parents' deaths, Arevin had been accepted as a member of his cousin's family group. There were six adult partners, two, now three, children, and Arevin. His responsibilities were not well defined, but he did feel responsible for the children. Especially now, with the trip to winter territory ahead, the clan needed the work of every member. From now until the end of the trip the musk oxen had to be watched night and day, or they would wander east, a few at a time, seeking the new pastures, and never be seen again. Finding food was an equally difficult problem for the human beings at this time of year. But if they left too early, they would arrive at the wintering grounds when the forage was still new-sprouted, tender and easily damaged.

"Cousin, tell me what you want to say."

"I know the clan can't spare anyone right now. I have respon sibilities here, to you, to this child . . . But the healer — how can she explain what happened here? How can she make her teachers understand when she can't understand it herself? I saw a sand viper strike her. I saw the blood and poison running down her hand. But she hardly even noticed it. She said she should never have felt it at all."

Arevin looked at his friend, for he had told no one about the sand viper before, thinking they would not be able to believe him. The leader was startled, but she did not dispute his word.

"How can she explain how we feared what she offered? She will tell her teachers she made a mistake and because of it the little serpent was killed. She blames herself. They will too, and they'll punish her."

The leader of the clan gazed across the desert. She reached up and pushed a lock of her graying hair back behind her ear.

"She is a proud woman," she said. "You're right. She wouldn't make excuses for herself."

"She won't come back if they exile her," Arevin said. "I don't know where she will go, but we would never see her again."

"The storms are coming," the leader said abruptly.

Arevin nodded.

"If you went after her — "

"I can't! Not now!"

"My dear," the leader said, "we do things the way we do them so we can all be as free as possible most of the time, instead of only some of us being free all of the time. You're enslaving yourself to responsibility when extraordinary circumstances demand freedom. If you were a partner in the group and it was your job to hold this child, the problem would be more difficult, but it would not necessarily be impossible to solve. As it is, my partner has had much more freedom since the child's birth than he expected to have when we decided to conceive it. That is because of your willingness to do more than your share."

"It isn't like that," Arevin said quickly. "I wanted to help with the child. I needed to. I needed — " He stopped, not knowing what he had started to say. "I was grateful to him for allowing me to help."

"I know. And I had no objection. But he was not doing you a favor. You were doing one for him. Perhaps now it's time to return his responsibilities." She smiled fondly. "He is inclined to get too engrossed in his work." Her partner was a weaver, the best in the clan, but she was right: he did often seem to drift through life in dreams.

"I should never have let her go," Arevin said abruptly. "Why didn't I see that before? I should have protected my sister, and I failed, and now I've failed the healer as well. She should have stayed with us. We would have kept her safe."

"We would have kept her crippled."

"She could still heal — !"

"My dear friend," Arevin's cousin said, "it's impossible to protect anyone completely without enslaving them. I think that's something you've never understood because you've always demanded too much of yourself. You blame yourself for your sister's death — "

"I didn't watch her carefully enough."

"What could you have done? Remember her life, not her death. She was brave and happy and arrogant, the way a child should be. You could only protect her more by chaining her to you with fear. She couldn't live that way, not and remain the person you loved. Nor, I think, could the healer."

Arevin stared down at the infant in his arms, knowing his cousin was right, yet still unable to throw off his feelings of confusion and guilt.

She patted his shoulder gently. "You know the healer best and you say she cannot explain our fear. I think you're right. I should have realized it myself. I do not want her to be punished for what we did, nor do I wish our people to be misunderstood." The handsome woman fingered the metal circle on the narrow leather thong around her neck. "You are right. Someone must go to the healers' station. I could go, because the clan's honor is my responsibility. My brother's partner could go, because he killed the little serpent. Or you could go, because you call the healer friend. The clan will have to meet to decide which. But any of us might be leader, and any of us might have feared her little serpent enough to kill it. Only you became her friend."

She looked from the horizon to Arevin, and he knew she had been leader long enough to reason as the clan would reason.

"Thank you," he said.

"You've lost so many people you've loved. There was nothing I could do when we lost your parents, or when your sister died. But this time I can help you, even if that might take you from us." She brushed her hand across his hair, which was graying like her own. "Please remember, my dear, that I would not like to lose you permanently."

She climbed quickly down to the desert floor, leaving him alone with her family group's new child. Her trust reassured him; he no longer needed to question if following the healer, if following Snake, was the right thing to do. It was, because it had to be done. At the very least the clan owed her that. Arevin eased his hand from the baby's damp grasp, moved the sling to his back, and climbed from the boulder to the desert floor.

On the horizon, the oasis hovered so green and soft in the dull dawn light that at first Snake thought it was a mirage. She did not feel quite capable of distinguishing illusion from reality. She had ridden all night to cross the lava flow before the sun rose and the heat grew intolerable. Her eyes burned and her lips were dry and cracked.

The gray mare, Swift, raised her head and pricked her ears, nostrils flaring at the scent of water, eager to reach it after so long on short rations. When the horse broke into a trot Snake did not rein her in.

The delicate summertrees rose around them, brushing Snake's shoulders with feathery leaves. The air beneath them was almost cool, and thick with the odor of ripening fruit. Snake pulled the end of her headcloth away from her face and breathed deeply.

She dismounted and led Swift to the dark clear pool. The mare plunged her muzzle into the water and drank. Even her nostrils were beneath the surface. Snake knelt nearby and cupped water in her hands. It splashed and ran between her fingers, brushing ripples across the pool's surface. The ripples widened and cleared, and Snake could see herself reflected above the black sand. Her face was masked with dust.

I look like a bandit, she thought. Or a clown.

But the laughter she deserved was of contempt, not joy. Tear tracks streaked the dirt on her face. She touched them, still staring down at her reflection.

Snake wished she could forget the past few days, but they would never leave her. She could still feel the dry fragility of Jesse's skin, and her light, questioning touch; she could still hear her voice. And she could feel the pain of Jesse's death, which she could do nothing to prevent, and nothing to ease. She did not want to see that pain or feel it again.

Plunging her hands into the cold water, Snake splashed it across her face, washing away the black dust, the sweat, and even the tracks of her tears.

She led Swift quietly along the shore, passing tents and silent campsites where the caravannaires still slept. When she reached Grum's camp she stopped, but the tent flaps were closed. Snake did not want to awaken the old woman or her grandchildren. Farther back from the shore Snake could see the horse corral. Squirrel, her tiger-pony, stood dozing with Grum's horses. His black and gold coat showed the effects of a week of energetic brushing, he was fat and content, and he no longer favored his shoeless foot. Snake decided to leave him with Grum another day, and disturb neither the tiger-pony nor the old caravannaire this morning.

Swift followed Snake along the shore, nibbling occasionally at her hip. Snake scratched the mare behind the ears, where sweat had dried underneath the bridle. Arevin's people had given her a sack of hay-cubes for Squirrel, but Grum had been feeding the pony, so the fodder should still be in camp.

"Food and a good brushing and sleep, that's what we both need," she said to the horse.

She had made her camp away from the others, beyond an outcropping of rock, in an area not much favored by the traders. It was safer for people and for her serpents if they were kept apart. Snake rounded the sloping stone ridge.

Everything was changed. She had left her bedroll rumpled and slept-in, but everything else had still been packed. Now someone had folded her blankets and piled them up, stacked her extra clothes nearby, and laid her cooking utensils in a row in the sand. She frowned and went closer. Healers were regarded with deference and even awe; she had not even thought of asking Grum to watch her belongings as well as her pony. That someone might bother her equipment while she was gone had never even occurred to her.

Then she saw that the utensils were dented, the metal plate bent in half, the cup crushed, the spoon twisted. She dropped Swift's reins and hurried to the neat array of her belongings. The folded blankets were slashed and torn. She picked up her clean shirt from the pile of clothing, but it was no longer clean. It had been trampled in the mud at the water's edge. It was old and soft and well worn, frayed and weak in spots, her comfortable, favorite shirt. Now it was ripped up the back and the sleeves were shredded; it was ruined.

The fodder bag lay in line with the rest of her things, but the scattered hay-cubes were crushed in the sand. Swift nibbled at the fragments, while Snake stood looking at the wreck around her. She could not understand why anyone would rifle her camp, then leave the ruined gear tidily folded. She could not understand why anyone would rifle her camp at all, for she had little of value. She shook her head. Perhaps someone believed she collected large fees of gold and jewels. Some healers were rewarded richly for their services. Still, there was much honor in the desert and even people who were unprotected by awe, by their professions, thought nothing of leaving valuables unguarded.

Her torn shirt still in her hand, Snake wandered around what had been her camp, feeling too tired and empty and confused to think about what had happened. Squirrel's packsaddle leaned against a rock; Snake picked it up for no particular reason except perhaps that it looked undamaged.

Then she saw that all its side pockets had been slashed open and torn away, though the flaps were secured only by buckles.

The side pockets had contained all her maps and records, and the journal of her unfinished proving year. She thrust her hands into corners, hoping for even a scrap of paper, but nothing at all remained. Snake flung the saddle to the ground. She hurried around the edges of her camp, looking behind rocks and kicking up the sand, hoping to see white discarded pages or to hear the crackle of paper beneath her feet, but she found nothing, there was nothing left.

She felt physically assaulted. Anything else she had, her blankets, her clothes, certainly the maps, could be useful to a thief, but the journal was worthless to anyone but her.

"Damn you!" she cried in a fury, at no one. The mare snorted and shied away, splashing into the pool. Shaking, Snake calmed herself, then turned and held out her hand and walked slowly toward Swift, speaking softly, until the horse let her take the reins. Snake stroked her.

"It's all right," she said. "It'll be all right, never mind." She was speaking as much to herself as to the horse. They were both up to their knees in the clear, cool water. Snake patted the mare's shoulder, combing the black mane with her fingers. Her vision suddenly blurred and she leaned against Swift's neck, shaking.

Listening to the strong steady heartbeat and the mare's quiet breathing, Snake managed to calm herself. She straightened and waded out of the water. On the bank, she unstrapped the serpent case, then unsaddled the horse and began to rub her down with a piece of the torn blanket. She worked with the grimness of exhaustion. The fancy saddle and bridle, now stained with dust and sweat, could wait, but Snake would not leave Swift dirty and sweaty while she herself rested.

"Snake-child, healer-child, dear girl — "

Snake turned. Grum hobbled toward her, helping herself along with a gnarled walking stick. One of her grandchildren, a tall ebony young woman, accompanied her, but all Grum's grandchildren knew better than to try to support the tiny, arthritis-bent old woman.

Grum's white headcloth lay askew on her sparse hair. "Dear child, how could I let you pass me? I'll hear her come in, I thought. Or her pony will smell her and neigh." Grum's dark-tanned age-wrinkled face showed extra lines of concern. "Snake-child, we never wanted you to see this alone."

"What happened, Grum?"

"Pauli," Grum said to her granddaughter, "take care of the healer's horse."

"Yes, Grum." When Pauli took the reins, she touched Snake's arm in a gesture of comfort. She picked up the saddle and led Swift back toward Grum's camp.

Holding Snake's elbow — not for support, but to support her — Grum guided her to a chunk of rock. They sat down and Snake glanced again around her camp, disbelief overcoming exhaustion. She looked at Grum.

Grum sighed. "It was yesterday, just before dawn. We heard noises and a voice, not yours, and when we came to look we could see a single figure, in desert robes. We thought he was dancing. But when we went closer, he ran away. He broke his lantern in the sand and we couldn't find him. We found your camp . . ." Grum shrugged. "We picked up all we could find, but nothing whole was left."

Snake looked around in silence, no closer to understanding why anyone would ransack her camp.

"By morning the wind had blown away the tracks," Grum said. "The creature must have gone out in the desert, but it was no desert person. We don't steal. We don't destroy."

"I know, Grum."

"You come with me. Breakfast. Sleep. Forget the crazy. We

all have to watch for crazies." She took Snake's scarred hand in her small, work-hardened one. "But you shouldn't have come to this alone. No. I should have seen you, Snake-child."

"It's all right, Grum."

"Let me help you move to my tents. You don't want to stay over here anymore."

"There's nothing left to move." Beside Grum, Snake stood staring at the mess. The old woman patted her hand gently.

"He wrecked everything, Grum. If he'd taken it all I could understand."

"Dear one, nobody understands crazies. They have no reasons."

That was exactly why Snake could not believe a real crazy would destroy so much so completely. The damage had been inflicted in a manner so deliberate and, in a strange way, rational, that the madness seemed less the result of insanity than of rage. She shivered again.

"Come with me," Grum said. "Crazies appear, they disappear. They're like sand flies, one summer you hear about them every time you turn around, the next year nothing."

"I suppose you're right."

"I am," Grum said. "I know about these things. He won't come back here, he'll go somewhere else, but soon we'll all know to look for him. When we find him we'll take him to the menders and maybe they can make him well."

Snake nodded tiredly. "I hope so."

She slung Squirrel's saddle over her shoulder and picked up the serpent case. The handle vibrated faintly as Sand slid across himself in his compartment.

She walked with Grum toward the old woman's camp, too tired to think anymore about what had happened, listening gratefully to Grum's soothing words of comfort and sympathy. The loss of Grass, and Jesse's death, and now this: Snake almost wished she were superstitious, so she could believe she had been cursed. People who believed in curses believed in ways of lifting them. Right now Snake did not know what to think or what to believe in, or how to change the course of misfortune her life had taken.

"Why did he only steal my journal?" she said abruptly. "Why my maps and my journal?"

"Maps!" Grum said. "The crazy stole maps? I thought you'd taken them with you. It *was* a crazy, then."

"I guess it was. It must have been." Still, she did not convince herself.

"Maps!" Grum said again.

Grum's anger and outrage seemed, for the moment, to take over for Snake's own. But the surprise in the old woman's voice disturbed her.

Snake started violently at the sharp tug on her robe. Equally startled, the collector jumped back. Snake relaxed when she saw who it was: one of the gleaners who picked up any bit of metal, wood, cloth, leather, the discards of other camps, and somehow made use of it all. The collectors dressed in multicolored robes of cloth scraps ingeniously sewn together in geometric patterns.

"Healer, you let us take all that? No good to you — "

"Ao, go away!" Grum snapped. "Don't bother the healer now. You should know better."

The collector stared at the ground but did not retreat. "She can't do with it. We can. Let us have it. Clean it up."

"This is a bad time to ask."

"Never mind, Grum." Snake started to tell the collector to take everything. Perhaps they could make use of torn blankets and broken spoons; she could not. She did not even want to see any of it again; she did not want to be reminded of what had happened. But the collector's request drew Snake from her questions and her confusion and back toward reality; she recalled something Grum had said about Ao's people when Snake first talked to her.

"Ao, when I vaccinate the others, will you all let me vaccinate you, too?"

The collector looked doubtful. "Creepty-crawlies, poisons, magics, witches — no, not for us."

"It's none of that. You won't even see the serpents."

"No, not for us."

"Then I'll have to take all that trash out to the middle of the oasis and sink it."

"Waste!" the collector cried. "No! Dirty the water? You shame my profession. You shame yourself."

"I feel the same way when you won't let me protect you against disease. Waste. Waste of people's lives. Unnecessary deaths."

The collector peered at her from beneath shaggy eyebrows. "No poisons? No magics?"

"None."

"Go last if you like," Grum said. "You'll see it doesn't kill me."

"No creepty-crawlies?"

Snake could not help laughing. "No."

"And then you give us that?" The collector gestured in the direction of Snake's battered camp.

"Yes, afterward."

"No disease afterward?"

"Fewer. I can't stop all. No measles. No scarlet fever. No lockjaw —"

"Lockjaw! You stop that?"

"Yes. Not forever but for a long time."

"We will come," the collector said, turned, and walked away.

In Grum's camp, Pauli was giving Swift a brisk rubdown while the mare pulled wisps of hay from a bundle. Pauli had the most beautiful hands Snake had ever seen, large yet delicate, long-fingered and strong, uncoarsened by the hard work she did. Even though she was tall, her hands still should have looked too big for her size, but they did not. They were graceful and expressive. She and Grum were as different as two people could be, except for the air of gentleness shared by grandmother and granddaughter, and by all Pauli's cousins that

Snake had met. Snake had not spent enough time in Grum's camp to know how many of her grandchildren she had with her, or even to know the name of the little girl who sat nearby polishing Swift's saddle.

"How's Squirrel?" Snake asked.

"Fine and happy, child. You can see him there, under the tree, too lazy to run. But he's sound again. You, now, you need a bed and rest."

Snake watched her tiger-pony, who stood among the summertrees, switching his tail. He looked so comfortable and content that she did not call him.

Snake was weary but she could feel all her muscles tight across her neck and shoulders. Sleep would be impossible until some of the tension had drained away. She wanted to think about her camp. Perhaps she would decide that it had, as Grum said, simply been vandalized by a crazy. If so, she must understand it and accept it. She was not used to so much happening by chance.

"I'm going to take a bath, Grum," she said, "and then you can put me someplace where I won't be in your way. It won't be for long."

"As long as you are here and we are here. You're welcome with us, healer-child."

Snake hugged her. Grum patted her shoulder.

Near Grum's camp one of the springs that fed the oasis sprang from stone and trickled down the rocks. Snake climbed to where sun-warmed water pooled in smooth basins. She could see the whole oasis: five camps on the shore, people, animals. The faint voices of children and the high yap of a dog drifted toward her through the heavy, dusty air. In a ring around the lake the summertrees stood like feathers, like a wreath of pale green silk.

At her feet, moss softened the rock around a bathing-basin. Snake pulled off her boots and stepped onto the cool living carpet.

She stripped and waded into the water. It was just below body temperature, pleasant but not shocking in the morning heat. There was a brisker pool higher in the rocks, a warmer one below. Snake lifted a stone from an outlet that allowed overflow water to spill down upon the sand. She knew better than to allow dirty water to continue flowing to the oasis. If she did, several angry caravannaires would come up to tell her to stop. They would do that as quietly and firmly as they would move animals corralled too close to the shore, or ask someone to leave who had the bad manners to relieve himself at water's edge. Diseases transmitted in fouled water did not exist in the desert.

Snake slid farther into the tepid water, feeling it rise around her, a pleasurable line crossing her thighs, her hips, her breasts. She lay back against the warm black stone and let tension flow slowly away. The water tickled the back of her neck.

She thought back over the last few days: somehow the incidents seemed spread over a long span of time. They were embedded in a fog of exhaustion. She looked at her right hand The ugly bruise was gone, and nothing was left of the sand viper's bite but two shiny pink puncture scars. She clenched her fist and held it: no stiffness, no weakness.

Such a short time for so many changes. Snake had never be fore encountered adversity. Her work and training had not been made easy, but they were possible, and no suspicions or uncertainties or crazies had marred the calm passage of days. She had never failed at anything. Everything had been crystal-clear, right and wrong well defined. Snake smiled faintly: if anyone had tried to tell her or the other students that reality was different, fragmentary and contradictory and surprising, she would not have believed. Now she understood the changes she had seen in students older than she, after they came back from their proving years. And, more, she understood why a few had never returned. Not all had died, perhaps not even most. Accidents and crazies were the only dangers that would have no respect for a healer. No, some had realized they were not meant for the healer's life, and had abandoned it for something else.

Snake, though, had discovered that no matter what, with all her serpents or none of them, she would always be a healer. The few worst days of self-pity over losing Grass were gone; the bad times of grief over Jesse had passed. Snake would never forget Jesse's death, but she could not excoriate herself for the manner of it forever. Instead she intended to carry out Jesse's wishes.

She sat up and scrubbed herself all over with sand. The stream flowed around her and spilled through the outlet onto the sand. Snake's hands lingered on her body. The pleasure of cool water, relaxation, and touch reminded her with an almost physical shock how long it was since anyone had touched her, since she had acted on desire. Lying back in the pool, she fantasied about Arevin.

Barefoot and bare-breasted, her robe slung over her shoulder, Snake descended from the bathing-pool. Halfway back to Grum's camp, she stopped short, listening again for a sound that had touched the edge of her hearing. It came again: the smooth slide of scales on rock, the sound of a moving serpent. Snake turned carefully toward the noise. At first she saw nothing, but then, finally, a sand viper slid from a crack in the stone. It raised its grotesque head, flicking its tongue out and in.

With a faint mental twinge, recalling the other viper's bite, Snake waited patiently until the creature crawled farther from its hiding place. It had none of the ethereal beauty of Mist, no striking patterns like Sand. It was simply ugly, with a head of lumpy protuberances and scales of a muddy dark brown. But it was a species unfamiliar to the healers, and, more, it was a threat to Arevin's people. She should have caught one near his camp, but she had not thought to. That she had regretted ever since.

She had not been able to vaccinate his clan because, not yet knowing what diseases were endemic, she could not prepare the right catalyst for Sand. When she returned, if she were ever permitted to return, she would do that. But if she could capture the viper sliding softly toward her, she could make a vaccine against its venom as well, as a gift.

The slight breeze blew from the viper to her; it could not scent her. If it had heat-receptors, the warm black rocks confused it. It did not notice Snake. Its vision, she supposed, was no better than any other serpent's. It crawled right in front of her, almost over her bare foot. She leaned down slowly, extending one hand toward its head and the other out in front of it. When the motion startled it, it drew back to strike and put itself right in her grasp. Snake held it firmly, giving it no chance to bite. It lashed itself around her forearm, hissed and struggled, showing its startlingly long fangs.

Snake shivered.

"You'd like a taste of me, wouldn't you, creature?" Awkwardly, one-handed, she folded her headcloth up and tied the serpent into the makeshift bag so it would frighten no one when she returned to camp.

She padded on down the smooth stone trail.

Grum had readied a tent for her. It was pitched in shade, its side flaps open to catch the faint cool early-morning breeze. Grum had left her a bowl of fresh fruit, the first ripe berries of the summertrees. They were blue-black, round, smaller than a hen's egg. Snake bit into one slowly, cautiously, for she had never eaten one fresh before. The tart thin juice spurted from the berry's broken skin. She ate it slowly, savoring it. The seed inside was large, almost half the volume of the fruit. It had a thick casing to protect it through the storms of winter and long months or years of drought. When she had finished the berry, Snake put the seed aside, for it would be planted near the oasis, where it would have a chance to grow. Lying down, Snake told herself to remember to take a few summertree seeds with her.

If they could be made to live in the mountains, they would be a good addition to the orchard. A moment later she fell asleep.

She slept soundly, dreamlessly, and when she awoke that evening, she felt better than she had for days; she felt good. The camp was quiet. For Grum and her grandchildren, this was a planned rest-stop for their pack animals and themselves. They were traders, returning home after a summer of bartering and buying and selling. Grum's family, like the other families camped here, held hereditary rights to a portion of the summertree berries. When the harvest was over and the fruit dried, Grum's caravan would leave the desert and travel the last few days to winter quarters. The harvest would begin soon: the air was bright with the fruit's sharp scent.

Grum stood near the corral, her hands folded across the top of her walking stick. Hearing Snake, she glanced around and smiled. "Sleep well, healer-child?"

"Yes, Grum, thanks."

Squirrel looked almost ordinary among Grum's horses; the old trader fancied appaloosas, piebalds, paints. She thought they made her caravan more noticeable, and probably she was right. Snake whistled and Squirrel tossed his head and cantered toward her, kicking his heels, completely sound.

"He's been lonely for you."

Snake scratched Squirrel's ears as he pushed her with his soft muzzle. "Yes, I can see he's been pining away."

Grum chuckled. "We do feed them well. No one ever accused me and mine of mistreating an animal."

"I'll have to coax him to leave."

"Then stay — come to our village with us and stay the winter. We're no healthier than any other people."

"Thank you, Grum. But I have something I have to do first." For a moment she had almost put Jesse's death out of her mind, but she knew it would never be far away. Snake ducked under the rope fence. Standing at the tiger-pony's shoulder, she lifted his foot.

"We tried to replace the shoe," Grum said. "But all ours are too big and there's no smith to reforge his or make him a new one. Not here, not this late."

Snake took the pieces of the broken shoe. It was nearly new, for she had had Squirrel reshod before ever entering the desert. Even the edges at the toe were still sharp and square. The metal itself must have been flawed. She handed the pieces back to Grum. "Maybe Ao can use the metal. If I take Squirrel carefully, can he get to Mountainside?"

"Oh, yes, since you can ride the pretty gray."

Snake regretted having ridden Squirrel at all. Usually she did not. Walking was fast enough for her, and Squirrel carried the serpents and her gear. But after leaving Arevin's camp she had felt the effects of the sand viper's bite again, when she thought she had overcome them. Intending to ride Squirrel only until she stopped feeling faint, Snake had got on him, and then actually fainted. He carried her patiently, slumped as she was over his withers, on across the desert. Only when he began to limp did she come to, hearing the clank of the broken iron.

Snake scratched her pony's forehead. "We'll go tomorrow, then, as soon as the heat fades. That leaves all day to vaccinate people, if they'll come to me."

"We'll come, my dear, many of us. But why leave us so soon? Come home with us. It's the same distance as to Mountainside."

"I'm going on to the city."

"Now? It's too late in the year. You'll be caught in the storms."

"Not if I don't waste any time."

"Healer-child, dear one, you don't know what they're like."

"Yes, I do. I grew up in the mountains. I watched them down below every winter."

"Watching from a mountaintop's nothing like trying to live through them," Grum said.

Squirrel wheeled away and galloped across the corral toward a group of horses dozing in the shade. Snake suddenly laughed.

"Tell me the joke, little one."

Snake looked down at the hunched old woman, whose eyes were as bright and clever as those of a fox.

"I just noticed which of your horses you put him in with."

Grum's deep tan flushed pink. "Healer, dear girl, I planned not to let you pay for his keep — I didn't think you'd mind."

"Grum, it's all right. I don't mind. I'm sure Squirrel doesn't. But I'm afraid you'll be disappointed come foaling time."

Grum shook her head wisely. "No, I won't, he's well behaved for a little stallion, but he knows what he's about. The spotty horses are what I like, especially the leopard ones." Grum had a leopard-spot appaloosa, her prize: white with coin-sized black spots all over. "And now I'll have stripy ones to go with them."

"I'm glad you like his color." Inducing a virus to encapsulate the proper genes had taken Snake a good bit of work. "But I don't think he can get you many foals."

"Why not? As I said —"

"He may surprise us — I hope he does, for you. But I think he's probably sterile."

"Ah," Grum said. "Ah, too bad. But I understand. He's from a horse and one of those stripy donkeys I heard about once."

Snake let it pass. Grum's explanation was quite wrong; Squirrel was no more a hybrid than any of Grum's horses, except at a single short gene complex. But Squirrel was resistant to the venom of Mist and Sand, and though the cause was different, the result was the same as if he were a mule. His immunities were so efficient that his system quite likely did not recognize haploid cells, the sperm, as "self," and so destroyed them.

"You know, Snake-child, I once had a mule that was a good stud. It happens sometimes. Maybe this time."

"Maybe," Snake said. The chance that her pony's immunities had left him fertile was no more remote than the chance of getting a fertile mule: Snake did not feel she was deceiving Grum with her cautious agreement.

Snake returned to her tent, let Sand out of the serpent case, and milked him of his venom. He did not fight the process. Holding him behind the head, she squeezed his mouth open gently and poured a vial of catalyst down his throat. He was much easier to drug than Mist. He would simply coil up sleepily in his compartment, little different from normal, while the poison glands manufactured a complicated chemical soup of several proteins, antibodies for a number of endemic diseases, stimulants to the immune systems of human beings. Healers had been using rattlers much longer than they had had cobras; compared to Mist, the diamondback was tens of generations and hundreds of genetic experiments more adapted to catalytic drugs and their changes.

In the morning, Snake milked Sand into a serum bottle. She could not use him to administer the vaccine, for each person required only a small amount. Sand would inject too much of it too deeply. For vaccinations, she used an inoculator, an instrument with a circle of short, needle-sharp points that pressed the vaccine down just beneath the skin. She returned the rattler to his compartment and went outside.

The people from the camps had begun to gather, adults and children, three or four generations in each family. Grum stood first in line with all her grandchildren around her. Altogether there were seven, from Pauli, the oldest, to a child about six, the little girl who had polished Swift's tack. They were not all Grum's direct descendants, for her clan's organization depended on a more extended family. The children of her long-deceased partner's siblings, of her sister, and of her sister's partner's siblings, were equally considered her grandchildren. All those people had not come with her, only those who were her apprentices as future caravannaires.

"Who's first?" Snake asked cheerfully.

"Me," Grum said. "I said me, so me it is." She glanced at the collectors, who stood in a colorful huddle off to one side. "You watch, Ao!" she called to the one who had asked for Snake's broken gear. "You'll see it doesn't kill me."

"Nothing could kill you, old rawhide-skin. I wait to see what happens to the others."

" 'Old rawhide-skin'? Ao, you old ragbag!"

"Never mind," Snake said. She raised her voice slightly. "I want to tell you all two things. First, some people are sensitive to the serum. If the mark turns bright red, if it hurts sharply, if the skin is hot, come back. I'll be here till evening. If anything is going to happen it'll happen before then, all right? If someone's sensitive I can keep them from getting sick. It's very important that you come to me if you feel anything worse than a dull ache. Don't try to be brave about it."

Among the nods and agreements Ao spoke up again. "This says you might kill."

"Are you foolish enough to pretend nothing's wrong if you break your leg?"

Ao snorted in derision.

"Then you're not foolish enough to pretend nothing's wrong and let yourself die if you overreact." Snake took off her robe and pushed up the very short sleeve of her tunic. "The second thing is this. The vaccination leaves a small scar, like this one." She went from group to group, showing them the mark of her first immunization against venom. "So if anyone wants the scar in a place less obvious, please tell me now."

Seeing the tiny innocuous scar calmed even Ao, who muttered without conviction that healers could stand any poison, and then shut up.

Grum came first in line, and Snake was surprised to see she was pale. "Grum, are you all right?"

"It's blood," Grum said. "Must be, Snake-child. I don't like to see blood."

"You'll hardly see any. Just let yourself relax." Talking to Grum in a soothing voice, Snake swabbed the old woman's arm with alcohol-iodine. She had only one bottle of the disinfectant left in the medicine compartment of the serpent case, but that was enough for today and she could get more at the chemist's in Mountainside. Snake squeezed a drop of serum onto Grum's upper arm and pressed the inoculator through it into her skin.

Grum flinched when the points entered, but her expression did not change. Snake put the inoculator into alcohol-iodine and swabbed Grum's arm again.

"There."

Grum peered at her in surprise, then glanced down at her shoulder. The pinpricks were bright red but not bleeding. "No more?"

"That's all."

Grum smiled and turned toward Ao. "You see, old pothole, it's nothing."

"We wait," Ao said.

The morning progressed smoothly. A few of the children cried, more because of the sting of the alcohol than the shallow pricks of the inoculator. Pauli had offered to help, and amused the little ones with stories and jokes while Snake worked. Most of the children, and not a few of the adults, remained to listen to Pauli after Snake had vaccinated them.

Apparently Ao and the other collectors were reassured about the safety of the vaccine, for no one had yet fallen down dead when their turn came. They submitted stoically to needle pricks and alcohol sting.

"No lockjaw?" Ao said again.

"This will protect you for ten years or so. After that it's safest to get another vaccination."

Snake pressed the inoculator against Ao's arm, then swabbed the skin. After a moment of grim hesitation, Ao smiled, for the first time, a wide, delighted smile. "We fear lockjaw. An evil disease. Slow. Painful."

"Yes," Snake said. "Do you know what causes it?"

Ao put one forefinger against the palm of the other hand and made a skewering gesture. "We are careful, but . . ."

Snake nodded. She could see how the collectors might get serious puncture wounds more often than other people, considering their work. But Ao knew the connection between the injury and the disease; a lecture about it would be patronizing.

"We never see healers before. Not on this side of the desert. People from other side tell us."

"Well, we're mountain people," Snake said. "We don't know much about the desert, so not many of us come here." That was only partly true, but it was the easiest explanation to give.

"None before you. You first."

"Maybe."

"Why?"

"I was curious. I thought I might be useful."

"You tell others to come too. No danger for them." Suddenly the expression on Ao's weather-creased face darkened. "Crazies, yes, but no more than in mountains. Crazies everywhere."

"I know."

"Sometime we find him."

"Will you do one thing for me, Ao?"

"Anything."

"The crazy took nothing but my maps and my journal. I suppose he'll keep the maps if he's sane enough to use them, but the journal's worthless to anyone but me. Maybe he'll throw it away and your people will find it."

"We keep it for you!"

"That's what I'd like." She described the journal. "Before I leave I'll give you a letter for the healers' station in the north mountains. If a messenger going that way took the journal and the letter there they'd be sure to get paid."

"We look. We find many things but not books too often."

"Probably it'll never turn up, I know that. Or the crazy thought it was something valuable and burned it when he realized it wasn't."

Ao flinched at the thought of perfectly good paper being burned to nothing. "We look hard."

"Thank you."

Ao went off after the other collectors.

As Pauli finished the story of Toad and the Three Tree Frogs,

Snake checked the children and was glad not to find the swelling and redness of any allergic reactions.

" 'And Toad didn't mind not being able to climb trees any more,' " Pauli said. "And that's the end. Go on home, now. You've all been very good."

They ran off in a bunch, yelling and making frog-croak sounds. Pauli sighed and relaxed. "I hope the real frogs don't think mating time's arrived out of season. We'll have them hopping all over camp."

"That's the kind of chance an artist takes," Snake said.

"An artist!" Pauli laughed and started rolling up her sleeve.

"You're as good as any minstrel I've ever heard."

"Storyteller, *maybe*," Pauli said. "But not a minstrel."

"Why not?"

"I'm tone-deaf, I can't sing."

"Most of the minstrels I've met can't make a story. You have a gift."

Snake prepared the inoculator and put it against Pauli's velvet-soft skin. The tiny needles sparkled in the drop of vaccine they held.

"Are you sure you want this scar here?" Snake asked suddenly.

"Yes, why not?"

"Your skin's so beautiful I hate to mark it." Snake showed Pauli her free hand, the scars. "I think I envy you a little bit."

Pauli patted Snake's hand, her touch as gentle as Grum's but steadier, and with more strength behind it. "Those are scars to take pride in. I'll be proud of the one you give me. Whoever sees it will know I've met a healer."

Reluctantly, Snake pressed the needles against Pauli's arm.

Snake rested through the hot afternoon, as did everyone else in camp. She had nothing else to do after she wrote Ao's letter, nothing to pack. She had nothing left. Squirrel would carry only his saddle, for the frame was intact and Snake could have the leather repaired. Other than that and the clothes she wore, she had only the serpent case, and Mist and Sand, and the ugly sand viper in the place where Grass should be.

Despite the heat, Snake lowered the tent flaps and opened two of the case's compartments. Mist flowed out like water, raising her head and spreading her hood, flicking out her tongue to taste the strangeness of the tent. Sand, as usual, crawled out at his leisure. Watching them glide through the warm dimness, with only the faint blue light of the bioluminescent lantern glinting on their scales, Snake wondered what would have happened if the crazy had ransacked her camp while she was there. Had the serpents been in their compartments he could have crept in unnoticed, for she had slept heavily while recovering from the viper bite. The crazy could have knocked her on the head and begun his vandalism, or his search. Snake still could not understand why a crazy would destroy everything so methodically unless he *were* making a search, and, therefore, not a crazy at all. Her maps were no different from those most desert people carried and shared. She would have let anyone who asked copy them. The maps were essential but easily obtained. The journal, though, was valueless except to Snake. She almost wished the crazy had attacked the camp while she was there, for if he had ripped open the serpent case he would not destroy anyone else's camp ever again. Snake was not pleased with herself for considering that possibility with any sort of pleasure, but it was exactly how she felt.

Sand slid across her knee and wrapped himself around her wrist, making a thick bracelet. He had fit there much better several years before, when he was small. A few minutes later Mist glided around Snake's waist and up and across her shoulders. In better times, if all were well, Grass would have circled her throat, a soft, living emerald necklace.

"Snake-child, is it safe?" Grum did not pull the tent flaps aside even enough to peek through.

"It's safe, if you aren't afraid. Shall I put them away?"

Grum hesitated. "Well . . . no."

She came through the entrance sideways, shouldering the tent flaps open. Her hands were full. While her eyes accustomed themselves to the dim light, she stood quite still.

"It's all right," Snake said. "They're both over here with me."

Blinking, Grum came closer. Next to the packsaddle she laid a blanket, a leather folder, a waterskin, a small cook-pot. "Pauli is getting provisions," she said. "None of this will make up for what happened, but — "

"Grum, I haven't even paid you for Squirrel's keep yet."

"Nor shall you," Grum said, smiling. "I explained about that."

"You have the bad end of a gamble that costs me nothing."

"Never mind. You visit us in the spring and see the little stripy foals your pony sires. I have a feeling."

"Then let me pay for the new equipment."

"No, we all talked, and we wanted to give it to you." She shrugged her left shoulder where she had been vaccinated. The place was probably sore by now. "To thank you."

"I don't want to seem ungrateful," Snake said, "but the vaccinations are something no healer ever accepts payment for. No one here was ill. I've done nothing for anyone."

"No one was ill, no, but had we been you would have helped. Am I right?"

"Yes, of course, but — "

"You would give, if someone could not pay. Should we do any less? Should we send you into the desert with nothing?"

"But I can pay." In her case she carried gold and silver coins.

"Snake!" Grum was scowling, and the endearments left her speech abruptly. "Desert people do not steal, and they do not allow their friends to be stolen from. We failed you. Leave us our honor."

Snake realized Grum did not intend, had never intended, to

be persuaded to take payment. Snake's accepting the gift was important to her.

"I'm sorry, Grum. Thank you."

The horses were saddled and ready to go. Snake put most of the equipment on Swift so Squirrel would not have much to carry. The mare's saddle, though decorated and intricately tooled, was functional. It fit the horse so well and was so comfortable and of such excellent quality that Snake began to feel less uneasy about the flamboyance of it.

Grum and Pauli had come to see her off. No one had had any adverse reaction to the vaccination, so it was safe for Snake to leave. She hugged both the women gently. Grum kissed her cheek, her lips soft and warm and very dry.

"Good-bye," Grum whispered as Snake mounted the mare. "Good-bye!" she called louder.

"Good-bye!" Snake rode away, turning in the saddle to wave back.

"If the storms come," Grum cried, "find a rock-cave. Don't forget the landmarks, they'll get you to Mountainside quicker!"

Smiling, Snake rode the mare between the summertrees, still able to hear Grum's advice and cautions about oases and water and the orientation of the sand dunes, the direction of the wind, the ways the caravannaires had of keeping their bearings in the desert; and about trails and roads and inns once Snake reached the central mountains, the high range separating the eastern and western deserts. Squirrel trotted at Snake's side, sound on his unshod forefoot.

The mare, well rested and well fed, would have galloped, but Snake held her to a jog. They had a long way to go.

Swift snorted and Snake woke abruptly, nearly hitting her head on the rock overhang. It was dead noon; in her sleep she had scrunched back into the only remaining shade.

"Who's there?"

No one answered. There was no reason for anyone to be nearby. Grum's oasis and the next one before the mountains were two nights apart: Snake had camped for today in rocky wilderness. There were no plants; there was no food or water.

"I'm a healer," she called, feeling foolish. "Be careful, my serpents are free. Speak or let me see you or make some signal and I'll put them away."

No one answered.

There's no one out there, that's why, Snake thought. For gods' sakes, no one's following you. Crazies don't follow people. They're just . . . crazy.

She lay down again and tried to fall asleep, but every touch of windblown sand against stone roused her. She did not feel comfortable until twilight came and she broke camp and headed east.

The rocky trail up the mountain slowed the horses and made Squirrel's forefoot tender again. Snake was limping slightly, too, for the change in altitude and temperature affected her bad right knee. But the valley sheltering Mountainside lay just ahead, another hour's walk. At its beginning the trail had been steep, but they were in the pass; soon they would be beyond the crest of the central mountains' eastern range. Snake dismounted to let Swift rest.

Scratching Squirrel's forehead as he nibbled at her pockets, Snake looked back over the desert. A thin haze of dust obscured the horizon, but the nearer black sand dunes lay in rolling opalescence before her, flashing back the reddened sunlight. Heat waves gave the illusion of movement. Once one of Snake's teachers had described the ocean to her, and this was what she imagined it to look like.

She was glad to leave the desert behind. Already the air had cooled, and grass and bushes clung tenaciously in crevices full of rich volcanic ash. Lower down, the wind scoured sand and earth and ash from each mountain's flanks. This high, hardy plants grew in sheltered spots, but there was not much water to help them.

Snake turned away from the desert and led the horse and the tiger-pony upward, her boots slipping on wind-polished rock. The desert robe encumbered her in this country, so she took it off and tied it behind the saddle. The loose pants and short-sleeved tunic she wore beneath flapped against her legs and body in the wind. As Snake neared the pass the wind rose, for the narrow cut in the rock acted as a funnel to strengthen any tiny breeze. In a few hours it would be cold. Cold — ! She could hardly imagine such a luxury.

Snake reached the summit and stepped into another world. Looking out over the green valley, Snake felt as if she must have left all the misfortunes of the desert behind. Squirrel and Swift both raised their heads and sniffed and snorted at the smell of fresh pasture, running water, other animals.

The town itself spread to either side of the main trail, clusters of stone buildings constructed against the mountain, cut into it, terraced black-on-black. The fields covered the floor of the valley, emerald and golden on the flood plain of a glittering gray river. The far side of the valley, sloping higher than Snake stood now, was wilderness, forest, to just below the western range's bare stony peaks.

Snake took a deep breath of the clean air and started downward.

The handsome people of Mountainside had encountered healers before. Their deference was colored by admiration and some caution, rather than the fear Snake had found on the other side of the desert. The caution Snake was used to; it was only common sense, for Mist and Sand could be dangerous to anyone but herself. Snake acknowledged respectful greetings with a smile as she led her horses through the cobblestone streets.

Shops were being closed and taverns being opened. By tomorrow, people would start coming to Snake to ask her aid, but she hoped that for tonight they would leave her to a comfortable room at the inn, a good dinner, a flask of wine. The desert had tired her to her bones. If anyone came now, this late, it would be because of serious illness. Snake hoped no one in Mountainside was dying tonight.

She left her horses outside a shop that was still open and bought new pants and a new shirt, choosing the fit by approximation and the owner's advice, for she was too tired to try them on.

"Never mind," the owner said. "I can alter them later, if you want. Or bring them back if you don't like them. I'll exchange things for a healer."

"They'll be fine," Snake said. "Thank you." She paid for the things and left the shop. There was a chemistry on the corner, and the proprietor was just shutting the door.

"Excuse me," Snake said.

The chemist turned, smiling resignedly. Then, glancing over Snake and her gear, she saw the serpent case. The smile turned to surprise.

"Healer!" she exclaimed. "Come in. What do you need?"

"Aspirin," Snake said. She had only a few grains left, and for her own sake she did not want to run out. "And alcohol-iodine, if you have it."

"Yes, of course. I make the aspirin myself and I purify the iodine again when I get it. There's no adulteration in my goods." She refilled Snake's bottles. "It's a long time since we've had a healer in Mountainside."

"Your people's health and beauty are renowned," Snake said, and she was not making any idle compliment. She glanced around the shop. "And your stocks are excellent. I expect you can handle nearly anything." On one section of the shelves the chemist kept painkillers, the strong and overwhelming kind that weakened the body instead of strengthening it. Ashamed to buy any, to have to admit the loss of Grass again so soon, Snake avoided looking at them. If anyone in

Mountainside were very ill, though, she would have to use them.

"Oh, we get along," the chemist said. "Where will you be staying? May I send people to you?"

"Of course." Snake named the inn Grum had recommended, paid for the chemicals, and left the shop with its owner, who turned in the other direction. Alone, Snake started down the street.

A shape in robes swirled at the edge of her vision. Snake spun, crouched down in defensive position. Swift snorted and sidestepped. The cloaked figure halted.

Embarrassed, Snake straightened up. The person who approached her was not in desert robes at all, but wrapped in a hooded cloak. She could not see the face, shadowed by the cowl, but it was not any crazy.

"May I speak with you a moment, healer?" His voice was hesitant.

"Of course." If he could ignore her unusual behavior, she could let it pass without comment, too.

"My name is Gabriel. My father is the town's mayor. I've come to invite you to be our guest at the residence."

"That's very kind of you. I'd planned to stop at the inn — "

"It's an excellent inn," Gabriel said. "And the keeper would be honored by your presence. But my father and I would dishonor Mountainside if we didn't offer you its best."

"Thank you," Snake said. She was beginning to feel, if not comfortable with, at least grateful for, the generosity and hospitality offered healers. "I accept your invitation. I should leave a message at the inn, though. The chemist said she might send people to me."

Gabriel glanced toward her. She could not see beyond the shadow of the hood, but she thought he might be smiling.

"Healer, by midnight everyone in the valley will know exactly where you are."

Gabriel guided her through streets that curved along the

mountain's contours, between one-story buildings of quarried black stone. The horses' hooves and Snake's and Gabriel's boots rang loudly on the cobblestones, echoing back and forth. The buildings ended and the street widened into a paved road separated from a sheer drop to the valley floor only by a thick, hip-high wall.

"Ordinarily my father would have greeted you himself," Gabriel said. His tone was not only apologetic but uncertain, as though he had something to tell her that he did not know how to phrase.

"I'm not used to being met by dignitaries," Snake said.

"I want you to know we would have invited you to stay with us under any circumstances, even if — " His voice trailed off.

"Ah," Snake said. "Your father's ill."

"Yes."

"You don't have to be hesitant about asking for my help," Snake said. "That's my profession, after all. And if I get a free room, that's an unexpected benefit."

Snake still did not see Gabriel's face, but the tension left his voice. "I just didn't want you to think we're the kind of people who never offer anything without expecting something in return."

They continued on in silence. The road curved, rounding an outcropping of rock that had cut off the line of sight, and Snake saw the mayor's residence for the first time. It was wide and high, built against the sloping face of a cliff. The usual black stone was highlighted with narrow stripes of white just below the roof, which presented a bank of shiny solar panels to the east and south. The windows of the upper rooms were tremendous panes curved to match the towers on either side of the main building. The lights shining through them revealed no flaws. Despite the windows and the carving on the tall wooden doors, the residence was as much fortress as showplace. It had no windows on its first floor, and the doors looked solid and heavy. Its far side was shielded by a second outcropping. The paved courtyard ended at the cliff, which at that spot was neither so steep nor so high as it was where Snake stood now. A lighted trail led to its foot, where lay stables and a bit of pastureland.

"It's very imposing," Snake said.

"It belongs to Mountainside, though my father has been living there since before I was born."

They continued along the stone road.

"Tell me about your father's illness." She felt sure it was not too serious, or Gabriel would have been much more worried.

"It was a hunting accident. One of his friends put a lance through his leg. He won't even admit it's infected. He's afraid someone will amputate it."

"What does it look like?"

"I don't know. He won't let me see it. He hasn't even let me see him since yesterday." He spoke with resigned sadness.

Snake glanced at him, concerned, for if his father were stubborn and frightened enough to stand considerable pain, his leg could be so badly infected that the tissue was dead.

"I hate amputations," Snake said quite sincerely. "You'd hardly believe the lengths I've gone to avoid doing them."

At the entrance to the residence Gabriel called, and the heavy doors swung open. He greeted the servant and had him take Squirrel and Swift to the stables below.

Snake and Gabriel entered the foyer, an echoing chamber of smooth-polished black stone that reflected movement and blurry images. Because there were no windows it was rather dark, but another servant hurried in and turned up the gaslights. Gabriel set Snake's bedroll on the floor, threw back his hood, and let his cloak slide off his shoulders. The polished walls mirrored his face erratically.

"We can leave your luggage here, someone will take it up."

Snake laughed to herself at having her bedroll called "luggage," as if she were a rich merchant about to set off on a buying trip.

Gabriel turned toward her. Seeing his face for the first time, Snake caught her breath. The inhabitants of Mountainside were very conscious of their beauty; this young man went out cloaked so heavily that Snake had wondered if he were plain, or even scarred or deformed. She was prepared for that. But in fact Gabriel was the most beautiful person she had ever seen. He was compactly built and well proportioned. His face was rather square, but not all planes and angles like Arevin's; it reflected more vulnerability, feelings closer to the surface. He neared her and she could see that his eyes were an unusually bright blue. His skin was tanned the same shade as his dark-blond hair. Snake could not say why he was so beautiful, whether it was the symmetry of his features, and their balance, and his flawless skin, or qualities less definable, or all those and more; but he was, quite simply, breathtaking.

Gabriel looked at Snake expectantly, and she realized he thought she would leave the leather case behind, too. He did not seem to notice his effect on her.

"My serpents are in here," she said. "I keep them with me."

"Oh — I'm sorry." He began to blush. The redness crept up his throat to his cheeks. "I should have known — "

"Never mind, it's not important. I think I'd better see your father as soon as possible."

"Of course."

They climbed a wide, curving staircase of stone blocks rounded at the corners by time and wear.

Snake had never met an extremely beautiful person who was as sensitive to criticism as Gabriel, especially unintended criticism. Compellingly attractive people often exuded an aura of self-confidence and assurance, sometimes to the point of arrogance. Gabriel, on the other hand, seemed exceedingly vulnerable. Snake wondered what had happened to make him so.

The thick-walled stone buildings of mountain towns kept their rooms at a nearly constant temperature. After so long in the desert Snake was glad of the coolness. She knew she was sweaty and dusty from the day's ride, but she did not feel tired now. The leather satchel made a satisfying weight in her hand. She would welcome a simple case of infection. Unless it was so bad she could do nothing but amputate, there would be small chance of complication, almost no chance of death. She was glad she would probably not have to face losing another patient so soon.

She followed Gabriel up a flight of spiral stairs. Gabriel did not even slow at the top, but Snake paused to glance around the enormous overpowering room. Its tall, smoke-colored window, the curved pane at the top of the tower, gave a spectacular view of the entire twilit valley. The scene dominated the whole room, and someone had realized that, for there was no furniture to detract from it except big wide pillows in neutral colors. The floor had two levels, an upper semicircle set against the back wall, to which the stairs led, and a lower, wider ring bordering the window.

Snake heard angry yelling, and a moment later an old man ran from the next room, bumping into Gabriel and knocking him off balance. The younger man, recovering, grabbed the older's elbows to steady him just as the old man clutched at him for the same reason. They looked at each other gravely, oblivious to the humor of the situation.

"How is he?" Gabriel asked.

"Worse," the old man said. He glanced beyond to Snake. "Is she — ?"

"Yes, I've brought the healer." He turned to introduce her to the old man. "Brian is my father's assistant. No one else can get near him."

"Not even me, now," Brian said. He pushed his thick white hair from his forehead. "He won't let me see his leg. It hurts him so much he's put a pillow under the blankets to hold them off his foot. Your father's a stubborn man, sir."

"No one knows better than me."

"Stop the noise out there!" Gabriel's father shouted. "Haven't you any respect? Get out of my rooms."

Gabriel straightened his shoulders and looked at Brian. "We'd better go in."

"Not me, sir," Brian said. "Me he ordered out. He said not to come back until he calls, if he calls." The old man looked downcast.

"Never mind. He doesn't mean it. He wouldn't hurt you."

"You believe that, sir, do you? That he doesn't mean to hurt?"

"He doesn't mean to hurt *you*. You're indispensable. I'm not."

"Gabriel — " the old man said, breaking his pose of servility.

"Don't go far," Gabriel said lightly. "I expect he'll want you soon." He entered his father's bedroom.

Snake followed him inside, her eyes slowly accustoming themselves to the darkness, for curtains hid this large room's windows and the lamps were not lit.

"Hello, father," Gabriel said.

"Get out. I told you not to bother me."

"I've brought a healer."

Like everyone else in Mountainside, Gabriel's father was handsome. Snake could see that, even beyond the lines of anxiety crossing his strong face. He had a pale complexion, black eyes, and black hair tousled by his stay in bed. In health he would be an imposing person, someone who would expect to control any group he joined. He was handsome in a completely different way from Gabriel, one that Snake could recognize but feel no attraction for.

"I don't need a healer," he said. "Go away. I want Brian."

"You frightened him and you hurt him, father."

"Call him."

"He'd come if I did. But he can't help you. The healer can. Please — " Gabriel's voice crept toward desperation.

"Gabriel, please light the lamps," Snake said. She stepped forward and stood beside the mayor's bed.

As Gabriel obeyed, his father turned away from the light.

His eyelids were puffy and his eyes bloodshot. He moved only his head.

"It will get worse," Snake said gently. "Until you won't dare move at all. Finally you won't be able to, because the poison from your wound will weaken you too much. Then you'll die."

"You're a fine one to talk about poisons!"

"My name is Snake. I'm a healer. I don't deal in poisons."

He did not react to her name's significance, but Gabriel did, turning to look at her with renewed respect and even awe.

"*Snakes!*" the mayor snarled.

Snake was not inclined to waste her energy in argument or persuasion. She went to the foot of the bed and pulled loose the blankets so she could look at the mayor's wounded leg. He started to sit up, protesting, but abruptly lay back, breathing heavily, his face pallid and shiny with sweat.

Gabriel came toward Snake.

"You'd better stay up there with him," she said. She could smell the cloying odor of infection.

The leg was an ugly sight. Gangrene had set in. The flesh was swollen, and angry red streaks reached all the way up the mayor's thigh. In a few more days the tissue would die and turn black, and then there would be nothing left to do but amputate.

The smell had grown strong and nauseating. Gabriel looked paler than his father.

"You don't have to stay," Snake said.

"I — " He swallowed and began again. "I'm all right."

Snake replaced the blankets, taking care not to put any pressure on the swollen foot. Curing the mayor would not be the problem. What she would have to deal with was his defensive belligerence.

"Can you help him?" Gabriel asked.

"I can speak for myself!" the mayor said.

Gabriel looked down with an unreadable expression, which his father ignored, but which to Snake seemed resigned and sorrowful and completely lacking in anger. Gabriel turned away and busied himself with the gas lamps.

Snake sat on the edge of the bed and felt the mayor's forehead. As she had expected, he had a high fever.

He turned away. "Don't look at me."

"You can ignore me," Snake said. "You can even order me to leave. But you can't ignore the infection, and it won't stop because you tell it to."

"You will not cut off my leg," the mayor said, speaking each word separately, expressionlessly.

"I don't intend to. It isn't necessary."

"I just need Brian to wash it."

"He can't wash away gangrene!" Snake was growing angry at the mayor's childishness. If he had been irrational with fever she would have offered him infinite patience; if he were going to die she would understand his unwillingness to admit what was wrong. He was neither. He seemed to be so used to having his own way that he could not deal with bad fortune.

"Father, listen to her, please."

"Don't pretend to care about me," Gabriel's father said. "You'd be quite happy if I died."

Ivory-white, Gabriel stood motionless for a few seconds, then slowly turned and walked from the room.

Snake stood up. "That was a dreadful thing to say. How could you? Anyone can see he wants you to live. He loves you."

"I want neither his love nor your medicines. Neither can help me."

Her fists clenched, Snake followed Gabriel.

The young man was sitting in the tower room, facing the window, leaning against the step formed by upper and lower levels. Snake sat beside him.

"He doesn't mean the things he says." Gabriel's voice was strained and humiliated. "He really — " He leaned forward with his face in his hands, sobbing. Snake put her arms around him and tried to comfort him, holding him, patting his strong shoulders and stroking his soft hair. Whatever the source of the animosity the mayor felt, Snake was certain it did not arise from hatred or jealousy in Gabriel.

He wiped his face on his sleeve. "Thanks," he said. "I'm sorry. When he gets like that . . ."

"Gabriel, does your father have a history of instability?"

For a moment Gabriel looked mystified. Abruptly he laughed, but with bitterness.

"In his mind, you mean? No, he's quite sane. It's a personal matter between us. I suppose . . ." Gabriel hesitated. "Sometimes he must wish I had died, so he could adopt a more suitable eldest child, or father one himself. But he won't even partner again. Maybe he's right. Maybe I do sometimes wish he were dead too."

"Do you believe that?"

"I don't want to."

"I don't believe it at all."

He looked at her, with the faint and tentative beginnings of what Snake thought would be an absolutely radiant smile, but sobered again. "What will happen if nothing is done?"

"He'll be unconscious in a day or so. Then — by then the choice will be to cut off his leg against his will, or let him die."

"Can't you treat him now? Without his consent?"

She wished she could give him an answer he would like better. "Gabriel, this isn't an easy thing to say, but if he lost consciousness still telling me to do nothing, I'd have to let him die. You say yourself he's rational. I have no right to go against his desires. No matter how stupid and wasteful they are."

"But you could save his life."

"Yes. But it's his life."

Gabriel rubbed his eyes with the heels of his hands, an exhausted gesture. "I'll talk to him again."

Snake followed him to his father's rooms, but agreed to stay outside when Gabriel went in. The young man had courage. Whatever his failings in his father's eyes — and apparently in his own — he did have courage. Yet perhaps on another level cowardice was not altogether absent, or why did he stay here and allow himself to be abused? Snake could not imagine herself remaining in this situation. She had thought her ties with other healers, her family, were as strong as relationships could be, but perhaps blood ties were even more compelling.

Snake felt not at all guilty about listening to the conversation.

"I want you to let her help you, father."

"No one can help me. Not any more."

"You're only forty-nine. Someone might come along you could feel about the way you felt about mother."

"You hold your tongue about your mother."

"No, not any more. I never knew her but half of me is her. I'm sorry I've disappointed you. I've made up my mind to leave here. After a few months you can say — no — in a few months a messenger will come and tell you I'm dead, and you'll never have to know if it isn't true."

The mayor did not answer.

"What do you want me to say? That I'm sorry I didn't leave sooner? All right — I am."

"That's one thing you've never done to me," Gabriel's father said. "You're stubborn and you're insolent, but you've never lied to me before."

Silence stretched on. Snake was about to go in when Gabriel spoke again.

"I hoped I might redeem myself. I thought if I could make myself useful enough — "

"I have to think of the family," the mayor said. "And the town. Whatever happened you'd always be my firstborn, even if you weren't my only child. I couldn't disavow you without humiliating you in public."

Snake was surprised to hear compassion in the harsh voice.

"I know. I understand that now. But it won't do any good if you die."

"Will you keep to your plan?"

"I swear it," Gabriel said.

"All right. Let the healer in."

If Snake had not taken an oath to help the injured and the sick, she might have left the castle right then. She had never heard such calm and reasoned rejection, and this was between a parent and a child —

Gabriel came to the doorway, and Snake entered the bedroom in silence.

"I've changed my mind," the mayor said. And then, as if he realized how arrogant he sounded, "If you would still consent to treat me."

"I will," Snake said shortly, and left the room.

Gabriel followed her, worried. "Is something wrong? You haven't changed your mind?"

Gabriel seemed calm and unhurt. Snake stopped. "I promised to help him. I will help him. I need a room and a few hours before I can treat his leg."

"We'll give you anything you ask."

He led her along the width of the top floor until they reached the south tower. Rather than containing a single imposing room, it was divided into several smaller chambers, less overwhelming and more comfortable than the mayor's quarters. Snake's room was a segment of the circumference of the tower. The curved hall behind the guest rooms surrounded a central common bath.

"It's nearly suppertime," Gabriel said as he showed her her room. "Would you join me?"

"No thank you. Not this time."

"Shall I bring something up?"

"No. Just come back in three hours." She paid him little attention, for she could not wonder about his problems while she was planning the operation on his father. Absently she gave him a few instructions on what to have ready in the mayor's room. Because the infection was so bad it would be a dirty, smelly job.

After she had finished he still did not leave.

"He's in a great deal of pain," Gabriel said. "Don't you have anything that would soothe it?"

"No," Snake said. "But it wouldn't hurt to get him drunk."

"Drunk? All right, I'll try. But I don't think it will help. I've never seen him unconscious from drink."

"The anesthetic value is secondary. Alcohol helps the circulation."

"Oh."

After Gabriel had left, Snake drugged Sand to make an antitoxin for gangrene. The new venom would have its own mild local anesthetic, but that would not be much help until after Snake had drained the mayor's wound and his circulation was not so seriously impeded. She was not glad she would have to hurt him, but she did not regret it as much as with other patients she had been forced to hurt in the course of a cure.

She took off the dusty desert clothes and her boots, which badly needed an airing. She had strapped her new pants and shirt to the bedroll. Whoever had brought it upstairs had laid them out. Getting back into the kind of clothes she was used to would be pleasant, but it would be a long time before they were worn as comfortable as what the crazy had destroyed.

The bathroom was softly lit with gas lamps. Most buildings as large as this one had their own methane generators. Whether private or communal, the generators used trash and garbage and human waste as a substrate for bacterial production of fuel. With a generator and the solar panels on the roof, the castle was probably at the very least self-sufficient in power. It might even have enough of a surplus to run a heat pump. If a summer came along that was hot enough to overwhelm the natural insulation of stone, the building could be cooled. The healers' station had similar amenities, and Snake was not sorry to come upon them again. She ran the deep tub full of hot water and bathed luxuriously. Even perfumed soap was an improvement over black sand, but when she reached for a towel and discovered it smelled of peppermint, she simply laughed.

Three hours passed slowly while the drug worked on Sand. Snake was lying fully clothed but barefoot, wide-awake, on the bed when Gabriel tapped on the door. Snake sat up, held Sand gently behind the head and let him wrap himself around her wrist and arm, and let Gabriel in.

The young man looked at Sand warily, fascinated enough to overcome an obvious trepidation.

"I won't let him strike," Snake said.

"I just wondered what they feel like."

Snake extended her arm toward him, and he reached out to stroke Sand's smooth patterned scales. He drew back his hand without comment.

Back in the mayor's bedchamber, Brian, looking not so downcast, was content to have his master under his care once more. The mayor was a lachrymose drunk. Moaning almost tunefully, he wept as Snake approached him, fat tears sliding down his cheeks. The moans ceased when the mayor saw Snake. She stopped at the foot of his bed. He watched her fearfully.

"How much has he drunk?"

"As much as he will," Gabriel said.

"It *would* be better if he were unconscious," Snake said, taking pity on him.

"I've seen him drink till dawn with the council members but I've never seen him unconscious."

The mayor squinted at them blearily. "No more brandy," he said. "No more." The words were forceful despite a slight slurring. "If I'm awake you can't cut off my leg."

"That's quite true," Snake said. "Stay awake, then."

His gaze fastened on Sand, the rattler's unblinking stare and flicking tongue, and he began to tremble. "Some other way," he said. "There must be another way — "

"You are trying my patience," Snake said. She knew she would lose her temper in another moment, or, worse, she would begin to cry for Jesse again. She could only remember how much she had wished to help her, while she could heal this man so easily.

The mayor lay back in his bed. Snake could feel him still trembling, but at least he was silent. Gabriel and Brian stood one on either side of him. Snake pulled the blankets loose from the foot of the bed and let them lie in a visual barricade across the mayor's knees.

"I want to see," he whispered.

His leg was purple and swollen. "You do not," Snake said. "Brian, please open the windows." The old servant hurried to obey, pulling aside the curtains, swinging glass panels open to the darkness outside. Cool fresh air drifted across the room.

"When Sand strikes you," Snake said, "you'll feel a sharp pain. Then the area around the bite will go numb. That will be just above the wound. The numbness will spread slowly, because your circulation is almost cut off. But when it spreads far enough I'll drain the wound. After that the antitoxin will work more effectively."

The mayor's flushed cheeks paled. He did not say anything, but Brian put a glass to his lips and the mayor drank deeply. The flush returned.

Well, Snake thought, some people you should tell, some people you shouldn't.

Snake tossed Brian a clean cloth. "Pour some of the brandy on this and lay it across his nose and mouth. You and Gabriel can do the same thing for yourselves if you want. This won't be pleasant. And both of you drink — one good gulp each. Then hold his shoulders easily. Don't let him sit up abruptly; he'll frighten the rattler."

"Yes, healer," Brian said.

Snake cleaned the skin above the deep wound in the mayor's calf.

Lucky not to have tetanus as well, she thought, remembering Ao and the other collectors. Healers came through Mountainside occasionally, though they had come more frequently in the past. Perhaps the mayor had been vaccinated, once he knew he would not have to see a serpent.

Snake unwrapped Sand from her arm and held him behind the bulge of his jaw, letting him flick his tongue against the discolored skin. He arranged himself into a thick coil on the bed. When Snake was satisfied with his position, she released his head.

He struck.

The mayor cried out.

Sand bit only once, and quickly, so fast he was back in his coil before an observer could be sure he had moved. But the mayor was sure. He had begun trembling violently again. Dark blood and pus oozed from the two small puncture wounds.

The rest of Snake's work was smelly and messy but routine. She opened the wound and let it drain. Snake hoped Gabriel had not eaten much dinner, for he looked ready to lose it, even with the brandy-soaked cloth over his face. Brian stood stoically by his master's shoulder, soothing him, keeping him still.

By the time Snake had finished, the swelling in the mayor's leg was already considerably reduced. He would be well in a few weeks.

"Brian, come here, would you?"

The old man obeyed her hesitantly, but he relaxed when he saw what she had done. "It looks better," he said. "Already better than when he last let me look at it."

"Good. It will keep draining, so it's got to be kept clean." She showed him how to dress the wound and bandage it. He called a young servant to take away the soiled cloths, and soon the stench of infection and dying flesh had dissipated. Gabriel was sitting on the bed, sponging his father's forehead. Sometime earlier the brandy-soaked cloth had slipped from his face to the floor, and he had not bothered to replace it. He no longer looked so pale.

Snake gathered Sand up and let him slide across her shoulders.

"If the wound hurts him badly, or his temperature rises again — if there's any change that isn't an improvement — come get me. Otherwise I'll see him in the morning."

"Thank you, healer," Brian said.

Snake hesitated as she passed Gabriel, but he did not look up. His father lay very still, breathing heavily, asleep or nearly so.

Snake shrugged and left the mayor's tower, returned to her room and put Sand in his compartment, then wandered downstairs until she found the kitchen. Another of the mayor's ubiquitous and innumerable servants made her some supper, and she went to bed.

The mayor felt better in the morning. Brian had clearly been up all night beside him, yet he accepted his orders — not exactly cheerfully, for that was not Brian's style, but without reservation or resentment.

"Will it leave a scar?" the mayor asked.

"Yes," Snake said, surprised. "Of course. Several. I took out quite a lot of dead muscle, and it will never all fill back in. You probably won't limp, though."

"Brian, where's my tea?" The tone of the mayor's voice revealed his annoyance at Snake's reply.

"It's coming, sir." The fragrance of spices drifted into the room. The mayor drank his tea alone, ignoring Snake while she rebandaged his leg.

When she left, scowling, Brian followed her to the hall outside.

"Healer, forgive him. He's not used to illness. He expects things to go his way."

"So I noticed."

"I mean . . . he thinks of himself scarred . . . He feels betrayed by himself . . ." Brian spread his hands, unable to find the right words.

It was not that uncommon to find people who did not believe they could get sick; Snake was used to difficult patients who wanted to get back to normal too soon, despite the need for recuperation, and who became querulous when they could not.

"That doesn't give him the right to treat people the way he does," Snake said.

Brian looked at the floor. "He's a good man, healer."

Sorry she had let her anger — no, her annoyance and hurt pride — touch him, Snake spoke again, more gently.

"Are you bound here?"

"No! Oh, no, healer, I'm free. The mayor doesn't allow bonding in Mountainside. Drivers who come with bondservants are sent out of the city, and their people can choose to go with them or give the city a year's service. If they stay the mayor buys their papers from the driver."

"Is that what happened with you?"

He hesitated but finally answered. "Not many know I used to be bound. I was one of the first to be freed. After one year he tore up my bonding papers. They were still valid for twenty years, and I'd already served five. Until then I wasn't sure I could trust him — or anyone. But I could." He shrugged. "I stayed on afterward."

"I understand why you feel grateful toward him," Snake said. "But it still doesn't give him the right to order you around twenty-four hours a day."

"I slept last night."

"In a chair?"

Brian smiled.

"Get someone else to watch him for a while," Snake said. "You come with me."

"Do you need help, healer?"

"No, I'm going down to the stables. But you can nap while I'm gone, at least."

"Thank you, healer. I'd rather stay here."

"Whatever you say."

She left the residence and crossed the courtyard. It felt good to walk in the cool morning, even down the steep hairpin turns of the cliff trail. The mayor's pastures spread out below her. The gray mare was alone in a green field, galloping back and forth with her head and tail high, bouncing stiff-legged to a halt at the fence, snorting, then wheeling to run in the opposite direction. If she had decided to keep on running, she could have cleared the chest-high fence and hardly noticed it, but she was running for no other reason than play.

Snake walked along the path to the barn. As she neared it she heard a slap and a cry, then a loud and furious voice.

"Get on with your work!"

Snake ran the last few steps to the stable and pulled open its doors. The inside was nearly dark. She blinked. She heard the rustling of straw and smelled the pleasant heavy odor of a clean horsebarn. After a moment her eyes became more accustomed to the dimness and she could see the wide straw-carpeted passageway, the two rows of box stalls, and the stablemaster turning toward her.

"Good morning, healer." The stablemaster was a tremendous man, at least two meters tall, and heavily built. His curly hair was bright red and his beard was blond.

Snake looked up at him. "What was that noise?"

"Noise? I don't — Oh, I was just countering the pleasures of laziness."

His remedy must have been effective, for whoever had been lazy had disappeared very quickly.

"At this hour of the morning laziness sounds like a good idea," Snake said.

"Well, we get started early." The stablemaster led her farther into the barn. "I stabled your mounts down here. The mare's out for a run, but I've kept the pony in."

"Good," Snake said. "He needs to be shod as soon as possible."

"I've sent for the blacksmith to come this afternoon."

"That's fine." She went inside Squirrel's stall. He nuzzled her and ate the piece of bread she had brought him. His coat shone his mane and tail were combed, and his hooves were even oiled. "Someone's taken very good care of him."

"We try to please the mayor and his guests," the big man said.

He stayed nearby, solicitously, until she left the stable to bring the mare inside. Swift and Squirrel had to be reintroduced to pasture slowly, after so long in the desert, or the rich grass would make them sick.

When she returned, riding Swift bareback and guiding her with her knees, the stablemaster was busy in another part of the building. Snake slid off the mare's back and led her into her stall.

"It was me, mistress, not him."

Startled, Snake turned, but whoever had whispered to her was not in the stall, nor in the passageway outside.

"Who's that?" Snake said. "Where are you?" Back in the stall she looked up and saw the hole in the ceiling where fodder was thrown down. She jumped on the manger, grabbed the edge of the hole, and chinned herself up so she could see into the loft. A small figure jumped back in fright and hid behind a bale of hay.

"Come out," Snake said. "I won't hurt you." She was in a ridiculous position, hanging down in the middle of the stall with Swift nibbling her boot, without the proper leverage to climb the rest of the way into the loft. "Come on down," she said, and let herself drop back to the ground.

She could see the form of the person in the hayloft, but not the features.

It's a child, she thought. Just a little kid.

"It's nothing, mistress," the child said. "It's just he always pretends he does all the work and there's others do too, is all. Never mind."

"Please come down," Snake said again. "You did a very nice job on Swift and Squirrel and I'd like to thank you."

"That's thanks enough, mistress."

"Don't call me that. My name's Snake. What's yours?"

But the child was gone.

*

People from town, both patients and messengers, already waited to see her when she reached the top of the cliff, leading Swift. She would get no leisurely breakfast today.

She saw a good deal of Mountainside before evening. For a few hours at a stretch she worked hard, busy and hurried but content, and then as she finished with one patient and went to hear about the next, apprehension swept over her and she thought that this time she might be asked to help someone who was dying, someone like Jesse whom she could not help at all.

Today, that did not happen.

In the evening she rode Swift north along the river, passing the town on her left, as the glow of the sun sank past the clouds and touched the west mountain peaks. The long shadows crept toward her as she reached the mayor's pasture and stables. Seeing no one around, she took Swift into the barn herself, unsaddled her, and began to brush her smooth dappled coat. She was not particularly anxious to return to the mayor's residence and its atmosphere of dogged loyalty and pain.

"Mistress, that's not for you to do. Let me. You go on up the hill."

"No, you come on down," Snake said to the disembodied whispery voice. "You can help. And don't call me mistress."

"Go on, now, mistress, please."

Snake brushed Swift's shoulder and did not answer. When nothing happened she thought the child had gone; then she heard a rustling in the hay above her. On impulse she stroked the brush backwards across Swift's flank. An instant later the child was beside her, taking the brush gently from her hand.

"You see, mistress — "

" 'Snake.' "

" — This is no job for you. You know healing, I know horse-brushing."

Snake smiled.

The little girl was only nine or ten, small and spare. She had not looked up at Snake; now she brushed Swift's ruffled hair straight again, her face turned down and close to the mare's side. She had bright red hair, and dirty, chewed fingernails.

"You're right," Snake said. "You are better at that than I am."

The child was silent for a moment. "You fooled me," she said sullenly, without turning around.

"A little," Snake admitted. "But I had to or you wouldn't let me thank you face to face."

The child spun around, glaring up. "Then thank me!" she cried.

The left side of her face was twisted with a terrible scar.

Third-degree burns, Snake thought. The poor child — ! And then she thought: If a healer had been near, the scar would not have been so bad.

But at the same time she noticed the bruise along the right side of the little girl's face. Snake knelt and the child shrank back from any contact, turning so the scar would be less visible. Snake touched the bruise gently.

"I heard the stablemaster yelling at someone this morning," Snake said. "It was you, wasn't it? He hit you."

The child turned back and stared at her, her right eye wide, the left held partly closed by scar tissue.

"I'm all right," she said. Then she slid out of Snake's hands and ran up a ladder into the darkness.

"Please come back," Snake called. But the child had disappeared, and even when Snake followed her into the loft she could not find her.

Snake hiked up the trail to the residence, her shadow pushed back and forth by the swaying of the lantern she carried. She thought about the nameless little girl ashamed to come into the light. The bruise was in a bad spot, just at the temple. But she had not flinched from Snake's touch — at least not the touch to the bruise — and she had none of the symptoms of a concussion. Snake did not have to worry about the child's immediate health. But in the future?

Snake wanted to help somehow, but she knew that if she had the stablemaster reprimanded, the little girl would be left with the consequences when Snake went away.

Snake climbed the stairs to the mayor's room.

Brian looked exhausted, but the mayor was fresh. Most of the swelling had left his leg. The punctures had scabbed over but Brian was doing a good job of keeping the main wound open and clean.

"When can I get up?" the mayor asked. "I have work to do. People to see. Disputes to settle."

"You can get up any time," Snake said. "If you don't mind having to stay in bed three times as long afterwards."

"I insist — "

"Just stay in bed," Snake said tiredly.

She knew he would disobey. Brian, as usual, followed her to the hall.

"If the wound bleeds in the night, come get me," she said. She knew it would, if the mayor got up, and she did not want the old servant to have to deal with the injury alone.

"He is all right? He will be?"

"Yes, if he doesn't push himself too hard. He's mending fairly well."

"Thank you, healer."

"Where's Gabriel?"

"He does not come up here any more."

"Brian, what's the matter between him and his father?"

"I'm sorry, healer, I cannot say."

You won't, you mean, Snake thought.

Snake stood looking out over the dark valley. She did not feel like going to sleep yet. That was one of the things she did not much like about her proving year: most of the time, she went to bed alone. Too many people in the places she had gone knew about healers by reputation only, and were afraid of her. Even Arevin feared her at the beginning, and by the time his fear ebbed, and their mutual respect changed to attraction, Snake had to leave. They had no chance together.

She leaned her forehead against the cool glass.

When Snake first crossed the desert, it was to explore, to see the places healers had not visited in decades or that they had never visited before. She had been presumptuous, perhaps, or even foolish, to do what her teachers no longer did and no longer considered doing. There were not even enough healers for the people on this side of the desert. If Snake succeeded on her visit to the city, all that might change. But Jesse's name was the only difference between Snake and any other healer to ask Center for knowledge. If she failed — Her teachers were good people, tolerant of differences and eccentricities, but how they would react to the errors Snake had made, she did not know.

The knock at her door came as a relief, for it interrupted her thoughts.

"Come in."

Gabriel entered, and she was struck once more by his beauty.

"Brian tells me my father's doing well."

"Well enough."

"Thank you for helping him. I know he can be difficult." He hesitated, glanced around, shrugged. "Well . . . I just came in to see if there's anything I can do for you."

Despite his preoccupation, he seemed gentle and pleasant, qualities that attracted Snake as much as his physical beauty. And she was lonely. She decided to accept his well-mannered offer.

"Yes," she said. "Thanks." She stopped before him, touched his cheek, took his hand and led him toward a couch. A flask of wine and some glasses stood on a low table near the window.

Snake realized that Gabriel was blushing scarlet.

If she did not know all the desert customs, she knew those of the mountains: she had not overstepped her privileges as a guest, and he *had* made the offer. She faced Gabriel and took his arms just above the elbows. Now he was quite pale.

"Gabriel, what's the matter?"

"I . . . I misspoke myself. I didn't mean — If you like I can send someone to you — "

She frowned. "If 'someone' was all I wanted I could have hired them from town. I wanted someone I like."

He gazed at her, with a quick faint grateful smile. Perhaps he had decided to stop repressing his beard and grow it out at the same time he decided to leave his father's house, for his cheeks showed a trace of fine red-gold hair.

"Thank you for that," he said.

She guided him to the couch, made him sit down, and sat beside him. "What's wrong?"

He shook his head. His hair fell across his forehead, half hiding his eyes.

"Gabriel, have you somehow not noticed that you are beautiful?"

"No." He managed a rueful grin. "I know that."

"Do I have to pry this out of you? Is it me? Gods know I can't match the looks of Mountainside people. Or if you prefer men, I understand." She had not hit on what made him draw away from her yet; he had not reacted to anything she had suggested. "Are you ill? I'm the first person you should tell!"

"I'm not ill," he said softly, not meeting her gaze. "And it isn't you. I mean, if I had my choice of anyone . . . I'm honored you think this much of me."

Snake waited for him to continue.

"It wouldn't be fair to you, if I stayed. I might — "

When he stopped again, Snake said, "This is the trouble between you and your father. This is why you're going away."

Gabriel nodded. "And he's right to want me to go."

"Because you haven't lived up to his expectations?" Snake shook her head. "Punishment is no help. It's stupid and self-gratifying. Come to bed with me, Gabriel. I won't make any demands on you."

"You don't understand," Gabriel said miserably. He took her

hand and lifted it to his face, rubbing her fingertips across the fine soft stubble. "I can't keep my side of the agreement lovers make between them. I don't know why. I had a good teacher. But biocontrol is all beyond my reach. I've tried. Gods, I've tried." His blue eyes were bright. He let his hand fall away from hers, to his side. Snake caressed his cheek once more and put her arm around his shoulders, hiding her surprise. Impotence she could comprehend, but lack of control — ! She did not know what to say to him, and he had more to tell her, something he desperately wanted to talk about: she could feel that from the stark tension of his whole body. His fists were clenched. She did not want to push him; he had been hurt enough that way already. She found herself searching for gentle and roundabout ways of saying things she would ordinarily deal with straightforwardly.

"It's all right," Snake said. "I understand what you're saying. Be easy. With me it doesn't matter."

He looked up at her, as wide-eyed and surprised as the little girl in the stable had been when Snake looked at the new bruise instead of the old, ugly scar.

"You can't mean that. I can't talk to anyone. They'd be disgusted, like my father. I don't blame them."

"You can talk to me. I won't judge you."

He hesitated a moment more, then the words, pent up for years, rushed out. "I had a friend named Leah," Gabriel said. "That was three years ago, when I was fifteen. She was twelve. The first time she decided to make love with anyone, more than just playing, you know, she chose me. She hadn't finished her training yet, of course, but it shouldn't have mattered because I'd finished mine. I thought."

He was leaning against Snake, now, with his head on her shoulder, gazing with unfocused eyes at the black windows.

"Maybe I should have taken other precautions," he said. "But I never even thought I might be fertile. I never heard of anybody who couldn't handle biocontrol. Well, maybe not deep trance, but fertility." He laughed bitterly. "And whiskers, but I hadn't started growing any then." Snake felt him shrug as the smooth material of his shirt slid across the rough new fabric of her own. "A few months later we had a party for her, because we thought she'd learned her biocontrol faster than usual. No one was surprised. Everything comes quickly to Leah. She's brilliant." He stopped for a moment and simply lay against Snake, breathing slowly and deeply. He glanced up at her. "But it wasn't her biocontrol that stopped her menstruation, it was that I had made her pregnant. She was twelve and my friend and she chose me, and I almost ruined her life."

Now Snake understood everything, Gabriel's shyness, his uncertainty, his shame, even why he cloaked his beauty when he went outside: he did not want to be recognized; even more, he did not want anyone to offer him their bed.

"You poor children," Snake said.

"I think we always assumed we'd partner, eventually, when we both knew what we were going to do. When we were settled. But who'd want an uncontrolled partner? They'd always know that if their control lapsed just a little, the other would have none. A partnering couldn't last that way." He shifted his weight. "Even so, she didn't want to humiliate me. She didn't tell anyone. She aborted it, but she was all alone. And her training wasn't far enough along for that. She almost bled to death."

"You shouldn't treat yourself as if you'd hurt her out of spite," Snake said, knowing that nothing as simple as words would be sufficient to make Gabriel stop despising himself, or to make up for the way his father treated him. He could not have known he was fertile, if he had not just been tested, and once one learned the technique it was not usually necessary to worry. Snake had heard of people incapable of biocontrol, but not very often. Only a person unable to care for anyone would have come unmarked through what Gabriel had undergone. And Gabriel quite obviously cared.

"She got well," Gabriel said. "But I turned what should have been pleasure into nightmare for her. Leah . . . I think she wanted to want to see me again, but couldn't make herself. If that makes sense."

"Yes," Snake said. Twelve years old: perhaps that had been Leah's first realization that other people could influence her life without her control or even knowledge; it was not a lesson children learned willingly or easily.

"She wants to be a glass-former, and she had an appointment to assist Ashley."

Snake whistled softly in admiration. Glass-forming was a demanding and respected profession. Only the best of its people could build solar mirrors; it took a long time just to learn to make decent tubed panels, or curved panes like the ones in the towers. Ashley was not one of the best. She was *the* best.

"Did Leah have to give it up?"

"Yes. It could have been permanently. She went the next year. But that was a year out of her life." He spoke slowly and carefully but without emotion, as if he had been through this so many times in his mind that he had forced some distance between himself and the memory. "Of course I went back to the teacher, but when they tracked my reactions longer they realized I could only keep the temperature differential a few hours at a time. Not enough."

"No," Snake said thoughtfully, wondering just how good Gabriel's teacher really could have been.

Gabriel drew back so he could look into her face. "So, you see, I can't stay with you tonight."

"You can. Please do. We're both lonely, and we can help each other."

He caught his breath and stood abruptly. "Don't you understand — " he cried.

"Gabriel."

He sat down slowly, but did not touch her.

"I am not twelve years old. You don't need to be afraid of giving me a child I don't want. Healers never have children. We take the responsibility for that ourselves, because we cannot afford to share it with our partners."

"You never have children?"

"Never. Women do not bear them and men do not father them."

He stared at her.

"Do you believe me?"

"You really still want me, even knowing — ?"

In answer, Snake stood up and began unbuttoning her shirt. The newness made the buttonholes stiff, so she stripped the shirt off over her head and dropped it on the floor. Gabriel stood up slowly, looking at her shyly. Snake unbuttoned his shirt and his pants as he reached out to hold her. When his pants slid off his narrow hips he began to blush.

"What's wrong?"

"I haven't been naked in front of anyone since I was fifteen."

"Well," Snake said, grinning, "high time." Gabriel's body was as beautiful as his face. Snake unfastened her pants and left them in a heap on the floor.

Taking Gabriel to her bed, Snake slipped under the sheet beside him. The soft glow of the lamp highlighted his blond hair and his fair skin. He was trembling.

"Relax," Snake whispered. "There's no hurry, and this is all for fun." As she massaged his shoulders the tightness slowly left them. She realized she too was tense, tense with desire and excitement and need. She wondered what Arevin was doing.

Gabriel turned on his side and reached for her. They caressed each other and Snake smiled to herself, thinking that though no single experience could compensate Gabriel for the last three years, she would do her best to make a start.

Soon, though, she realized he was not prolonging the foreplay by intent. He was working to please her, still thinking and worrying much too much, as if she were Leah, a twelve year old whose first sexual pleasure was his responsibility. Snake got no joy out of being worked on, out of being someone's duty. And, as well, he was trying hard to respond to her, failing, and growing more embarrassed by the second. Snake touched him gently, brushing his face with her lips.

Gabriel flung himself away from her with a curse and hunched over on his side with his back to her.

"I'm sorry," he said. His voice was so rough Snake knew he was crying. She sat up beside him and stroked his shoulder.

"I told you I'd make no demands."

"I keep thinking . . ."

She kissed the point of his shoulder, letting her breath tickle him. "Thinking isn't the idea."

"I can't help it. All I can offer anyone is trouble and pain. And now without even giving them any pleasure first. Maybe it's just as well."

"Gabriel, an impotent man can satisfy another person. You must know that. What we're talking about now is *your* pleasure."

He did not answer, did not look at her: he had flinched when she said "impotent," for that was one difficulty Gabriel had not talked himself into until now.

"You don't believe you're safe with me, do you?"

He rolled over and looked up. "Leah wasn't safe with me."

Snake drew her knees up against her breasts and rested her chin on her fists. She gazed at Gabriel for a long time, sighed, and held out her hand so he could see the scars and slashes of snakebites.

"Any of those bites would have killed anyone but a healer. Quickly and unpleasantly or slowly and unpleasantly."

She paused to let what she had said sink in.

"I spent a lot of time developing immunities to those venoms," she said. "And a good deal of discomfort. I never get sick. I never have infections. I can't get cancer. My teeth don't decay. Healers' immunities are so active they respond to anything unusual. Most of us are sterile because we even form antibodies to our own sex cells. Let alone anyone else's."

Gabriel pushed himself up on one elbow. "Then . . . if you can't have children, why did you say healers can't afford to have them? I thought you meant you didn't have time. So if I — "

"We raise children!" Snake said. "We adopt them. But the first healers tried to bear them. Most of them couldn't. A few could, but the infants were deformed, and they had no minds."

Gabriel turned on his back and gazed at the ceiling. He sighed deeply. "Gods."

"We learn fertility control very well," Snake said.

Gabriel did not answer.

"You're still worried." Snake leaned on her elbow beside him, but she did not reach out to touch him yet.

He glanced at her with an ironic and humorless smile, his face strained with self-doubt. "I'm scared, I guess."

"I know."

"Have you ever been afraid? Really frightened?"

"Oh, yes," Snake said.

She rested her hand on his belly, brushing her fingers across his smooth skin and the delicate dark-gold hairs. He was not visibly shaking but Snake could feel his deep, steady, frightened trembling.

"Lie still," she said. "Don't move until I tell you." She began stroking his belly and thighs, his hips and the sides of his buttocks, ending each stroke closer to his genitals but not actually touching them.

"What are you doing?"

"Sh-h. Lie still." She kept stroking him; and she talked to him, letting her voice slip into a hypnotic, soothing monotone. She could feel him fighting not to move as she teased him: he fought himself, and the trembling stopped without his noticing.

"Snake!"

"What?" she asked innocently. "Is something wrong?"

"I can't — "

"Sh-h."

He groaned. This time he was not shaking with fear. Snake smiled, eased herself down beside him, and drew him around to face her.

"Now you can move," she said.

For whatever reason — because of her teasing, or because Snake had made herself as vulnerable to him as he was to her, and he could trust her, or more probably simply because he was young and healthy and eighteen and at the end of three years' guilty self-deprivation, he was all right after that.

Snake felt like an observer, not a salacious eavesdropper but an imperturbable watcher, almost disinterested. And that was strange. Gabriel was innately gentle, and Snake drew him on to abandonment as well. Though her own climax was satisfying, a welcome release of emotional tensions that had been building as long as she had been alone, she was concerned mostly for Gabriel. Though she returned his passion eagerly, she could not keep from wondering how sex would be with Arevin.

Snake and Gabriel lay close together, both sweaty and breathing heavily, their arms around each other. For Snake, the companionship was as important as the sex itself. More important, for sexual tensions were easily enough dealt with. Aloneness, and loneliness, were something else altogether. She leaned over Gabriel and kissed his throat and the edge of his jaw.

"Thank you," he whispered. Snake could feel the vibration of his words against her lips.

"You're welcome," she said. "But I didn't ask you for selfless reasons."

He lay silent for a while, his fingers spread along the curve of her waist. Snake patted his hand. He was a sweet boy. She knew the thought was condescending, but she could not help it, nor could she help wishing, with the detached observer part of herself, that Arevin was with her instead. She wanted someone she could share with, not someone who would be grateful to her.

Gabriel suddenly held her tight and hid his face against her shoulder. She stroked the short curls at the back of his neck.

"What am I going to do?" His voice was muffled, his breath warm on her skin. "Where will I go?"

Snake held him and rocked him. Suddenly she wondered if it might have been kinder to let him leave her when he had offered to send someone else, to allow him to continue his life of abstinence unbroken. Yet she could not believe he was really one of the unfocused pitiful human beings who could never learn any biocontrol at all.

"Gabriel, what kind of training did you have? When they tested you, how long could you hold the temperature differential? Didn't they give you a token?"

"What kind of token?"

"A little disc with a chemical inside that changes color with temperature. Most of the ones I've seen turn red when a man raises his genital temperature high enough." She grinned, remembering an acquaintance who was rather vain about the intensity of his disc's color, and had to be talked into removing it when he went to bed.

But Gabriel was frowning at her. "High enough?"

"Yes, of course, high enough. Isn't that how *you* do it?"

His fair eyebrows drew together, distress and surprise mixing in his expression. "Our teacher instructs us on keeping the temperature low."

The memory of her vain friend and any number of bawdy jokes came together in Snake's mind. She wanted to laugh out loud. Somehow she managed to reply to Gabriel with a perfectly straight face.

"Gabriel, dear friend, how old was your teacher? A hundred?"

"Yes," Gabriel said. "At least. A very wise old man. He still is."

"Wise, I'm sure, but out of touch," Snake said. "Out of date by eighty years. Lowering the temperature of your scrotum will make you infertile. But raising the temperature is much more effective. And it's supposed to be a good deal easier to learn."

"But he said I could never control myself properly — "

Snake frowned but did not say what she thought: that no teacher should ever say that to a student about anything. "Well, often one person doesn't get along well with another and all that's needed is a different teacher."

"Do you think I could learn?"

"Yes." She restrained another sharp comment about the wisdom and ability of Gabriel's first teacher. It would be better if the young man realized the teacher's faults himself. Clearly, he still felt too much admiration and respect; Snake did not want to push him into a defense of the old man, the person who perhaps had done most to hurt him.

Gabriel grasped Snake's hand. "What do I do? Where do I go?" This time he spoke with hope and excitement.

"Anywhere the men's teacher knows techniques less than a century old. Which direction are you going when you leave?"

"I . . . I haven't decided." He looked away.

"It's hard to go," Snake said. "I know it is. But it's best. Spend some time exploring. Decide what will be good for you."

"Find a new place," Gabriel said sadly.

"You could go to Middlepath," Snake said. "The best teachers I've heard of live there. And then when you've finished you can come back. There'll be no reason not to."

"I think there will. I think I'll never be able to come home again, because even if I do learn what I need, people here will always wonder about me. The rumors will still be there." He shrugged. "But I have to go anyway. I promised. I'll go to Middlepath."

"Good." Snake reached back and turned down the lamp to a tiny spark. "The new technique has other benefits, I'm told."

"What do you mean?"

She touched him. "It requires you to increase the circulation in the genital area. That's supposed to increase endurance. And sensitivity."

"I wonder if I have any endurance now?"

Snake began to answer him seriously, then realized Gabriel had made his first, tentative, joke about sex.

"Let's see," she said.

A hurried knock on the door woke Snake well before dawn. The room was gray and ghostly, highlighted in shades of pink and orange from the lamp's low flame. Gabriel slept soundly, smiling faintly, his long blond eyelashes gently brushing his cheeks. He had pushed away the bedclothes and his long beautiful body lay uncovered to mid-thigh. Snake turned reluctantly toward the door.

"Come in."

A stunningly lovely young servant entered hesitantly, and light from the corridor spilled over the bed.

"Healer, the mayor — " She gasped and stood staring at Gabriel, the blood on her hands forgotten. "The mayor . . ."

"I'll be right there." Snake got up, slipped into her new pants and the stiff new shirt, and followed the young woman to the mayor's suite.

Blood from the opened wound soaked the bedding, but Brian had done the proper emergency things: the bleeding had nearly stopped. The mayor was ghastly pale, and his hands trembled.

"If you didn't look so sick," Snake said, "I'd give you the tongue-lashing you deserve." She busied herself with the bandages. "You're blessed with a superb nurse," she said when Brian returned with fresh sheets and was easily within hearing. "I hope you pay him what he's worth."

"I thought . . ."

"Think all you like," Snake said. "An admirable occupation. But don't try to stand up again."

"All right," he muttered, and Snake took it as a promise.

She decided she did not need to help change the sheets. When it was necessary, or when it was for people she liked, she did not mind giving menial services. But sometimes she could be inordinately prideful. She knew she had been unforgiveably short with the mayor, but she could not help it.

The young servant was taller than Snake, easily stronger than Brian; Snake expected she could handle her share of lifting the mayor and most of Brian's as well. But she watched with a distressed expression as Snake left the room to go back to bed and padded barefoot down the hallway.

"Mistress — ?"

Snake turned. The young servant glanced around as if afraid someone might see them together.

"What's your name?"

"Larril."

"Larril, my name is Snake, and I hate being called 'mistress.' All right?"

Larril nodded but did not use Snake's name.

Snake sighed to herself. "What's the matter?"

"Healer . . . in your room I saw . . . a servant should not see some things. I don't want to shame any member of this family." Her voice was shrill and strained. "But . . . but Gabriel — he is — " Her words caught in confusion and shame. "If I asked Brian what to do he would have to tell his master. That would be . . . unpleasant. But you mustn't be hurt. I never thought the mayor's son would — "

"Larril," Snake said, "Larril, it's all right. He told me everything. The responsibility is mine."

"You know the — the danger?"

"He told me everything," she said again. "There's no danger to me."

"You've done a kind thing," Larril said abruptly.

"Nonsense. I wanted him. And I have a good deal more experience at control than a twelve year old. Or an eighteen year old, for that matter."

Larril avoided her gaze. "So do I," she said. "And I've felt so sorry for him. But I — I was afraid. He is so beautiful, one might think of . . . one might lapse, without meaning to. I couldn't take the chance. I still have another six months before my life is mine again."

"You were bonded?"

Larril nodded. "I was born in Mountainside. My parents sold me. Before the mayor's new laws, they were allowed to do that." The tension in her voice belied her matter-of-fact words. "It was a long time before I heard the rumors that bonding had been forbidden here, but when I did, I escaped and came back." She looked up, almost crying. "I didn't break my word — " She straightened and spoke more confidently. "I was a child, and I had no choice in the bonding. I owed no driver my loyalty. But the city bought my papers. I *do* owe loyalty to the mayor."

Snake realized how much courage it had taken Larril to speak as she had. "Thank you," Snake said. "For telling me about Gabriel. None of this will go any farther. I'm in your debt."

"Oh, no, healer, I did not mean — "

There was something in Larril's voice, a sudden shame, that Snake found disturbing. She wondered if Larril thought her own motives in speaking to Snake were suspect.

"I did mean it," Snake said again. "Is there some way I can help you?"

Larril shook her head, once, quickly, a gesture of denial that said no to her more than to Snake. "No one can help me, I think."

"Tell me."

Larril hesitated, then sat on the floor and angrily jerked up the cuff of her pants.

Snake sat on her heels beside her.

"Oh, my gods," Snake said.

Larril's heel had been pierced, between the bone and the Achilles tendon. It looked to Snake as if someone had used a hot iron on her. The scar accommodated a small ring of a gray, crystalline material. Snake took Larril's foot in one hand and touched the ring. It showed no visible joining.

Snake frowned. "This was nothing but cruelty."

"If you disobey them they have the right to mark you," Larril said. "I'd tried to escape before and they said they had to make me remember my place." Anger overcame the quietness of her voice. Snake shivered.

"Those will always bind me," Larril said. "If it was just the scars I wouldn't mind so much." She withdrew her foot from Snake's hands. "You've seen the domes in the mountains? That's what the rings are made of."

Snake glanced at her other heel, also scarred, also ringed. Now she recognized the gray, translucent substance. But she had never before seen it made into anything except the domes, which lay mysterious and inviolable in unexpected places.

"The smith tried to cut that one," Larril said. "When he didn't even mark it he was so embarrassed he broke an iron rod with one blow, just to prove he could." She touched the fine tough strand of her tendon, trapped within the delicate ring. "Once the crystal hardens it's there forever. Like the domes. Unless you cut the tendon, and then you're lame. Sometimes I think I could almost stand that." She jerked the cuff of her pants down to cover the ring. "As you see, no one can help. It's vanity, I know it. Soon I *will* be free no matter what those things say."

"I can't help you here," Snake said. "And it would be dangerous."

"You mean you could do it?"

"It could be done, it could be tried, at the healers' station."

"Oh, healer — "

"Larril, there would be a risk." On her own ankle she showed what would have to be done. "We wouldn't cut the tendon, we'd detach it. Then the ring could come off. But you'd be in a cast for quite a while. And there's no certainty that the tendons would heal properly, your legs might never be as strong as they are now. The tendons might not even re-attach at all."

"I see . . ." Larril said, with hope and joy in her voice, perhaps not really hearing Snake at all.

Will you promise me one thing?"

"Yes, healer, of course."

"Don't decide what to do yet. Don't decide right after your service to Mountainside is over. Wait a few months. Be certain. Once you're free you might decide it doesn't matter to you any more."

Larril glanced up quizzically and Snake knew she would have asked how the healer would feel in her position, but thought the question insolent.

"Will you promise?"

"Yes, healer. I promise."

They stood up.

"Well, good night," Snake said.

"Good night, healer."

Snake started down the corridor.

"Healer?"

"Yes?"

Larril flung her arms around Snake and hugged her. "Thank you!" Embarrassed, she withdrew. They both turned to go their ways, but Snake glanced back.

"Larril, where do the drivers get the rings? I never heard of anyone who could work the dome material."

"The city people give it to them," Larril said. "Not enough to make anything useful. Just the rings."

"Thank you."

Snake went back to bed, musing about Center, which gave chains to slavers but refused to talk to healers.

7

Snake awoke before Gabriel, at the very end of night. As dawn broke, the faint gray light illuminated the bedroom. Snake lay on her side, propped on her elbow, and watched Gabriel sleep. He was, if that were possible, even more beautiful asleep than awake.

Snake reached out, but stopped before she touched him. Usually she liked to make love in the morning. But she did not want Gabriel to wake up.

Frowning, she lay back and tried to trace her reaction. Last night had not been the most memorable sexual encounter of her life, for Gabriel was, though not exactly clumsy, still awkward with inexperience. Yet, though she had not completely been satisfied, neither had she found sleeping with Gabriel at all unpleasant.

Snake forced her thoughts deeper, and found that they disturbed her. They were all too much like fear. Certainly she did not fear Gabriel: the very idea was ridiculous. But she had never before been with a man who could not control his fertility. He made her uneasy, she could not deny it. Her own control was complete; she had confidence in herself on that matter. And even if by some freakish accident she did become pregnant, she could abort it without the overreaction that had nearly killed Gabriel's friend Leah. No, her uneasiness had little basis in the reality of what could happen. It was merely the knowledge of Gabriel's incapability that made her hold back from him, for she had grown up knowing her lovers would be controlled, knowing they had exactly the same confidence in her. She could not give that confidence to Gabriel, even though his difficulties were not his fault.

For the first time she truly understood how lonely he had been for the last three years, how everyone must have reacted to him and how he must have felt about himself. She sighed in sadness for him and reached out to him, stroking his body with her fingertips, waking him gradually, leaving behind all her hesitation and uneasiness.

Carrying her serpent-case, Snake hiked down the cliff to get Swift. Several of her town patients needed looking at again, and she would spend the afternoon giving vaccinations. Gabriel remained in his father's house, packing and preparing for his trip.

Squirrel and Swift gleamed with brushing. The stablemaster, Ras, was nowhere in sight. Snake entered Squirrel's stall to inspect his newly shod feet. She scratched his ears and told him aloud that he needed exercise or he would founder. Above her, the loose hay in the loft rustled softly, but though Snake waited, she heard nothing more.

"I'll have to ask the stablemaster to chase you around the field," she said to her pony, and waited again.

"I'll ride him for you, mistress," the child whispered.

"How do I know you can ride?"

"I can ride."

"Please come down."

Slowly the child climbed through the hole in the ceiling, hung by her hands, and dropped to Snake's feet. She stood with her head down.

"What's your name?"

The little girl muttered something in two syllables. Snake went down on one knee and grasped her shoulders gently. "I'm sorry, I couldn't hear you."

She looked up, squinting through the terrible scar. The

bruise was fading. "M-Melissa." After the first hesitation she said the name defensively, as if daring Snake to deny it to her. Snake wondered what she had said the first time. "Melissa," the child said again, lingering over the sounds.

"My name is Snake, Melissa." Snake held out her hand and the child shook it watchfully. "Will you ride Squirrel for me?"

"Yes."

"He might buck a little."

Melissa grabbed the bars of the stall door's top half and chinned herself up. "See him over there?"

The horse across the way was a tremendous piebald, well over seventeen hands. Snake had noticed him before; he flattened his ears and bared his teeth whenever anyone passed.

"I ride him," Melissa said.

"Good lords," Snake said in honest admiration.

"I'm the only one can," Melissa said. "Except that other."

"Who, Ras?"

"No," Melissa said with contempt. "Not him. The one from the castle. With the yellow hair."

"Gabriel."

"I guess. But he doesn't come down much, so I ride his horse." Melissa jumped back to the floor. "He's fun. But your pony is nice."

In the face of the child's competence, Snake gave no more cautions. "Thank you, then. I'll be glad to have someone ride him who knows what they're doing."

Melissa climbed to the edge of the manger, about to hide herself in the hayloft again, before Snake could think of a way to interest her enough to talk some more. Then Melissa turned halfway toward her. "Mistress, you tell him I have permission?" All the confidence had crept from her voice.

"Of course I will," Snake said.

Melissa vanished.

Snake saddled Swift and led her outside, where she encountered the stablemaster.

"Melissa's going to exercise Squirrel for me," Snake told him. "I said she could."

"Who?"

"Melissa."

"Someone from town?"

"Your stable-hand," Snake said. "The redheaded child."

"You mean Ugly?" He laughed.

Snake felt herself flushing scarlet with shock, then anger. "How dare you taunt a child that way?"

"Taunt her? How? By telling her the truth? No one wants to look at her and it's better she remembers it. Has she been bothering you?"

Snake mounted her horse and looked down at him. "You use your fists on someone nearer your size from now on." She pressed her heels to Swift's sides and the mare sprang forward, leaving the barn and Ras and the castle and the mayor behind.

The day slipped by more rapidly than Snake had expected. Hearing that a healer was in Mountainside, people from all the valley came to her, bringing young children for the protection she offered and older people with chronic ailments, some of whom, like Grum with her arthritis, she could not help. Her good fortune continued, for though she saw a few patients with bad infections, tumors, even a few contagious diseases, no one came who was dying. The people of Mountainside were nearly as healthy as they were beautiful.

She spent all afternoon working in a room on the ground floor of the inn where she had intended to lodge. It was a central spot in town, and the innkeeper made her welcome. In the evening, the last parent led the last weepy child from the room. Wishing Pauli had been here to tell them jokes and stories, Snake leaned back in her chair, stretching and yawning, and let herself relax, arms still raised, her head thrown back, eyes closed. She heard the door open, footsteps, the swish of a long garment, and smelled the warm fragrance of herb tea.

Snake sat up as Lainie, the innkeeper, placed a tray on the table nearby. Lainie was a handsome and pleasant woman of middle age, rather stout. She seated herself, poured two mugs of tea, and handed one to Snake.

"Thanks." Snake inhaled the steam.

After they sipped their tea for a few minutes, Lainie broke the silence. "I'm glad you came," she said. "We've not had a healer in Mountainside for too long."

"I know," Snake said. "We can't get this far south very often." She wondered if Lainie knew as well as she did that it was not the distance between Mountainside and the healers' station that was the problem.

"If a healer were to settle here," Lainie said, "I know the town would be liberal in its gratitude. I'm sure the mayor will speak to you about this when he's better. But I'm on the council and I can assure you his proposal would be supported."

"Thank you, Lainie. I'll remember that."

"Then you might stay?"

"Me?" She stared at her tea, surprised. It had not even occurred to her that Lainie meant the invitation to be direct. Mountainside, with its beautiful, healthy people, was a place for a healer to settle after a lifetime of hard work, a place to rest for someone who did not wish to teach. "No, I can't. I'm leaving in the morning. But when I go home I'll tell the other healers about your offer."

"Are you sure you don't wish to stay?"

"I can't. I haven't the seniority to accept such a position."

"And you must leave tomorrow?"

"Yes. There's really not much work in Mountainside. You're all entirely too healthy." Snake grinned.

Lainie smiled quickly, but her voice remained serious. "If you feel you must go because the place you are staying . . . because you need a place more convenient to your work," she said hesitantly, "my inn is always open to you."

"Thanks. If I were staying longer I'd move. I wouldn't want to

. . . abuse the mayor's hospitality. But I really do have to go."

She glanced at Lainie, who smiled again. They understood each other.

"Will you stay the night?" Lainie asked. "You must be tired, and it's a long way."

"Oh, it's a pleasant ride," Snake said. "Relaxing."

Snake rode toward the mayor's residence through darkened streets, the rhythmic sound of Swift's hooves a background for her dreams. She dozed as the mare walked on. The clouds were high and thin tonight; the waning moon cast shadows on the stones.

Suddenly Snake heard the rasp of boot heels on pavement. Swift shied violently to the left. Losing her balance, Snake grabbed desperately for the pommel of the saddle and the horse's mane, trying to pull herself back up. Someone snatched at her shirt and hung on, dragging her down. She let go with one hand and struck at the attacker. Her fist glanced off rough cloth. She hit out again and connected. The man grunted and let her go. She dragged herself onto Swift's back and kicked the mare's sides. Swift leaped forward. The assailant was still holding onto the saddle. Snake could hear his boots scraping as he tried to keep up on foot. He was pulling the saddle toward him. Suddenly it righted with a lurch as the man lost his grip.

But a split second later Snake reined the mare in. The serpent case was gone.

Snake wheeled Swift around and galloped her after the fleeing man.

"Stop!" Snake cried. She did not want to run Swift into him, but he was not going to obey. He could duck into an alley too narrow for a horse and rider, and before she could get down and follow he could disappear.

Snake leaned down, grabbed his robe, and launched herself at him. They went down hard in a tangle. He turned as he fell, and Snake hit the cobbled street, slammed against it by his weight. Somehow she kept hold of him as he struggled to escape her and she fought for breath. She wanted to tell him to drop the case, but she could not yet speak. He struck out at her and she felt a sharp pain across her forehead at the hairline. Snake hit back and they rolled and scuffled on the street. Snake heard the case scrape on stone: she lunged and grabbed it and so did the hooded man. As Sand rattled furiously inside, they played tug of war like children.

"Let it go!" Snake yelled. It seemed to be getting darker and she could hardly see. She knew she had not hit her head, she did not feel dizzy. She blinked her eyes and the world wavered around her. "There's nothing you can use!"

He pulled the case toward him, moaning in desperation. For an instant Snake yielded, then snatched the case back and freed it. She was so astonished when the obvious trick worked that she fell backward, landed on her hip and elbow, and yelped with the not-quite-pain of a bruised funny bone. Before she could get up again the attacker fled down the street.

Snake climbed to her feet, holding her elbow against her side and tightly clutching the handle of the case in her other hand. As fights went, that one had not amounted to much. She wiped her face, blinking, and her vision cleared. She had blood in her eyes from a scalp cut. Taking a step, she flinched; she had bruised her right knee. She limped toward the mare, who snorted skittishly but did not shy away. Snake patted her. She did not feel like chasing horses, or anything else, again tonight. Wanting to let Mist and Sand out to be sure they were all right, but knowing that would strain the mare's tolerance beyond its limit, Snake tied the case back on the saddle and remounted.

Snake halted the mare in front of the barn when it loomed up abruptly before them in the darkness. She felt high and dizzy. Though she had not lost much blood, and the attacker never hit her hard enough to give her a concussion, the adrenalin from the fight had worn off, leaving her totally drained of energy.

She drew in her breath. "Stablemaster!"

No one answered for a moment, then, five meters above her, the loft door rumbled open on its tracks.

"He's not here, mistress," Melissa said. "He sleeps up in the castle. Can I help?"

Snake looked up. Melissa remained in the shadows, out of the moonlight.

"I hoped I wouldn't wake you . . ."

"Mistress, what happened? You're bleeding all over!"

"No, it's stopped. I was in a fight. Would you mind going up the hill with me? You can sit behind me on the way up and ride Swift back down."

Melissa grabbed both sides of a pulley rope and lowered herself hand-over-hand to the ground. "I'd do anything you asked me to, mistress," she said softly.

Snake reached down and Melissa took her hand and swung up behind her. All children worked, in the world Snake knew, but the hand that grasped hers, a ten year old's hand, was as calloused and rough and hard as any adult manual laborer's.

Snake squeezed her legs against Swift's sides and the mare started up the trail. Melissa held the cantle of the saddle, an uncomfortable and awkward way of balancing. Snake reached back and drew the child's hands around her waist. Melissa was as stiff and withdrawn as Gabriel, and Snake wondered if Melissa had waited even longer than he for anyone to touch her with affection.

"What happened?" Melissa asked.

"Somebody tried to rob me."

"Mistress, that's awful. Nobody ever robs anybody in Mountainside."

"Someone tried to rob me. They tried to steal my serpents."

"It must have been a crazy," Melissa said.

Recognition shivered up Snake's spine. "Oh, gods," she said. She remembered the desert robe her attacker had worn, a garment seldom seen in Mountainside. "It was."

"What?"

"A crazy. No, not a crazy. A crazy wouldn't follow me this far. He's looking for something, but what is it? I haven't got anything anybody would want. Nobody but a healer can do anything with the serpents."

"Maybe it was Swift, mistress. She's a good horse and I've never seen such fancy tack."

"He tore up my camp, before Swift was given to me."

"A really crazy crazy, then," Melissa said. "Nobody would rob a healer."

"I wish people wouldn't keep telling me that," Snake said. "If he doesn't want to rob me, what does he want?"

Melissa tightened her grip around Snake's waist, and her arm brushed the handle of Snake's knife.

"Why didn't you kill him?" she asked. "Or stab him good, anyway."

Snake touched the smooth bone handle. "I never even thought of it," she said. "I've never used my knife against anyone." She wondered, in fact, if she could use it against anyone. Melissa did not reply.

Swift climbed the trail. Pebbles spun from her hooves and clattered down the sheer side of the cliff.

"Did Squirrel behave himself?" Snake finally asked.

"Yes, mistress. And he isn't lame at all now."

"That's good."

"He's fun to ride. I never saw a horse striped like him before."

"I had to do something original before I was accepted as a healer, so I made Squirrel," she said. "No one ever isolated that gene before." She realized Melissa would have no idea what she was talking about; she wondered if the fight had affected her more than she thought.

"You made him?"

"I made . . . a medicine . . . that would make him be born the color he is. I had to change a living creature without hurting it to prove I was good enough to work on changing the serpents. So we can cure more diseases."

"I wish I could do something like that."

"Melissa, you can ride horses I wouldn't go near."

Melissa said nothing.

"What's wrong?"

"I was going to be a jockey."

She was a small, thin child, and she could certainly ride anything. "Then why — " Snake cut herself off, for she realized why Melissa could not be a jockey in Mountainside.

Finally the child said, "The mayor wants jockeys as pretty as his horses."

Snake took Melissa's hand and squeezed it gently. "I'm sorry."

"It's okay here, mistress."

The lights of the courtyard reached toward them. Swift's hooves clattered on the stone. Melissa slipped from the mare's back.

"Melissa?"

"Don't worry, mistress, I'll put your horse away. Hey!" she called. "Open the door!"

Snake got down slowly and unfastened the serpent case from the saddle. She was already stiff, and her bad knee ached fiercely.

The residence door opened and a servant in nightclothes peered out. "Who's there?"

"It's Mistress Snake," Melissa said from the darkness. "She's hurt."

"I'm all right," Snake said, but with a shocked exclamation the servant turned away, calling for help, and then came running into the courtyard.

"Why didn't you bring her inside?" He reached out to support Snake. She gently held him away. Other people came running out and milled around her.

"Come get the horse, you foolish child!"

"Leave her alone!" Snake said sharply. "Thank you, Melissa."

"You're welcome, mistress."

As Snake entered the vaulted hallway, Gabriel came clattering down the huge curved staircase. "Snake, what's wrong? — Good lords, what happened?"

'I'm all right," she said again. "I just got in a fight with an incompetent thief." It was more than that, though. She knew it now.

She thanked the servants and went upstairs to the south tower with Gabriel. He stood uneasily and restlessly by while she checked Mist and Sand, for he had urged her to take care of herself first. The two serpents had not been hurt, so Snake left them in their compartments and went into the bathroom.

She caught a glimpse of herself in the mirror: her face was covered with blood and her hair was matted against her scalp. Her blue eyes stared out at her.

"You look like you've almost been murdered." He turned on the water and brought out washcloths and towels.

"I do, don't I?"

Gabriel dabbed at the gash across her forehead and up above the hairline. Snake could see its edges in the mirror: it was a shallow, thin cut that must have been made with the edge of a ring, not a knuckle.

"Maybe you should lie down."

"Scalp wounds always bleed like that," Snake said. "It isn't as bad as it looks." She glanced down at herself and laughed sadly. "New shirts are never very comfortable but this is a hard way to age one." The shoulder and elbow were ripped out, and the right knee of her pants, from her fall to the cobblestones; and dirt was ground into the fabric. Through the holes she could see bruises forming.

"I'll get you another," Gabriel said. "I can't believe this happened. There's hardly any robbery in Mountainside. And everybody knows you're a healer. Who would attack a healer?"

Snake took the cloth from him and finished washing the cut. Gabriel had cleaned it too gently; Snake did not much want it to heal over dirt and bits of gravel.

"I wasn't attacked by anyone from Mountainside," she said.

Gabriel sponged the knee of her pants to loosen the material where dry blood glued it to her skin. Snake told him about the crazy.

"At least it wasn't one of our people," Gabriel said. "And a stranger will be easier to find."

"Maybe so." But the crazy had escaped the search of the desert people; a town had many more hiding places.

She stood up. Her knee was getting sorer. She limped to the big tub and turned on the water, very hot. Gabriel helped her out of the rest of her clothes and sat nearby while she soaked the aches away. He fidgeted, angry at what had happened.

"Where were you when the crazy attacked you? I'm going to send the town guards out to search."

"Oh, Gabriel, leave it for tonight. It's been at least an hour — he'll be long gone. All you'll do is make people get up out of their warm beds to run around town and get other people up out of their warm beds."

"I want to do *something*."

"I know. But there's nothing to be done for now." She lay back and closed her eyes.

"Gabriel," she said suddenly after several minutes of silence, "what happened to Melissa?"

She glanced over at him; he frowned.

"Who?"

"Melissa. The little stable-hand with burn scars. She's ten or eleven and she has red hair."

"I don't know — I don't think I've seen her."

"She rides your horse for you."

"Rides my horse! A ten-year-old child? That's ridiculous."

"She told me she rides him. She didn't sound like she was lying."

"Maybe she sits on my horse's back when Ras leads him out to pasture. I'm not even sure he'd stand for that, though. Ras can't ride him — how could a child?"

"Well, never mind," Snake said. Perhaps Melissa had simply

wanted to impress her; she would not be surprised if the child lived in fantasies. But Snake found she could not dismiss Melissa's claim so lightly. "That doesn't matter," she said to Gabriel. "I just wondered how she got burned."

"I don't know."

Exhausted, feeling that if she stayed in the bath any longer she would fall asleep, Snake pushed herself out of the tub. Gabriel wrapped a big towel around her and helped her dry her back and her legs, for she was still very sore.

"There was a fire down at the stable," he said abruptly. "Four or five years ago. But I thought no one was hurt. Ras even got most of the horses out."

"Melissa hid from me," Snake said. "Could she have been hiding for four years?"

Gabriel remained silent for a moment. "If she's scarred . . ." He shrugged uneasily. "I don't like to think of it this way, but I've been hiding from almost everyone for three years. I guess it's possible."

He helped her back to the bedroom and stopped just inside the doorway, suddenly awkward. Snake realized all at once that she had been as good as teasing him again, without intending to. She wished she could offer him a place in her bed tonight; she would have liked the companionship. But she was not inexhaustible. Right now she had no energy for sex or even for sympathy, and she did not want to tease him even more by expecting him to lie chaste all night beside her.

"Good night, Gabriel," she said. "I wish we had last night to live over again."

He controlled disappointment well, disappointment and the embarrassment of realizing he was disappointed, though he knew she was hurt and tired. They merely kissed good night. Snake felt a sudden surge of desire. All that kept her from asking him to stay was the knowledge of how she would feel in the morning after tonight's physical and emotional stress. More exertion of body and mind, even pleasurable passion, would only make things worse.

"Damn," Snake said as Gabriel stepped back. "That crazy keeps adding to what he owes."

A sound roused Snake from deep, exhausted sleep. She thought Larril had come about the mayor, but no one spoke. Light from the hallway illuminated the room for an instant, then the door closed, leaving darkness again. Snake lay very still. She could hear her heart pounding as she readied herself for defense, remembering what Melissa had said about her knife. In a camp it was always nearby, though she no more expected to be attacked while traveling than while sleeping in the mayor's castle. But tonight her belt and knife lay somewhere on the floor where she had dropped them, or perhaps even in the bathroom. She did not remember. Her head ached and her knee hurt.

What am I thinking of? she wondered. I don't even know how to fight with a knife.

"Mistress Snake?" The voice was so soft she could barely hear it.

Turning, Snake sat bolt upright, fully awake, her fist relaxing even as reflex had clenched it.

"What — Melissa?"

"Yes, mistress."

"Thank gods you spoke — I almost hit you."

"I'm sorry. I didn't really mean to wake you up. I just . . . I wanted to be sure . . ."

"Is anything wrong?"

"No, but I didn't know if you were all right. I always see lights up here and I thought nobody went to bed till way late. I thought maybe I could ask somebody. Only . . . I couldn't. I better go."

"No, wait." Snake's eyes were better accustomed to the darkness and she could see Melissa's form, the ghost of faint light on the sun-bleached streaks in her red hair; and she could smell the pleasant odor of hay and clean horses.

"It was sweet of you to come all this way to ask about me." She drew Melissa closer, leaned down, and kissed her forehead.

The thick curly bangs could not completely hide the irregularity of scar tissue beneath them.

Melissa stiffened and pulled away. "How can you stand to touch me?"

"Melissa, dear — " Snake reached out and turned up the light before Melissa could stop her. The child turned away. Snake took her by the shoulder and gently brought her around until they were facing each other. Melissa would not look at her.

"I like you. I always touch the people I like. Other people would like you, too, if you gave them a chance."

"That's not what Ras says. He says nobody in Mountainside wants to look at uglies."

"Well, I say Ras is a hateful person, and I say he has other reasons for making you afraid of everyone. He takes credit for what you do, doesn't he? He pretends he's the one who gentles the horses and rides them."

Melissa shrugged, her head down so the scar was less visible.

"And the fire," Snake said. "What really happened? Gabriel said Ras saved the horses, but you're the one who got hurt."

"Everybody knows a little eight-year-old kid couldn't get horses out of a fire," Melissa said.

"Oh, Melissa . . ."

"I don't care!"

"Don't you?"

"I get a place to live. I get to eat. I get to stay with the horses, they don't mind . . ."

"Melissa, gods! Why do you stay here? People need more than food and somewhere to sleep!"

"I can't leave. I'm not fourteen."

"Did he tell you you're bound to him? Bonding isn't allowed in Mountainside."

"I'm not a bondservant," Melissa said irritably. "I'm twelve. How old did you think I was?"

"I thought you were about twelve," Snake said, not wanting

to admit how much younger she had really thought Melissa was. "What difference does that make?"

"Could you go where you wanted when you were twelve?"

"Yes, of course I could. I was lucky enough to be in a place I didn't want to leave, but I could have gone."

Melissa blinked. "Oh," she said. "Well . . . here it's different. If you leave, your guardian comes after you. I did it once and that's what happened."

"But why?"

"Because I can't hide," Melissa said angrily. "You think people wouldn't mind, but they told Ras where I was so he'd take me back — "

Snake reached out and touched her hand. Melissa fell silent.

"I'm sorry," Snake said. "That isn't what I meant. I meant what gives anyone the right to make you stay where you don't want to? Why did you have to hide? Couldn't you just take your pay and go where you wanted?"

Melissa laughed sharply. "My pay! Kids don't get paid. Ras is my guardian. I have to do what he says. I have to stay with him. That's law."

"It's a terrible law. I know he hurts you — the law wouldn't make you stay with someone like him. Let me talk to the mayor, maybe he can fix it so you can do what you want."

"Mistress, no!" Melissa flung herself down at the side of the bed, kneeling, clutching the sheets. "Who else would take me? Nobody! They'd leave me with him, but they would've made me say bad things about him. And then he'll just, he'll just be meaner. Please don't change anything!"

Snake drew her from her knees and put her arms around her, but Melissa huddled in on herself, pulling back from Snake's embrace, then, suddenly, flinching forward with a sharp gasp as Snake, releasing her, slid her hand across the child's shoulder blade.

"Melissa, what is it?"

"Nothing!"

Snake loosened Melissa's shirttail and looked at her back. She had been beaten with a piece of leather, or a switch: something that would hurt but not draw blood, not prevent Melissa from working.

"How — " She stopped. "Oh, damn. Ras was angry at me, wasn't he? I reprimanded him and just got you into trouble, didn't I?"

"Mistress Snake, when he wants to hit, he hits. He doesn't plan it. It's the same whether it's me or the horses." She stepped back, glancing at the door.

"Don't go. Stay here tonight. Tomorrow we can think of something to do."

"No, please, mistress, it's all right. Never mind. I've been here all my life. I know how to get along. Don't do anything. Please. I've got to go."

"Wait — "

But Melissa slipped out of the room. The door closed behind her. By the time Snake climbed out of bed and stumbled after her, she was halfway to the stairs. Snake supported herself against the doorjamb, leaning out into the hall. "We have to talk about this!" she called, but Melissa ran silently down the stairs and vanished.

Snake limped back to her luxurious bed, got under her warm blankets, and turned down the lamp, thinking of Melissa out in the dark, chilly night.

Awakening slowly, Snake lay very still, wishing she could sleep through the day and have it over. She was so seldom sick that she had difficulty making herself take it easy when she was ill. Considering the stern lectures she had given Gabriel's father, she would make quite a fool of herself if she did not follow her own advice now. Snake sighed. She could work hard all day; she could make long journeys on foot or on horseback, and she would be all right. But anger and adrenalin and the violence of a fight combined against her.

Gathering herself, she moved slowly. She caught her breath

and froze. The ache in her right knee, where the arthritis was worst, turned sharp. Her knee was swollen and stiff and she ached in all her joints. She was used to the aches. But today, for the first time, the worst twinges had spread to her right shoulder. She lay back. If she forced herself to travel today, she would be laid up even longer soon, somewhere out on the desert. She could make herself ignore pain when that was necessary, but it took a great deal of energy and had to be paid for afterwards. Right now her body had no energy to spare.

She still could not remember where she had left her belt, nor, now that she thought about it, why she had been looking for it during the night — Snake sat up abruptly, remembering Melissa, and almost cried out. But guilt was as strong as the protests of her body. She had to do something. Yet confronting Ras would not help her young friend. Snake had seen that already. She did not know what she could do. For the moment she did not even know if she could get herself into the bathroom.

That much, at least, she managed. And her belt pouch was there as well, neatly hung on a hook with her belt and knife. As far as she recalled she had left all her things where they fell. She was slightly embarrassed, for she was not ordinarily quite so untidy.

Her forehead was bruised and the long shallow cut thickly scabbed: nothing to be done about that. Snake got her aspirin from the belt pouch, took a heavy dose, and limped back to bed. Waiting for sleep she wondered how much more frequent the arthritis attacks would get as she grew older. They were inevitable, but it was not inevitable that she would have such a comfortable place in which to recover.

The sun was high and scarlet beyond thin gray clouds when she woke again. Her ears rang faintly from the aspirin. She bent her right knee tentatively and felt relief when she found it more limber and less sore. The hesitant knock that had awakened her came again.

"Come in."

Gabriel opened the door and leaned inside.

"Snake, are you all right?"

"Yes, come on in."

Gabriel entered as she sat up.

"I'm sorry if I woke you but I looked in a couple of times and you never even moved."

Snake pulled aside the bedclothes and showed him her knee. Much of the swelling had gone down, but it was clearly not normal, and the bruises had turned black and purple.

"Good lords," Gabriel said.

"It'll be better by morning," Snake said. She moved over so he could sit beside her. "Could be worse, I guess."

"I sprained my knee once and it looked like a melon for a week. Tomorrow, you say? Healers must heal fast."

"I didn't sprain it last night, I only bruised it. The swelling's mostly arthritis."

"Arthritis! I thought you never get sick."

"I never catch contagious diseases. Healers always get arthritis, unless we get something worse." She shrugged. "It's because of the immunities I told you about. Sometimes they go a little wrong and attack the same body that formed them." She saw no reason to describe the really serious diseases healers were prone to. Gabriel offered to get her some breakfast and she found to her surprise that she was hungry.

Snake spent the day taking hot baths and lying in bed, asleep from so much aspirin. That was the effect it had on her, at least. Every so often Gabriel came in and sat with her for a while, or Larril brought a tray, or Brian reported on how the mayor was getting along. Gabriel's father had not needed Snake's care since the night he had tried to get up; Brian was a much better nurse than she.

She was anxious to leave, anxious to cross the valley and the next ridge of mountains, anxious to get started on her trip to the city. Its potentialities fascinated her. And she was anxious to leave the mayor's castle. She was as comfortable as she had ever been, even back home in the healers' station. Yet the residence was an unpleasant place in which to live: familiarity with it brought a clearer perception of the emotional strains between the people. There was too much building and not enough family; too much power and no protection against it. The mayor kept his strengths to himself, without passing them on, and Ras's strength was misused. As much as Snake wanted to leave, she did not know how she could without doing something for Melissa. Melissa . . .

The mayor had a library, and Larril had brought Snake some of its books. She tried to read. Ordinarily she would have absorbed several in a day, reading much too fast, she knew, for proper appreciation. But this time she was bored and restless and distracted and disturbed.

Midafternoon. Snake got up and limped to a chair by the window where she could look out over the valley. Gabriel was not even here to talk to, for he had gone to Mountainside to give out the description of the crazy. She hoped someone would find the madman, and she hoped he could be helped. A long trip lay ahead of her and she did not relish the thought of having to worry about her pursuer the whole time. This season of the year she would find no caravans heading toward the city; she would travel alone or not at all.

Grum's invitation to stay the winter at her village was even more attractive now. But the idea of spending half a year crippled in her profession, without knowing whether she would ever be able to redeem herself, was unendurable. She would go to the city, or she would return to the healers' station and receive her teachers' judgment.

Grum. Perhaps Melissa could go to her, if Snake could free the child from Mountainside. Grum was neither beautiful nor obsessed with physical beauty; Melissa's scars would not repel her.

But it would take days to send a message to Grum and receive an answer, for her village lay far to the north. Snake had to admit to herself, too, that she did not know Grum well enough to ask her to take on a responsibility like this one. Snake sighed and combed her fingers through her hair, wishing the problem would submerge in her subconscious and reemerge solved, like a dream. She stared around the room as if something in it would tell her what to do.

The table by the window held a basket of fruit, a plate of cookies, cheese, and a tray of small meat pies. The mayor's staff was too generous in its treatment of invalids; during the long day Snake had not even had the diversion of waiting for and looking forward to meals. She had urged Gabriel, and Larril and Brian and the other servants who had come to make the bed, polish the windows, brush away the crumbs (she still had no idea how many people worked to manage the residence and to serve Gabriel and his father; every time she learned another name a new face would appear) to help themselves to the treats, but most of the serving dishes were still almost full.

On impulse, Snake emptied the basket of all but the most succulent pieces of fruit, then refilled it with cookies and cheese and meat pies wrapped in napkins. She started to write a note, changed her mind, and drew a coiled serpent on a bit of paper. She folded the slip in among the bundles and tucked a napkin over everything, then rang the call-bell.

A young boy appeared — still another servant she had not encountered before — and she asked him to take the basket to the stable and put it in the loft above Squirrel's stall. The boy was only thirteen or fourteen, lanky with rapid growth, so she made him promise not to raid the basket. In turn she promised him all he wanted of what remained on the table. He did not look underfed, but Snake had never known a child undergoing a growth-spurt who was not always a little bit hungry.

"Is that a satisfactory bargain?" she asked.

The boy grinned. His teeth were large and white and very slightly crooked; he would be a handsome young man. Snake reflected that in Mountainside even adolescents had clear complexions.

"Yes, mistress," he said.

"Good. Be sure the stablemaster doesn't see you. He can hunt up his own meals as far as I'm concerned."

"Yes, mistress!" The boy grinned again, took the basket, and left the room. From his voice, Snake decided Melissa was not the only defenseless child to feel Ras's temper. But that was no help to Melissa. The servant boy was in no better position to speak against Ras than Melissa was.

She wanted to talk to the child, but the day passed and Melissa did not appear. Snake was afraid to send any more definite message than the one in the basket; she did not want Melissa beaten again because of a stranger's meddling.

It was already dark when Gabriel returned to the castle and came to Snake's room. He was preoccupied, but he had not forgotten his promise to replace Snake's ruined shirt.

"Nothing," he said. "No one in desert robes. No one acting strangely."

Snake tried on the shirt, which fit surprisingly well. The one she had bought had been brown, a rough homespun weave. This one was of a much softer fabric, silky thin strong white material block-printed with intricate blue designs. Snake shrugged and held out her arms, brushing her fingertips over the rich color. "He buys new clothes — he's a different person. A room at an inn, and nobody sees him. He probably isn't any more unusual than any other stranger passing through."

"Most of the strangers came through weeks ago," Gabriel said, then sighed. "But you're right. Even now he wouldn't be remarked on."

Snake gazed out the window. She could see a few lights, those of valley farms, widely scattered.

"How's your knee?"

"It's all right now." The swelling was gone and the ache had subsided to what was normal during changeable weather. One thing she had liked about the black desert, despite the heat, was the constancy of its weather. There she had never awakened in the morning feeling like some infirm centenarian.

"That's good," Gabriel said, with a hopeful, questioning, tentative note in his voice.

"Healers *do* heal fast," Snake said. "When we have good reason to." She thrust aside her worries, grinned, and was rewarded with Gabriel's radiant smile.

This time the sound of the door opening did not frighten Snake. She awakened easily and pushed herself up on her elbow.

"Melissa?" She turned the lamp up just enough for them to see each other, for she did not want to disturb Gabriel.

"I got the basket," Melissa said. "The things were good. Squirrel likes cheese but Swift doesn't."

Snake laughed. "I'm glad you came up here. I wanted to talk."

"Yeah." Melissa let her breath out slowly. "Where would I go? If I could."

"I don't know if you can believe this, after all Ras has said. You could be a jockey, if that's what you want, almost anyplace but Mountainside. You might have to work a little harder at first, but people would value you for who you are and what you can do." The words sounded hollow even to Snake: You fool, she thought, you're telling a frightened child to go out in the world and succeed all alone. She searched for something better to say.

Lying beside her, one hand flung over her hip, Gabriel shifted and muttered. Snake glanced over her shoulder and put her hand on his. "It's all right, Gabriel," she said. "Go back to sleep." He sighed and the instant of wakefulness passed.

Snake turned back to Melissa. For a moment the child stared at her, ghostly pale in the dim light. Suddenly she spun away and fled.

Snake jumped out of bed and followed her. Sobbing, Melissa fumbled at the door and got it open just as Snake reached her. The child plunged into the hallway, but Snake caught up to her and stopped her.

"Melissa, what's wrong?"

Melissa hunched away, crying uncontrollably. Snake knelt and hugged her, drawing her slowly around, stroking her hair.

"It's all right, it's all right," Snake murmured, just to have something to say.

"I didn't know, I didn't understand . . ." Melissa jerked away from her. "I thought you were stronger — I thought you could do what you want, but you're just like me."

Snake would not let go of Melissa's hand. She led her into one of the other guest rooms and turned up the light. Here the floor was not heated, and the stone seemed to pull the warmth out through the soles of Snake's bare feet. She dragged a blanket off the neat bed and wrapped it around her shoulders as she took Melissa to the window seat. They sat down, Melissa reluctantly.

"Now. Tell me what's wrong."

With her head down, Melissa hugged her knees to her chest. "You have to do what they want, too."

"I don't *have* to do what anybody wants."

Melissa looked up. From her right eye, the tears slid straight down her cheek. From the left, the ridges of scar tissue led tear-tracks sideways. She put her head down again. Snake moved nearer and put an arm around her shoulders.

"Just relax. There's no hurry."

"They . . . they do things . . ."

Snake frowned, totally confounded. "What things? Who's 'they'?"

"Him."

"Who? Not Gabriel!"

Melissa nodded quickly without meeting her gaze.

Snake could not imagine Gabriel hurting anyone deliberately. "What happened? If he hurt you, I'm sure it was an accident."

Melissa stared at her. "He didn't do anything to *me*." Her voice was contemptuous.

"Melissa, dear, I haven't understood a word you've said. If Gabriel didn't do anything to you, why were you so upset when you saw him? He's really very nice." Perhaps Melissa had heard about Leah and was afraid for Snake.

"He makes you get in his bed."

"That's my bed."

"It doesn't matter whose bed! Ras can't find where I sleep, but sometimes . . ."

"Ras?"

"Me and him. You and the other."

"Wait," Snake said. "Ras makes you get in his bed? When you don't want to?" That was a stupid question, she thought, but she could not think of a better one.

"Want to!" Melissa said with disgust.

With the calmness of disbelief, Snake said carefully, "Does he make you do anything else?"

"He said it would stop hurting, but it never did . . ." She hid her face against her knees.

What Melissa had been trying to say came clear to Snake in a rush of pity and disgust. Snake hugged Melissa, patting her and stroking her hair until gradually, as if afraid someone would notice and make her stop, Melissa slipped her arms around Snake and cried against her shoulder.

"You don't have to tell me any more," Snake said. "I didn't understand, but now I do. Oh, Melissa, it's not supposed to be like that. Didn't anybody ever tell you?"

"He said I was lucky," Melissa whispered. "He said I should be grateful he would touch me." She shuddered violently.

Snake rocked her back and forth. "He was lucky," she said. "He's been lucky no one knew."

The door opened and Gabriel looked in. "Snake — ? Oh, there you are." He came toward her, the light glinting off his golden body. Startled, Melissa glanced toward him. Gabriel froze, shock and horror spreading over his face. Melissa ducked her head again and held Snake tighter, shaking with the effort of controlling her sobs.

"What — ?"

"Go back to bed," Snake said, even more harshly than she had meant to but less harshly than she felt toward him right now.

"What's going on?" he asked plaintively. Frowning, he looked at Melissa.

"Go away! I'll talk to you tomorrow."

He started to protest, saw Snake's expression change, cut off his words, and left the room. Snake and Melissa sat together in silence for a long time. Melissa's breathing slowly grew quieter and more regular.

"You see how people look at me?"

"Yes, dear. I see." After Gabriel's reaction Snake hardly felt she could paint any more rosy pictures of people's tolerance. Yet now Snake hoped even more that Melissa would decide to leave this place. Anything would be better. Anything.

Snake's anger rose in a slow, dangerous, inexorable way. A scarred and hurt and frightened child had as much right to a gentle sexual initiation as any beautiful, confident one, perhaps a greater right. But Melissa had only been scarred and hurt and frightened more. And humiliated. Snake held her and rocked her. Melissa clung contentedly to her like a much younger child.

"Melissa . . ."

"Yes, mistress."

"Ras is an evil man. He's hurt you in ways no one who wasn't evil would ever hurt anyone. I promise you he'll never hurt you again."

"What does it matter if it's him or somebody else?"

"Remember how surprised you were that someone tried to rob me?"

"But that was a crazy. Ras isn't a crazy."

"There are more crazies like that than people like Ras."

"That other one is like Ras. You had to be with him."

"No, I didn't. I invited him to stay with me. There are things people can do for each other — "

Melissa glanced up. Snake could not tell if her expression was curiosity or concern, her face was so stiff with the terrible scars of burning. For the first time Snake could see that the scars extended beneath the collar of the child's shirt. Snake felt the blood drain from her face.

"Mistress, what's wrong?"

"Tell me something, dear. How badly were you burned? Where are the scars?"

Melissa's right eye narrowed; that was all she could make of a frown. "My face." She drew back and touched her collarbone, just to the left of her throat. "Here." Her hand moved down her chest to the bottom of her rib cage, then to her side. "To here."

"No farther down?"

"No. My arm was stiff for a long time." She rotated her left shoulder: it was not as limber as it should have been. "I was lucky. If it was worse and I couldn't ride, then I wouldn't be worth keeping alive to anybody."

Snake released her breath slowly with great relief. She had seen people burned so badly they had no sex left at all, neither external organs nor capacity for pleasurable sensation. Snake thanked all the gods of all the people of the world for what Melissa had told her. Ras had hurt her, but the pain was because she was a child and he was a large and brutal adult, not because the fire had destroyed all other feeling except pain.

"People can do things for each other that give them both pleasure," Snake said. "That's why Gabriel and I were together. I wanted him to touch me and he wanted me to touch him. But when someone touches another person without caring how they feel — against their wishes!" She stopped, for she could not understand anyone twisted enough to turn sexuality into assault. "Ras is an evil man," she said again.

"The other one didn't hurt you?"

"No. We were having fun."

"All right," Melissa said reluctantly.

"I can show you."

"No! Please don't."

"Don't worry," Snake said. "Don't worry. From now on nobody will do anything to you that you don't want."

"Mistress Snake, you can't stop him. I can't stop him. You have to go away, and I have to stay here."

Anything would be better than staying here, Snake had thought. Anything. Even exile. Like the dream she had been searching for, the answers slipped up into Snake's mind, and she laughed and cried at herself for not seeing them sooner.

"Would you come with me, if you could?"

"Come with *you?*"

"Yes."

"Mistress Snake — !"

"Healers adopt their children, did you know that? I didn't realize it before, but I've been looking for someone for a long time."

"But you could have anybody."

"I want you, if you'll have me as your parent."

Melissa huddled against her. "They'll never let me go," she whispered. "I'm scared."

Snake stroked Melissa's hair and stared out the window at the darkness and the scattered lights of wealthy, beautiful Mountainside. Some time later, just on the edge of sleep, Melissa whispered, "I'm scared."

Snake woke at the first rays of scarlet morning sun. Melissa was gone. She must have slipped out and returned to the stable, and Snake was afraid for her.

Snake unfolded herself from the window seat and padded back to her room, the blanket wrapped around her shoulders. The tower was silent and cool. Her room was empty. Just as well that Gabriel had left, for though she was annoyed at him she did not want to dissipate her anger. It was not he who deserved it, and she had better uses for it. After washing she dressed, looking out over the valley. The eastern peaks still shadowed much of its floor. As she watched, the darkness crept back from the stable and its geometric white-fenced paddocks. Everything was still.

Suddenly, a horse strode from shade to sunlight. Tremendously lengthened, its shadow sprang from its hooves and marched like a giant through the sparkling grass. It was the big piebald stallion, with Melissa perched on his back.

The stallion broke into a canter and moved smoothly across the field. Snake wished she too were riding through the morning with the wind on her face; she could almost hear the hollow drumming of hooves on earth, smell the fragrance of new grass, see glistening dewdrops flung up by her passing.

The stallion galloped across the field, mane and tail flying. Melissa hunched close over his withers. One of the high stone boundary walls loomed before them.

Snake caught her breath, certain the stallion was out of

Melissa's control. His pace never slackened. Snake leaned forward as if she could reach out and stop them before the horse threw the child against the wall. She could see the tension in him, but Melissa sat still and calm. The horse steadied and sailed over the barrier, clean.

A few paces later his canter slowed; he trotted a few steps and then walked, sedately, grandly, toward the stable, as if he, like Melissa, were in no hurry to return.

If she had had any doubts about the truth of anything Melissa had told her, they were gone now. She had not doubted that Ras abused the child: Melissa's distress and confusion were all too real. Snake had wondered if riding Gabriel's horse had been an understandable fantasy, but it was equally real and it made Snake understand how difficult it might be to free her young friend. Melissa was valuable to Ras and he would not want to let her go. Snake was afraid to go straight to the mayor, with whom she had no rapport, and denounce Ras for the twisted thing he was. Who would believe her? In daylight she herself had trouble believing such a thing could ever happen, and Melissa was too frightened to accuse Ras directly. Snake did not blame her.

Snake went to the other tower and knocked on the mayor's door. As the noise echoed in the stone hallways she realized how early it was. But she did not really care; she was in no mood for conventional courtesy.

Brian opened the door. "Yes, mistress?"

"I've come to speak to the mayor about my payment."

He bowed her inside. "He's awake. I'm sure he'll see you."

Snake lifted one eyebrow at the implication that he might choose not to see her. But the servant had spoken the way a man does who worships another person beyond consideration for any other customs. Brian did not deserve her anger either.

"He's been wakeful all night," Brian said, leading her toward the tower room. "The scab itches so badly — perhaps you could — ?"

"If it isn't infected it's a matter for the chemist, not for me," Snake said coldly.

Brian glanced back at her. "But, mistress — "

"I'll speak to him alone, Brian. Will you please send for the stablemaster and for Melissa?"

"Melissa?" It was his turn to raise his eyebrows. "Is that the red-haired child?"

"Yes."

"Mistress, are you sure you wish her to come here?"

"Please do as I ask."

He bowed slightly, his face again the mask of a perfect servant. Snake stepped past him into the mayor's bedroom.

The mayor lay contorted on his bed, sheets and blankets in a tangle around him and on the floor. The bandages and dressing sagged away from his leg and the clean brown scab. His expression one of pleasure and relief, he scratched the healing wound slowly.

He saw Snake and tried to pull the bandages back up, smiling guiltily.

"It does itch," he said. "I suppose that means it's getting well?"

"Scratch all you want," Snake said. "I'll be two days gone by the time you reinfect it."

He snatched his hand away and pushed himself back up on his pillows. Awkwardly trying to straighten the bedclothes, he looked around, irritable again. "Where's Brian?"

"He's doing a favor for me."

"I see." Snake detected more annoyance in his tone, but the mayor let the subject drop. "Did you want to see me about something?"

"My payment."

"Of course — I should have brought it up myself. I had no idea you were leaving us so soon, my dear."

Snake hated endearments from people toward whom she did not feel dear. Grum must have said the same words to her fifty times, a hundred times a day, and they had not grated the way this man's did.

"I know of no town that refuses Mountainside currency," he said. "They know we never adulterate the metal or short-weigh the coins. However, we can pay you in precious stones if you prefer."

"I want neither," Snake said. "I want Melissa."

"Melissa? A citizen? Healer, it took me twenty years to overcome Mountainside's reputation as a place of bonding! We free bondservants, we don't take them."

"Healers don't keep bondservants. I should have said I want her freedom. She wants to leave with me, but your stablemaster Ras is — what do you call it? — her guardian."

The mayor stared at her. "Healer, I can't ask a man to break up his family."

Snake forced herself not to react. She did not want to have to explain her disgust. When she did not reply, the mayor fidgeted, rubbed his leg, pulled his hand away from the bandage again.

"This is very complicated. Are you sure you won't choose something else?"

"Are you refusing my request?"

He recognized her tone as the veiled threat it was; he touched the call-bell and Brian reappeared.

"Send a message to Ras. Ask him to come up as soon as he can. He's to bring his child as well."

"The healer has sent for them already, sir."

"I see." He gazed at Snake as Brian withdrew. "Suppose he refuses your demands?"

"Anyone is free to refuse payment to a healer," Snake said. "We carry weapons only for defense and we never make threats. But we do not go where we are not welcome."

"You mean you boycott any place that doesn't please you."

Snake shrugged.

"Ras is here, sir," Brian said from the doorway.

"Ask him to come in."

Snake tensed, forcing herself to control contempt and revulsion. The big man entered the room, ill at ease. His hair was damp and haphazardly slicked back. He bowed slightly to the mayor.

Behind Ras, next to Brian, Melissa hung back. The old servant drew her into the room, but she did not look up.

"It's all right, child," the mayor said. "You aren't here for punishment."

"That's hardly the way to reassure anyone!" Snake snapped.

"Healer, please, sit down," the mayor said gently. "Ras — ?" He nodded to two chairs.

Ras seated himself, glancing at Snake with dislike. Brian urged Melissa forward until she was standing between Snake and Ras, but she kept her gaze fixed on the floor.

"Ras is your guardian," the mayor said. "Is that correct?"

"Yes," she whispered.

Ras reached out, put one finger against Melissa's shoulder, and shoved lightly but deliberately. "Show some respect when you speak to the mayor."

"Sir." Melissa's voice was soft and shaky.

"Melissa," Snake said, "he asked you up here to find out what it is you want to do."

Ras swung around. "What she wants to do? What's that supposed to mean?"

"Healer," the mayor said again, his cautioning tone a little more emphatic, "please. Ras, I'm in considerable difficulty. And only you, my friend, can help me."

"I don't understand."

"The healer saved my life, you know, and now it's time to pay her. It seems she and your child have taken a fancy to one another."

"So what is it you want me to do?"

"I'd not ask you to make this sacrifice if not for the good of the town. And according to the healer it's what your child wishes."

"*What's* what she wishes?"

"Your child — "

"Melissa," Snake said.

"Her name isn't Melissa," Ras said shortly. "It isn't that now and it never has been."

"Then you tell the mayor what you call her!"

"What I call her is more honest than the airs she puts on. She gave herself that name."

"Then it's all the more hers."

"Please," the mayor said. "We're talking about the child's guardianship, not her name."

"Her guardianship? Is that what this is all about? You mean you want me to give her away?"

"That's a harsh way of putting it, but . . . accurate."

Ras glanced at Melissa, who had not moved, and then at Snake. Before he turned back to the mayor he concealed the quick flash of insight and triumph that Snake saw clearly.

"Send her off with a stranger? I've been her guardian since she was three. Her parents were my friends. Where else could she go where she'd be happy and people wouldn't stare at her?"

"She isn't happy here," Snake said.

"Stare at her? Why?"

"Raise your head," Ras said to Melissa. When she did not obey he prodded her again, and slowly she looked up.

The mayor's reaction was more controlled than Gabriel's had been, but still he flinched. Melissa avoided his stare quickly, gazing stolidly at the floor again and letting her hair fall in front of her face.

"She was burned in the stable fire, sir," Ras said. "She nearly died. I took care of her."

The mayor turned toward Snake. "Healer, won't you change your mind?"

"Doesn't it matter if she wants to come with me? Anywhere else that would be all there is to it."

"Do you want to go with her, child? Ras has been good to you, hasn't he? Why do you want to leave us?"

Her hands clenched tightly together behind her back, Melissa did not answer. Snake willed her to speak, but knew she would not; she was too frightened, and with good reason.

"She's just a child," the mayor said. "She can't make a decision like this. The responsibility has to be mine, just like the responsibility for guarding Mountainside's children has been mine for twenty years."

"Then you must realize I can do more for her than either of you," Snake said. "If she stays here she'll spend her life hiding in a stable. Let her go with me and she won't have to hide any more."

"She'll always hide," Ras said. "Poor little scar-face."

"You've made sure she'll never forget that!"

"He hasn't necessarily done an unkindness there, healer," the mayor said gently.

"All you people see is beauty!" Snake cried, and knew they would not understand what she was saying.

"She needs me," Ras said. "Don't you, girl? Who else would take care of you like I do? And now you want to leave?" He shook his head. "I don't understand. Why would she want to go? And why do you want her?"

"That's an excellent question, healer," the mayor said. "Why do you want this child? People might be all too willing to say we've gone from selling our beautiful children to disposing of our disfigured ones."

"She can't spend her whole life hiding," Snake said. "She's a talented child, she's smart and she's brave. I can do more for her than anyone can here. I can help her have a profession. I can help her be someone who won't be judged on her scars."

"A healer?"

"It's possible, if that's what she wants."

"What you're saying is, you'd adopt her."

"Yes, of course. What else?"

The mayor turned to Ras. "It would be quite a coup for Mountainside if one of our people became a healer."

"She wouldn't be happy away from here," Ras said.

"Don't you want to do what's best for the child?" The mayor's voice had softened, taking on a cajoling tone.

"Is sending her away from her home what's best? Would you send your — " Ras cut himself off, paling.

The mayor lay back against his pillows. "No, I wouldn't send my own child away. But if he chose to go, I'd let him." He smiled at Ras sadly. "You and I have similar problems, my friend. Thank you for reminding me." He put his hands behind his head and stared up at the ceiling for long moments.

"You can't send her away," Ras said. "It's just the same as selling her as a bondservant."

"Ras, my friend," the mayor said gently.

"Don't try to tell me any different. I know better and so will everyone else."

"But the benefits — "

"Do you really believe anyone would offer this poor little thing the chance to be a healer? The idea's crazy."

Melissa glanced quickly, surreptitiously, at Snake, her emotions as always masked, then lowered her gaze again.

"I don't like being called a liar," Snake said.

"Healer, Ras didn't mean that the way it sounded. Let's all be calm. We aren't talking so much about reality as appearances. Appearances are very important and they're what people believe. I have to take that into account. Don't think it's easy keeping this office. More than one young firebrand — and some who aren't so young — would move me out of my home if I gave them a chance. No matter that I've been here twenty years. A charge of bonding — " He shook his head.

Snake watched him talk himself back toward refusal, helpless to turn him toward acceptance. Ras had known exactly what arguments would affect him most, while Snake had assumed that she would be trusted, or at the very least be given her own way. But the possible healer's interdict against Mountainside was a future problem, made even more serious by how rare healers' visits to the town had become in recent years.

If the mayor could risk accepting her ultimatum, Snake could not risk bringing it into force. She could not chance leaving Melissa with Ras another day, another hour; Snake had put her in too much danger. What was more, she had shown her dislike of the stablemaster, so the mayor might not believe what she said about him. Even if Melissa accused him, there was no proof. Snake searched desperately for another way to win Melissa's freedom; she hoped she had not already ruined any chance of gaining it directly.

She spoke as calmly as she could. "I withdraw my request."

Melissa caught her breath but did not look up again. The mayor's expression turned to one of relief, and Ras sat back in his chair.

"On one condition," Snake said. She paused to choose her words well, to say only what could be proven. "On one condition. When Gabriel leaves, he's going north. Let Melissa go with him, as far as Middlepath." Snake said nothing about Gabriel's plans; they were his business and no one else's. "A fine women's teacher lives there, and she wouldn't turn down anyone who needed her guidance."

A small damp patch widened on the front of Melissa's shirt, as tears fell silently on the rough material. Snake hurried on.

"Let Melissa go with Gabriel. Her training might take longer than usual because she's so old to start. But it's for her health and her safety. Even if Ras loves — " she almost choked on the word — "loves her too much to give her up to the healers, he won't keep her from this."

Ras's ruddy complexion paled.

"Middlepath?" The mayor scowled. "We have perfectly good teachers here. Why does she need to go to Middlepath?"

"I know you value beauty," Snake said, "but I think you also value self-control. Let Melissa learn the skills, even if she has to go elsewhere to find a teacher."

"Do you mean to tell me this child has never been to one?"

"Of course she has!" Ras cried. "It's a trick to get the girl out of our protection! You think you can come to a place and change everybody around to suit yourself!" Ras yelled at Snake. "Now you think people will believe anything you and that ungrateful little brat can make up about me. Everybody else is afraid of you and your slimy reptiles, but I'm not. Set one on me, go ahead, and I'll mash it flat!" He stopped abruptly and glanced right and left as if he had forgotten where he was. He had no way to make a dramatic exit.

"You needn't guard yourself against serpents," Snake said.

Ignoring him, ignoring Snake, the mayor leaned toward Melissa. "Child, have you been to a women's teacher?"

Melissa hesitated, but finally she answered. "I don't know what that is."

"No one would accept her," Ras said.

"Don't be ridiculous. Our teachers don't refuse people. Did you take her to one or not?"

Ras stared at his knees and said nothing more.

"It's easy enough to check."

"No, sir."

"No! *No?*" The mayor flung off the bedclothes and got up, stumbling but catching himself. He stood over Ras, a big man confronting another big man, two huge handsome creatures facing each other, one livid, one pale before the other's rage.

"Why not?"

"She doesn't need a teacher."

"How dare you do such a thing!" The mayor leaned forward until Ras was pressed back in the chair away from him. "How dare you endanger her! How dare you condemn her to ignorance and discomfort!"

"She isn't in danger! She doesn't need to protect herself — who would ever touch her?"

"You touch me!" Melissa ran to Snake and flung herself against her. Snake hugged the child close.

"You — " The mayor straightened and stepped back. Brian, appearing silently, supported him before his leg failed him. "What does she mean, Ras? Why is she so frightened?"

Ras shook his head.

"Make him say it!" Melissa cried, facing them squarely. "Make him!"

The mayor limped to her and stooped down awkwardly. He looked Melissa directly in the face. Neither he nor she flinched.

"I know you're frightened of him, Melissa. Why is he so frightened of you?"

"Because Mistress Snake believes me."

The mayor drew in a long breath. "Did you want him?"

"No," she whispered.

"Ungrateful little brat!" Ras yelled. "Spiteful ugly thing! Who else but me would ever touch her?"

The mayor ignored Ras and took Melissa's hand in both his.

"The healer's your guardian from now on. You're free to go with her."

"Thank you. Thank you, sir."

The mayor lurched back to his feet. "Brian, find me her guardianship papers in the city records — Sit down, Ras — And Brian, I'll want a messenger to ride into town. To the menders."

"You slaver," Ras growled. "So this is how you steal children. People will — "

"Shut up, Ras." The mayor sounded exhausted far beyond his brief exertion, and he was pale. "I can't exile you. I have a responsibility to protect other people. Other children. Your troubles are my troubles now, and they must be resolved. Will you talk to the menders?"

"I don't need the menders."

"Will you go voluntarily or would you prefer a trial?"

Ras lowered himself slowly back into the chair, and finally nodded. "Voluntarily," he said.

Snake stood up, her arm around Melissa's shoulders, Melissa with an arm around her waist and her head turned slightly so the scar was almost concealed. Together they walked away.

"Thank you, healer," the mayor said.

"Good-bye," Snake said, and shut the door.

She and Melissa walked through the echoing hallway to the second tower.

"I was so scared," Melissa said.

"So was I. For a little while I thought I'd have to steal you."

Melissa looked up. "Would you really do that?"

"Yes."

Melissa was silent for a moment. "I'm sorry," she said.

"Sorry! What for?"

"I should have trusted you. I didn't. But I will from now on. I won't be scared any more."

"You had a right to be scared, Melissa."

"I'm not now. I won't be any more. Where are we going?" For the first time since Melissa had offered to ride Squirrel, her voice held self-confidence and enthusiasm with no undertone of dread.

"Well," Snake said, "I think you should go on up north to the healers' station. Home."

"What about you?"

"I have one more thing I have to do before I can go home. Don't worry, you can go almost halfway with Gabriel. I'll write a letter for you to take, and you'll have Squirrel. They'll know I sent you."

"I'd rather go with you."

Realizing how shaken Melissa was, Snake stopped. "I'd rather have you come too, please believe me. But I have to go to Center and it might not be safe."

"I'm not afraid of any crazy. Besides, if I'm along we can keep watch."

Snake had forgotten about the crazy; the reminder brought a quick shock of memory.

"Yes, the crazy's another problem. But the storms are coming, it's nearly winter. I don't know if I can get back from the city before then." And it would be better for Melissa to become established at the station, before Snake returned, in case the trip to Center failed. Then, even if Snake had to leave, Melissa would be able to remain.

"I don't care about the storms," Melissa said. "I'm not afraid."

"I know you're not. It's just that there's no reason for you to be in danger."

Melissa did not reply. Snake knelt down and turned the child toward her.

"Do you think *I'm* trying to avoid you now?"

After a few moments, Melissa said, "I don't know what to think, Mistress Snake. You said if I didn't live here I could be responsible for myself and do what I thought was right. But I don't think it's right for me to leave you, with the crazy and the storms."

Snake sat back on her heels. "I did say all that. I meant it, too." She looked down at her scarred hands, sighed, and glanced up again at Melissa. "I better tell you the real reason I want you to go home. I should have told you before."

"What is it?" Melissa's voice was tight, controlled; she was ready to be hurt again. Snake took her hand.

"Most healers have three serpents. I only have two. I did something stupid and the third one was killed." She told Melissa about Arevin's people, about Stavin and Stavin's younger father and Grass.

"There aren't very many dreamsnakes," Snake said. "It's hard to make them breed. Actually we never make them breed, we just wait and hope they might. The way we get more is something like the way I made Squirrel."

"With the special medicine," Melissa said.

"Sort of." The alien biology of dreamsnakes lent itself neither to viral transduction nor to microsurgery. Earth viruses could not interact with the chemicals the dreamsnakes used in place of DNA, and the healers had been unsuccessful in isolating anything comparable to a virus from the alien serpents. So they could not transfer the genes for dreamsnake venom into another serpent, and no one had ever been successful in synthesizing all the venom's hundreds of components.

"I made Grass," Snake said, "and four other dreamsnakes. But I can't make them anymore. My hands aren't steady enough, the same thing's wrong with them that was wrong with my knee yesterday." Sometimes she wondered if her arthritis was as much psychological as physical, a reaction against sitting in the laboratory for hours at a time, delicately manipulating the controls of the micropipette and straining her eyes to find each of the innumerable nuclei in a single cell from a dreamsnake. She had been the first healer in some years to succeed in transplanting genetic material into an unfertilized ovum. She had had to prepare several hundred to end up with Grass and his four siblings; even so, her percentage was better than that of anyone else who had ever managed the task. No one at all had ever discovered what made the serpents mature. So the healers had a small stock of frozen immature ova, gleaned from the bodies of dreamsnakes that had died, but no one could clone them; and a frozen stock of what was probably dreamsnake sperm, cells too immature to fertilize the ova when they were mixed in a test tube.

Snake believed her success to be a matter of luck as much as technique. If her people had the technology needed to build one of the electron microscopes described in their books, she felt sure they would find genes independent of the nuclear bodies, molecules so small they could not be seen, too small to transplant unless the micropipette sucked them up by chance.

"I'm going to Center to deliver a message, and to ask the people there to help us get more dreamsnakes. But I'm afraid they'll refuse. And if I have to go home without any, after I lost mine, I don't know what will happen. A few dreamsnakes might have hatched since I left, some might even have been cloned, but if not, I might not be allowed to be a healer. I can't be a good one without a dreamsnake."

"If there aren't any others they should give you one of the ones you made," Melissa said. "That's the only thing that's fair."

"It wouldn't be fair to the younger healers I gave them to, though," Snake said. "I'd have to go home and say to a brother or sister that they couldn't be a healer unless the dreamsnakes we have reproduce again." She let out her breath in a long sigh. "I want you to know all that. That's why I want you to go home before I do, so everyone gets a chance to know you. I had to get you away from Ras, but if you go home with me, I don't know for sure that things will be much better."

"Snake!" Melissa was angry. "No matter what, being with you will be better than — than being in Mountainside. I don't care what happens. Even if you hit me — "

"Melissa!" Snake said, as shocked as the child had been.

Melissa grinned, the right side of her mouth curving up slightly. "See?" she said.

"Okay."

"It'll be all right," Melissa said. "I don't care what happens at the healers' station. And I know the storms are dangerous. And I saw you after you fought the crazy, so I know he's dangerous too. But I still want to go with you. Please don't make me go with anybody else."

"You're sure."

Melissa nodded.

"All right," Snake said. She grinned. "I never adopted anybody before. Theories aren't the same when you actually have to start using them. We'll go together." In truth, she appreciated the complete confidence that Melissa, at least, had in her.

They walked down the hall hand in hand, swinging their arms like two children instead of a child and an adult. Then they rounded the last corner and Melissa suddenly pulled back. Gabriel was sitting outside Snake's door, saddle-pack by his side, his chin on his drawn-up knees.

"Gabriel," Snake said.

He looked up, and this time he did not flinch when he saw Melissa.

"Hello," he said to her. "I'm sorry."

Melissa had turned toward Snake so the worst of the scar was hidden. "It's all right. Never mind. I'm used to it."

"I wasn't really awake last night . . ." Gabriel saw the look on Snake's face and fell silent.

Melissa glanced at Snake, who squeezed her hand, then at Gabriel, and back at Snake. "I better — I'll go get the horses ready."

"Melissa — " Snake reached for her but she fled. Snake watched her go, sighed, and opened the door to her room. Gabriel stood up.

"I'm sorry," he said again.

"You do have a knack." She went inside, picked up her saddlebags, and tossed them on the bed.

Gabriel followed her. "Please don't be angry with me."

"I'm not angry." She opened the flaps. "I was last night, but I'm not now."

"I'm glad." Gabriel sat on the bed and watched her pack. "I'm ready to leave. But I wanted to say good-bye. And thank you. And I'm sorry . . ."

"No more of that," Snake said.

"All right."

Snake folded her clean desert robes and put them in the saddlebag.

"Why don't I go with you?" Gabriel leaned forward anxiously with his elbows on his knees. "It must be easier to travel with someone to talk to than alone."

"I won't be alone. Melissa's coming with me."

"Oh." He sounded hurt.

"I'm adopting her, Gabriel. Mountainside isn't a place for her — no more it is for you, right now. I can help her, but I can't do anything for you. Except make you dependent on me. I don't want to do that. You'll never find your strengths without your freedom."

Snake put the sack with her toothpowder and comb and aspirin and soap into the saddlebag, buckled the flap, and sat down. She took Gabriel's soft strong hand.

"Here they make it too hard for you. I could make it too easy. Neither way is right."

He lifted her hand and kissed it, the tanned, scarred back and the cup of her palm.

"You see how fast you learn?" She brushed her other hand across his fair fine hair.

"Will I ever see you again?"

"I don't know," Snake said. "Probably not." She smiled. "You won't need to."

"I'd like to," he said wistfully.

"Go out in the world," Snake said. "Take your life in your hands and make it what you want."

He stood up, leaned down, and kissed her. Rising, she kissed him back more gently than she wanted to, wishing they had more time, wishing she had met him first in a year or so. She spread her fingers across his back and turned the embrace into a hug.

"Good-bye, Gabriel."

"Good-bye, Snake."

The door closed softly behind him.

Snake let Mist and Sand out of the serpent case for a short spell of freedom before the long trip. They glided over her feet and around her legs as she looked out the window.

There was a knock on Snake's door.

"Just a minute." She let Mist crawl up her arm and over her shoulder, and picked Sand up in both hands. It would not be long before he would grow too large to coil comfortably around her wrist.

"You can come in now."

Brian entered, then stepped back abruptly.

"It's all right," Snake said. "They're calm."

Brian retreated no farther but watched the serpents carefully. Their heads turned in unison whenever Snake moved; their tongues flicked out and in as the cobra and the rattler peered at Brian and tasted his odor.

"I brought the child's papers," Brian said. "They prove you are her guardian now."

Snake coiled Sand around her right arm and took the papers left-handed. Brian gave them to her gingerly. Snake looked at them with curiosity. The parchment was stiff and crinkly, heavy with wax seals. The mayor's spidery signature was on one corner, Ras's opposite, elaborate and shaky.

"Is there any way Ras can challenge this?"

"He could," Brian said. "But I think he will not. If he claims he was compelled to sign, he will have to say what the compulsion was. And then he would have other . . . compulsions . . . to explain. I think he prefers a voluntary retreat to a publicly enforced one."

"Good."

"Something else, healer."

"Yes?"

He handed her a small heavy bag. Inside, coins touched with the clear hard sound of gold. Snake glanced at Brian quizzically.

"Your payment," he said, and offered her a receipt and a pen to sign it with.

"Is the mayor still afraid he'll be accused of bonding?"

"It could happen," Brian said. "It's best to be on guard."

Snake amended the receipt to read "Accepted for my daughter, in payment of her wages for horse training," signed it, and handed it back.

Brian read it slowly.

"I think that's better," Snake said. "It's only fair to Melissa, and if she's being paid she obviously isn't bonded."

"It's more proof you've adopted her," Brian said. "I think it will satisfy the mayor."

Snake slipped the coin bag into a pocket and let Mist and Sand slide back into their compartments. She shrugged. "All right. It doesn't matter. As long as Melissa can leave." Suddenly she felt depressed, and she wondered if she had held so firmly and arrogantly to her own will that she had disarranged the lives of others to no benefit for them. She did not doubt she had done the right thing for Melissa, at least in freeing her from Ras. Whether Gabriel was better off, or the mayor, or even Ras . . .

Mountainside was a rich town, and most of the people seemed happy; certainly they were more content and safer now than they had been before the mayor took office twenty years before. But what good had that done the children of his own household? Snake was glad to be leaving, and she was glad, for good or ill, that Gabriel was going too.

"Healer?"

"Yes, Brian?"

From behind, he touched her shoulder quickly and withdrew. "Thank you." When Snake turned a moment later, he had already, silently, disappeared.

As the door to her room swung softly shut, Snake heard the hollow thud of the big front door closing in the courtyard. She looked out the window again. Below, Gabriel mounted his big pinto horse. He looked down into the valley, then slowly turned until he faced the window of his father's room. He gazed at it for a long time. Snake did not look across at the other tower, for she could tell from watching the young man that his father did not appear. Gabriel's shoulders slumped, then straightened, and when he glanced toward Snake's tower his expression was calm. He saw her and smiled a sad, self-deprecating smile. She waved to him. He waved back.

A few minutes later Snake still watched as the pinto horse switched his long black and white tail and disappeared around the last visible turn in the northbound trail. Other hooves clattered in the courtyard below. Snake returned her thoughts to her own journey. Melissa, riding Squirrel and leading Swift, looked up and beckoned to her. Snake smiled and nodded, threw her saddlebags over her shoulder, picked up the serpent case, and went to join her daughter.

The wind in Arevin's face felt cool and clean. He was grateful for the mountain climate, free of dust and heat and the ever present sand. At the crest of a pass he stood beside his horse and looked out over the countryside Snake had been raised in. The land was bright and very green, and he could both see and hear great quantities of free-flowing water. A river meandered through the center of the valley below, and a stone's throw from the trail a spring gushed across mossy rock. His respect for Snake increased. Her people did not migrate; they lived here all year around. She would have had little experience with extreme climates when she entered the desert. This was no preparation for the black sand waste. Arevin himself had not been prepared for the central desert's severity. His maps were old; no member of the clan still living had ever used them. But they had led him safely to the other side of the desert, following a line of trustworthy oases. It was so late in the season that he had met no one at all: no one to ask advice about the best route, no one to ask about Snake.

He mounted his horse and rode down the trail into the healers' valley.

Before he encountered any dwellings he reached a small orchard. It was unusual: the trees farthest from the road were full-grown, gnarled, while the nearest ones were merely saplings, as if a few trees had been planted every year for many years. A youth of fourteen or fifteen lounged in the shade, eating a piece of fruit. When Arevin stopped, the young man glanced up, rose, and started toward him. Arevin urged his horse across the grassy edge of the meadow. They met in a row of trees that seemed perhaps five or six years old.

"Hi," the young man said. He picked another piece of fruit and held it out toward Arevin. "Have a pear? The peaches and the cherries are all gone and the oranges aren't quite ripe yet."

Arevin saw that, in fact, each tree bore fruit of several different shapes, but leaves of only a single shape. He reached uncertainly for the pear, wondering if the ground the trees grew on was poisoned.

"Don't worry," the young man said. "It isn't radioactive. There aren't any craters around here."

At this Arevin drew back his hand. He had not said a word, yet the youth seemed to know what he was thinking.

"I made the tree myself, and I never work with hot mutagens."

Arevin had no idea what the boy was talking about except that he seemed to be assuring him that the fruit was safe. He wished he understood the boy as well as the boy understood him. Not wishing to be impolite, he took the pear.

"Thank you." Since the youth was watching him both hopefully and expectantly, Arevin bit into the fruit. It was sweet and tart at the same time, and very juicy. He took another bite. "It's very good," he said. "I've never seen a plant that would produce four different things."

"First project," the boy said. He gestured back toward the older trees. "We all do one. It's pretty simple-minded but it's traditional."

"I see," Arevin said.

"My name's Thad."

"I am honored to meet you," Arevin said. "I am looking for Snake."

"Snake!" Thad frowned. "I'm afraid you've had a long ride for nothing. She isn't here. She isn't even due back for months."

"But I could not have passed her."

Thad's pleasant and helpful expression changed to one of worry. "You mean she's coming home already? What happened? Is she all right?"

"She was well when I saw her last," Arevin said. Surely she should have reached her home well ahead of him, if nothing had happened. Thoughts of accidents, unlike viper bites, to which she would be vulnerable, assailed him.

"Hey, are you all right?"

Thad was beside him, holding his elbow to steady him.

"Yes," Arevin said, but his voice was shaky.

"Are you sick? I'm not done with my training yet but one of the other healers can help you."

"No, no, I'm not ill. But I can't understand how I reached this place before she did."

"But why's she coming home so early?"

Arevin gazed down at the intent young man, now as concerned as Arevin himself.

"I do not think I should tell her story for her," he said. "Perhaps I should speak to her parents. Will you show me where they live?"

"I would if I could," Thad said. "Only she doesn't have any. Won't I do? I'm her brother."

"I'm sorry to cause you distress. I did not know your parents were dead."

"They aren't. Or they might be. I don't know. I mean I don't know who they are. Or who Snake's are."

Arevin felt thoroughly confused. He had never had any trouble understanding what Snake said to him. But he did not think he had comprehended half of what this youth had told him in only a few minutes.

"If you do not know who your parents are, or whose Snake's are, how can you be her brother?"

Thad looked at him quizzically. "You really don't know much about healers, do you?"

"No," Arevin said, feeling that the conversation had taken

still another unexplained turn. "I do not. We have heard of you, of course, but Snake is the only one to visit my clan."

"The reason I asked," Thad said, "is because most people know we're all adopted. We don't have families, exactly. We're all one family."

"Yet you said you are her brother, as if she did not have another." Except for his blue eyes, and they were not the same shade at all, Thad did not look anything like Snake.

"That's how we think of each other. I used to get in trouble a lot when I was a kid and she'd always stick up for me."

"I see." Arevin dismounted and adjusted his horse's bridle, considering what the boy had told him. "You are not blood kin with Snake," he said, "but you feel a special relationship to her. Is this correct?"

"Yes." Thad's easygoing attitude had vanished.

"If I tell you why I have come, will you advise me, thinking first of Snake, even if you should have to go against your own customs?"

Arevin was glad the youth hesitated, for he would not have been able to depend on an impulsive and emotional answer.

"Something really bad has happened, hasn't it?"

"Yes," Arevin said. "And she blames herself."

"You feel a special relationship for her, too, don't you?"

"Yes."

"And she for you?"

"I think so."

"I'm on her side," Thad said. "Always."

Arevin unbuckled the horse's bridle and slipped it off so his mount could graze. He sat down beneath Thad's fruit tree and the boy sat nearby.

"I come from the other side of the western desert," Arevin said. "There we have no good serpents, only sand vipers whose bite means death . . ."

Arevin told his story and waited for Thad to respond, but the young healer stared at his scarred hands for a long time.

"Her dreamsnake was killed," he said finally.

Thad's voice held shock and hopelessness; the tone chilled Arevin all the way to his almost impervious, controlled center.

"It was not her fault," Arevin said again, though he had continually stressed that fact. Thad now knew about the clan's fear of serpents and even about Arevin's sister's horrible death. But Arevin could see quite clearly that Thad did not understand.

The boy looked up at him. "I don't know what to tell you," he said. "This is really awful." He paused and looked around and rubbed the heel of his hand across his forehead. "I guess we better talk to Silver. She was one of Snake's teachers and she's the eldest now."

Arevin hesitated. "Is that wise? Pardon me, but if you, Snake's friend, cannot comprehend how all this happened, will any of the other healers be able to?"

"I understand what happened!"

"You know what happened," Arevin said. "But you do not understand it. I do not want to offend you, but I fear what I say is true."

"It doesn't matter," Thad said. "I still want to help her. Silver will think of something to do."

The exquisite valley in which the healers lived combined areas of total wilderness with places of complete civilization. What appeared to Arevin to be virgin climax forest, ancient and unchanging, spread as far as he could see, beginning on the north slope of the valley. Yet immediately downhill from the tremendous dark old trees, an array of windmills spun gaily. The forest of trees and the forest of windmills harmonized.

The station was a serene place, a small town of well-built wood and stone houses. People greeted Thad or waved to him, and nodded to Arevin. The faint shouts of a children's game drifted down the breeze.

Thad left Arevin's horse loose in a pasture, then led Arevin to a building somewhat larger than the others, and somewhat removed from the main group. Inside, Arevin was surprised to observe, the walls were not of wood but of smooth white glazed ceramic tile. Even where there were no windows, the illumination was as bright as day, neither the eerie blue glow of bioluminescence nor the soft yellow light of gas flames. The place possessed a feeling of activity quite different from the placid atmosphere of the town itself. Through a half-open door Arevin saw several young people, younger even than Thad, bending over complicated instruments, completely absorbed in their work.

Thad gestured toward the students. "These are the labs. We grind the lenses for the microscopes right here at the station. Make our own glassware too."

Almost all the people Arevin saw here — and, now that he thought of it, most of the people in the village — were either very young or elderly. The young ones in training, he thought, and the old ones teaching. Snake and the others out practicing their profession.

Thad climbed a flight of stairs, went down a carpeted hall, and knocked softly on a door. They waited for several minutes, and Thad seemed to think this quite ordinary, for he did not become impatient. Finally a pleasant, rather high-pitched voice said, "Come in."

The room beyond was not so stark and severe as the labs. It was wood-paneled, with a large window overlooking the windmills. Arevin had heard of books, but he had never actually seen one. Here, two walls lined with shelves were full of them. The old healer sitting in a rocking chair held a book in her lap.

"Thad," she said, nodding, with a welcoming yet questioning tone.

"Silver." He brought Arevin in. "This is a friend of Snake's. He's come a long way to talk to us."

"Sit down." Her voice and her hands shook slightly. She was very old, her joints swollen and twisted. Her skin was smooth and soft and translucent, deeply lined on the cheeks and forehead. Her eyes were blue.

Following Thad's lead, Arevin sat on a chair. He felt uncomfortable; he was accustomed to sitting cross-legged on the ground.

"What do you wish to say?"

"Are you Snake's friend?" Arevin asked. "Or only her teacher?"

He thought she might laugh, but she gazed at him somberly. "Her friend."

"Silver nominated her for her name," Thad said. "Did you think I wanted you to talk to just anybody?"

Still, Arevin wondered if he should tell his story to this kindly old woman, for he remembered Snake's words all too clearly: "My teachers seldom give the name I bear, and they'll be disappointed." Perhaps Silver's disappointment would be great enough to exile Snake from her people.

"Tell me what's wrong," Silver said. "Snake is my friend, and I love her. You need not fear me."

Arevin told his story for the second time that day, watching Silver's face intently. Her expression did not change. Surely, after all the experiences she must have had, she could understand what had happened better than young Thad could.

"Ah," she said. "Snake went across the desert." She shook her head. "My brave and impulsive child."

"Silver," Thad said, "what can we do?"

"I don't know, my dear." She sighed. "I wish Snake had come home."

"Surely the small serpents die," Arevin said. "Surely others have been lost in accidents. What is done?"

"They live a long time," Thad said. "Longer than their healers, sometimes. They don't breed well."

"Every year we train fewer people because we have too few dreamsnakes," Silver said in her feathery voice.

"Snake's excellence must entitle her to another serpent," Arevin said.

"One cannot give what one does not have," Silver said.

"She thought some might have been born."

"Only a few ever hatched," the old woman said sadly.

Thad glanced away. "One of us might decide not to finish their training . . ."

"Thad," Silver said, "we haven't enough for all of you now. Do you think Snake would ask you to return the dreamsnake she gave you?"

Thad shrugged, still not meeting Silver's gaze or Arevin's. "She shouldn't have to ask. I should give it to her."

"We cannot decide without Snake," Silver said. "She must come home."

Arevin looked down at his hands, realizing that there would be no easy solution to this dilemma, no simple explanation of what had happened, then forgiveness for Snake.

"You mustn't punish her for my clan's error," he said again.

Silver shook her head. "It is not a question of punishment. But she cannot be a healer without a dreamsnake. I have none to give her."

They sat together in silence. After a few minutes Arevin wondered if Silver had fallen asleep. He started when she spoke to him without glancing away from the view out her window.

"Will you keep looking for her?"

"Yes," he said without hesitation.

"When you find her, please tell her to come home. The council will meet with her."

Thad rose, and with a deep sense of failure and depression Arevin understood that they had been dismissed.

They went back outside, leaving the workrooms and their strange machines, their strange light, their strange smells. The sun was setting, joining the long shadows together into darkness.

"Where shall I look?" Arevin said suddenly.

"What?"

"I came here because I believed Snake was coming home. Now I don't know where she might be. It's nearly winter. If the storms have started . . ."

"She knows better than to get stuck out on the desert in winter," Thad said. "No, what must have happened is somebody needed help and she had to go off the route home. Maybe her patient was even in the central mountains. She'll be somewhere south of here, in Middlepass or New Tibet or Mountainside."

"All right," Arevin said, grateful for any possibility. "I will go south." But he wondered if Thad were speaking with the unquestioning self-confidence of extreme youth.

Thad opened the front door of a long low house. Inside, rooms opened off a central living-space. Thad threw himself down on a deep couch. Putting aside careful manners, Arevin sat on the floor.

"Dinner's in a while," Thad said. "The room next to mine is free right now, you can use it."

"Perhaps I should go on," Arevin said.

"Tonight? It's crazy to ride at night around here. We'd find you at the bottom of a cliff in the morning. At least stay till tomorrow."

"If that is your advice." In fact, he felt a great heavy lethargy. He followed Thad into the spare room.

"I'll get your pack," Thad said. "You take a rest. You look like you need it."

Arevin sat down slowly on the edge of the bed.

At the door, Thad turned back. "Listen, I'd like to help. Is there anything I can do for you?"

"No," Arevin said. "Thank you. I am very comfortable."

Thad shrugged. "Okay."

The black-sand desert stretched to the horizon, flat and empty, unmarred by any sign that it had ever been crossed. Heat waves rose like smoke. There was no steady wind yet, but all the marks and detritus of the traders' route had already been obliterated: erased or covered by the shifting breezes that preceded winter. At the crest of the central mountains' eastern range, Snake and Melissa looked out toward their invisible destination. They dismounted to rest the horses. Melissa adjusted a strap on Squirrel's new riding saddle, then glanced back the way they had come, down into the high valley that had been her home. The town clung to the steep mountain slope, above the fertile valley floor. Windows and black glass panels glittered in the noon sun.

"I've never been this far from there before," Melissa said with wonder. "Not in my whole life." She turned away from the valley, toward Snake. "Thank you, Snake," she said.

"You're welcome, Melissa."

Melissa dropped her gaze. Her right cheek, the unscarred one, flushed scarlet beneath her tan. "I should tell you something about that."

"About what?"

"My name. It's true, what Ras said, that it isn't really — "

"Never mind. Melissa is your name as far as I'm concerned. I had a different child-name, too."

"But they gave you your name. It's an honor. You didn't just take it like I did mine."

They remounted and started down the well-used switchback trail.

"But I could have turned down the name they offered me," Snake said. "If I'd done that, I would have picked my own adult name like the rest of the healers do."

"You could have turned it down?"

"Yes."

"But they hardly ever give it! That's what I heard."

"That's true."

"Has anybody ever said they didn't want it?"

"Not as far as I know. I'm only the fourth one, though, so not very many people have had the chance. Sometimes I wish I hadn't accepted it."

"But why?"

"Because of the responsibility." Her hand rested on the corner of the serpent case. Since the crazy's attack she had begun to touch it more often. She drew her hand away from the smooth leather. Healers tended to die fairly young or live to a very old age. The Snake immediately preceding her had been only forty-three when he died, but the other two had each outlasted a century. Snake had a tremendous body of achievement to live up to, and so far she had failed.

The trail led downward through forever trees, among the gnarled brown trunks and dark needles of the trees legend said never bore seeds and never died. Their resin sharpened the air with a piny tang.

"Snake . . ." Melissa said.

"Yes?"

"Are you . . . are you my mother?"

Taken aback, Snake hesitated a moment. Her people did not form family groups quite the way others did. She herself had never called anyone "mother" or "father," though all the older healers bore exactly that relationship to her. And Melissa's tone was so wistful . . .

"All healers are your family now," Snake said, "but I adopted you, and I think that makes me your mother."

"I'm glad."

"So am I."

Below the narrow band of scraggly forest, almost nothing grew on the mountain's flanks but lichen, and though the altitude was still high and the path steep, Snake and Melissa might as well have been on the desert floor already. Below the trees, the heat and the dryness of the air increased steadily. When they finally did reach the sand, they stopped for a moment to change, Snake into the robes Arevin's people had given her, Melissa into desert clothes they had bought for her in Mountainside.

They saw no one all day. Snake glanced over her shoulder from time to time, and kept on guard whenever the horses passed through dunefields where someone could hide and ambush unsuspecting passersby. But there was no trace of the crazy. Snake began to wonder if the two attacks might have been coincidence, and her memories of other noises around her camp a dream. And if the crazy *was* a crazy, perhaps his vendetta against her had by now been diverted by some other irresistible concern.

She did not convince herself.

By evening the mountains lay far behind them, forming an abrupt wall. The horses' hooves crunched in the sand, but the underlying silence was complete and unearthly. Snake and Melissa rode and talked as darkness fell. The heavy clouds obscured the moon; the constant glow of the lightcells in Snake's lantern, relatively brighter now, provided just enough illumination for the travelers to continue. Hanging from the saddle, the lantern swung with Swift's walk. The black sand reflected light like water. Squirrel and Swift moved closer together. Gradually, Snake and Melissa talked more and more softly, and finally they did not speak at all.

Snake's compass, the nearly invisible moon, the direction of the wind, the shapes of sand dunes all helped them proceed in the right direction, but Snake could not put aside the pervasive wilderness fear that she was traveling in circles. Turning in the saddle, Snake watched the invisible trail behind them for several minutes, but no other light followed. They were alone; there was nothing but the darkness. Snake settled back.

"It's spooky," Melissa whispered.

"I know. I wish we could travel by day."

"Maybe it'll rain."

"That would be nice."

The desert received rain only once every year or two, but

when it came, it usually arrived just before winter. Then the dormant seeds exploded into growth and reproduction and the sharp-grained desert softened with green and bits of color. In three days the delicate plants shriveled to brown lace and died, leaving hard-cased seeds to endure another year, or two, or three, until the rain roused them again. But tonight the air was dry and quiet and gave no hint of any change.

A light shimmered in the distance. Snake, dozing, woke abruptly from a dream in which the crazy was following and she saw his lantern moving closer and closer. Up until now she had not realized how sure she was that somehow he was still following her, still somewhere near, fired by incomprehensible motives.

But the light was not a carried lantern, it was steady and stationary and ahead of her. The sound of dry leaves drifted toward her on faint wind: they were nearing the first oasis on the route to Center.

It was not even dawn. Snake reached forward and patted Swift's neck. "Not much farther now," she said.

"What?" Melissa, too, started awake. "Where — ?"

"It's all right," Snake said. "We can stop soon."

"Oh." Melissa looked around, blinking. "I forgot where I was."

They reached the summertrees ringing the oasis. Snake's lantern illuminated leaves already split and frayed by windblown sand. Snake did not see any tents and she could not hear any sounds of people or animals. All the caravannaires, by now, had retreated to the safety of the mountains.

"Where's that light?"

"I don't know," Snake said. She glanced at Melissa, for her voice sounded strange: it was muffled by the end of her headcloth, pulled across her face. When no one appeared, she let it drop as if unaware that she had been hiding herself.

Snake turned Swift around, worried about the light.

"Look," Melissa said.

Swift's body cut off the lantern's light in one direction, and there against the darkness rose a streak of luminescence. Closer, Snake could see that it was a dead summertree, close enough to the water to rot instead of drying. Lightcells had invaded its fragile trunk, transforming it into a glowing signal. Snake breathed softly with relief.

They rode farther, circling the still, black pool until they found a site with trees thick enough to give some shelter. As soon as Snake reined in, Melissa jumped down and began unsaddling Squirrel. Snake climbed down more slowly, for despite the constant desert climate, her knee had stiffened again during the long ride. Melissa rubbed Squirrel with a twist of leaves, talking to him in a barely audible voice. Soon they were all, horses and people, bedded down to wait through the day.

Snake padded barefoot toward the water, stretching and yawning. She had slept well all day, and now she wanted a swim before starting out again. It was still too early to leave the shelter of the thick summertrees. Hoping to find a few pieces of ripe fruit still on the branches, she glanced up and around, but the desert dwellers' harvest had been thorough.

Only a few days before, on the other side of the mountains, the foliage at the oases had been lush and soft; here, now, the leaves were dry and dying. They rustled as she brushed past. The brittle fronds crumbled in her hand.

She stopped where the beach began. The black strip was only a few meters wide, a semicircle of sand around a minuscule lagoon that reflected the overhanging latticework of branches. In the secluded spot, Melissa was kneeling half-naked on the sand. She leaned out over the water, staring silently downward. The marks of Ras's beating had faded, and the fire had left her back unscarred. Her skin was fairer than Snake would have guessed from her deep-tanned hands and face. As Snake watched, Melissa reached out slowly and touched the surface of the dark water. Ripples spread from her fingertips.

*

Melissa watched, fascinated, as Snake let Mist and Sand out of the case. Mist glided around Snake's feet, tasting the scents of the oasis. Snake picked her up gently. The smooth white scales were cool against her hands.

"I want her to smell you," Snake said. "Her instinctive reaction is to strike at anything that startles her. If she recognizes your scent, it's safer. All right?"

Melissa nodded slowly, clearly frightened. "She's very poisonous, isn't she? More than the other?"

"Yes. As soon as we get home I can immunize you, but I don't want to start that here. I have to test you first and I don't have the right things with me."

"You mean you can fix it so she'd bite me and nothing would happen?"

"Not quite nothing. But she's bitten me by mistake a few times and I'm still here."

"I guess I better let her smell me," Melissa said.

Snake sat down next to her. "I know it's hard not to be afraid of her. But breathe deeply and try to relax. Close your eyes and just listen to my voice."

"Horses know it, too, when you're afraid," Melissa said, and did as Snake told her.

The cobra's forked tongue flickered over Melissa's hands, and the child remained still and silent. Snake remembered the first time she had seen the albino cobras: a terrifying, exhilarating moment when a mass of them, coiled together in infinite knots, felt her footsteps and lifted their heads in unison, hissing, like a many-headed beast or an alien plant in violent and abrupt full bloom.

Snake kept her hand on Mist as the cobra glided over Melissa's arms.

"She feels nice," Melissa said. Her voice was shaky, and a little scared, but the tone was sincere.

Melissa had seen rattlers before; their danger was a known one and not so frightening. Sand crawled across her hands and she stroked him gently. Snake was pleased; her daughter's abilities were not limited to horses.

"I hoped you'd get along with Mist and Sand," she said. "It's important for a healer."

Melissa looked up, startled. "But you didn't mean — " She stopped.

"What?"

Melissa drew in a deep breath. "What you told the mayor," she said hesitantly. "About what I could do. You didn't really mean it. You had to say it so he'd let me go."

"I meant everything I said."

"But I couldn't be a healer."

"Why not?" Melissa did not answer, so Snake continued. "I told you healers adopt their children, because we can't have any of our own. Let me tell you some more about us. A lot of healers have partners who have different professions. And not all our children become healers. We aren't a closed community. But when we choose someone to adopt, we usually pick someone we think could be one of us."

"Me?"

"Yes. If you want to. That's the important thing. For you to do what you want to do. Not what you think anyone else wants or expects you to do."

"A healer . . ." Melissa said.

The quality of wonder in her daughter's voice gave Snake another compelling reason to make the city people help her find more dreamsnakes.

The second night Snake and Melissa rode hard. There was no oasis, and in the morning Snake did not stop at dawn, though it was really too hot to travel. Sweat drenched her. The sticky beads rolled down her back and sides. They slid halfway down her face and dried into salty grit. Swift's coat darkened as sweat streamed down her legs. Every step flung droplets from her fetlocks.

"Mistress . . ."

The formality startled Snake and she glanced over at Melissa with concern. "Melissa, what's wrong?"

"How much farther before we stop?"

"I don't know. We have to go on as long as we can." She gestured toward the sky, where the clouds hung low and threatening. "That's what they look like before a storm."

"I know. But we can't go much longer. Squirrel and Swift have to rest. You said the city is in the middle of the desert. Well, once we get in we have to get back out, and the horses have to take us."

Snake slumped back in her saddle. "We have to go on. It's too dangerous to stop."

"Snake . . . Snake, you know about people and storms and healing and deserts and cities, and I don't. But I know about horses. If we let them stop and rest for a few hours, they'll take us a far way tonight. If they have to keep going, by dark we'll have to leave them behind."

"All right," Snake said finally. "We'll stop when we get to those rocks. At least there'll be some shade."

At home in the healers' station, Snake did not think of the city from one month to the next. But in the desert, and in the mountains where the caravannaires wintered, life revolved around it. Snake had begun to feel that her life too depended on it when at last, at dawn after the third night, the high, truncated mountain that protected Center appeared before her. The sun rose directly behind it, illuminating it in scarlet like an idol. Scenting water, sensing an end to their long trek, the horses raised their heads and quickened their tired pace. As the sun rose higher the low, thickening clouds spread the light into a red wash that covered the horizon. Snake's knee ached with every step Swift took, but she did not need the signal of swollen joints to tell her a storm approached. Snake clenched her fists around the reins until the leather dug painfully into her palms, then slowly she relaxed her hands and stroked her horse's damp neck. She had no doubt that Swift ached as much as she did.

They approached the mountain. The summertrees were brown and withered, rustling stalks surrounding a dark pond and deserted firepits. The wind whispered between the dry leaves and over the sand, coming first from one direction, then another, in the manner of winds near a solitary mountain. The city's sunrise shadow enveloped them.

"It's a lot bigger than I thought," Melissa said quietly. "I used to have a place where I could hide and listen to people talk, but I always thought they were making up stories."

"I think I did too," Snake said. Her own voice sounded very lost and far away. As she approached the great rock cliffs, cold sweat broke out on her forehead, and her hands grew clammy despite the heat. The tired mare carried her forward.

The times the city had dominated the healers' station were the year Snake was seven, and again when she was seventeen. In each of those years a senior healer undertook the long hard journey to Center. Each of those years was the beginning of a new decade, when the healers offered the city dwellers an exchange of knowledge and of help. They were always turned away. Perhaps this time, too, despite the message Snake had to give them.

"Snake?"

Snake started and glanced over at Melissa. "What?"

"Are you okay? You looked so far away, and, I don't know— "

" 'Scared' would be a good word, I think," Snake said.

"They'll let us in."

The dark clouds seemed to grow thicker and heavier every minute.

"I hope so," Snake said.

At the base of Center's mountain, the wide dark pool had neither inlets nor outlets. The water oozed up into it from below, then flowed invisibly away into the sand. The summer-trees were dead, but the ground cover of grass and low bushes grew lushly. Fresh grass already sprouted in the trampled areas of abandoned camps and the paths between, but not on the wide road to the city's gate.

Snake did not have the heart to ride Swift past the water. She handed her reins to Melissa at the edge of the pool.

"Follow me when they're finished drinking. I won't go in without you, so don't worry. If the wind rises, though, come running. Okay?"

Melissa nodded. "A storm couldn't come that quick, could it?"

"I'm afraid it could," Snake said.

She drank quickly and splashed water on her face. Wiping the drops on the corner of her headcloth she strode along the bare road. Somewhere close beneath the black sand lay a smooth, unyielding surface. An ancient road? She had seen remains in other places, disintegrating concrete flesh and even the rusting steel bones in places the collectors had not yet worked.

Snake stopped before Center's gate. It was five times her height. Generations of sandstorms had brushed the metal to a lustrous finish. But it had no handle, no bellpull, no door knocker, no way Snake could see of summoning someone to let her in.

She stepped forward, raised her fist, and banged it against the metal. The solid thud sounded not at all hollow. She pounded on the door, thinking it must be very thick. As her eyes grew more accustomed to the dim light in the recessed doorway, she saw that the front of the door was actually concave, perceptibly worn down by the fury of the storms.

Her hand aching, she stepped back for a moment.

"About time you stopped that noise."

Snake jumped at the voice and turned toward it, but no one was there. Instead, in the side of the alcove, a panel clicked away into the rock and a window appeared. A pale man with bushy red hair glared out at her.

"What do you mean, beating on the door after we've closed?"

"I want to come in," Snake said.

"You're not a city dweller."

"No. My name is Snake. I'm a healer."

He did not answer — as politeness dictated where Snake had been raised — with his name. She hardly noticed, for she was getting used to the differences that made politeness in one place an offense somewhere else. But when he threw back his head and laughed, she was surprised. She frowned and waited until he stopped.

"So they've quit sending old crocks to beg, have they? It's young ones now!" He laughed again. "I'd think they could choose somebody handsome."

From his tone, Snake assumed she had been insulted. She shrugged. "Open the gate."

He stopped laughing. "We don't let outsiders in."

"I've brought a message from a friend to her family. I want to deliver it."

He did not answer for a moment, glancing down. "All the people who went out came back in this year."

"She left a long time ago."

"You don't know much about this city if you expect me to go running around it looking for some crazy's family."

"I know nothing about your city. But from the looks of you, you're related to my friend."

"What's that supposed to mean?" For the first time he was taken aback.

"She told me her family was related to the keepers of the gate. And I can see it — the hair, the forehead . . . the eyes are different. Hers are brown." This city dweller's eyes were pale green.

"Did she happen to mention," the young man said, attempting sarcasm, "just exactly which family she's supposed to belong to?"

"The ruling one."

"Just a minute," he said slowly. He glanced down and his

hands moved, out of Snake's view, but when she moved closer she could see nothing beyond the edge of the "window," for it was not a window but a glass panel carrying a moving image. Though startled, she did not permit herself to react. She had known, after all, that the city dwellers had more mechanical technology than her people. That was one of the reasons she was here.

The young man looked up slowly, one eyebrow arched in astonishment. "I'll have to call someone else to talk to you." The image on the glass panel dissolved in multicolored lines.

Nothing happened for some time. Snake leaned outside the shallow alcove and looked around.

"Melissa!"

Neither the child nor the horses were in sight. Snake could see most of the pool's near shore through a translucent curtain of withered summertrees, but in a few places enough vegetation remained to hide two horses and a child.

"Melissa!" Snake called again.

Again there was no answer, but the wind could have carried her voice away. The false window had turned dead black. Snake was about to leave it to find her daughter when it wavered back to life.

"Where are you?" a new voice called. "Come back here."

Snake glanced outside one last time and returned reluctantly to the image-carrier.

"You upset my cousin rather badly," the image said.

Snake stared at the panel, speechless, for the speaker was astonishingly like Jesse, much more so than the younger man. This was Jesse's twin, or her family was highly inbred. As the figure spoke again the thought passed through Snake's mind that inbreeding was a useful way of concentrating and setting desired traits, if the experimenter were prepared for a few spectacular failures among the results. Snake was unprepared for the implied acceptance of spectacular failures in human births.

"Hello? Is this working?"

The red-haired figure peered out at her worriedly, and a loud hollow scratching noise followed the voice. The voice: Jesse's had been pleasant and low, but not this low. Snake realized she was speaking to a man, not to a woman as she had thought from the resemblance. Not Jesse's twin, then, certainly. Snake wondered if the city people cloned human beings. If they did it often and could even handle cross-sex clones, perhaps they had methods that would be more successful than those the healers used in making new dreamsnakes.

"I can hear you, if that's what you mean," Snake said.

"Good. What do you want? It must be worrisome from the look on Richard's face."

"I have a message for you if you're direct kin of the prospector Jesse," Snake said.

The man's pink cheeks whitened abruptly. "Jesse?" He shook his head, then regained his composure. "Has she changed that much in all these years, or do I look like anything but direct kin?"

"No," Snake said. "You look like kin."

"She's my older sister," he said. "And now I suppose she wants to come back and be the eldest again, while I'm to go back to being nothing but a younger?"

The bitterness of his voice was like a betrayal; Snake felt it like a shock. The news of Jesse's death would not bring sorrow to her brother, only joy.

"She's coming back, isn't she?" he said. "She knows the council would put her back at the head of our family. Damn her! I might as well not have existed for the last twenty years."

Snake listened to him, her throat tightening with grief. Despite the brother's resentment, if Snake had been able to keep Jesse alive, her people *would* have taken her back, welcomed her back: if they could, they would have healed her.

Snake spoke with some difficulty. "This council — perhaps I should give the message to them." She wanted to speak to someone who cared, someone who had loved Jesse, not to someone who would laugh and thank her for her failure.

"This is family business, not a matter for the council. You should give Jesse's message to me."

"I would prefer speaking to you face to face."

"I'm sure you would," he said. "But that's impossible. My cousins have a policy against letting in outsiders — "

"Surely, in this case — "

" — and besides, I couldn't even if I wanted to. The gate's locked till spring."

"I don't believe you."

"It's true."

"Jesse would have warned me."

He snorted. "She never believed it. She left when she was a child, and children never really believe. They play at staying out till the last minute, pretending they might get locked out. So sometimes we lose one who tests the rules too far."

"She stopped believing almost everything you say." Anger tightened Snake's voice.

Jesse's brother glanced away, intently watching something else for a moment. He looked at Snake again. "Well, I hope you believe what I tell you now. A storm's gathering, so I suggest you give me the message and leave yourself time to find shelter."

Even if he was lying to her, he was not going to let her inside. Snake no longer even hoped for that.

"Her message is this," Snake said. "She was happy out here. She wants you to stop lying to your children about what it's like outside your city."

Jesse's brother stared at Snake, waiting, then suddenly smiled and laughed once, quickly and sharply. "That's all? You mean she isn't coming back?"

"She cannot come back," Snake said. "She's dead."

A strange and eerie mixture of relief and sorrow passed over the face that was so like Jesse's.

"Dead?" he said softly.

"I could not save her. She broke her back — "

"I never wished her dead." He drew in a long breath, then let it out slowly. "Broke her back . . . a quick death, then. Better than some."

"She did not die when she broke her back. Her partners and I were going to bring her home, because you could heal her."

"Perhaps we could have," he said. "How did she die?"

"She prospected in the war craters. She couldn't believe the truth that they are dangerous, because you told her so many lies. She died of radiation poisoning."

He flinched.

"I was with her," Snake said. "I did what I could, but I have no dreamsnake. I could not help her die."

He seemed to be staring at Snake, through her.

"We are in your debt, healer," he said. "For service to a family member, for bringing us news of her death." He spoke in a distressed, distracted tone, then suddenly looked up, glaring at her. "I don't like my family to be in debt. There's a payment slot at the base of the screen. The money — "

"I want no money," Snake said.

"I can't let you in!" he cried.

"I accept that."

"Then what do you want?" He shook his head quickly. "Of course. Dreamsnakes. Why won't you believe we have none? I can't discharge our debt with dreamsnakes — and I'm not willing to exchange my debt to you for a debt to the offworlders. The offworlders — " He stopped; he seemed upset.

"If the offworlders can help me, let me speak to them."

"Even if I could, they'd refuse you."

"If they're human, they'll listen to me."

"There's . . . some question about their humanity," Jesse's brother said. "Who can tell, without tests? You don't understand, healer. You've never met them. They're dangerous and unpredictable."

"Let me *try*." Snake held out her hands, palms up, a quick, beseeching gesture, trying to make him understand her. "Other people die as Jesse died, in agony, because there aren't enough healers. There aren't enough dreamsnakes. I want to talk to the offworlders."

"Let me pay you now, healer," Jesse's brother said sadly, and Snake might as well have been back at Mountainside. "The power in Center is precariously balanced. The council would never permit an outsider to deal with the offworlders. The tensions are too great, and we won't chance altering them. I'm sorry my sister died in pain, but what you ask would risk too many more lives."

"How can that be true?" Snake said. "A simple meeting, a single question — "

"You can't understand, I told you that. One has to grow up here and deal with the forces here. I've spent my life learning."

"I think you have spent your life learning how to explain away your obligations," Snake said angrily.

"That's a lie!" Jesse's brother was enraged. "I would give you anything I had it in my power to give, but you demand impossibilities. I can't help you find new dreamsnakes."

"Wait," Snake said suddenly. "Maybe you can help us in another way."

Jesse's brother sighed and looked away. "I've no time for plots and schemes," he said. "And neither do you. The storm is coming, healer."

Snake glanced over her shoulder. Melissa was still nowhere to be seen. In the distance the clouds hugged the horizon, and flurries of windblown sand skittered back and forth between earth and sky. It was growing colder, but it was for other reasons that she shivered. The stakes were too high to give up now. She felt sure that if she could just get inside the city, she could seek out the offworlders by herself. She turned back to Jesse's brother.

"Let me come inside, in the spring. You have techniques our

technology isn't advanced enough to let us discover." Suddenly, Snake smiled. Jesse was beyond help, but others were not. Melissa was not. "If you could teach me how to induce regeneration — " She was astonished that she had not thought of the possibility before. She had been completely and selfishly concerned with dreamsnakes, with her own prestige and honor. But so many people would benefit if the healers knew how to regenerate muscle and nerves . . . but first she would learn how to regenerate skin so her daughter could live unscarred. Snake watched Jesse's brother and found to her joy that his expression was relieved.

"That is possible," he said. "Yes. I'll discuss that with the council. I'll speak for you."

"Thank you," Snake said. She could hardly believe that finally, *finally*, the city people were acceding to the request of a healer. "This will help us more than you know. If we can improve our techniques we won't have to worry about getting new dreamsnakes — we'll be better at cloning them."

Jesse's brother had begun to frown. Snake stopped, confused by the abrupt change.

"You'll have the gratitude of the healers," Snake said quickly, not knowing what she had said wrong, so not knowing how to repair it. "And of all the people we serve."

"Cloning!" Jesse's brother said. "Why do you think we'd help you with cloning?"

"I thought you and Jesse — " She caught herself, thinking that would upset him even more. "I merely assumed, with your advanced — "

"You're talking about genetic manipulation!" Jesse's brother looked ill. "Turning our knowledge to making monsters!"

"What?" Snake asked, astonished.

"Genetic manipulation — Gods, we have enough trouble with mutation without inducing it deliberately! You're lucky I couldn't let you in, healer. I'd have to denounce you. You'd spend your life in exile with the rest of the freaks."

Snake stared at the screen as he changed from rational acquaintance to accuser. If he was not a clone with Jesse, then his family was so highly inbred that deformities were inevitable without genetic manipulation. Yet what he was saying was that the city people refused themselves that method of helping themselves.

"I won't have my family indebted to a freak," he said without looking at her, doing something with his hands. Coins clattered into the payment slot beneath the screen. "Take your money and go!"

"People out here die because of the information you hoard!" she shouted. "You help the drivers enslave people with your crystal rings, but you won't help cure people who are crippled and scarred!"

Jesse's brother started forward in a rage. "Healer — " He stopped, looking beyond Snake. His expression changed to horror. "How dare you come here with a changeling? Do they exile the mother as well as the offspring out there? And you lecture me on humanity!"

"What are you talking about?"

"You want regeneration, and you don't even know you can't reform mutants! They come out the same." He laughed bitterly, hysterically. "Go back where you came from, healer. There can be no words between us."

Just as his image began to fade, Snake scooped up the coins and flung them at him. They clattered against the screen, and one jammed in the protective panel. Gears whined, but the panel would not completely close, and Snake felt a certain perverse satisfaction.

Snake turned away from the screen and the city to look for Melissa, and came face to face with her daughter. Melissa's cheeks were wet with tears. She grabbed Snake's hand and blindly pulled her out of the alcove.

"Melissa, we've got to try to set up a shelter — " Snake tried to draw back toward the alcove. It was nearly dark, though it was morning. The clouds were no longer gray but black, and Snake could see two separate whirlwinds.

"I found a place." The words came hard: Melissa was still crying. "I — I hoped they'd let you in but I was afraid they wouldn't, so I went looking."

Snake followed her, nearly blinded by the windblown sand. Swift and Squirrel came unwillingly, heads down and ears flattened. Melissa took them to a low fissure in the abrupt cliff of the mountain's flank. The wind rose by the moment, howling and moaning, flinging sand against their faces.

"They're scared," Melissa yelled above the whining wind. "Blindfolds — " She uncovered her face, squinting hard, and covered Squirrel's eyes with her headcloth. Snake did the same for the gray mare. When she uncovered her mouth and nose the wind took her breath away. Eyes streaming, holding her breath, she led the mare after Squirrel into the cave.

The wind died away abruptly. Snake could hardly open her eyes, and she felt as if sand had been driven into her lungs. The horses snorted and blew while Snake and Melissa coughed and tried to blink the overwhelming sand away, brush it from their hair and clothes, spit it out. Finally Snake managed to rub or brush or cough away the worst of the scratchy particles, and tears washed her eyes clean.

Melissa unwrapped her headcloth from Squirrel's eyes, then with a sob flung her arms around his neck.

"It's my fault," she said. "He saw me and sent you away."

"The gate was locked," Snake said. "He couldn't have let us in if he'd wanted to. If it weren't for you we'd be out there in the storm."

'But they don't want you to come back. Because of me."

"Melissa, he'd already decided not to help us. Believe me. What I asked him for scared him. They don't understand us."

"But I heard him. I saw him looking at me. You asked for help for — for me, and he said go away."

Snake wished Melissa had not understood that part of the

conversation, for she had not wanted her to hope for what might never happen. "He didn't know you'd been burned," Snake said. "And he didn't care. He was looking for excuses to get rid of me."

Unconvinced, Melissa blankly stroked Squirrel's neck, slipped off his bridle, uncinched his saddle.

"If this is anybody's fault," Snake said, "it's mine. I'm the one who brought us here — " The full impact of their situation hit her as violently as the storm winds. The faint glow of lightcells barely illuminated the cave in which they were trapped. Snake's voice broke in fear and frustration. "I'm the one who brought us here, and now we're locked outside — "

Melissa turned from Squirrel and took Snake's hand. "Snake — Snake, I knew what could happen. You didn't make me follow you. I knew how sneaky and mean all these people here can be. Everybody who trades with them says so." She hugged Snake, comforting her as Snake had comforted Melissa only a few days before.

All in an instant, she froze and the horses screamed and Snake heard the furious echoing snarl of a big cat. Swift rushed past the healer and knocked her down. As Snake struggled back to her feet to grab the bridle she glimpsed the black panther, lashing its tail at the entrance of the cave. It snarled again and Swift reared, pulling Snake off her feet. Melissa tried to hold Squirrel as pony and child backed quivering into a corner. The panther sprang toward them. Snake caught her breath as it brushed by like the wind itself, and its sleek coat touched her hand. The panther leaped four meters up the back wall and disappeared through a narrow fissure.

Melissa laughed shakily with relief and release of terror. Swift blew out her breath in a high, loud, frightened snort.

"Good gods," Snake said.

"I heard — I heard somebody say wild animals are as scared of you as you are of them," Melissa said. "But I don't think I believe it any more."

Snake unfastened the lantern from Swift's saddle and held it high, toward the fissure, wondering if human beings could follow where a big cat led. She mounted the skittish mare and balanced herself standing on the saddle. Melissa took Swift's reins and calmed her.

"What are you doing?"

Snake leaned against the cave wall, stretching to cast the lantern's light into the passageway.

"We can't stay here," she said. "We'll die of thirst or starve. Maybe there's a way to the city through here." She could not see very far into the opening; she was too far below it. But the panther had vanished. Snake heard her own voice echo and return as if there were many chambers beyond the narrow crack. "Or a way to something." She turned and slid down into the saddle, dismounted, and untacked the gray mare.

"Snake," Melissa said softly.

"Yes?"

"Look — cover the lantern — " Melissa pointed to the rock over the entrance of the cave. Snake shielded the lantern, and the indistinct luminous shape brightened and reached toward her. She felt a quick chill up her spine. She held out the lantern and moved closer to the form.

"It's a drawing," she said. It had only appeared to move; it was a spidery shape crawling against the wall, merely paint. A clever optical illusion that now, though Snake knew better, looked as if it were creeping toward her.

"I wonder what it's for." Melissa's voice, too, whispered against the rock.

"Maybe it's to lead people out — that would mean there *is* something farther inside."

"But what about Swift and Squirrel? We can't leave them here."

"If we don't find something for them to eat," Snake said gently, "they'll starve too."

Melissa looked up toward the panther's ledge, the blue light ghostly on her scarred face.

"Melissa," Snake said suddenly, "do you hear something?" It

was a change, but she could not figure out what it was. The black panther, screaming in the distance? Whoever had painted the spider symbol on the wall? Her fingers curled around the handle of the knife on her belt.

"The wind stopped!" Melissa said. She ran toward the cave entrance.

Snake followed close behind, at every instant ready to pull Melissa back from the storm's violence. But her daughter was right: what she had heard was not a sound but the abrupt end of a sound she had become accustomed to.

Nothing happened. Outside, the air was absolutely still. The low dust clouds had swept across the desert and disappeared, leaving puffy, towering thunderheads arrayed around with rich blue sky. Snake stepped out into the strange luminosity of the morning, and a cold breeze fluttered the robe at her ankles.

All at once, the rain began.

Snake ran out into the drops, lifting her arms to them like a child. Squirrel trotted past her and broke into a gallop. Swift sped by him, and they cavorted and bucked like foals. Melissa stood still, gazing upward, letting the rain wash her face.

The clouds, a long, wide bank of them, passed slowly overhead, now shedding rain, now breaking for an instant of hummingbird-bright sun. Snake and Melissa finally retreated to the shelter of the rocks, soaked and chilly and happy. A triple rainbow arched across the sky. Snake sighed and sank down on her heels to watch it. She was so wrapped in awe of the colors, as they alternated back and forth through the spectrum, that she did not notice exactly when Melissa sat close beside her. First she was not there, then she was, and Snake slipped her arm around her daughter's shoulders. This time Melissa relaxed against her, not quite so poised to tear herself away from any human contact.

The clouds passed, the rainbow faded, and Squirrel trotted back to Snake, so wet that the texture of his stripes, as well as their color, was visible. Snake scratched him behind the ears and under the jaw; then for the first time in perhaps half an hour looked out across the desert.

In the direction from which the clouds had come, a pale, delicate green already softened the low black hills. The desert plants grew so quickly that Snake imagined she could almost see the boundary slipping nearer like a gentle tide, following the progress of the rain.

Snake realized reluctantly that she could not stay at Center. It was simply too dangerous to spend any time exploring the mountain caves, though they drew her strongly. They might lead eventually to the city, but they might as easily trap her, and Melissa, in a mesh of sterile stone tunnels. The rain offered a single reprieve: if Snake did not accept it, she and her daughter, the horses and the serpents, would have no second chance.

Somehow it did not seem fair or right to Snake that her return to the mountains was as easy as a pleasure trip through meadowlands. For that was what the desert metamorphosed into after a rain. All day the horses snatched mouthfuls of tender leaves as they walked, while their riders picked great bouquets of honeycups and sucked the flowers' ends for their nectar. Pollen hung heavy in the air. Leading the horses, Snake and Melissa walked far into the night, while the aurora borealis danced; the desert became luminous and neither horses nor riders seemed tired. Snake and Melissa ate at random intervals, chewing on dry fruit or jerky as they traveled; near dawn, they flung themselves on soft, lush grass where only sand had been a few hours before. They slept a short while and woke at sunrise, refreshed.

The plants on which they rested had already budded. By afternoon flowers covered the dunes in drifts of color, one hill white, the next bright purple, a third multicolored in streamers of species that led from crest to valley. The flowers moderated the heat, and the sky was clearer than Snake had ever seen it. Even the contours of the dunes were altered by the rain, from soft rolling billows to sharp-edged eroded ridges, marked by the narrow canyons of short-lived streams.

The third morning the dust clouds began to gather again. The rain had all seeped away or evaporated; the plants had captured all they could. Now dryness mottled the leaves with brown as the plants shriveled and died. Their seeds drifted across Snake's path in eddies of the wind.

The vast desert's peace wrapped itself around her shoulders, but the eastern foothills of the central mountain range rose before her, reminding her again of failure. She did not want to go home.

Swift, responding to some unconscious movement of Snake's body, her reluctance to go on, stopped abruptly. Snake did not urge her forward. A few paces farther along, Melissa reined in and looked back.

"Snake?"

"Oh, Melissa, what am I taking you to?"

"We're going home," Melissa said, trying to soothe her.

"I might not even have a home anymore."

"They won't send you away. They couldn't."

Snake wiped tears fiercely away on her sleeve, the fabric silky against her cheek. Hopelessness and frustration would give her no comfort and no relief. She leaned down against Swift's neck, clenching her fists in the mare's long black mane.

"You said it was your home, you said they were all your family. So how could they send you away?"

"They wouldn't," Snake whispered. "But if they said I couldn't be a healer, how could I stay?"

Melissa reached up and patted her awkwardly. "It'll be all right. I know it will. How can I make you not be so sad?"

Snake let out her breath in a long sigh. She looked up. Melissa gazed at her steadily, never flinching. Snake turned and kissed Melissa's hand; she enfolded it in her own.

"You trust me," she said. "And maybe that's what I need most right now."

Melissa half smiled in embarrassment and encouragement and they started onward, but after a few paces Snake reined Swift in again. Melissa stopped too, looking up at her with worry.

"Whatever happens," Snake said, "whatever my teachers decide about me, you're still their daughter as much as mine. You can still be a healer. If I have to go away — "

"I'll go with you."

"Melissa — "

"I don't care. I never wanted to be a healer anyway," Melissa said belligerently. "I want to be a jockey. I wouldn't want to stay with people who made you leave."

The intensity of Melissa's loyalty troubled Snake. She had never known anyone who was so completely oblivious to self-interest. Perhaps Melissa could not yet think of herself as someone with a right to her own dreams; perhaps so many of her dreams had been taken from her that she no longer dared to have them. Snake hoped that somehow she could give them back to her daughter.

"Never mind," she said. "We aren't home yet. We can worry about it then."

Melissa's set mask of decision relaxed slightly, and they rode on.

By the end of the third day the tiny plants had fallen to dust beneath the horses' hooves. A fine brown haze covered the desert. Now and then a cloud of feathery seeds drifted by, cast to the air. When the wind was stronger, heavier seeds skittered along the sand like tides. When night fell Snake and Melissa had already entered the foothills, and the desert had turned bare and black behind them.

They had returned to the mountains traveling straight west, the quickest way to safety. Here, the foothills rose more gently than the steep cliffs at Mountainside, far to the north; the climb was easier but much longer than at the northern pass. At the first crest, before they started toward the next, higher, hills, Melissa reined Squirrel in and turned around, gazing back at the darkening desert. After a moment she grinned at Snake.

"We made it," she said.

Snake smiled slowly in return. "You're right," she said. "We did." Her most immediate fear, of the storms, dissolved slowly in the clearer, colder air of the hills. The clouds hung oppressively low, disfiguring the sky. No one, caravannaire or mountain dweller, would see even a patch of blue, or a star, or the moon, until next spring, and the sun's disc would fade duller and duller. Now, sinking beneath the mountain peaks, it cast Snake's shadow back toward the darkening stark sand plain. Beyond the reach of the most violent wind, beyond the heat and waterless sand, Snake urged Swift on, toward the mountains where they all belonged.

Snake kept a lookout for a place to camp. Before the horses descended very far she heard the welcome trickle of running water. The trail led past a small hollow, the source of a spring, a spot that looked as if it had been used as a campsite, but long ago. The water sustained a few scrubby forever trees and some grass for the horses. In the center of a bare-beaten patch of ground the earth was smudged with charcoal, but Snake had no firewood. She knew better than to try chopping down the forever trees, unlike some travelers who had left futile ax marks, now grown half together, in the rough bark. The wood beneath was as hard and resilient as steel.

Night travel in the mountains was as difficult as day travel in the desert, and the easy return from the city had not wiped out the strain of the complete journey. Snake dismounted. They would stop for the night, and at sunrise —

At sunrise, what? She had been in a hurry for so many days, rushing against sickness or death or the implacable sands, that she had to stop and make herself realize that she had no reason for hurrying any more, no overwhelming need to get from here to anywhere else, nor to sleep a few hours and rise yawning at sunrise or sunset. Her home awaited her, and she was not at all sure it would still be her home once she reached it. She had nothing to take back but failure and bad news and one violent-tempered sand viper that might or might not be useful. She untied the serpent case and laid it gently on the ground.

When the horses were rubbed down, Melissa knelt by the packs and started getting out food and the paraffin stove. This was the first time since they started out that they had made a proper camp. Snake sat on her heels by her daughter to help with dinner.

"I'll do it," Melissa said. "Why don't you rest?"

"That doesn't seem quite fair," Snake said.

"I don't mind."

"That isn't the point."

"I like to do things for you," Melissa said.

Snake put her hands on Melissa's shoulders, not forcing or even urging her to turn. "I know you do. But I like to do things for you, too."

Melissa's fingers fumbled with buckles and straps. "That isn't right," she said finally. "You're a healer, and I — I work in a stable. It's right for me to do things for you."

"Where does it say that a healer has more rights than someone who used to work in a stable? You're my daughter, and we're a partnership."

Melissa flung herself around and hugged Snake tightly, hiding her face against her shirt. Snake embraced her and held her, rocking back and forth on the hard ground, comforting Melissa as if she were the much younger child she had never had the chance to be.

After a few minutes Melissa's arms loosened and she pulled back, self-contained again, glancing away in embarrassment.

"I don't like not doing anything."

"When did you ever have the chance to try?"

Melissa shrugged.

"We can take turns," Snake said, "or split the chores every day. Which would you rather do?"

Melissa met her gaze with a quick, relieved smile. "Split the chores every day." She glanced around as if seeing the camp for the first time. "Maybe there's dead wood farther on," she said. "And we need some water." She reached for the woodstrap and the waterskin.

Snake took the waterskin from her. "I'll meet you back here in a few minutes. If you don't find anything don't spend a lot of time looking. Whatever falls during the winter probably gets used up by the first traveler every spring. If there is a first traveler every spring." The place not only looked as though no one had been here for many years, it had an undefinable aura of abandonment.

The spring flowed swiftly past the camp and there was no sign now of mud where Swift and Squirrel had drunk, but Snake walked a short distance upstream anyway. Near the source of the spring she put the waterskin down and climbed to the top of a tremendous boulder that provided a view of most of the surrounding area. No one else was in sight, no horses, no camps, no smoke. Snake was finally almost willing to let herself believe the crazy was gone, or never really there at all, a coincidence of her meeting one real crazy and a misguided and incompetent thief. Even if they were the same person, she had seen no sign of him since the street fight. That was not as long ago as it seemed, but perhaps it was long enough.

Snake climbed back down to the spring and held the waterskin just beneath the silvery surface. Water gurgled and bubbled into the opening and slipped over her hands and through her fingers, cold and quick. Water was a different being in the mountains. The leather bag bulged up full. Snake looped a couple of half hitches around its neck and slung the strap over her shoulder.

Melissa had not yet returned to camp. Snake puttered around for a few minutes, getting together a meal of dried provisions that looked the same even after they had been soaked. They tasted the same, too, but they were a little bit easier to eat. She unrolled the blankets. She opened the serpent case but Mist remained inside. The cobra often stayed in her dark compartment after a long trip, and grew bad-tempered if disturbed. Snake felt uneasy with Melissa out of sight. She could not dispel her discomfort by reminding herself that Melissa was tough and independent. Instead of opening Sand's compartment so the rattler could come out, or even checking on the sand viper, a task she did not much enjoy, she refastened the case and stood up to call her daughter. Suddenly Swift and Squirrel shied violently, snorting in fear, Melissa cried "Snake! Look out!" in a voice of warning and terror, and rocks and dirt clattered down the side of the hill.

Snake ran toward the sound of scuffling, the knife on her belt half-drawn. She rounded a boulder and slid to a stop.

Melissa struggled violently in the grasp of a tall, cadaverous figure in desert robes. He had one hand over her mouth and the other around her, pinning her arms. She fought and kicked, but the man did not react in either pain or anger.

"Tell her to stop," he said. "I won't hurt her." His words were thick and slurred, as if he were intoxicated. His robes were torn and soiled and his hair stood out wildly. The irises of his eyes seemed paler than the bloodshot whites, giving him a blank, inhuman look. Snake knew immediately that this was the crazy, even before she saw the ring that had cut her forehead when he attacked her on the streets of Mountainside.

"Let her go."

"I'll trade you," he said. "Even trade."

"We don't have much, but it's yours. What do you want?"

"The dreamsnake," he said. "No more than that." Melissa struggled again and the man moved, gripping her more tightly and more cruelly.

"All right, " Snake said. "I haven't any choice, have I? He's in my case."

He followed her back to camp. The old mystery was solved, a new one created.

Snake pointed to the case. "The top compartment," she said.

The crazy sidled toward it, pulling Melissa awkwardly along. He reached toward the clasp, then jerked back his hand. He was trembling.

"You do it," he said to Melissa. "For you it's safe."

Without looking at Snake, Melissa reached for the clasp. She was very pale.

"Stop it," Snake said. "There's nothing in there."

Melissa let her hand fall to her side, looking at Snake with mixed relief and fear.

"Let her go," Snake said again. "If the dreamsnake is what you want, I can't help you. He was killed before you even found my camp."

Narrowing his eyes, he stared at her, then turned and reached for the serpent case. He flicked the catch open and kicked the whole thing over.

The grotesque sand viper lurched out in a tangle, writhing and hissing. It raised its head for an instant as if to strike in retaliation for its captivity, but both the crazy and Melissa stood frozen. The viper slithered around and slid toward the rocks. Snake sprang forward and pulled Melissa away from the crazy, but he did not even notice.

"Trick me!" Suddenly he laughed hysterically and raised his hands to the sky. "That would give me what I need!" Laughing and crying, with tears streaming down his face, he sank to the ground.

Snake moved quickly toward the rocks, but the sand viper had disappeared. Scowling, gripping the handle of her knife, she stood over the crazy. The vipers were rare enough on the desert: they were nonexistent in the foothills. Now she could not make the vaccine for Arevin's people, and she had nothing at all to take back to her teachers.

"Get up," she said. Her voice was harsh. She glanced at Melissa. "Are you okay?"

"Yeah," Melissa said. "But he let that viper go."

The crazy remained in his crumpled heap, crying quietly.

"What's wrong with him?" Melissa stood at Snake's elbow, peering down at the sobbing man.

"I don't know." Snake toed him in the side. "You. Stop it. Get up."

The man moved weakly at their feet. His wrists protruded from ragged sleeves; his arms and hands were like bare branches.

"I should have been able to get away from *him*," Melissa said in disgust.

"He's stronger than he looks," Snake said. "For gods' sakes, man, stop all that howling. We're not going to do anything to you."

"I'm already dead," he whispered. "You were my last chance so I'm dead."

"Your last chance for what?"

"For happiness."

"That's a lousy kind of happiness, that makes you wreck things and jump out on people," Melissa said.

He glared up at them, tears streaking his skeletal face. Deep lines creased his skin. "Why did you come back? I couldn't follow you anymore. I wanted to go home to die, if they'd let me. But you came back. Right back to me." He buried his face in the tattered sleeves of his desert robe. He had lost his headcloth. His hair was brown and dry. He sobbed no longer, but his shoulders trembled.

Snake knelt down and urged him to his feet. She had to support most of his weight herself. Melissa stood warily by for a moment, then shrugged and came to help. As they started forward, Snake felt a hard, square-edged shape beneath the crazy's clothes. Dragging him around, she pulled open his robe, fumbling through layers of grimy material.

"What are you doing? Stop it!" He struggled with her, flailing about with his bony arms, trying to pull his clothing back across his scrawny body.

Snake found the inside pocket. As soon as she touched the hidden shape she knew it was her journal. She snatched it and let the crazy go. He backed up a step or two and stood shivering, frantically rearranging the folds of his garments. Snake ignored him, her hands clenched tight around the book.

"What is it?" Melissa asked.

"The journal of my proving year. He stole it from my camp."

"I meant to throw it away," the crazy said. "I forgot I had it."

Snake glared at him.

"I thought it would help me, but it didn't. It was no help at all."

Snake sighed.

Back in their camp, Snake and Melissa lowered the crazy to the ground and pillowed his head on a saddle, where he lay staring blankly at the sky. Every time he blinked, a fresh tear rolled down his face and washed the dirt and dust away in streaks. Snake gave him some water and sat on her heels watching him, wondering what, if anything, his strange remarks meant. He was a crazy, after all, but not a spontaneous one. He was driven by desperation.

"He isn't going to do anything, is he?" Melissa asked.

"I don't think so."

"He made me drop the wood," Melissa said. Clearly disgusted, she strode toward the rocks.

"Melissa — "

She glanced back.

"I hope that sand viper just kept on going, but he might still be over there someplace. We better do without a fire tonight."

Melissa hesitated so long tha. Snake wondered if she might say she preferred the company of the sand viper to that of the crazy, but in the end she shrugged and went over to the horses.

Snake held the water flask to the crazy's lips again. He swallowed once, then let the water drip from the corners of his mouth through several days' growth of beard. It pooled on the hard ground beneath him and dribbled away in tiny rivulets.

"What's your name?" Snake waited, but he did not answer. She had begun to wonder if he had gone catatonic, when he shrugged, deeply and elaborately.

"You must have a name."

"I suppose," he said; he licked his lips, his hands twitched, he blinked and two more tears cut through the dust on his face, "I suppose I must have had one once."

"What did you mean, all that about happiness? Why did you want my dreamsnake? Are you dying?"

"I told you that I was."

"Of what?"

"Need."

Snake frowned. "Need for what?"

"For a dreamsnake."

Snake sighed. Her knees hurt. She shifted her position and sat cross-legged near the crazy's shoulder. "I can't help you if you don't help me know what's wrong."

He jerked himself upright, scrabbling at the robe he had arranged so carefully, pulling at the worn material until it ripped. He flung it open and bared his throat, lifting his chin. "That's all you need to know!"

Snake looked closer. Among the rough dark hairs of the crazy's growing beard she could see numerous tiny scars, all in pairs, clustered over the carotid arteries. She rocked back, startled. A dreamsnake's fangs had left those marks, she had no doubt of that, but she could not even imagine, much less recall, a disease so severe and agonizing that it would require so much venom to ease the pain, yet in the end leave its victim alive. Those scars had been made over a considerable time, for some were old and white, some so fresh and pink and shiny that they must still have been scabbed over when he first rifled her camp.

"Now do you understand?"

"No," Snake said. "I don't. What was the matter — " She stopped, frowning. "Were you a healer?" But that was impossible. She would have known him, or at least known about him. Besides, dreamsnake venom would have no more effect on a healer than the poison of any serpent.

She could not think of any reason for one person to use so much dreamsnake venom over so long a time. People must have died in agony because of this man, whoever or whatever he was.

Shaking his head, the crazy sank back to the ground. "No, never a healer . . . not me. We don't need healers in the broken dome."

Snake waited, impatient but unwilling to take the chance of sidetracking him. The crazy licked his lips and spoke again.

"Water . . . please?"

Snake held the flask to his lips and he drank greedily, not spilling and slobbering as before. He tried to sit up again but his elbow slipped beneath him and he lay still, without even trying to speak. Snake's patience ended.

"Why have you been bitten so often by a dreamsnake?"

He looked at her, his pale, bloodshot eyes quite steady. "Because I was a good and useful supplicant and I took much treasure to the broken dome. I was rewarded often."

"Rewarded!"

His expression softened. "Oh, yes." His eyes lost their focus; he seemed to be looking through her. "With happiness and forgetfulness and the reality of dreams."

He closed his eyes and would not speak again, even when Snake prodded him roughly.

She joined Melissa, who had found a few dry branches on the other side of camp and now sat by the tiny fire, waiting to find out what was going on.

"Someone has a dreamsnake," Snake said. "They're using the venom as a pleasure-drug."

"That's stupid," Melissa said. "Why don't they just use something that grows around here? There's lots of different stuff."

"I don't know," Snake said. "I don't know for myself what the venom feels like. Where they got the dreamsnake is what I'd like to know. They didn't get it from a healer, at least not voluntarily."

Melissa stirred the soup. The firelight turned her red hair golden.

"Snake," she finally said, "when you came back to the stable that night — after you fought with him — he would have killed you if you'd let him. Tonight he would've killed me if he'd had a chance. If he has some friends and they decided to take a dreamsnake from a healer . . ."

"I know." Healers killed for their dreamsnakes? It was a difficult idea to accept. Snake scratched intersecting lines on the ground with a sharp pebble, a meaningless design. "That's almost the only explanation that makes any sense."

They ate dinner. The crazy was too deeply alseep to be fed, though he was far from being in danger of dying, as he claimed. He was, in fact, surprisingly healthy under the dirt and rags: he was thin but his muscle tone was good, and his skin bore none of the signs of malnutrition. He was, without question, very strong.

But all that, Snake thought, was why healers carried dreamsnakes to begin with. The venom did not kill, and it did not make death inevitable. Rather, it eased the transition between life and death and helped the dying person accept finality.

Given time, the crazy could no doubt will himself to die. But Snake had no intention of letting him carry out his will before she found out where he came from and what was going on there. She also had no intention of staying up half the night trading watches over him with Melissa. They both needed a good night's sleep.

The crazy's arms were as limp as the ragged robes covering them. Snake drew his hands above his head and tied his wrists to her saddle with two sets of its packstraps. She did not tie him tightly or cruelly, just firmly enough so she would hear him if he tried to get away. The evening had turned chilly, so she threw a spare blanket over him, then she and Melissa spread their own blankets on the hard ground and went to sleep.

It must have been midnight when Snake woke again. The fire had gone out, leaving the camp pitch-dark. Snake lay without moving, expecting the sound of the crazy trying to escape.

Melissa cried out in her sleep. Snake slid toward her, groping in the dark, and touched her shoulder. She sat beside her, stroking her hair and her face.

"It's all right, Melissa," Snake whispered. "Wake up, you're just having a bad dream."

After a moment Melissa sat bolt upright. "What — "

"It's me, it's Snake. You were having a nightmare."

Melissa's voice shook. "I thought I was back in Mountainside," she said. "I thought Ras . . . "

Snake held her, still stroking her soft curly hair. "Never mind. You never have to go back there."

She felt Melissa nod.

"Do you want me to stay here next to you?" Snake asked. "Or would that bring the nightmares back?"

Melissa hesitated. "Please stay," she whispered.

Snake lay down and pulled both blankets over them. The night had turned cold, but Snake was glad to be out of the desert, back in a place where the ground did not tenaciously hold the day's heat. Melissa huddled against her.

The darkness was complete, but Snake could tell from Melissa's breathing that she was already asleep again. Perhaps she had never completely awakened. Snake did not go back to sleep for some time. She could hear the crazy's rough breath, nearly a snore, above the trickle of water from the spring, and she could feel the vibrations of Swift and Squirrel's hooves on the hard-packed earth as the horses shifted in the night. Beneath her shoulder and hip the ground yielded not at all, and above her not a star or a sliver of moon broke through into the sky.

The crazy's voice was loud and whiny, but much stronger than it had been the night before.

"Let me up. Untie me. You going to torture me to death? I need to piss. I'm thirsty."

Snake threw off the blankets and sat up. She was tempted to offer him the drink of water first, but decided that was the unworthy fantasy of being awakened at dawn. She got up and stretched, yawning, then waved at Melissa, who was standing between Swift and Squirrel as they nudged her for their breakfast. Melissa laughed and waved back.

The crazy pulled at the straps. "Well? You going to let me up?"

"In a minute." She used the privy they had dug behind some bushes, and walked over to the spring to splash water on her face. She wanted a bath, but the spring did not provide that much water, nor did she intend to make the crazy wait quite so long. She returned to camp and untied the thongs around his wrists. He sat up, rubbing his hands together and grumbling, then rose and started away.

"I don't want to invade your privacy," Snake said, "but don't go out of my sight."

He snarled something unintelligible but did not let the natural screen hide him completely. Scuffing back to Snake, he squatted down and grabbed for the water flask. He drank thirstily and wiped his mouth on his sleeve, looking around hungrily.

"Is there breakfast?"

"I thought you were planning to die."

He snorted.

"Everyone in my camp works for their food," Snake said. "You can talk for yours."

The man looked at the ground and sighed. He had dark bushy eyebrows that shadowed his pale eyes.

"All right," he said. He sat cross-legged and rested his forearms on his knees, letting his hands droop. His fingers trembled.

Snake waited, but he did not speak.

Two healers had vanished in the past few years. Snake still thought of them by their child-names, the names by which she had known them until they left on their proving years. She had not been extremely close to Philippe, but Jenneth had been her favorite older sister, one of the three people she had been closest to. She could still feel the shock of the winter and spring of Jenneth's testing year, as the days passed and the community slowly realized she would not return. They never found out what happened to her. Sometimes when a healer died a messenger would bring the bad news to the station, and sometimes even the serpents were returned. But the healers never had any message from Jenneth. Perhaps the crazy slumping before Snake had leapt on her in a dark alley somewhere, and killed her for her dreamsnake.

"Well?" Snake asked sharply.

The crazy started. "What?" He squinted at her, struggling to focus his eyes.

Snake kept her temper. "Where are you from?"

"South."

"What town?" Her maps showed this pass, but nothing beyong it. In the mountains as well as in the desert, people had good reason to avoid the extreme southern lands.

He shrugged. "No town. No town left, there. Just the broken dome."

"Where did you get the dreamsnake?"

He shrugged.

Snake leaped to her feet and grabbed his dirty robe. The cloth at his throat bunched in her fist as she pulled him upright. "Answer me!"

A tear trickled down his face. "How can I? I don't understand you. Where did I get it? I never had one. They were always there, but not mine. They were there when I went there and they were there when I left. Why would I need yours if I had some of my own?" The crazy sank to the ground as Snake slowly unclenched her fingers.

"'Some' of your own?"

He held out his hands, raising them to let the sleeves fall back to his elbows. His forearms, too, at the inside of the elbow, at the wrists, everywhere the veins were prominent, showed the scars of bites.

"It's best if they strike you all over at once," he said dreamily. "In the throat, that's quick and sure, that's for emergencies, for sustenance. That's all North will give you, usually. But all over, if you do something special for him, that's what he gives you." The crazy hugged himself and rubbed his arms as if he were cold. He flushed with excitement, rubbing harder and faster. "Then you feel, you feel — everything lights up, you're on fire, everything — it goes on and on."

"Stop it!"

He let his hands drop to the ground and looked at her, blank-eyed again. "What?"

"This North — he has dreamsnakes."

The crazy nodded eagerly, letting memory excite him again.

"A lot of them?"

"A whole pitful. Sometimes he lets someone down in the pit, he rewards them — but never me, not since the first time."

Snake sat down, gazing at the crazy yet at nothing, imagining the delicate creatures trapped in a pit, exposed to the elements.

"Where does he get them? Do the city people trade with him? Does he deal with the offworlders?"

"Get them? They're there. North has them."

Snake was shaking as hard as the crazy. She clasped her hands hard around her knees, tensing all her muscles, then slowly making herself relax. Her hands steadied.

"He got angry at me, and he sent me away," the crazy said. "I was so sick . . . and then I heard about a healer and I went to find you, but you weren't there and you took the dreamsnake with you — " His voice rose as the words came quicker. "And the people chased me away but I followed you, and followed you and followed you until you went back into the desert again, I couldn't follow you there anymore, I just couldn't, I tried to go home but I couldn't, so I lay down to die but I couldn't do that either. Why did you come right back to me when you don't have the dreamsnake? Why don't you let me die?"

"You aren't about to die," Snake said. "You're going to live until you take me to North and the dreamsnakes. After that whether you live or die is your own business."

The crazy stared at her. "But North sent me away."

"You don't have to obey him any more," Snake said. "He has no more power over you, if he won't give you what you want. Your only chance is to help me get some of the dreamsnakes."

The crazy stared at her for a long time, blinking, frowning in deep thought. Suddenly his expression cleared. His face grew serene and joyful. He started toward her, stumbled, and crawled. On his knees beside her, he caught her hands. His own were dirty and callused. The ring that had cut Snake's forehead was a setting that had lost its stone.

"You mean you'll help me get a dreamsnake of my own?" He smiled. "To use any time?"

"Yes," Snake said through clenched teeth. She drew her hands back as the crazy bent to kiss them. Now she had promised him, and though she knew it was the only way she could get his cooperation, she felt as if she had committed a terrible sin.

Moonlight shone dimly on the excellent road to Mountainside. Arevin rode late into the night, so immersed in his thoughts that he did not notice when sunset burned daylight into dusk. Though the healers' station lay days behind him to the north, he still had not encountered anyone with news of Snake. Mountainside was the last place she could be, for there was nothing south of Mountainside. Arevin's maps of the central mountains showed a herders' trail, an old unused pass that cut only through the eastern range, and ended. Travelers in the mountains, as well as in Arevin's country, did not venture into the far southern regions of their world.

Arevin tried not to wonder what he would do if he did not find Snake here. He was not close enough to the crest of the mountains to catch glimpses of the eastern desert, and for that he was glad. If he did not see the storms begin, he could imagine the calm weather lasting longer than usual.

He rounded a wide curve, looked up, and shielded his lantern, blinking. Lights ahead: soft yellow gaslights. The town looked like a basket of sparks spilled out on the slope, all resting together but for a few scattered separately on the valley floor.

Though he had added several towns to his experience, Arevin still found astonishing how much work and business their people did after dark. He decided to continue on to Mountainside tonight: perhaps he could have news of Snake before morning. He wrapped his robe more tightly around himself against the coldness of the night.

Despite himself, Arevin dozed, and did not awaken until his horse's hooves rang on cobblestones. There was no activity here, so he rode on until he reached the town's center with its taverns and other places of entertainment. Here it was almost as bright as day, and the people acted as if night had never come. Through a tavern entrance he saw several workers with their arms around each other's shoulders, singing, the contralto slightly flat. The tavern was attached to an inn, so he stopped his horse and dismounted. Thad's advice about asking for information at inns seemed sound, though as yet none of the proprietors Arevin had talked to had possessed any information to give him.

He entered the tavern. The singers were still singing, drowning out their accompaniment, or whatever tune the flute player in the corner might have been trying to construct. She rested her instrument across her knee, picked up an earthenware mug, and sipped from it: beer, Arevin thought. The pleasant yeasty odor permeated the tavern.

The singers began another song, but the contralto closed her mouth quite suddenly and stared at Arevin. One of the men glanced at her. The song died raggedly as he and her other companions followed her gaze. The flute melody drifted hollowly up, down, and stopped. The attention of everyone in the room centered on Arevin.

"I greet you," he said formally. "I would like to speak to the proprietor, if that is possible."

No one moved. Then the contralto stumbled abruptly to her feet, knocking over her stool.

"I'll — I'll see if I can find her." She disappeared through a curtained doorway.

No one spoke, not even the bartender. Arevin did not know what to say. He did not think he was so dusty and dirty as to stun anyone mute, and certainly in a trader's town like this one people would be accustomed to his manner of dress. All he could think of to do was gaze back at them and wait. Perhaps they would return to their singing, or drink their beer, or ask him if he was thirsty.

They did nothing. Arevin waited.

He felt faintly ridiculous. He took a step forward, intending to break the tension by acting as if everything were normal. But as soon as he moved everyone in the tavern seemed to catch their breath and flinch away from him. The tension in the room was not that of people inspecting a stranger, but of antagonists awaiting an enemy. Someone whispered to another person; the words were inaudible but the tone sounded ominous.

The curtains across the doorway parted and a tall figure paused in the shadows. The proprietor stepped into the light and looked at Arevin steadily, without any fear.

"You wished to speak with me?"

She was as tall as Arevin, elegant and stern. She did not smile. These mountain people were quick to express their feelings, so Arevin wondered if he had perhaps blundered into a private house, or broken a custom he did not know.

"Yes," he said. "I am looking for the healer Snake. I hoped I might find her in your town."

"Why do you think you'd find her here?"

If all travelers were spoken to so rudely in Mountainside, Arevin wondered how it managed to be so prosperous.

"If she isn't here, she must never have reached the mountains at all — she must still be in the western desert. The storms are coming."

"Why are you looking for her?"

Arevin permitted himself a slight frown, for the questions had passed the limits of mere rudeness.

"I do not see that that is any of your business," he said. "If common civility is not the custom in your house, I will ask elsewhere."

He turned and nearly walked into two people with insignia on their collars and chains in their hands.

"Come with us, please."

"For what reason?"

"Suspicion of assault," the other one said.

Arevin looked at him in utter astonishment. "Assault? I've not been here more than a few minutes."

"That will be determined," the first one said. She reached for his wrist to lock shackles on him. He pulled back with revulsion, but she kept her grip. He struggled and both people came at him. In a moment they were all flailing away at each other, with the bar patrons shouting encouragement. Arevin hit at his two assailants and lurched almost to his feet. Something smacked against the side of his head. He felt his knees go weak, and collapsed.

Arevin woke in a small stone room with a single high window. His head ached fiercely. He did not understand what had happened, for the traders to whom his clan sold cloth spoke of Mountainside as a place of fair people. Perhaps these town bandits only preyed on solitary travelers, and left well-protected caravans alone. His belt, with all his money and his knife, was gone. Why he was not lying dead in an alley somewhere, he did not know. At least he was no longer chained.

Sitting up slowly, pausing when movement dizzied him, he looked around. He heard footsteps in the corridor, jumped to his feet, stumbled, and pulled himself up to look out through the bars on the tiny opening in the door. The footsteps receded, running.

"Is this how you treat visitors to your town?" Arevin shouted. His even temper took a considerable amount of perturbation to disarrange, but he was angry.

No one answered. He unclenched his hands from the bars and let himself back to the floor. He could see nothing outside his prison but another stone wall. The window was too high to reach, even if he moved the heavy-timbered bed and stood on it. All the light in the room was reflected downward from a vague sunny patch on the wall above. Someone had taken Arevin's robe, and his boots, and left him nothing but his long loose riding trousers.

Calming himself slowly, he set himself to wait.

Halting footsteps — a lame person, a cane — came down the stone corridor toward his cell. This time Arevin simply waited.

The key clattered and the door swung open. Guards, wearing the same insignia as his assailants of the night before, entered first, cautiously. There were three of them, which seemed strange to Arevin since he had not even been able to overpower two the night before. He did not have much experience at fighting. In his clan, adults gently parted scuffling children and tried to help them settle their differences with words.

Supported by a helper as well as by the cane, a big dark-haired man entered the cell. Arevin did not greet him or rise. They stared at each other steadily for several moments.

"The healer is safe, from you at least," the big man said. His helper left him for an instant to drag a chair in from the hall. As the man sat down Arevin could see that he was not congenitally lame, but injured: his right leg was heavily bandaged.

"She helped you, too," Arevin said. "So why do you set upon those who would find her?"

"You feign sanity well. But I expect once we watch you for a few days you'll go back to raving."

"I have no doubt I'll begin raving if you leave me here for long," Arevin said.

"Do you think we'd leave you loose to go after the healer again?"

"Is she here?" Arevin asked anxiously, abandoning his reserve. "She must have got out of the desert safely if you've seen her."

The dark-haired man gazed at him for some seconds. "I'm surprised to hear you speak of her safety," he said. "But I suppose inconsistency is what one should expect of a crazy."

"A crazy!"

"Calm yourself. We know about your attack on her."

"Attack — ? Was she attacked? Is she all right? Where is she?"

"I think it would be safer for her if I told you nothing."

Arevin looked away, seeking some means of concentrating his thoughts. A peculiar mixture of confusion and relief possessed him. At least Snake was out of the desert. She must be safe.

A flaw in a stone block caught the light. Arevin gazed at the sparkling point, calming himself.

He looked up, nearly smiling. "This argument is foolish. Ask her to come see me. She'll tell you we are friends."

"Indeed? Who should we tell her wants to see her?"

"Tell her . . . the one whose name she knows."

The big man scowled. "You barbarians and your superstitions — !"

"She knows who I am," Arevin said, refusing to submit to his anger.

"You'd confront the healer?"

"Confront her!"

The big man leaned back in his chair and glanced at his assistant. "Well, Brian, he certainly doesn't talk like a crazy."

"No, sir," the older man said.

The big man stared at Arevin, but his eyes were really focused on the wall of the cell behind him. "I wonder what Gabriel — " He cut off his words, then glanced at his assistant. "He did sometimes have good ideas in situations like this." He sounded slightly embarrassed.

"Yes, mayor, he did."

There was a longer and more intense silence. Arevin knew that in a few moments the guards and the mayor and the old man Brian would get up and leave him alone in the tiny squeezing cell. Arevin felt a drop of sweat roll down his side.

"Well . . ." the mayor said.

"Sir — ?" One of the guards spoke in a hesitant voice.

The mayor turned toward her. "Well, speak up. I've no stomach for imprisoning innocents, but we've had enough madmen loose recently."

"He was surprised last night when we arrested him. Now I believe his surprise was genuine. Mistress Snake fought with the crazy, mayor. I saw her when she returned. She won the fight, and she had serious abrasions. Yet this man is not even bruised."

Hearing that Snake was injured, Arevin had to restrain himself from asking again if she was all right. But he would not beg anything of these people.

"That seems true. You're very observant," the mayor said to the guard. "Are you bruised?" he asked Arevin.

"I am not."

"You'll forgive me if I insist you prove it."

Arevin stood up, intensely disliking the idea of stripping himself before strangers. But he unfastened his pants and let them fall around his ankles. He let the mayor look him over, then slowly turned. At the last moment he remembered he had been in a fight the night before and could very well be visibly bruised somewhere. But no one said anything, so he turned around again and put his pants back on.

Then the old man came toward him. The guards stiffened. Arevin stood very still. These people might consider any move threatening.

"Be careful, Brian," the mayor said.

Brian lifted Arevin's hands, looked at the backs, turned them over, peered at the palms, let them drop. He returned to his place by the mayor's side.

"He wears no rings. I doubt he's ever worn any. His hands are tanned and there's no mark. The healer said the cut on her forehead was made by a ring."

The mayor snorted. "So what do you think?"

"As you said, sir, he doesn't talk like a crazy. Also, a crazy would not necessarily be stupid, and it would be stupid to ask after the healer while wearing desert robes, unless one was in fact innocent — of both the crime and the knowledge of it. I am inclined to take this man at his word."

The mayor glanced up at his assistant and over at the guard. "I hope," he said, in a tone not altogether bantering, "that you'll give me fair warning if either of you ever decides to run for my job." He looked at Arevin again. "If we let you see the healer, will you wear chains until she identifies you?"

Arevin could still feel the iron from the night before, trapping him, enclosing him, cold on his skin all the way to his bones. But Snake would laugh at them when they suggested chains. This time Arevin did smile.

"Give the healer my message," he said. "Then decide whether I need to be chained."

Brian helped the mayor to his feet. The mayor glanced at the guard who believed in Arevin's innocence. "Stay ready. I'll send for him."

She nodded. "Yes, sir."

The guard returned, with her companions and with chains. Arevin stared horrified at the clanking iron. He had hoped Snake would be the next person through that door. He stood up blankly as the guard approached him.

"I'm sorry," she said. She fastened a cold metal band around his waist, shackled his left wrist and passed the chain through a ring on the waistband, then locked the cuff around his right wrist. They led him into the hall.

He knew Snake would not have done this. If she had, then the person who existed in his mind had never existed in reality at all. A real, physical death, hers or even his own, would have been easier for Arevin to accept.

Perhaps the guards had misunderstood. The message that came to them might have been garbled, or it was sent so quickly that no one remembered to tell them not to bother about the chains. Arevin resolved to bear this humiliating error with pride and good humor.

The guards led him into daylight that momentarily dazzled him. Then they were inside again, but his eyes were misadjusted to the dimness. He climbed stairs blindly, stumbling now and then.

The room they took him to was also nearly dark. He paused in the doorway, barely able to make out the blanket-wrapped figure sitting in a chair with her back to him.

"Healer," one of the guards said, "here is the one who says he's your friend."

She did not speak or move.

Arevin stood frozen with terror. If someone had attacked her — if she was badly injured, if she could no longer talk or move, or laugh when they suggested chains — He took one fearful step toward her, another, wanting to rush to her and say he would care for her, wanting to flee and never have to remember her except as alive and whole and strong.

He could see her hand, limply dangling. He fell to his knees beside the shrouded form.

"Snake — "

The shackles made him awkward. He took her hand and bent to kiss it.

As soon as he touched her, even before he saw the smooth, unscarred skin, he knew this was not Snake. He flung himself backward with a cry of despair.

"Where is she?"

The shrouded figure threw off the blanket with a cry of her own, one of shame. She knelt before Arevin, hands outstretched to him, tears on her cheeks. "I'm sorry," she said. "Please forgive me — " She slumped down, her long hair hanging around her beautiful face.

The mayor limped out of the darkness in a corner of the room. Brian helped Arevin up this time, and in a moment the chains clattered to the floor.

"I had to have some better assurance than bruises and rings," the mayor said. "I believe you now."

Arevin heard the sounds but not the meanings. He knew Snake was not here at all, not anywhere. She would never have participated in this farce.

"Where is she?" he whispered.

"She's gone. She went to the city. To Center."

Arevin sat on a luxurious couch in one of the mayor's guest rooms. It was the same room where Snake had stayed, but try as he might, Arevin could feel nothing of her presence.

The curtains were open to the darkness. Arevin had not moved since returning from the observation point, where he had looked down upon the eastern desert and the rolling masses of storm clouds. The killing winds turned sharp-edged sand grains into lethal weapons. In the storm, heavy clothing would not protect Arevin, nor would any amount of courage or desperation. A few moments in the desert would kill him; an hour would strip his bones bare. In the spring no trace of him would be left.

If Snake was still in the desert, she was dead.

He did not cry. When he knew she was gone he would mourn her. But he did not believe she was dead. He wondered if it were foolish to believe he would know if Snake no longer lived. He had thought many things about himself, but never before that he was a fool. Stavin's older father, Arevin's cousin, had known when the little one was ill; he had come back a month early with one of the herds. His ties with Stavin were ties of love and of family, not of blood. Arevin made himself believe the same abilities would work in him.

Someone knocked on Arevin's door.

"Come in," he said reluctantly.

Larril, the servant woman who had pretended to be Snake, entered the room.

"Are you all right?"

"Yes."

"Would you like some dinner?"

"I thought she was safe," Arevin said. "But she's in the desert and the storms have begun."

"She had time to get to Center," Larril said. "She left in plenty of time."

"I've learned a great deal about that city," Arevin said. "Its people can be cruel. Suppose they would not let her in?"

"She even had time to come back."

"But she isn't back. No one has seen her. If she were here, everyone would know."

He took Larril's silence as acquiescence and they both stared morosely out the window.

"Maybe — " Larril cut herself off.

"What?"

"Maybe you should rest and wait for her, you've been searching so many places — "

"That isn't what you planned to say."

"No . . ."

"Please tell me."

"There's one more pass, to the south. No one ever uses it any more. But it's closer to Center than we are."

"You're right," he said slowly, trying to reconstruct the map precisely in his mind. "Might she have gone there?"

"You must have heard these words so often," she said.

"Yes."

"I'm sorry."

"But I thank you," Arevin said. "I might have seen it myself when I looked at the map again, or I might have given up hope. I'll leave for there tomorrow." He shrugged. "I tried to wait for her once and I could not. If I try again I'll become the crazy you all feared me to be. I'm in your debt."

She looked away. "Everyone in this house owes you a debt, one that can't even be paid."

"Never mind," he said. "It's forgotten."

That seemed to give her some comfort. Arevin looked out the window again.

"The healer was kind to me, and you are her friend," Larril said. "Is there anything I can do for you?"

"No," Arevin said. "Nothing."

She hesitated, turned, and walked away. After a moment Arevin realized he had not heard the door close. He glanced over his shoulder just as it swung shut.

The crazy still could not or would not remember his name.

Or maybe, Snake thought, he comes from a clan like Arevin's, and he doesn't tell his name to strangers.

Snake could not imagine the crazy in Arevin's clan. His people were steady and self-possessed; the crazy was dependent and erratic. One minute he thanked her for the promised dreamsnake, the next he wept and moaned that he was as good as dead, for North would kill him. Telling him to keep silent made no difference at all.

Snake was glad to be back in the mountains where they could travel by day. The morning was cool and eerie, the trails narrow and fog-laden. The horses waded through the mist like aquatic creatures, tendrils swirling around their legs. Snake inhaled deeply until the cold air hurt her lungs. She could smell the fog, and the rich humus, and the faint spicy tang of pitch. The world lay green and gray around her, for the leaves on the overhanging trees had not yet begun to turn. Higher on the mountain, the darker evergreens looked almost black through the fog.

Melissa rode right next to her, silent and watchful. She would not stay any closer to the crazy than she had to. He was audible but not visible, somewhere behind them. His old horse could not quite keep up with Swift and Squirrel, but at least Snake did not have to stand for riding double anymore.

His voice grew fainter and fainter. Impatiently, Snake reined Swift in to let him catch up. Melissa stopped even more reluctantly. The crazy had refused to ride any better animal; only this one was calm enough for him. Snake had had to press payment on the horse's owners, and she did not think the young herders had tried to refuse to sell it to her because they were not glad to get rid of it or because they wanted a higher price. Jean and Kev had been embarrassed. Well, no less was Snake.

The horse shambled through the mist, eyelids drooping, ears flopping. The crazy hummed tunelessly.

"Does the trail look familiar yet?"

The crazy gazed smiling at her. "It's all the same to me," he said, and laughed.

Snapping at him, cajoling him, threatening him did no good. He did not seem to be in pain or in need anymore, since being promised a dreamsnake, as if the expectation were sufficient to maintain him. He hummed and muttered contentedly and made incomprehensible jokes, and sometimes straightened up, looked around, exclaimed "Ever southward!" and subsided into tuneless songs again. Snake sighed and let the crazy's broken down old horse pass them so the crazy could lead.

"I don't think he's taking us anyplace, Snake," Melissa said. "I think he's just leading us around so we have to take care of him. We ought to leave him here and go somewhere else."

The crazy stiffened. Slowly, he turned around. The old horse stopped. Snake was surprised to see a tear spill from the crazy's eye and drip down his cheek.

"Don't leave me," he said. His expression and his tone of voice were simply pitiful. Before this he had not seemed capable of caring so much about anything at all. He gazed at Melissa, blinking his lashless eyelids. "You're right not to trust me, little one," he said. "But please don't abandon me." His eyes became unfocused and his words came from very far away. "Stay with me to the broken dome, and we'll both have our own dreamsnakes. Surely your mistress will give you one." He leaned toward her, reaching out, his fingers curved like claws. "You forget bad memories and troubles, you'll forget your scars — "

Melissa jerked back from him with an incoherent curse of surprise and anger. She clamped her legs against Squirrel's sides and put the tiger-pony into a gallop from a standstill, leaning close over his neck and never looking back. In a moment the trees obscured all but the muffled thud of Squirrel's hooves.

Snake glared at the crazy. "How could you say such a thing to her?"

He blinked, confused. "What did I say wrong?"

"You follow us, you understand? Don't go off the trail. I'll find her and we'll wait for you." She touched Swift's sides with her heels and cantered after Melissa. The crazy's uncomprehending voice drifted after her.

"But why did she do that?"

Snake was not worried about Melissa's safety, or Squirrel's. Her daughter could ride any horse in these mountains all day and never put herself or her mount in danger. On the dependable tiger-pony she was doubly safe. But the crazy had hurt her and Snake did not want to leave her alone right now.

She did not have to go far. Where the trail started to rise again, turning toward the slope of the valley and another mountain, Melissa stood beside Squirrel, hugging his neck as he nuzzled her shoulder. Hearing Swift approach, Melissa wiped her face on her sleeve and looked around. Snake dismounted and went toward her.

"I was afraid you'd go a long way," she said. "I'm glad you didn't."

"You can't expect a horse to run uphill just after he's been lame," Melissa said matter-of-factly, but with a trace of resentment.

Snake held out the reins of Swift's bridle. "If you want to ride hard and fast for a while you can take Swift."

Melissa stared at her as if trying to perceive some sarcasm in her expression that had been absent from her tone. She did not find it.

"No," Melissa said. "Never mind. Maybe it would help, but I'm all right. It's just — I don't want to forget. Not like that, anyway."

Snake nodded. "I know."

Melissa embraced her with one of her abrupt, self-conscious hugs. Snake held her and patted her shoulder. "He *is* crazy."

"Yeah." Melissa drew back slowly. "I know he can help you. I'm sorry I can't keep from hating him. I've tried."

"So have I," Snake said.

They sat down to wait for the crazy to come at his own slow pace.

Before the crazy had even begun to recognize the countryside or the trail, Snake saw the broken dome. She looked at its hulking shape several moments before she realized, with a start, what it was. At first it looked like another peak of the mountain ridge; its color, gray instead of black, attracted Snake's attention. She had expected the usual hemisphere, not a tremendous irregular surface that lay across the hillside like a quiescent amoeba. The main translucent gray was streaked with colors and reddened by afternoon sunlight. Whether the dome had been constructed in an asymmetrical form or whether it began as a round plastic bubble and was melted and deformed by the forces of the planet's former civilization, Snake could not tell. But it had been in its present shape for a long, long time. Dirt had settled in the hollows and valleys in its surface, and trees and grass and bushes grew thick in the sheltered pockets.

Snake rode in silence for a minute or two, hardly able to believe she had finally reached this goal. She touched Melissa's shoulder; the child looked up abruptly from the indeterminate spot on Squirrel's neck at which she had been staring. Snake pointed. Melissa saw the dome and exclaimed softly, then smiled with excitement and relief. Snake grinned back.

The crazy sang behind them, oblivious to their destination. A *broken dome*. The words fit together strangely. Domes did not break, they did not weather, they did not change. They simply existed, mysterious and impenetrable.

Snake stopped, waiting for the crazy. When the old horse shambled up and stopped beside her, she pointed upward. The crazy followed with his gaze. He blinked as if he could not quite believe what he was seeing.

"Is that it?" Snake asked.

"Not yet," the crazy said. "No, not yet, I'm not ready."

"How do we get up there? Can we ride?"

"North will see us . . ."

Snake shrugged and dismounted. The way to the dome was steep and she could see no trail. "We walk, then." She unfastened the girth straps of the mare's saddle. "Melissa — "

"No!" Melissa said sharply. "I won't stay down here while you go up there alone with that one. Squirrel and Swift will be okay and nobody will bother the case. Except maybe another crazy and they'll deserve what they get."

Snake was beginning to understand why her own strong will had so often exasperated the older healers, when she was Melissa's age. But at the station there had never been much serious danger, and they could afford to indulge her.

Snake sat down on a fallen log and motioned to her daughter to sit beside her. Melissa did so, without looking up at Snake, her shoulders set in defiance.

"I need your help," Snake said. "I can't succeed without you. If something happens to me — "

"That's not succeeding!"

"In a way it is. Melissa . . . the healers need dreamsnakes. Up in that dome they have enough to use them for play. I have to find out how they got them. But if I can't, if I don't come back down, you're the only way the other healers will be able to know what happened to me. And why it happened. You're the only way they'll know about the dreamsnakes."

Melissa stared at the ground, rubbing the knuckles of one hand with the fingernails of the other. "This is very important to you, isn't it?"

"Yes."

Melissa sighed. Her hands were fists. "All right," she said. "What do you want me to do?"

Snake hugged her. "If I'm not back in, oh, two days, take Swift and Squirrel and ride north. Keep on going past Mountainside and Middlepass. It's a long way, but there's plenty of money in the case. You know how to get it safely."

"I have my wages," Melissa said.

"All right, but the other's just as much yours. You don't need to open the compartments Mist and Sand are in. They can survive until you get home." For the first time she actually considered the possibility that Melissa might have to make the trip alone. "Sand is getting too fat anyway." She forced a smile.

"But — " Melissa cut herself off.

"What?"

"If something does happen to you, I couldn't get back in time to help, not if I go all the way to the healers' station."

"If I don't come back on my own, there won't be any way to help me. Don't come after me by yourself. Please. I need to know you won't."

"If you don't come back in three days, I'll go tell your people about the dreamsnakes."

Snake let her have the extra day, with some gratitude, in fact. "Thank you, Melissa."

They let the tiger-pony and the gray mare loose in a clearing near the trail. Instead of galloping toward the meadow and rolling in the grass, they stood close together, watchful and nervous, their ears swiveling, nostrils wide. The crazy's old horse stood in the shade alone, his head down. Melissa watched them, her lips tight.

The crazy stood where he had dismounted, staring at Snake, tears in his eyes.

"Melissa," Snake said, "if you do go home alone, tell them I adopted you. Then — then they'll know you're their daughter too."

"I don't want to be their daughter. I want to be yours."

"You are. No matter what." She took a deep breath and let it out slowly. "Is there a trail?" she asked the crazy. "What's the quickest way up?"

"No trail . . . it opens before me and closes behind me."

Snake could feel Melissa restraining a sarcastic remark. "Let's go, then," she said, "and see if your magic will work for more than one."

She hugged Melissa one last time. Melissa held tight, reluctant to let her go.

"It'll be all right," Snake said. "Don't worry."

The crazy climbed surprisingly quickly, almost as if a path really did open up for him, and for him alone. Snake had to work hard to keep up with him, and sweat stung her eyes. She scrambled up a few meters of harsh black stone and grabbed his robe. "Not so fast."

His breath came quickly, from excitement, not effort. "The dreamsnakes are near," he said. He jerked his robe from her hand and scuttled up sheer rock. Snake wiped her forehead on her sleeve, and climbed.

The next time she caught him she grabbed him by the shoulder and did not let go until he sank down on a ledge.

"We'll rest here," she said, "and then we'll go on, more slowly and more quietly. Otherwise your friends will know we're coming before we're ready to have them know."

"The dreamsnakes — "

"North is between us and the dreamsnakes. If he sees you first will he let you go on?"

"You'll give me a dreamsnake? One of my own? Not like North?"

"Not like North," Snake said. She sat in a narrow wedge of shade, leaning her head back against the volcanic rock. In the valley below, an edge of the meadow showed between dark evergreen branches, but neither Swift nor Squirrel was in that part of the clearing. It looked like a small scrap of velvet from this distance. Suddenly Snake felt both isolated and lonely.

Nearby, the rock was not so barren as it appeared from below. Lichen lay in green-gray patches here and there, and small fat-leaved succulents nestled in shady niches. Snake leaned forward to see one more closely. Against black rock, in shadow, its color was indistinct.

She sat back abruptly.

Picking up a shard of rock, Snake leaned forward again and knelt over the squat blue-green plant. She poked at its leaves. They closed down tight.

It's escaped, Snake thought. It's from the broken dome.

She should have expected something like this; she should have known she would find things that did not belong on the earth. She prodded it again, from the same side. It was, indeed, moving. It would crawl all the way down the mountain if she let it. She slipped the rock's point beneath it and lifted the plant out of the crevice, rolling it upside down. Except for the bristle of rootlets in its center, it looked just the same, its brilliant turquoise leaves rotating on their bases, seeking a hold. Snake had never seen this species before, but she had seen similar creatures, plants — they did not fit into the normal classifications — take over a field in a night, poisoning the ground so nothing else would grow. One summer several years before she and the other healers had helped burn off a swarm of them from nearby farms. They had not swarmed again, but little colonies of them still turned up from time to time, and the fields they had taken over were barren.

She wanted to burn this one but could not risk a fire now. She pushed it out of the shadows into sunlight and it closed up tight. Now Snake noticed that here and there lay the shriveled hulls of other crawlies, dead and sun-dried, defeated by the barren cliff.

"Let's go," Snake said, more to herself than to the crazy.

She chinned herself over the edge of the cliff to the broken dome's hollow. The strangeness of the place hit Snake like a physical blow. Alien plants grew all around the base of the tremendous half-collapsed structure, nearly to the cliff, leaving no clear path at all. What covered the ground resembled nothing Snake knew, not grass or scrub or bushes. It was a flat, borderless expanse of bright red leaf. Looking closer, Snake could see that it was more than a single huge leaf: each section was perhaps twice as long as she was tall, irregularly shaped, and joined at the edges to neighboring leaves by a system of intertwining hairs. Wherever more than two leaves touched, a delicate frond rose a few handsbreadths from the intersection. Wherever a fissure split the stone, a turquoise streak of crawlies parted the red ground cover, seeking shadow as deliberately as the red leaves spread themselves for light. Someday several crawlies at once would overcome the long sloping exposed cliff face and then they would take over the valley below: someday, when weather and heat and cold opened more sheltering cracks in the stone.

The depressions in the surface of the dome retained some normal vegetation, for the crawlies' reproductive tendrils could not reach that far. If this species was anything like the similar one Snake had seen, it produced no seeds. But other alien plants had reached the top of the dome, for the melted hollows were filled randomly, some with ordinary green, others with bold, unearthly colors. In a few of the seared, heat-sunken pockets, high above the ground, the colors warred together, one not yet having overcome the other.

Inside the translucent dome, tall shapes showed as shadows, indistinct and strange. Between the edge of the cliff and the dome there was no cover, nor was there any other approach.

Snake became painfully aware of her visibility, for she was standing silhouetted against the sky.

The crazy clambered up beside her. "We follow the path," he said, pointing across the flat-leaves that no trail parted. In more than one place dark veins of crawlies cut the line he indicated.

Snake stepped forward and put her boot carefully on the edge of a flat-leaf. Nothing happened. It was no different from stepping on an ordinary leaf. Beneath it, the ground felt as solid as any other stone.

The crazy passed her, striding toward the dome. Snake grabbed his shoulder.

"The dreamsnakes!" he cried. "You promised!"

"Have you forgotten that North banished you? If you could just come back here, why did you look for me?"

The crazy stared at the ground. "He won't like to see me," he whispered.

"Stay behind me," she said. "Everything will be all right."

Snake started across the barely yielding leaves, placing her feet cautiously in case the wide red sheets hid a crack the blue creepers had not yet taken over. The crazy followed.

"North likes new people," he said. "He likes it when they come and ask him to let them dream." His voice grew wistful. "Maybe he'll like me again."

Snake's boots left marks on the red flat-leaves, blazing her path across the outcropping that held the broken dome. She only looked back once: her footsteps lay in livid purple bruises against red all the way back to the cliff edge. The crazy's trail was much fainter. He crept along behind her, a little to one side so he could always see the dome, not quite as frightened of this person North as he was attracted by the dreamsnakes.

The oblong bubble was even larger than it looked from the cliff. Its translucent flank rose in an immense and gentle curve to the highest point of the surface, many times Snake's height. The side she approached was streaked with multicolored veins.

They did not fade to the original gray until they reached the far end of the dome, a long way to Snake's right. To her left, the streaks grew brighter as they approached the structure's narrower end.

Snake reached the dome. The flat-leaves grew up along its sides to the level of her knees, but above that the plastic was clean. Snake put her face up close to the wall, peering between a stripe of orange and one of purple, cutting off the exterior light with her hands, but the shapes inside were still indistinct and strange. Nothing moved.

She followed the intensifying bands of color.

As she rounded the narrow end, she saw why it was called the broken dome. Whatever had melted the surface had a power Snake could not comprehend, for it had also blasted an opening in a material she believed indestructible. The rainbow streaks radiated from the hole along buckled plastic. The heat must have crystallized the substance, for the edges of the opening had broken away, leaving a huge, jagged entrance. Globs of plastic, fluorescent colors glowing between the leaves of alien plants, lay all over the ground.

Snake approached the entrance cautiously. The crazy began his half-humming moan again.

"Sh-h!" Snake did not turn back, but he subsided.

Fascinated, Snake climbed through the hole. She felt the sharp edges against her palms but did not really notice them. Beyond the opening, where the side wall, when intact, had curved inward to form the roof, an entire archway of plastic was slumped to barely more than Snake's height. Here and there the plastic had run and dripped and formed ropes from ceiling to floor. Snake reached out and touched one gently. It thrummed like a giant harp string, and she grabbed it quickly to silence it.

The light inside was reddish and eerie; Snake kept blinking her eyes, trying to clear her vision. But nothing was wrong with her sight except that it could not become accustomed to the alien landscape. The dome had enclosed an alien jungle, now gone wild, and many more species than crawlies and flat-leaves crowded the ground. A great vine with a stem bigger around than the largest tree Snake had ever seen climbed up the wall, huge suckers probing the now brittle plastic, punching through to precarious holds in the dome. The vine spread a canopy across the ceiling, its bluish leaves tiny and delicate, its flowers tremendous but made up of thousands of white petals even smaller than the leaves.

Snake moved farther inside, to where the melting, less severe, had not collapsed the ceiling. Here and there a vine had crept up the edge, then, where the plastic was both too strong to break and too slick to grasp, dropped back to earth. After the vines, the trees took over, or what passed for trees inside the dome. One stood on a hummock nearby: a tangled mass of woody stalks, or limbs, piled and twisted far above Snake's head, spreading slowly as it rose to shape the plant into a cone.

Recalling the crazy's vague description, Snake pointed toward a central hill that rose almost to touch the plastic sky. "That way, hm?" She found herself whispering.

Crouched behind her, the crazy mumbled something that sounded affirmative. Snake set out, passing beneath the lacy shadows of the tangle-trees and through occasional areas of colored light where the dome's rainbow wounds filtered sunlight. As Snake walked she listened carefully, for the sound of another human voice, for the faint hissing of nested serpents, for anything. But even the air was still.

The ground began to rise: they reached the foot of the hill. Here and there black volcanic rock pierced the topsoil, the alien earth for all Snake knew. It looked ordinary enough, but the plants growing from it did not. Here the ground cover looked like fine brown hair and had the same slick texture. The crazy led on, following a trail that was not there. Snake trudged after him. The hillside steepened and sweat beaded on her forehead. Her knee began to ache again. She cursed softly under her breath. A pebble rolled beneath the hair plants she stepped on and her boot slipped out from under her. Snake snatched at the grass to break her fall. It held long enough to steady her, but when she stood again she held a handful of the thin stalks. Each piece had its own delicate root, as if it really were hair.

They climbed higher, and still no one challenged them. The sweat on Snake's forehead dried: the air was growing cooler. The crazy, grinning and mumbling to himself, climbed more eagerly. The coolness became a whisper of air running downhill like water. Snake had expected the hilltop, right up under the crown of the dome, to be warm with trapped heat. But the higher she climbed, the colder and stronger the breeze became.

They passed through the area of hill-hair and entered another stand of trees. These were similar to the ones below, formed of tangled branches and compact twisted roots, with tiny fluttering leaves. Here, though, they grew only a few meters high, and they clustered together in small groves of three or more, deforming each other's symmetry. The forest thickened. Finally, winding between the twisted trunks, a pathway appeared. As the forest closed in over her, Snake caught up with the crazy and stopped him.

"From now on stay behind me, all right?"

He nodded without looking at her.

The dome diffused sunlight so nothing cast a shadow, and the light was barely bright enough to penetrate the twisting, knotted branches overhead. Tiny leaves shivered in the cold breeze blowing through the forest corridor. Snake moved forward. The rocks beneath her boots had given way to a soft trail of humus and fallen leaves.

To the right a tremendous chunk of rock rose up out of the hillside at a gentle slant, forming a ledge that would overlook the larger part of the dome. Snake considered climbing out on it, but it would put her in full view. She did not want North and his people to be able to accuse her of spying, nor did she want them to know of her presence until she walked into their camp. Pressing on, she shivered, for the breeze had become a cold wind.

She glanced around to be sure the crazy was following her. As she did, he scurried up toward the rock ledge, waving his arms. Startled, Snake hesitated. Her first thought was that he had decided again to die. In that instant Melissa dashed after him.

"North!" he cried, and Melissa flung herself at his knees, hitting him with her shoulder and knocking him down. Snake ran toward them as Melissa fought to keep him from getting up and he fought to free himself. His single shout echoed and re-echoed, rebounding from the walls and the melted undulations of the dome. Melissa struggled with the crazy, half-tangled in his emaciated limbs and his voluminous desert robes, fumbling for her knife and somehow managing to keep her hold on his legs.

Snake pulled Melissa away from him, as gently as she could. The crazy lurched around, ready to scream again, but Snake drew her own knife and held it beneath his chin. Her other hand was clenched in a fist. She opened it slowly, forcing her anger away.

"Why did you do that? Why? We had an agreement."

"North — " he whispered. "North will be angry with me. But if I bring him new people . . ." His voice trailed off.

Snake looked at Melissa, and Melissa looked at the ground.

"I didn't promise not to follow you," she said. "I made sure of that. I know it's cheating, but . . ." She raised her head and met Snake's gaze. "There are things you don't know about people. You trust them too much. There are things I don't know, too, I know that, but they're different things."

"It's all right," Snake said. "You're right, I did trust him too much. Thank you for stopping him."

Melissa shrugged. "A lot of good I did. They know we're here now, wherever they are."

The crazy began to giggle, rolling back and forth with his arms wrapped around him. "North will like me again."

"Oh, shut up," Snake said. She slid her knife back into its sheath. "Melissa, you've got to get out of the dome before anyone comes."

"Please come with me," Melissa said. "Nothing makes any sense around here."

"Someone has to tell my people about this place."

"I don't care about your people! I care about you! How can I go to them and tell them I let you get killed by a crazy?"

"Melissa, please, there isn't time to argue."

Melissa twined the end of her headcloth in her fingers, pulling it forward so the material covered the scar on the side of her face. Though Snake had changed back to her regular clothes when they left the desert, Melissa had not.

"You should let me stay with you," she said. She turned around, shoulders slumped, and started down the trail.

"You'll get your wish, little one." The voice was deep and courteous.

For an instant Snake thought the crazy had spoken in a normal tone, but he was cowering on the bare rock beside her, and a fourth person now stood on the trail. Melissa, stopping short, stared up at him and then backed away.

"North!" the crazy cried. "North, I brought new people. And I warned you, I didn't let them sneak up on you. Did you hear me?"

"I heard you," North said. "And I wondered why you disobeyed me by coming back."

"I thought you'd like these people."

"And that's all?"

"Yes!"

"Are you sure?" The courteous tone remained, but behind it lay great pleasure in its taunting, and the man's smile was more cruel than kind. His form was eerie in the dim light, for he was very tall, so tall he had to hunch over in the leafy tunnel, pathologically tall: pituitary gigantism, Snake thought. Emaciation accentuated every asymmetry of his body. He was dressed all in white, and he was albino as well, with chalk-white hair and eyebrows and eyelashes, and very pale blue eyes.

"Yes, North," the crazy said. "That's all."

Heavy with North's presence, silence lay over the woods. Snake thought she could see other movement between the trees, but she could not be sure, and the growth seemed too close and heavy for other people to be hiding there. Perhaps in this dark alien forest the trees twined and untwined their branches as easily as lovers clasp hands. Snake shivered.

"Please, North — let me come back. I've brought you two followers — "

Snake touched the crazy's shoulder; he fell silent.

"Why are you here?"

In the last few weeks, Snake had grown wary enough not to tell North immediately that she was a healer. "For the same reason as anyone else," she said. "I've come about the dreamsnakes."

"You don't look like the kind of person who usually finds out about them." He came forward, looming over her in the dimness. He glanced from her to the crazy, and then to Melissa. His hard gaze softened. "Ah, I see. You've come for her."

Melissa nearly snarled a denial: Snake saw her start with anger, then forcibly hold herself calm.

"We've all three come together," Snake said. "All for the same reason." She felt the crazy move, as if to rush toward North and fling himself at his feet. She clamped her hand harder around the bony point of his shoulder and he slumped into lethargy again.

"And what did you bring me, to initiate you?"

"I don't understand," Snake said.

North's brief, annoyed frown dissolved in a laugh. "That's just what I'd expect from this poor fool. He brought you here without explaining our customs."

"But I brought them, North. I brought them for you."

"And they brought you for me? That's hardly sufficient payment."

"Payment can be arranged," Snake said, "when we reach an agreement." That North had set himself up as a minor god, requiring tribute, using the power of the dreamsnakes to enforce his authority, angered Snake as much as anything else she had heard. Or, rather, offended her. Snake had been taught, and believed very deeply, that using healers' serpents for self-aggrandizement was immoral and unforgivable. While visiting other people she had heard children's stories in which villains or tragic heroes used magical abilities to make tyrants of themselves; they always came to bad ends. But healers had no such stories. It was not fear that kept them from misusing what they had. It was self-respect.

North hobbled a few steps closer. "My dear child, you don't understand. Once you join my camp, you don't leave again until I'm certain of your loyalty. In the first place, you won't want to leave. In the second, when I send someone out it's proof that I trust them. It's an honor."

Snake nodded toward the crazy. "And him?"

North laughed without cheer. "I didn't send him out. I exiled him."

"But I know where their things are, North!" The crazy pulled away from Snake. This time, in disgust, she let him go. "You don't need them, just me." Kneeling, he wrapped his arms around North's legs. "Everything's in the valley. We only need to take it."

Snake shrugged when North glanced from the crazy to her. "It's well protected. He could lead you to my gear but you couldn't take it." Still she did not tell him what she was.

North extricated himself from the crazy's arms. "I am not strong," he said. "I don't travel to the valley."

A small, heavy bag landed at North's feet. He and Snake both looked at Melissa.

"If you need to be paid just to talk to somebody," Melissa said belligerently, "there."

North bent painfully down and picked up Melissa's wages. He opened the sack and poured the coins out into his hand. Even in the dim forest light, the gold glittered. He shook the gold pieces up and down thoughtfully.

"All right, this will do as a beginning. You'll have to give up your weapons, of course, and then we'll go on to my home."

Snake took her knife from her belt and tossed it on the ground.

"Snake — " Melissa whispered. She looked up at her, stricken, clearly wondering why she had done what she had done, her fingers clenched around the handle of her own knife.

"If we want him to trust us, we have to trust him," Snake said. Yet she did not trust him, and she did not want to trust him. Still, knives would be of little use against a group of people, and she did not think North had come alone.

My dear daughter, Snake thought, I never said this would be easy.

Melissa flinched back as North took one step toward her. Her knuckles were white.

"Don't be afraid of me, little one. And don't try to be clever. I have more resources than you might imagine."

Melissa looked at the ground, slowly drew her knife, and dropped it at her feet.

North ordered the crazy to Melissa with a quick jerk of his head. "Search her."

Snake put her hand on Melissa's shoulder. The child was taut and trembling. "He need not search her. I give you my word that Melissa carries no other weapons." Snake could sense that Melissa had controlled herself nearly to her limit. Her dislike of and disgust for the crazy would push her farther than her composure would stretch.

"All the more reason to search her," North said. "We'll not be fanatic about the thoroughness. Do you want to go first?"

"That would be better," Snake said. She raised her hands, but North prodded her, turned her around, and made her reach out and lean forward and grasp the twisted branches of a tree. If she had not been worried about Melissa she would have been amused by the theatricality of it all.

Nothing happened for what seemed a long time. Snake started to turn around again, but North touched the fresh shiny puncture scars on her hand with the tip of one pale finger. "Ah," he said, very softly, so close she could feel his warm, unpleasant breath. "You're a healer."

Snake heard the crossbow just after the bolt plunged into her shoulder, just as the pain spread over her in a wave. Her knees swayed but she could not fall. The force of the bolt dissipated through the trunk of the twisted tree, in vibrations up and down her body. Melissa screamed in fury. Snake heard other people behind her. Blood ran hot down her shoulder blade, down her breast. With her left hand, she fumbled for the shaft of the thin crossbow bolt where it ripped out of her flesh and into the tree, but her fingers slipped and the living wood held the bolt's tip fast. Melissa was at her side, holding her up as best she could. Voices wove themselves together into a tapestry stretching behind her.

Someone grabbed the crossbow bolt and jerked it loose, wrenching it through muscle. The scrape of wood on bone wrung a gasp from her. The cool smooth metal point slid from the wound.

"Kill her now," the crazy said. The words came fast with excitement. "Kill her and leave her here as a warning."

Snake's heart pumped hot blood down her shoulder. She staggered, caught herself, and fell to her knees. The force hit the small of her back, vibrating with the pain, and she tried but failed to cringe away from it, like poor little Grass writhing with a severed spine.

Melissa stood before her, her scarred face and red hair uncovered as she tried clumsily, blinded with tears, whispering comfort as she would to a horse, to wind her headcloth over the wound.

So much blood from such a small arrow, Snake thought.

She fainted.

The coldness roused Snake first. Even as she regained consciousness, Snake was surprised to be aware at all. The hatred in North's voice when he recognized her profession had left her no hope. Her shoulder ached fiercely, but without the stabbing, thought-destroying pain. She flexed her right hand. It was weak, but it moved.

She struggled up, shivering, blinking, her vision blurred. "Melissa?" she whispered.

Nearby, North laughed. "Not being a healer yet, she hasn't been hurt."

Cold air flowed around her. Snake shook her head and drew her sleeve across her eyes. Her sight cleared abruptly. The effort of sitting up made her break out in a sweat that the air turned icy. North sat before her, smiling, flanked by his people, who closed the human circle around her. The blood on her shirt, except immediately over the wound, was brown: she had been unconscious for some time.

"Where is she?"

"She's safe," North said. "She can stay with us. You needn't worry, she'll be happy here."

"She didn't want to come in the first place. This isn't the kind of happiness she wants. Let her go home."

"As I said before, I have nothing against her."

"What is it you have against healers?"

North gazed at her steadily for a long time. "I should think that would be obvious."

"I'm sorry," Snake said. "We could probably give you some ability to form melanin, but we aren't magicians." The frigid air flowed from a cave behind her, billowing around her, raising goose bumps on her arms. Her boots were gone; the cold stone sucked heat from the bare soles of her feet. But it also numbed the ache in her shoulder. Then she shivered violently and pain struck with even more ferocity than before. She gasped and closed her eyes for a moment, then sat very still in her own inner darkness, breathing deeply and shutting away her perception of the wound. It was bleeding again, in back where it would be hard to reach. She hoped Melissa was somewhere warmer, and she wondered where the dreamsnakes were, for they needed warmth to survive. Snake opened her eyes.

"And your height —" she said.

North laughed bitterly. "Of all the things I've said about healers, I never said they didn't have nerve!"

"What?" Snake asked, confused. She was lightheaded from loss of blood, and in the middle of replying to North. "We might have helped if we'd seen you early. You must have been grown before anyone took you to a healer — "

North's pale face turned scarlet with fury. "Shut up!" He leaped to his feet and dragged Snake up. She hugged her right arm to her side.

"Do you think I want to hear that? Do you think I want to keep hearing that I *could* have been ordinary?" He pushed her toward the cave. She stumbled into the wind but he dragged her up again. "Healers! Where were you when I needed you? I'll let you see how I feel — "

"North, please, North!" Snake's crazy sidled out of the crowd of North's emaciated followers, whom Snake now only perceived as vague shapes. "She helped me, North, I'll take her place." He plucked at North's sleeve, moaning and pleading. North pushed him away and he fell and lay still.

"Your brain's addled," North said. "Or you think mine is."

The interior of the cave glittered in the dim light of smoking torches, its walls flawed jewels of ice. Above the torches sooty stone showed in large round patches. Melt-water trickled into pools of slush that spread across the floor and ran together in a rivulet. Water dripped everywhere with a cold sound of crystal clarity. Every step Snake took jarred her shoulder again, and she no longer had the strength to force the sensation away. The air was heavy with the smell of burning pitch. Gradually she became aware of a low hum of machinery, felt rather than heard. It crept through her body, into her bones.

Ahead the tunnel grew lighter. It ended suddenly, opening out into a depression in the top of the hill, like the crater of a volcano but clearly human-made. Snake stood in the mouth of the icy tunnel and blinked, looking stupidly around. The black eyes of other caves stared back at her. The dome above formed a gray, directionless sky. Across from her the cold air flowed from the largest tunnel, forming an almost palpable lake, drained by the smaller tunnels. North pushed Snake forward again. She saw things, felt things, but reacted to nothing. She could not.

"Down there. Climb." North kicked a coil of rope and wood and it clattered into the deep crack in the rock in the center of the crater. The tangle unrolled: a rope ladder. Snake could see its top but its lower end was in darkness.

"Climb," North said again. "Or be thrown."

"North, please," the crazy moaned, and Snake suddenly realized where she was being sent. North stared at her while she laughed. She felt as if strength were flowing into her, drawn from the wind and the earth.

"Is this how you torture a healer?" she said. She swung herself down into the crevasse, clumsily but eagerly. One-handed, she lowered herself by steps into the freezing darkness, catching each rung with her bare toes and pulling it outward so she had a foothold. Above, she heard the crazy break down in helpless sobs.

"We'll see how you feel in the morning," North said.

The crazy's voice rose in terror. "She'll kill all the dreamsnakes, North! North, that's what she came here for."

"I'd like to see that," North said. "A healer killing dreamsnakes."

From the echoes as the rungs clattered against the walls of the crevasse, Snake knew she was nearing the bottom. It was not quite dark, but her eyes accustomed themselves slowly. Damp with sweat and shivering again, she had to pause. She rested her forehead against cold stone. Her toes and the knuckles of her left hand were scraped raw, for the ladder lay flush against stone.

It was then, finally, that she heard the soft rustling slide of small serpents. Clutching the ropes, Snake hung against the stone and squinted into the dimness below. Light penetrated in a long narrow streak down the center of the crevasse.

A dreamsnake slid smoothly from one edge of darkness to the other.

Snake fumbled her way the last few meters, stepping to the floor as cautiously as she could, feeling around with her numb bare foot until she was certain nothing moved beneath it. She knelt. Cold jagged chunks of stone cut into her knees, and the only warmth was the fresh blood on her shoulder. But she reached out among the shards, feeling carefully. Her fingertips brushed the smooth scales of a serpent as it slid silently away. She reached out again, ready this time, and caught the next one she touched. Her hand stung at two tiny points. She smiled and held the dreamsnake gently behind the head, by habit conserving its venom. She brought it close enough to see. It was wild, not tame and gentle as Grass had been. It writhed and lashed itself around her hand; its delicate trident tongue flicked out at her, and in again to taste her scent. But it did not hiss, just as Grass had never hissed.

As her eyes became more and more used to the darkness, Snake gradually perceived the rest of the crevasse, and all the other dreamsnakes, all sizes of them, lone ones, clumps of them, tangles of them, more than she had ever seen before in her life, more than her people could gather together at the station, if all the healers brought their dreamsnakes home at the same time.

The dreamsnake she held grew quiet in the meager warmth

of her hand. One drop of blood collected over each puncture of its bite, but the sting of its venom had lasted only an instant. Snake sat back on her heels and stroked the dreamsnake's head. Once more she began to laugh. She knew she had to control herself: this was more hysteria than joy. But, for the moment, she laughed.

"Laugh away, healer." North's voice echoed darkly against stone. "We'll see how long you laugh."

"You're a fool," she cried with glee, with dreamsnakes all around her and in her hand. She laughed at the hilarity of this punishment, like a child's story come true. She laughed until she cried, but for an instant the tears were real. She knew that when this torture could not harm her, North would find some other way. She sniffed and coughed and wiped her face on the tail of her shirt, for at least she had a little time.

And then she saw Melissa.

Her daughter lay crumpled on the broken stone in the narrow end of the crevasse. Snake moved carefully to her side, trying not to injure any of the serpents she passed, nor to startle those that lay curled around Melissa's arms, or coiled together against her body. They made green tendrils in her bright red hair.

Snake knelt beside Melissa and gently, carefully plucked the wild serpents away. North's people had taken Melissa's robe, and cut her pants off at the knees. Her arms were bare, and her boots, like Snake's, were gone. Rope bound her hands and feet, chafing her wrists raw where she had struggled. Small bloody bites spotted her bare arms and legs. A dreamsnake struck: its fangs sank into Snake's flesh and the creature jerked back almost too fast to see. Her teeth clenched, Snake remembered the crazy's words: "It's best if they strike you all over at once . . ."

With her own body, Snake blocked the serpents away from Melissa and freed her wrists, fumbling left-handed with the knots. Melissa's skin was cold and dry. Snake cradled her in her left arm as the wild dreamsnakes crawled over her own bare feet and ankles. Once more she wondered how they lived in the cold. She would never have dared let Grass loose in this temperature. Even the case would have been too cold: she would have brought him out, warmed him in her hands, and let him loop himself around her throat.

Melissa's hand slid limply against the rocks. Blood smeared in streaks from the puncture wounds where her skin rubbed cloth or stone. Snake managed to get Melissa in her lap, off the freezing ground. Her pulse was heavy and slow, her breathing deep. But each new breath came so long after the last that Snake was afraid she would stop altogether.

The cold pressed down around them, pushing back the ache in Snake's shoulder and draining her energy again. Stay awake, she thought. Stay awake. Melissa might stop breathing; her heart might stop from so much venom, and then she will need help. Despite herself, Snake's eyes went out of focus and her eyelids drooped; each time she nodded asleep she jerked herself awake again. A pleasant thought insinuated itself into her mind: No one dies of dreamsnake venom. They live, or they die of their illness, in peace, when their time comes. It's safe to sleep, she will not die. But Snake knew of no one who had ever been given such a large dose of the venom, and Melissa was only a child.

A tiny dreamsnake slid between her leg and the side of the crevasse. She reached out with her numb right hand and picked it up with wonder. It lay coiled in her palm, staring toward her with its lidless eyes, its trident tongue tasting the air. Something about it was unusual: Snake looked closer.

It was an eggling, just hatched, for it still had the beak of horny tissue common to the hatchlings of many species of serpents. It was final proof of how North obtained his dreamsnakes. He had not found an offworld supply. He did not clone them. He had a breeding population. In this pit were all sizes and all ages, from egglings to mature individuals larger than any dreamsnakes Snake had ever seen.

She turned to lay the hatchling down behind her, but her hand knocked against the wall. Startled, the dreamsnake struck. The sharp stab of its tiny fangs made Snake flinch. The creature slid from her hand to the ground and on into shadows.

"North!" Snake's voice was hoarse. She cleared her dry throat and tried again. "North!"

In time, his silhouette appeared at the rim of the crevasse. By his easy smile Snake knew he expected her to beg him for her freedom. He looked down at her, noting the way she had positioned herself between Melissa and the serpents.

"She could be free if you'd let her," he said. "Don't keep her from my creatures."

"Your creatures are wasted here, North," Snake said. "You should take them out into the world. You'd be honored by everyone, particularly the healers."

"I'm honored here," North said.

"But this must be a difficult life. You could live in comfort and ease — "

"There's no comfort for me," North said. "You of all people should realize that. Sleeping on the ground or wrapped in featherbeds, it's all the same to me."

"You've made dreamsnakes breed," Snake said. She glanced down at Melissa. Several of the serpents had insinuated themselves past Snake. She grabbed one just before it reached her daughter's bare arm. The serpent struck and bit her. She put it and the others behind her with stinging hands, ignoring their fangs. "However you do it, you should take the knowledge out and give it to others."

"And what's your place in this plan? Should I bring you up to be my herald? You could dance into each new town and tell them I was coming."

"I admit I wouldn't care to die down here."

North laughed harshly.

"You could help so many people. There was no healer when you needed one because we haven't got enough dreamsnakes. You could help people like you."

"I help the people who come to me," North said. "Those are the people who are like me. They're the only ones I want." He turned away.

"North!"

"What?"

"At least give me a blanket for Melissa. She'll die if I can't keep her warm."

"She won't die," North said. "Not if you leave her to my creatures." His shadow and his form disappeared.

Snake hugged Melissa closer, feeling each slow, heavy beat of the child's heart through her own body. She was so cold and tired that she could not think any longer. Sleep would start to heal her, but she had to stay awake, for Melissa's sake and for her own. One thought remained strong: defy North's wishes. Above everything, she knew she and her daughter were both lost if they obeyed him.

Moving slowly so the work of drawing pain from her shoulder would not be undone, Snake took Melissa's hands in her own and chafed them, trying to bring back circulation and warmth. The blood on the dreamsnake bites was dry now. One of the serpents wrapped itself around Snake's ankle. She wiggled her toes and flexed her ankle, hoping the dreamsnake would crawl away again. Her foot was so chilled she barely felt the serpent's fangs sink into her instep. She continued to rub Melissa's hands. She breathed on them and kissed them. Her breath plumed out before her. The dim light was failing. Snake looked up. The slice of gray dome visible between the edges of the crevasse had turned nearly black with gathering night. Snake felt an overwhelming sensation of grief. This was how it had been the night Jesse died, lacking only stars, the sky as clear and dark, the rock walls surrounding her just as steep, the cold as exhausting as the desert's heat. Snake hugged Melissa closer and bent over her, sheltering her from shadows. Because of the dreamsnakes, she could do nothing for Jesse; because of the dreamsnakes, she could do nothing for Melissa.

The dreamsnakes massed together and slithered toward her,

the sound of their scales on fogdamp stone whispering around her — Snake came abruptly awake out of the dream.

"Snake?" Melissa's voice was the rough whisper she had heard.

"I'm here." She could just see her daughter's face. The last diffused light shone dully on her curly hair and the thick stiff scars. Her eyes held a faraway dazed look.

"I dreamed . . ." She let her voice trail away. "He was right!" she cried in sudden fury. "Damn him, he was right!" She flung her arms around Snake's neck and hid her face. Her voice was muffled. "I did forget, for a little while. But I won't again. I won't . . ."

"Melissa — " Melissa stiffened at the tone of her voice. "I don't know what's going to happen. North says he won't hurt you." Melissa was trembling, or shivering. "If you say you'll join him — "

"No!"

"Melissa — "

"No! I won't! I don't care." Her voice was high and tight. "It'd be just like Ras again . . ."

"Melissa, dear, you have a place to go now. It's the same as when we talked before. Our people need to know about this place. You have to give yourself a chance to get away."

Melissa huddled against her in silence.

"I left Mist and Sand," she said finally. "I didn't do what you wanted, and now they'll starve to death."

Snake stroked her hair. "They'll be all right for a while."

"I'm scared," Melissa whispered. "I promised I wouldn't be any more, but I am. Snake, if I say I'll join him and he says he'll let me be bitten again I don't know what I'll do. I don't want to forget myself . . . but I did for a while, and . . ." She touched the heavy scar around her eye. Snake had never seen her do that before. "This went away. Nothing hurt any more. After a while I'd do anything for that." Melissa closed her eyes.

Snake grabbed one of the dreamsnakes and flung it away,

handling it more roughly than she would have believed she could.

"Would you rather die?" she asked harshly.

"I don't know," Melissa said faintly, groggily. Her arms slipped from Snake's neck and her hands lay limp. "I don't know. Maybe I would."

"Melissa, I'm sorry, I didn't mean it — "

But Melissa was asleep or unconscious again. Snake held her as the last of the light faded away. She could hear the dreamsnakes' scales on the damp slick rocks. She imagined again that they were coming closer, approaching her in a solid aggressive wave. For the first time in her life she felt afraid of serpents. Then, to reassure herself when the noises seemed to close in, she reached out to feel the bare stone. Her hand plunged into a mass of sleek scales, writhing bodies. She jerked back as a constellation of tiny stinging points spread across her arm. The dreamsnakes were seeking warmth, but if she let them find what they needed they would find her daughter as well. She shrank back into the narrow end of the crevasse. Her numb hand closed involuntarily around a heavy chunk of sharp volcanic rock. She lifted it clumsily, ready to smash it down on the wild dreamsnakes.

Snake lowered her hand and willed her fingers open. The rock clattered away, among other rocks. A dreamsnake slid across her wrist. She could no more destroy them than she could float out of the crevasse on the cold, thick air. Not even for Melissa. A hot tear rolled down her cheek. When it reached her chin it felt like ice. There were too many dreamsnakes to protect Melissa against, yet North was right. Snake could not kill them.

Desperate, she pushed herself to her feet, using the crevasse wall as support and wedging herself into the narrow space. Melissa was small for her age, and still very thin, but her limp weight seemed immense. Snake's cold hands were too numb to keep a secure grip, and she could hardly feel the rocks beneath her bare feet. But she could feel the dreamsnakes coiling around her ankles. Melissa slipped in her arms, and Snake clutched at her with her right hand. The pain shot through her shoulder and up and down her spine. She managed to brace herself between the converging rock walls, and to hold Melissa above the serpents.

The cultivated fields and well-built houses of Mountainside lay far behind Arevin at the end of his third day's travel south. The road was now a trail, rising and falling along the edges of successive mountains, leading now casually through a pleasant valley, now precariously across scree. The country grew higher and wilder. Arevin's stolid horse plodded on.

No one had passed him all day, in either direction. He could easily be overtaken by anyone else traveling south: anyone who knew the trail better, anyone who had a destination, would surely catch and pass him. But he remained alone. He felt chilled by the mountain air, enclosed and oppressed by the mountains' sheer walls and the dark overhanging trees. He was conscious of the beauty of the countryside, but the beauty he was used to was that of his homeland's arid plains and plateaus. He was homesick, but he could not go home. He had the proof of his own eyes that the eastern desert's storms were more powerful than those in the west, but the difference was one of quantity rather than kind. A western storm killed unprotected creatures in twenty breaths; an eastern one would do it in ten. He must stay in the mountains until spring.

He could not simply wait, at the healers' station or in Mountainside. If he did nothing but wait, his imagination would overpower his conviction that Snake was alive. And if he began to believe she was dead: that was dangerous, not only to his sanity but to Snake herself. Arevin knew he could not perform magic any more than Snake could, magical as her accomplishments might appear, but he was afraid to imagine her death.

She was probably safe in the underground city, gathering new knowledge that would atone for the actions of Arevin's cousin. Arevin reflected that Stavin's younger father was lucky he did not have to pay for his terror himself. Lucky for him, unlucky for Snake. Arevin wished he had good news to give her when he did find her. But all he would be able to say was, "I have explained, I have tried to make your people understand my people's fear. But they gave me no answer: they want to see you. They want you to go home."

At the edge of a meadow, thinking he heard something, he stopped his horse. The silence was a presence of its own, all around him, subtly different from the silence of a desert.

Have I begun imagining sounds, now, he wondered, as well as her touch in the night?

But then, from the trees ahead, he heard again the vibrations of animals' hooves. A small herd of delicate mountain deer appeared, trotting across the glade toward him, their twig-thin legs flashing white, long supple necks arched high. Compared to the huge musk oxen Arevin's clan herded, the fragile deer were like toys. They were nearly silent; it was the horses of their herders that had alerted him. His horse, lonely for its own kind, neighed.

The herders, waving, cantered up to him and pulled their mounts to flamboyant stops. They were both youngsters, with sun-bronzed skin and short-cut pale blond hair, kin by the look of them. At Mountainside Arevin had felt out of place in his desert robes, but that was because people mistook him for the crazy. He had not thought it necessary to change his manner of dress after he made his intentions clear. But now, the two children looked at him for a moment, looked at each other, and grinned. He began to wonder if he should have purchased new clothes. But he had little money and he did not wish to use it for what was not absolutely necessary.

"You're a long way from the trade routes," the older herder said. His tone was not belligerent but matter-of-fact. "Need any help?"

"No," Arevin said. "But I thank you." Their deer herd milled around him, the animals making small sounds of communion with each other, more like birds than hoofed creatures. The younger herder gave a sudden whoop and waved her arms. The deer scattered in all directions. Another difference between this herd and the one Arevin kept: a musk ox's response to a human on horseback flailing their arms would be to amble over and see what the fun was.

"Gods, Jean, you'll scare off everything from here to Mountainside." But he did not seem perturbed about the deer, and in fact they reassembled into a compact group a little way down the trail. Arevin was struck again by the willingness to reveal personal names in this country, but he supposed he had better get used to it.

"Can't talk with the beasties underfoot," she said, and smiled at Arevin. "It's good to see another human face after looking at nothing but trees and deer. And my brother."

"Have you seen no one else on the trail, then?" That was more a statement than a question. If Snake had returned from Center and the herders had overtaken her, it would have made much more sense for them all to travel together.

"Why? You looking for someone?" The young man sounded suspicious, or perhaps just wary. Could he have met Snake after all? Arevin, too, might ask impertinent questions of a stranger in order to safeguard a healer. And he would do considerably more than that for Snake.

"Yes," he said. "A healer. A friend. Her horse is a gray, and she has a tiger-pony as well, and a child riding with her. She would be coming north, back from the desert."

"She's not, though."

"Jean!"

Jean scowled at her brother. "Kev, he doesn't look like anybody who would hurt her. Maybe he needs her for somebody sick."

"And maybe he's friends with that crazy," the brother said. "Why are you looking for her?"

"I'm a friend of the healer," Arevin said again, alarmed. "Did you see the crazy? Is Snake safe?"

"This one's all right," Jean said to Kev.

"He didn't answer my question."

"He said he was her friend. Maybe it's none of your business."

"No, your brother has the right to question me," Arevin said. "And perhaps the obligation. I'm looking for Snake because I told her my name."

"What is your name?"

"Kev!" Jean said, shocked.

Arevin smiled for the first time since meeting these two. He was growing used to abrupt customs. "That is not something I would tell either of you," he said pleasantly.

Kev scowled in embarrassment.

"We do know better," Jean said. "It's just all this time out here away from people."

"Snake is coming back," Arevin said, his voice a little strained with excitement and joy. "You saw her. How long ago?"

"Yesterday," Kev said. "But she isn't coming this way."

"She's going south," Jean said.

"South!"

Jean nodded. "We were up here getting the herd before it snows. We met her when we came down from high pasture. She bought one of the pack horses for the crazy to ride."

"But why is she with the crazy? He attacked her! Are you sure he was not forcing her to go with him?"

Jean laughed. "No, Snake was in control. No doubt about that."

Arevin did not doubt her, so he could put aside the worst of his fear. But he was still uneasy. "South," he said. "What lies south of here? I thought there were no towns."

"There aren't. We come about as far as anybody. We were surprised to see her. Hardly anybody uses that pass, even coming from the city. But she didn't say where she was going."

"Nobody ever goes farther south than we do," Kev said. "It's dangerous."

"In what way?"

Kev shrugged.

"Are you going after her?" Jean asked.

"Yes."

"Good. But it's time to make camp. Do you want to stop with us?"

Arevin glanced past them, southward. In truth, the mountain shadows were passing over the glade, and twilight closed in toward him.

"You can't get much farther tonight, that's true," Kev said. "And this is the best place to camp in half a day's ride."

Arevin sighed. "All right," he said. "Thank you. I will camp here tonight."

Arevin welcomed the warmth of the fire that crackled in the center of camp. The fragrant burning wood snapped sparks. The mountain deer were a dim moving shadow in the center of the meadow, completely silent, but the horses stamped their hooves now and then; they grazed noisily, tearing the tender grass blades with their teeth. Kev had already rolled himself up in his blankets; he snored softly at the edge of the firelight. Jean sat across from Arevin, hugging her knees to her chest, the firelight red on her face. She yawned.

"I guess I'll go to sleep," she said. "You?"

"Yes. In a moment."

"Is there anything I can do for you?" she asked.

Arevin glanced up. "You've already done a great deal," he said.

She looked at him curiously. "That isn't exactly what I meant."

The tone of her voice was not quite annoyance; it was milder than that, but enough changed that Arevin knew something was wrong.

"I don't understand what you do mean."

"How do your people say it? I find you attractive. I'm asking if you'd like to share a bed with me tonight."

Arevin looked at Jean impassively, but he was embarrassed. He thought — he hoped — he was not blushing. Both Thad and Larril had asked him the same question, and he had not understood it. He had refused them offhandedly, and they must have thought him discourteous at best. Arevin hoped they had realized that he did not understand them, that his customs were different.

"I'm healthy, if you're worried," Jean said with some asperity. "And my control is excellent."

"I beg your pardon," Arevin said. "I did not understand you at all. I'm honored by your invitation and I did not doubt your health or your control. Nor would you need to doubt me. But if I will not offend you I must say no."

"Never mind," Jean said. "It was just a thought."

Arevin could tell she was hurt. Having so abruptly and unwittingly turned down Thad and Larril, Arevin felt he owed Jean, at least, some explanation. He was not sure how to explain his feelings, for he was not sure he understood them himself.

"I find you very attractive," Arevin said. "I would not have you misunderstand me. Sharing with you would not be fair. My attention would be . . . elsewhere."

Jean looked at him through the heat waves of the fire. "I can wake Kev up if you like."

Arevin shook his head. "Thank you. But I meant my attention would be elsewhere than this camp."

"Oh," she said with sudden comprehension. "I see now. I don't blame you. I hope you find her soon."

"I hope I have not offended you."

"It's okay," Jean said, a little wistfully. "I don't suppose it'd make any difference if I told you I'm not looking for anything permanent? Or even anything beyond tonight?"

"No," Arevin said. "I'm sorry. It's still the same."

"Okay." She picked up her blanket and moved to the edge of the firelight. "Sleep well."

Later, lying in his bedroll, the blankets not quite keeping off the chill, Arevin reflected on how pleasant and warm it would be to be lying next to another person. He had casually coupled with people in his and neighboring clans all his life, but until he met Snake he had found no one he thought he might be able to partner with. Since meeting her he had felt no desire for anyone else; what was even stranger, he had not noticed that he was not attracted to anyone else. He lay on the hard ground, thinking about all that, and trying to remind himself that he had no evidence but one brief touch, and a few ambiguous words, that Snake felt any more than casually attracted to him. Yet he could hope.

For a long time Snake did not move; in fact, she did not think she could move. She kept expecting dawn to come, but night remained. Perhaps North's people had covered the crevasse to keep it in the dark, but Snake knew that was ridiculous, if only because North would want to be able to see her and laugh at her.

As she was considering darkness, light glimmered above her. She looked up, but everything was blurs and shadows and strange noises that grew louder. Ropes and wood scraped against the crevasse wall and Snake wondered what other poor cripple had found North's refuge, and then, as a platform sank smoothly toward her, lowered on pulleys, she saw North himself descending. She could not hold Melissa tighter, or hide her from him, or even stand up and fight for her. North's lights illuminated the crevasse and Snake was dazzled.

He stepped from his platform as the pulley ropes drooped

down to its corners. Two of his followers flanked him, carrying lanterns. Two sets of shadows flowed and rippled on the walls.

When North came close enough, the light enveloped both of them and Snake could see his face. He smiled at her.

"My dreamsnakes like you," he said, nodding toward her feet where the serpents coiled around her legs, halfway to her knees. "But you mustn't be so selfish about them."

"Melissa doesn't want them," Snake said.

"I must say," he said, "I hardly expected you to be so lucid."

"I'm a healer."

North frowned a little, hesitating. "Ah. I see. Yes, I should have thought of that. You would have to be resistant, would you not." He nodded to his people and they put down their lanterns and came toward Snake. The light illuminated North's face from below, shadowing his paper-white skin with strange black shapes. Snake shrank away from his people, but the rock was at her back; she had nowhere to go. The followers walked gently among the jagged stones and the dreamsnakes. Unlike Snake they were heavily shod. One reached out to take Melissa from her. Snake felt the serpents uncoiling from her ankles, and heard them slide across the rock.

"Stay away!" Snake cried, but an emaciated hand tried to ease Melissa from her arms. Snake lunged down and bit. It was the only thing she could think of to do. She felt the cold flesh yield between her teeth until she met bone; she tasted the warm blood. She wished she had sharper teeth, sharp teeth with channels for poison. As it was, all she could do was hope the wound became infected.

North's follower pulled back with a yelp, tearing his hand away, and Snake spat out his blood. There was a flurry of motion as North and the others grabbed her by the hair and by her arm and by her clothes and held her while they took Melissa away from her. North twined his long fingers in her hair, holding her head back against the wall so she could not bite again. They forced her out of the narrow end of the crevesse. Fighting them, she staggered to her feet as one of the followers turned toward the platform with Melissa. North jerked her hair again and pulled her backward. Her knees collapsed. She tried to get up but she had nothing left to fight with, no more strength to overcome exhaustion and injury. Her left hand around her right shoulder, blood trickling between her fingers, she sagged to the ground.

North let go of Snake's hair and went to Melissa, looking at her eyes and feeling her pulse. He glanced back at Snake.

"I told you not to keep her from my creatures."

Snake raised her head. "Why are you trying to kill her?"

"Kill her! I? You don't know a tenth what you think you know. You're the one who's endangered her." He left Melissa and came back to Snake, bending down to capture several serpents. He put them in a basket, holding them carefully so they could not bite.

"I'll have to take her out of here to save her life. She'll hate you for ruining her first experience. You healers flaunt your arrogance."

Snake wondered if he was right about arrogance; if he was, then perhaps he was right, too, about Melissa, about everything. She could not think properly to argue with him. "Be kind to her," she whispered.

"Don't worry," North said. "She'll be happy with me." He nodded to his two followers. As they came toward Snake she tried to rise and prepare herself for one last defense. She was on one knee when the man she had bitten grabbed her by the right arm and pulled her to her feet, wrenching her shoulder again. The second follower held her up from the other side.

North leaned over her, holding a dreamsnake. "How certain are you of your immunities, healer? Are you arrogant about them, too?"

One of his people forced Snake's head back, exposing her throat. North was so tall that Snake could still watch him lower the dreamsnake.

The fangs sank into her carotid artery. Nothing happened.

She knew nothing would happen. She wished North would realize it and let her go, let her lie down on the cold sharp rocks to sleep, even if she never woke up. She was too tired to fight any more, too tired to react even when North's follower relaxed his hold. Blood trickled down her neck to her collarbone. North picked up another dreamsnake and held it at her throat.

When the second dreamsnake bit her, she felt a sudden flash of pain, radiating from her throat all through her body. She gasped as it receded, leaving her trembling.

"Ah," North said. "The healer is beginning to understand us." He hesitated a moment, watching her. "One more, perhaps," he said. "Yes."

When he bent over her again, his face was in shadow and the light formed a halo of his pale, fine hair. In his hands, the third dreamsnake was a silent shadow. Snake drew back, and the grip of North's followers on her arms did not change. The people who held her acted as if hypnotized by the black gaze of the serpent. Snake lunged forward, and for a moment she was free, but fingers like claws dug into her flesh and the man she had bitten snarled in fury. He dragged her back, twisting her right arm with one hand and digging the nails of his other into her wounded shoulder.

North, who had stepped away from the scuffle, came forward again. "Why fight, healer? Allow yourself to share the pleasure my creatures give." He brought the third dreamsnake to her throat.

It struck.

This time the pain radiated through her as before, but when it faded it was followed with her pulsebeat by another wave of agony. Snake cried out.

"Ah," she heard North say. "Now she does understand."

"No . . ." she whispered.

She silenced herself. She would not give North the satisfaction of her pain.

The followers released her and she fell forward, trying to

support herself with her left hand. This time the intensity of the sensation did not fade. It built, echoing and re-echoing through the canyon of her body, reinforcing itself, resonating. Snake shuddered with every beat of her heart. Trying to breathe between the agonizing spasms, she collapsed onto the cold hard rock.

Daylight filtered into the crevasse. Snake lay as she had fallen, one hand flung out before her. Frost silvered the ragged edges of her sleeve. A thick white coat of ice crystals covered the tumbled rock fragments of the floor and crept up the side of the crevasse. Fascinated by the lacy pattern, Snake let her mind drift among the delicate fronds. As she gazed at them they became three-dimensional. She was in a prehistoric forest of moss and ferns, all black and white.

Here and there wet trails cut the traceries, throwing them abruptly back into two-dimensionality, forming a second, harsher pattern. The stone-dark lines looked like the tracks of dreamsnakes, but Snake knew better than to expect any of the serpents to be active in this temperature, active enough to slide over ice-covered ground. Perhaps North, to safeguard them, had taken them to a warmer place.

While she was hoping that was true, she heard the quiet rustle of scales on stone. One of the creatures, at least, had been left behind. That gave her comfort, for it meant she was not entirely alone.

This one must be a hardy beast, she thought.

It might be the big one that had bitten her, one large enough to produce and conserve some body heat. Opening her eyes, she tried to reach out toward the sound. Before her hand could move, if it would move, she saw the serpents.

Because many more than one remained. Two, no, three dreamsnakes twined themselves around each other only an arm's length away. None was the huge one; none was much larger than Grass had been. They writhed and coiled together, marking the frost with dark hieroglyphics that Snake could not read. The symbols had a meaning, of that she was sure, if she could only decipher them. Only part of the message lay within her view, so, slowly and stiffly, she turned her head to follow the connecting tracks. The dreamsnakes remained at the edge of her sight, rubbing against each other, their bodies forming triple-stranded helices.

The serpents were freezing and dying, that must be it, and somehow she had to call North and make him save them. Snake pushed herself up on her elbows, but she could move no farther. She struggled, trying to speak, but a wave of nausea overcame her. North and his creatures: Snake retched dryly, but there was nothing in her stomach to come up and help purge her of her revulsion. She was still under the effects of the venom.

The stabbing pain had faded to a deep, throbbing ache. She forced it back, forced herself to feel it less and less, but she could not maintain the necessary energy. Overwhelmed, she fainted again.

Snake roused herself from sleep, not unconsciousness. All the hurts remained, but she knew she had beaten them when she forced them away, one by one, and they did not return. She was still free, and North could not enslave her with the dreamsnakes. The crazy had described ecstasy, so the venom had not affected Snake as it affected North's followers. She did not know if that was because of her healer's immunities, or because of the resistance of her will. It did not really matter.

She did understand why North had been so certain Melissa would not freeze to death. The cold remained, and Snake was aware of it, but she felt warm, even feverish. How long her body could sustain the increased metabolism she did not know, but she could feel her blood coursing through her and she knew she did not have to fear frostbite.

She remembered the dreamsnakes, active beyond possibility on the frost-jeweled ground.

That all must have been a dream, she thought.

But she looked around, and there among the dark hieroglyphics of their trails coiled a triplet of small serpents. She saw a second triplet, then a third, and suddenly in pure astonishment and delight she understood the message this place and its creatures had been trying to give her. It was as if she were the representative of all the generations of healers, sent here on purpose to accept what was offered.

Even as she wondered at how long it had taken to discover the dreamsnakes' secrets, she understood the reasons. Now that she had fought the venom off, she could understand what the hieroglyphics told her, and she saw much more than the many triplets of dreamsnakes copulating on the frigid stones.

Her people, like all the other people on earth, were too self-centered, too introspective. Perhaps that was inevitable, for their isolation was well enforced. But as a result the healers had been too shortsighted; by protecting the dreamsnakes, they had kept them from maturing. That, too, was inevitable: dreamsnakes were too valuable to risk to experimentation. It was safer to count on nuclear-transplant clones for a few new dreamsnakes than to threaten the lives of those the healers already had.

Snake smiled at the clarity and simplicity of the solution. Of course the healers' dreamsnakes never matured. At some point in their development they needed this bitter cold. Of course they seldom mated, even the few that spontaneously matured: the cold triggered reproduction as well. And finally: hoping mature serpents would meet each other, the healers followed tedious plans to put them together . . . two by two.

Isolated from new knowledge, the healers had understood that their dreamsnakes were alien, but they had not been able to comprehend just how alien.

Two by two. Snake laughed silently.

She recalled passionate arguments with other healers in training, in classes, over lunch, about whether dreamsnakes might be diploid or hexaploid, for the number of nuclear bodies made either state a possibility. But in all those passionate arguments, no one had been on the side of the truth. Dreamsnakes were triploid, and they required a triplet, not a pair. Snake's mental laughter faded away into a sad smile of regret for all the mistakes she and her people had made for so many years, hampered as they were by lack of the proper information, by a mechanical technology insufficient to support the biological possibilities, by ethnocentrism. And by the forced isolation of earth from other worlds, by the self-imposed isolation of too many groups of people from each other. Her people had made mistakes: with dreamsnakes, they had only succeeded by mistake.

Now that Snake understood, perhaps it was all too late.

Snake felt warm and calm and sleepy. It was thirst that roused her to wakefulness; thirst, then memory. The crevasse was perhaps as bright as it ever got, and the stones Snake lay on were dry. She moved her hand and felt heat seep into it from the black rock.

She eased herself upright, testing herself. Her knee hurt but it was not swollen. Her shoulder merely ached. She did not know how long she had slept, but the healing had already begun.

Water dripped in a tiny quick rivulet through the other end of the crevasse. Snake stood up and went toward it, bracing herself against the rock wall. She felt unsteady, as if she had suddenly become very old. But her strength was still there; she could feel it gradually returning. Kneeling beside the stream, she cupped water in her hand and drank cautiously. The water tasted clean and cold. She drank deeply, trusting her decision. It was exceedingly difficult to poison a healer, but she did not much care right now to challenge her body with more toxins.

The near-freezing water ached in her empty stomach. She put thoughts of food aside and stood up in the center of the crevasse, turning slowly to inspect it in daylight. The walls were rough but not fissured; she could see no toe- or fingerholds. The edge was three times higher than she could leap even if she were not injured. But, somehow, she had to get out. She had to find Melissa, and they had to escape.

Snake felt lightheaded. Afraid she would panic herself, she breathed deeply and slowly for a few long breaths, keeping her eyes closed. It was difficult to concentrate because she knew North would return, perhaps any second. He would want to gloat over her while she was awake, since he had overcome her immunities and affected her with the venom. His hatred must wish to see her groveling like the crazy, begging until he obliged her and growing weaker each time he did. She shivered and opened her eyes. Once he realized its true effect on her, he would use it to kill her, if he could.

Snake sat down and unwrapped Melissa's headcloth from her shoulder. The material was caked and stiff with blood, and she had to soak away the layer next to her skin. But the scab on the wound was thick and she did not begin to bleed again. The wound was not exactly clean: the scar would be full of dirt and grit unless she did something about it soon. But it would not become infected and she could not take any time over it now. She ripped a couple of narrow strips off one edge of the square of cloth and gathered the rest into a makeshift bag. Four big dreamsnakes lay languorously on the rocks almost within reach. She captured them, put them in the sack, and looked for more. The ones she had were certainly mature, at that size, and perhaps one or two were even forming fertile eggs. She caught three more, but the rest of the dreamsnakes had vanished. She walked across the stones more carefully, looking for any sign of lairs, but found nothing.

She wondered if she had imagined or dreamt the mating scene. It had seemed so real . . .

Whether she had dreamt it or not, there had been many more dreamsnakes in the crevasse. Either their holes were too well concealed for her to find without a more careful search, or North had taken all the rest of the serpents away.

A green motion at the edge of her vision drew her around. She reached for the dreamsnake and it struck at her. She pulled her hand back, glad to see that even after all that had happened her reflexes were quick enough to avoid the fangs. She was not afraid of the bite of one of the serpents: her immunity to the venom would be extremely high right now. Each time she was exposed to it, it would take even more to affect her the next time. But she did not want to experience a next time.

She captured the last big dreamsnake and put it in her bag, tied the cloth shut with one strip of material, and tied the whole thing to her belt with the other, leaving a long tether.

Snake could see only one way to escape. Well, there *was* another way, but she doubted she had enough time to build herself a ramp of fragmented stone and stroll out. She returned to the far end of the crevasse, to the narrow space where the walls came together, where she had held Melissa.

Something tickled her bare foot. She looked down and saw the eggling dreamsnake gliding away. She bent down and picked it up, gently so as not to startle it. The horny tissue had fallen away, and the scales beneath were pale pink all around its mouth. In time they would turn scarlet. The tiny serpent tasted the air with its three-pronged tongue, butted its nose against her palm, and flowed around her thumb. She slipped it into the breast pocket of her torn shirt, where she could feel it moving only a layer of material away. It was young enough to tame. The warmth of her body lulled it.

Snake braced herself in the narrow space. Leaning back, she pressed her shoulders and her spine against the rock. The wound had not yet begun to hurt again, but she did not know how much stress she could stand. She set herself not to feel the injury, but exhaustion and hunger made concentration difficult. Snake put her right foot against the opposite wall and pushed, bracing herself. Carefully, she placed her other foot on the wall and hung suspended between the two faces of the crevasse. She pushed with both feet, sliding her shoulders upward, pushing back and down with her hands. She slipped her feet a little higher and pushed again, creeping upward.

A pebble came free beneath her foot and she slid, falling sideways. She scratched at the wall, scrabbling to keep herself in position. Rock tore at her elbows and back. She slammed down, landing hard and badly. Struggling for breath, Snake tried to rise and then lay still. Down and up reversed and shimmered. When they finally steadied, she drew in a long breath and pushed herself to her feet again. Her bad knee trembled slightly with the strain.

She had not, at least, fallen on the dreamsnakes. She put her hand to her pocket and felt the little one moving easily.

Gritting her teeth, Snake leaned back against the wall. She pushed herself upward again, moving more carefully, feeling for broken stone before she put any pressure on a new spot. Rock scraped her back and her hands grew slippery with sweat. She kept herself going; she imagined being able to look over the edge of her prison and she imagined hard ground and horizons.

She heard a noise and froze.

It's nothing, she thought. One piece of stone hitting another. Volcanic rock always sounds alive when it clashes against itself.

The muscles in her thighs trembled with strain. Her eyes stung and her vision sparkled with sweat.

The sound came again. It was no clattering rock but two voices, and one of them was North's.

Nearly sobbing with frustration, Snake slid back into the crevasse. Going down was just as hard, and it seemed to take an interminable length of time before she was far enough to jump the rest of the way. Her back and her hands and feet scraped against stone. The noise was so loud in the enclosed space that she was sure North would hear it. As a rock clattered down the side of the crevasse, Snake flung herself to the ground, curling her body around the sack of dreamsnakes. She froze there, by sheer will concealing the tremors of fatigue. Needing desperately to pant for breath, she forced herself to breath slowly, as if she were still asleep. She kept her eyes nearly closed, but she saw the shadow that fell over her.

"Healer!"

Snake did not move.

"Healer, wake up!"

She heard the scuff of a boot against stones. A shower of rock fragments rained down on her.

"She's still sleeping, North," Snake's crazy said. "Like everybody else, everybody but you and me. Let's go to sleep, North. Please let me sleep."

"Shut up. There isn't any venom left. The serpents are exhausted."

"They could give just one more bite. Or let me go down and get another, North. A nice big one. Then I can make sure the healer's really sleeping."

"What do I care if she's really sleeping or not?"

"You can't trust her, North. She's sneaky. She tricked me into bringing her to you . . ."

The crazy's voice faded away with his and North's footsteps. As far as Snake could hear, North did not bother to reply again.

As they left, Snake moved only enough to put her hand over the pocket of her shirt. The eggling was, somehow, still all right; she could feel it moving slowly and calmly beneath her fingers. She began to believe that if she ever got out of the crevasse alive, the tiny dreamsnake would too. Or perhaps she had the order reversed. Her hand was shaking; she drew it away so it would not frighten her serpent. Turning slowly over on her back, she looked at the sky. The top of the crevasse seemed an immense distance from her, as if each time she had tried to scale the walls they had risen higher. A hot tear trickled from the corner of her eye back into her hair.

Snake sat up all at once. Getting to her feet was slower and clumsier, but finally she stood in the narrow space between the walls and stared straight ahead at the face of the rock. The scraped places on her back rubbed against the stone, and the wound in her shoulder was perilously close to tearing open. Without looking upward, Snake put one foot against the wall, braced herself, wedged herself in with her other foot, and started up again.

As she crept higher and higher, she could feel the cloth of her shirt shredding beneath her shoulders. The knotted headcloth rose from the ground and scraped up the wall beneath her. It started to swing; it was just heavy enough to disturb her balance. She stopped, suspended like a bridge from nowhere leading nowhere, until the pendulum below shortened its oscillation. The tension in her leg muscles increased until she could hardly feel the rock against her feet. She did not know how near the top she was and she would not look.

She was higher than she had got before; here the walls of the crevasse gaped wider and it was harder for her to brace herself. With every tiny step she took up the wall she had to stretch her legs a little farther. Now she was held only by her shoulders, by her hands pushing hard against the rock, and by the balls of her feet. She could not keep going much longer. Beneath her right hand, the stone was wet with blood. She forced herself upward one last time. Abruptly the back of her head slipped over the rim of the crevasse and she could see the ground and the hills and the sky. The sharp change nearly destroyed her balance. She flailed out with her left arm, catching the edge of the crevasse with her elbow and then with her hand. Her body spun around and she snatched at the ground with her right hand. The wound in her shoulder stabbed her from spine to fingertips. Her nails dug into the ground, slipped, held. She scrabbled for a toehold and somehow found one. She hung against the wall for a moment, gasping for breath and feeling the bruises over her hipbones where she had slammed into the stone. Just above her breast, in her pocket, squeezed but not quite crushed, the eggling dreamsnake squirmed unhappily.

With the last bit of strength in her arms, Snake heaved herself over the edge and lay panting on the horizontal surface, her feet and legs still dangling. She crawled the rest of the way out. The torn headcloth scraped over stone, the fabric stretching and fraying. Snake pulled it gently until the makeshift sack lay beside her. Only then, with one hand on the serpents and the other almost caressing the solid ground, could Snake look around and be sure that she had climbed out unobserved. For the moment, at least, she was free.

She unbuttoned her pocket and looked at the eggling, hardly believing that it was unharmed. Rebuttoning her pocket, she took one of the baskets from the pile beside the crevasse and put the mature serpents in it. She slung it across her back, rose shakily to her feet, and started toward the tunnels circling the crater.

But the tunnels surrounded her like infinite reflections, and she could not remember which one had let her in. It was opposite the single large refrigeration duct, but the crater was so large that any one of three exits might have been the one she wanted.

Maybe it's better, Snake thought. Maybe they always go in through the same one and I'll get another that's deserted.

Or maybe no matter which one I take I'll meet someone, or maybe all the others lead to dead ends.

At random, Snake entered the left-hand tunnel. Inside it looked different, but that was because the frost had melted. This tunnel, too, held torches, so North's people must use it for something. But most of them had burned to stubs, and Snake crept through darkness from one vague, flickering point to another, trailing her hand against the wall so she could return if this did not lead her outside. Each new light had to be the tunnel's mouth, but each time she found another fading torch. The corridor stretched onward. However harried she had been before, however exhausted she was now, she knew the first tunnel had not been this long.

One more light, she thought. And then — ?

The sooty smoke drifted around her, not even revealing an air current to show her the way. She stopped at the torch and turned around. Only blackness lay behind her. The other flames had gone out, or she had rounded a curve that blotted them from her view. She could not bring herself to backtrack.

She walked through a great deal of darkness before she saw the next light. She wanted it to be daylight, made bargains and bets with herself that it would be daylight, but knew it was merely another torch before she reached it. It had nearly died; it flickered to an ember. She could smell the acrid smoke of an ebbing flame.

Snake wondered if she were being herded to another crevasse, one lying in wait in the dark. From then on she walked more carefully, sliding one foot forward without shifting her weight until she was sure of solid ground.

When the next torch appeared she hardly noticed it. It did not cast enough light to help her make her way. The basket grew heavier and a reaction to all that had happened set in. Her knee ached fiercely and her shoulder hurt so much that she had to slide her hand beneath her belt and hug her arm in close against her body. As she scuffed along the untrustworthy path, she did not think she could have lifted her feet higher even if caution had allowed it.

Suddenly she was standing on a hillside in daylight beneath the strange twisted trees. She looked around blankly, then stretched out her left hand and stroked rough tree bark. She touched a fragile leaf with an abraded, broken-nailed fingertip.

Snake wanted to sit down, laugh, rest, sleep. Instead, she turned right and followed the hillside around, hoping the long tunnel had not led her half the hill or half the dome away from North's camp. She wished North or the crazy had said something about where they had put Melissa.

The trees ended abruptly. Snake almost walked into the clearing before she stopped herself and pulled back into the shadows. Thick low round-leafed bushes carpeted the meadow with a solid layer of scarlet vegetation. On the natural mattress lay all the people she had seen with North, and more. They were all asleep, dreaming, Snake supposed. Most lay face up with their heads thrown back, their throats exposed, revealing puncture wounds and thin trickles of blood among many sets of scars. Snake looked from person to person, recognizing no one, until her search reached the other side of the clearing. There, touched by the shade of an alien tree, the crazy lay sleeping. His position differed from that of everyone else: he was face down, stripped to the waist, and he had stretched out his arms before him as if in supplication. His legs and feet were bare. As Snake skirted the clearing, moving closer to the crazy, she saw the many fang marks on his inner arms and behind his knees. So North had found an unexhausted serpent, and the crazy had finally got what he wanted.

But North was not in the clearing, and Melissa was not there either.

A well-used trail led back into the forest. Snake followed it cautiously, ready to slip between the trees at any warning. But nothing happened. She could even hear the rustling of small animals or birds or indescribably alien beasts as she padded barefoot over the hard ground.

The trail ended just above the entrance to the first tunnel. There, next to a large basket, alone with a dreamsnake in his hands, sat North.

Snake watched him curiously. He held the serpent in the safe way, behind the head so it could not strike. With the other hand he stroked its smooth green scales. Snake had noticed that North had no throat scars, and she had assumed that for himself he used the slower and more pleasurable method of taking the venom. But now the sleeves of his robe had fallen back and she could see quite clearly that his pale arms were unscarred too.

Snake frowned. Melissa was nowhere in sight. If North had put her back in the caves Snake might search futilely for days and still not find her. She had no strength left for a long search. She stepped out into the clearing.

"Why don't you let it bite you?" she said.

North started violently, but did not lose control of the serpent. He stared at Snake with an expression of pure confusion. He glanced quickly around the clearing as if noticing for the first time that his people were not near him.

"They're all asleep, North," Snake said. "Dreaming. Even the one who brought me here."

"Come to me!" North shouted, but Snake did not obey his commanding voice, and no one at all answered.

"How did you get out?" North whispered. "I've killed healers — they were never magic. They were as easy to kill as any creature."

"Where's Melissa?"

"How did you get out?" he screamed.

Snake approached him without any idea what she would do. It was true that North was not strong, but sitting down he was still nearly as tall as she was standing, and right now she was not strong either. She stopped in front of him.

North thrust the dreamsnake toward her, as if it would frighten her or bind her with desire to his will. Snake was so close that she reached out and stroked the serpent with the tip of her finger.

"Where's Melissa?"

"She's mine," he said. "She doesn't belong in the world outside. She belongs here."

But his pale eyes, flicking sideways, betrayed him. Snake followed his gaze: to the huge basket, nearly as long as she was tall and half that deep. Snake went to it and carefully lifted its lid. She took one involuntary backward step, drawing in a long angry breath. The basket was nearly filled with a solid mass of dreamsnakes. She swung toward North, furious.

"How could you?"

"It was what she needed."

Snake turned her back on him and slowly, carefully began lifting dreamsnakes from the basket. There were so many of them she could not see Melissa, even as a vague shape. She took dreamsnakes out of the basket by pairs, and, once they could no longer reach her daughter, dropped them on the ground. The first one slid over her foot and coiled itself around her ankle, but the second one glided rapidly away toward the trees.

North scrambled up. "What are you doing? You can't — " He started after the freed serpents, but one of them raised itself to strike and North flinched back. Snake dropped two more serpents on the ground. North tried once again to capture a dreamsnake, but it struck at him and he nearly fell avoiding it. North abandoned the serpent and flung himself toward Snake, using his height to threaten her, but she held a dreamsnake out toward him and he stopped.

"You're afraid of them, aren't you, North?" She took one step toward him. He tried to stand firm but when Snake took a second step he backed abruptly away.

"Don't you accept your own advice?" She was angrier than she had ever been before: the sane part of her mind, driven deep, watched with shock how glad she was to be able to frighten him.

"Stay away — "

As Snake approached him he fell backward. Scrabbling at the ground he pulled himself away, and stumbled again when he tried to rise. Snake was near enough to smell the odor of him, musty and dry, nothing like human scent. Panting, like an animal at bay, he stopped and faced her, his fists clenched to strike as she brought the dreamsnake closer.

"Don't," he said. "Don't do it — '

Thinking of Melissa, Snake did not reply.

North stared at the dreamsnake, mesmerized. "No — " His voice broke. "Please — "

"Is it pity you want from me?" Snake cried with joy, knowing she would give him no more mercy than he had offered her daughter.

Suddenly North's fists unclenched and he leaned toward her, stretching out his hands to her, exposing the fine blue veins of his wrists.

"No," he said. "I want peace." He trembled visibly as he waited for the dreamsnake's strike.

Astonished, Snake drew back her hands.

"Please!" North cried again. "Gods, don't play with me!"

Snake looked at the serpent, then at North. Her pleasure in his capitulation turned to revulsion. Was she so much like him, that she needed power over other human beings? Perhaps his accusations had been true. Honor and deference pleased her as much as they pleased him. And she had certainly been guilty of arrogance, she had always been guilty of arrogance. Perhaps the difference between her and North was not of kind, but only of degree. Snake was not sure, but she knew that if she forced this serpent on him now, while he was helpless, whatever differences there might be would have even less meaning. She stepped back, dropping the dreamsnake on the ground.

"Stay away from me." Her voice, too, trembled. "I'm going to take my daughter and go home."

"Help me," he whispered. "I discovered this place, I used its creatures to help others, don't I deserve help now?" He looked pitiably at Snake but she did not move.

Suddenly he moaned and lunged for the dreamsnake, grasping it in one hand and forcing it to bite his other wrist. He whimpered as the fangs sank in, once, again.

Snake backed away from him, but he no longer paid any attention to her. She turned toward the huge wicker basket.

The dreamsnakes had begun to escape of their own accord now. One slithered over the basket's side and fell to the earth with a soft thud. Several more peered over, and gradually the weight of the whole mass of them bulged out the wicker and tilted the basket. It tipped over, and the serpents squirmed out in a writhing pile.

But Melissa was not there.

North swept past Snake, oblivious to her, and plunged his pale blood-spotted hands into the mass of dreamsnakes.

Snake grabbed him and pulled him around. "Where is she?"

"What — ?" He strained feebly toward the serpents, his translucent eyes glassy.

"Melissa — where is she?"

"She was dreaming . . ." He gazed at the dreamsnakes. "With them."

Somehow, Melissa had got away. Somehow, her will had defeated North, the venom, the lure of forgetfulness. Snake looked around the camp, searching again, seeing everything but what she wished to see.

North moaned in frustration and Snake let him go. He grabbed at escaping serpents as they slid away into the forest. His arms were a mass of bloody pinpricks, and each time he recaptured another of his creatures he forced it to strike at him.

"Melissa!" Snake called, but there was no answer.

Suddenly North grunted; then, after a moment, he made a strange moaning sound. Snake looked over her shoulder. North rose slowly, a serpent in his bloody hands, thin trickles of blood flowing from a bite in his throat. He stiffened, and the dreamsnake writhed. North fell to his knees and balanced there. He toppled forward and lay still, and his power drained away from him as the alien dreamsnakes escaped back into their alien forest.

By reflex, Snake went to him. He breathed evenly. He was not hurt, not by such a gentle fall. Snake wondered if the venom would affect him as it affected his followers. But even if it did not, even if his dread of it caused him to react badly, she could do nothing for him.

The dreamsnake he still held squirmed and flailed itself from his grasp. Snake caught her breath in memory and sorrow. Its spine was broken. Snake knelt beside it and ended its pain, killing it as she had killed Grass.

With the taste of its blood chill and salty on her lips, she fumbled for the strap of her small wicker basket and hoisted it across her shoulders. It did not occur to her to look for Melissa anywhere but on the trail leading down the hill, toward the break in the dome.

The tangle-trees cast a deeper, darker shade here than in the first place Snake had passed among them, and the opening through them was narrower and lower. With chills on her back, Snake pushed herself as fast as she could go. The alien forest that surrounded her could harbor any sort of creature, from dreamsnakes to silent carnivores. Melissa was completely unprotected; she did not even have her knife anymore.

When Snake had begun to believe she was on the wrong trail, she reached the rock outcropping where the crazy had betrayed her. It was a long way from North's camp to the ledge, and Snake wondered how Melissa could have got this far.

Maybe she escaped and hid herself, Snake thought. Maybe she's still up near North's camp, sleeping, or dreaming . . . and dying.

She went a few steps farther, hesitated, decided, and plunged ahead.

Stretched out on the trail, her fingers digging into the ground to pull her even a little farther, Melissa lay unconscious just around the next turn. Snake ran to her, stumbled, fell to her knees beside her.

Snake gently turned her daughter over. Melissa did not move, and she was very limp and cold. Snake searched for a pulse, now thinking it was there, now certain it was not. Melissa was in deep shock, and Snake could do nothing for her here.

Melissa, my daughter, she thought, you tried so hard to keep your promise to me, and you nearly succeeded. I made promises to you, too, and they've all been broken. Please let me have another chance.

Awkwardly, forced to use her nearly crippled right arm, Snake wrestled Melissa's small body up on her left shoulder. She staggered to her feet, nearly losing her balance. If she fell she did not think she would be able to rise again. The trail stretched before her, and she knew how long it was.

Snake trudged across the flat-leaves, stumbling once crossing a crevice full of blue-green crawlies, slipping, nearly falling, on a surface made slick and slimy by recent rain. Melissa never moved. Afraid to put her down, Snake kept going.

There's nothing I can do for her up here, she thought again, and fixed her attention on the downward climb.

Melissa seemed terribly cold, but Snake could not trust her own perceptions. She was pushing herself beyond sensation of any kind. She plodded on like a machine, watching her body from a faraway vantage point, knowing she could get to the bottom of the hill but ready to scream in frustration because the body moved so slowly, stolidly onward, one step, another, and would not go any faster.

The cliff looked much steeper, viewed from above, than it had appeared when Snake climbed up it. Standing at its edge she could not even recall how she had made her way to the top. But the forest and meadow below, the lovely shades of green, reassured her.

Snake sat and eased herself over the edge of the cliff. At first she slid slowly, braking herself with her sore bare feet and managing to keep her balance. She bumped over the stone; the wicker basket scraped and bounced along behind her. But near the bottom she picked up speed, Melissa's limp weight pulled her off balance, and she slipped and skidded sideways. She fought to keep from rolling, succeeded at the cost of some skin on her back and elbows, and stopped finally at cliff's end in a shower of dirt and pebbles. She lay still for a moment, with Melissa limp against her and the battered wicker carrier crunched up under her shoulder. The dreamsnakes slithered over each other, but found no holes quite large enough to crawl through. Snake passed her hand over her breast pocket and felt the eggling dreamsnake move beneath her fingers.

Only a little farther, she thought. I can almost see the meadow. If I lie here very quietly I'll be able to hear Squirrel eating grass . . .

"Squirrel!" She waited a moment, then whistled. She called him again and thought she heard him neigh, but could not be sure. He would usually follow her around if he were nearby, but he only responded to his name or a whistle when he was in the proper mood. Right now he did not seem to be in the proper mood.

Snake sighed and rolled over and struggled to her knees. Melissa lay pale and cold before her, her arms and legs streaked with dry blood. Snake lifted Melissa to her shoulder; her right arm was nearly useless. Gathering her strength, Snake pushed herself to her feet. The strap of the carrier slipped and hung in the crook of her arm. She took one step forward. The basket bumped against her leg. Her knees were shaking. She took another step, her vision blurred with fear for Melissa's life.

She called to her pony again as she stumbled into the meadow. She heard hoofbeats but saw neither Squirrel nor Swift, just the crazy's old pack horse lying in the grass with his muzzle resting on the ground.

Arevin's robes of musk-ox wool protected him from rain as well as they did from heat and wind and desert sand. He rode through the fresh-washed day, brushing past overhanging branches that showered him with captured droplets. As yet he had seen no sign of Snake, but there was only the single trail.

His horse raised its head and neighed loudly. An answering

call came from beyond a dense stand of trees. Arevin heard the drumming of hooves on hard, wet ground, and a gray horse and the tiger-pony Squirrel galloped into sight along the curving trail. Squirrel slid to a stop and pranced nearer, neck arched. The gray mare trotted past, wheeled around, galloped a few steps in play, and stopped again. As the three horses blew their breath into each others' nostrils in greeting, Arevin reached down and scratched Squirrel's ears. Both of Snake's horses were in splendid condition. The gray and the tiger-pony would not be free if Snake had been ambushed: they were too valuable. Even if the horses had escaped during an attack they would still be saddled and bridled. Snake must be safe.

Arevin started to call her name, but changed his mind at the last instant. No doubt he was too suspicious, but after all that had happened he felt it wise to be cautious. A few more moments of waiting would not kill him.

He glanced up the slope, which rose into rocky cliffs and succeeding mountain peaks, stunted vegetation, lichen . . . and the dome.

Once he had realized what it was he could not understand why he had not seen it instantly. It was the only one he had ever encountered that showed any sign at all of damage: that fact served to disguise it. But it was still, unquestionably, one of the ancients' domes, the largest he had ever seen or heard of. Arevin had no doubt that Snake was up there somewhere. That was the only possibility that made any sense.

He urged his horse forward, backtracking the other horses' deep muddy footprints. Thinking he heard something, he stopped. It had not been his imagination: the horses listened with ears pricked. He heard the call again and tried to shout a reply, but the words caught in his throat. He squeezed his legs around his horse so abruptly that the beast sprang into a gallop from a standstill, toward the sound of the healer's voice, toward Snake.

*

Followed by the tiger-pony and the gray mare, a small black horse burst through the trees on the far side of the meadow. Snake cursed in an instant of fury that one of North's people should return to him right now.

And then she saw Arevin.

Astonished, she was unable to move toward him or even speak. He swung down from his mount while the horse was still galloping; he ran to Snake, his robe swirling around him. She stared at him as if he were an apparition, for she was sure he must be, even when he stopped near enough to her to touch.

"Arevin?"

"What happened? Who did this to you? The crazy — "

"He's in the dome," she said. "With some others. They're no danger right now. It's Melissa, she's in shock. I have to get her back to camp . . . Arevin, are you real?"

He lifted Melissa from her shoulder; he held Snake's daughter in one arm and supported Snake with the other.

"Yes, I'm real. I'm here."

He helped her across the meadow. When they reached the spot where her gear was piled, Arevin turned to lay Melissa down. Snake knelt by her serpent case and fumbled at the catch. She opened the medicine compartment shakily.

Arevin put his hand on her uninjured shoulder, his touch gentle.

"Let me tend your wound," he said.

"I'm all right," she said. "I will be. It's Melissa — " She glanced up at him and froze at the look in his eyes.

"Healer," he said, "Snake, my friend — "

She tried to stand up; he tried to restrain her.

"There's nothing to be done."

"Nothing to be done — ?" She struggled to her feet.

"You're hurt," Arevin said desperately. "Seeing the child now will only hurt you more."

"Oh, gods," Snake said. Arevin still tried to hold her back. "Let go of me!" she cried. Arevin stepped away, startled. Snake did not stop to apologize. She could not allow anyone, even him, to protect her: that was too easy, too tempting.

Melissa lay in the deep shade of a pine tree. Snake knelt on the thick mat of brown needles. Behind her, Arevin remained standing. Snake took Melissa's cold, pale hand. The child did not move. Dragging herself along the ground, she had torn her fingernails to the quick. She had tried so hard to keep her promise . . . She had kept her promises to Snake much better than Snake had kept her promises to Melissa. Snake leaned over her, smoothing her red hair back from the terrible scars. Snake's tears fell on Melissa's cheek.

"There's nothing to be done," Arevin said again. "Her pulse is gone."

"Sh-h," Snake whispered, still searching for a beat in Melissa's wrist, at her throat, now thinking she had found the pulse, now certain she had not.

"Snake, don't torture yourself like this. She's dead! She's cold!"

"She's alive." She knew he thought she was losing her mind with grief; he did not move, but stared sadly down at her. She turned toward him. "Help me, Arevin. Trust me. I've dreamed about you. I love you, I think. But Melissa is my daughter and my friend. I've got to try to save her."

The phantom pulse faintly touched her fingers. Melissa had been bitten so often . . . but the metabolic increase brought on by the venom was over, and instead of returning to normal it had fallen sharply to a level barely sustaining life. And mind, Snake hoped. Without help, Melissa would die of exhaustion, of hypothermia, almost as if she were dying of exposure.

"What should I do?" His tone was resigned, depressed.

"Help me move her."

Snake spread blankets on a wide, flat rock that had soaked up the sunlight all day. She was clumsy with everything. Arevin picked Melissa up and laid her on the warm blanket. Leaving her daughter for a moment, Snake spilled her saddlebags out on the ground. She pushed the canteen, the paraffin stove, and the cook-pot toward Arevin, who watched her with troubled eyes. She had hardly had the chance to look at him.

"Heat some water, please, Arevin. Not too much." She cupped her hands together to indicate the amount. She grabbed the packet of sugar from the medicine compartment of the serpent case.

By Melissa's side again, Snake tried to rouse her. The pulse appeared, disappeared, returned.

It's there, Snake told herself. I'm not imagining it.

She scattered a pinch of sugar onto Melissa's tongue, hoping there was enough moisture to dissolve it. Snake dared not force her to drink; she might choke if the water went into her lungs. Time was short, but if Snake rushed she would kill her daughter as surely as North might have done. Every minute or so, as she waited for Arevin, she gave Melissa a few more grains of ıgar.

Saying nothing, Arevin brought the steaming water. Snake put one more pinch of sugar on Melissa's tongue and handed Arevin the pouch. "Dissolve as much of this in there as you can." She chafed Melissa's hands and patted her cheek. "Melissa, dear, try to wake up. Just for a moment. Daughter, help me."

Melissa gave no response. But Snake felt the pulse, once, again, this time strong enough to make her sure. "Is that ready?"

Arevin swirled the hot water around in the pan: a bit too eagerly and some splashed on his hand. Alarmed, he looked at Snake.

"It's all right. It's sugar." She took the pan from him.

"Sugar!" He wiped his fingers on the grass.

"Melissa! Wake up, dear." Melissa's eyelids flickered. Snake caught her breath with relief.

"Melissa! You need to drink this."

Melissa's lips moved slightly.

"Don't try to talk yet." Snake held the small metal container to her daughter's mouth and let the thick, sticky liquid flow in slowly, bit by bit, waiting until she was certain Melissa had swallowed each portion of the stimulant before she gave her any more.

"Gods . . ." Arevin said in wonder.

"Snake?" Melissa whispered.

"I'm here, Melissa. We're safe. You're all right now." She felt like laughing and crying at the same time.

"I'm so cold."

"I know." She wrapped the blanket around Melissa's shoulders. That was safe, now that Melissa had the warm drink in her stomach, and the stimulant exploding energy into her blood.

"I didn't want to leave you there, but I promised . . . I was afraid that crazy would get Squirrel, I was afraid Mist and Sand would die . . ."

Her last fears gone, Snake eased Melissa back on the warm rock. Nothing in Melissa's speech or words indicated brain damage; she had survived whole.

"Squirrel's here with us, and so are Mist and Sand. You can go back to sleep, and when you wake up everything will be fine." Melissa might have a headache for a day or so, depending on how sensitive she was to the stimulant. But she was alive, she was well.

"I tried to get away," Melissa said, not opening her eyes. "I kept going and going, but . . ."

"I'm very proud of you. No one could do what you did without being brave and strong."

The unscarred side of Melissa's mouth twisted into a half smile, and then she was asleep. Snake shaded her face with a corner of the blanket.

"I would have sworn my life she was dead," Arevin said.

"She'll be all right," Snake said, to herself more than to Arevin. "Thank gods, she will be all right."

The urgency that had possessed her, tne fleeting strength

brought on by adrenalin, had slowly drained away without her noticing. She could not move, even to sit down again. Her knees had locked; all that was left for her to do was fall. She could not even tell if she was swaying or if her eyes were playing tricks on her, for objects seemed to approach and recede randomly.

Arevin touched her left shoulder. His hand was just as she remembered it, gentle and strong.

"Healer," he said, "the child is safe. Think of yourself now." His voice was completely neutral.

"She's been through so much," Snake whispered. The words came out with difficulty. "She'll be afraid of you . . ."

He did not reply, and she shivered. Arevin supported her and eased her to the ground. His hair had come loose; it fell around his face and he looked just as he had the last time she had seen him.

He held his flask to her dry lips, and she drank warm water freshened with wine.

"Who did this to you?" he asked. "Are you still in danger?"

She had not even thought what could happen when North and his people revived. "Not now, but later, tomorrow — " Abruptly, she struggled to rise. "If I sleep, I won't wake up in time — "

He soothed her. "Rest. I'll keep watch till morning. Then we can move to a safer place."

With his reassurance, she could rest. He left her for a moment, and she lay flat on the ground, her fingers spread wide and pressing down, as if the earth held her to it yet gave something back. Its coolness helped ease her returning awareness of the crossbow wound. She heard Arevin kneel beside her, and he laid a cool, wet cloth across her shoulder to soak loose the frayed material and dry blood. She watched him through her eyelashes, again admiring his hands, the long lines of his body. But his touch was as neutral as his words had been.

"How did you find us?" she asked. "I thought you were a dream."

"I went to the healers' station," he said. "I had to try to make your people understand what happened and that the fault was my clan's, not yours." He glanced at her, then away, sadly. "I failed, I think. Your teacher said only that you must go home."

Before, there had been no time for Arevin to respond to what she had said to him, that she dreamed about him and loved him. But now he acted as if she had never said those things, as if he had done what he had done out of duty alone. Snake wondered, with a great empty feeling of loss and regret, if she misunderstood his feelings. She did not want more gratitude and guilt.

"But you're here," she said. She pushed herself up on her elbow, and with some effort sat to face him. "You didn't have to follow me, if you had a duty it ended at my home."

He met her gaze. "I . . . dreamed about you, too." He leaned toward her, forearms resting on his knees, hands outstretched. "I never exchanged names with another person."

Slowly, gladly, Snake slid her dirty, scarred left hand around his clean, dark-tanned right one.

He looked up at her. "After what happened — "

Wishing even more now that she was not hurt, Snake released his hand and reached into her pocket. The eggling dreamsnake coiled itself around her fingers. She brought it out and showed it to Arevin. Nodding toward the wicker basket, she said, "I have more in there, and I know how to let them breed."

He stared at the small serpent, then at her, in wonder. "Then you did reach the city. They accepted you."

"No," she said. She glanced toward the broken dome. "I found dreamsnakes up there. And a whole alien world, where they live." She let the eggling slip back into her pocket. It was growing used to her already; it would make a good healer's serpent. "The city people sent me away, but they haven't seen the last of healers. They still owe me a debt."

"My people owe you a debt, too," Arevin said. "A debt I've failed to repay."

"You helped save my daughter's life! Do you think that

counts for nothing?" Then, more calmly, Snake said, "Arevin, I wish Grass were still alive. I can't pretend I don't. But my negligence killed him, nothing else. I've never thought anything but that."

"My clan," Arevin said, "and my cousin's partner — "

"Wait. If Grass hadn't died, I'd never have started home when I did."

Arevin smiled slightly.

"And if I hadn't come back then," Snake said, "I never would have gone to Center. I never would have found Melissa. And I never would have encountered the crazy or heard about the broken dome. It's as if your clan acted as a catalyst. If not for you we would have kept on begging the city people for dreamsnakes, and they would have kept on refusing us. The healers would have gone on unchanging until there were no dreamsnakes and no healers left. That's all different now. So maybe I'm in as much debt to you as you think you are to me."

He looked at her for a long time. "I think you are making excuses for my people."

Snake clenched her fist. "Is guilt all that can exist between us?"

"No!" Arevin said sharply. More quietly, as if surprised by his own outburst, he said, "At least, I've hoped for something more."

Relenting, Snake took his hand. "So have I." She kissed his palm.

Slowly, Arevin smiled. He leaned closer, and a moment later they were embracing each other.

"If we've owed each other, and repaid each other, our people can be friends," Arevin said. "And perhaps you and I have earned the time you once said we needed."

"We have," Snake said.

Arevin brushed the tangled hair back from her forehead. "I've learned new customs since I came to the mountains," he said. "I want to take care of you while your shoulder heals. And when you're well, I want to ask if there's anything else I can do for you."

Snake returned his smile; she knew they understood each other. "That's a question I've wanted to ask you, too," she said, and then she grinned. "Healers mend quickly, you know."